APPRENTICE

THE BLACK MAGE BOOK 2

RACHEL E. CARTER

Apprentice (The Black Mage Book 2)

Copyright © 2016 Rachel E. Carter

ISBN: 1-946155-01-2

ISBN-13: 978-1-946155-01-6

Publisher's Note: This is a work of fiction. Names, characters, places, and incidents are a product of the author's imagination. Locales and public names are sometimes used for atmospheric purposes. Any resemblance to actual people, living or dead, or to businesses, companies, events, institutions, or locales is completely coincidental.

Cover Design by Deranged Doctor Designs

Edited by Hot Tree Editing

To The Boy Who Never Reads,

Too bad you are marrying an author.
I'm sorry for all the times I ignored you to write this book.
Thanks for putting a ring on it anyway.
I love you.

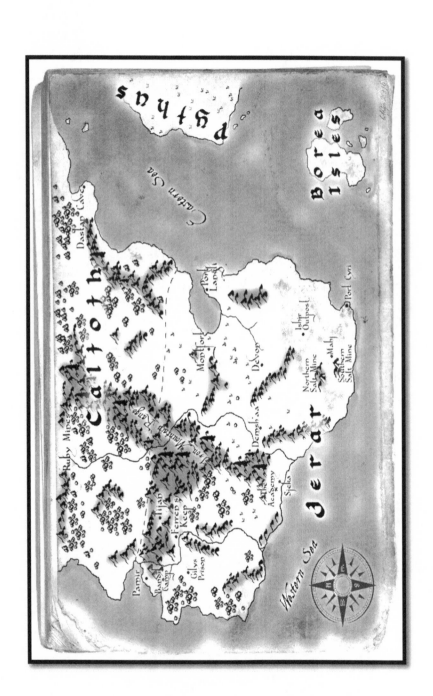

YEAR ONE

ONE

I WATCHED THE two figures dance, twisting and turning as they exchanged matching blows in the stifling morning heat of the desert sun. The sand shifted and clouded beneath their feet, small swells of dirt temporarily blinding my vision as the two continued to reposition their lightning-quick blows.

I studied their forms. Lissome, dangerous. I couldn't help but notice how the sweat glistened off their tanned skin, highlighting the contours of taut arms and shoulders. It was an observation I'd partaken in many times but had yet to grow tired of watching.

The two fighters continued their match. The taller of the two, a young man with sandy brown curls and laughing green eyes, seemed the most at ease with the procession. He countered his partner's rapid attacks with an almost lazy defense that spoke of a lifetime of training. The second young man was the opposite, trying to hide his building frustration in every blocked attempt. Garnet eyes flared underneath black bangs, and my heart skipped a beat. The shorter of the two might have been less skilled in hand-to-hand combat, yet my eyes clung to him just a second too long.

The bout carried on for several more minutes. I fanned myself with my hand, desperately wishing our faction had been assigned a cooler terrain to train in. I certainly hadn't expected the desert, and I had yet to grow accustomed to its sweltering heat. Many of the other apprentices seemed to share my opinion; there was not a full water skin to be found anywhere in the audience.

The tall boy caught the second off guard with a swift, sweeping kick that sent his partner sprawling into the sand. The second shot the older boy a look of pure venom that would've sent most people to their knees. The tall boy just chuckled, offering the second his hand, which the second blatantly ignored, as the rest of the class hooted and cheered.

A man in stiff black robes stepped forward with a scowl. "That will do, Ian." Then he addressed the young man on the ground in a much friendlier tone: "Darren, that was very good for a second-year. You have no reason to be disappointed."

The expression on Darren's face didn't change as he stood, brushing sand from his breeches and belt. His eyes stated very clearly he did not share Master Byron's confidence. I hadn't the slightest doubt that the prince would be training in private for weeks to come. Though we couldn't be more different, it was amazing how similar the two of us were when it came to performance. The master had been praising him for weeks, but until he was the best, Darren wouldn't be satisfied.

"Ryiah. Lynn. You two are up."

Nerves tingling, I made my way to the front. A young

woman with dark bangs and amber eyes gripped my elbow as I passed. "Good luck, Ry," Ella whispered.

Standing where the two boys had fought just moments before was a girl of Borean descent, who I had sparred with many times before. Lynn gave me a reassuring smile. I tried to return the sentiment as I took my position across from my mentor.

Palms sweating, I waited for the master of Combat to start our drill.

"And begin."

Lynn was the first to make a move, ducking into my circle with a low jab to the ribs. I held my guard and countered her strike with a low block of my own. The girl pulled back, long ponytail flying, and I quickly launched a high kick, narrowly missing as she fell back out of reach. My fingers itched to send a casting, but I quickly squelched the urge.

No magic, Ryiah.

Refocusing on the task at hand, I studied my opponent, seeking any tell in her stance that might foreshadow her next attack. Lynn's hazel eyes met mine, sparkling with a delicate innocence that matched her doll-like features. It was a lie. She might be petite, but I had long ago learned the truth. The olive-skinned third-year was lethal in hand-to-hand combat and anything with a pole.

I exhaled slowly. I'd lost every single match to my mentor since we'd started these duels, but like Darren, I wanted to win. I was the sixth apprentice to join Combat months before, and I still had something to prove.

Every time I lost, I wondered if the others were questioning the Black Mage's decision to admit me to their ranks.

A snicker came from somewhere in the audience. I didn't need to look to identify the girl. Priscilla of Langli was impossible to mistake.

Lynn shifted her hips, weight transferring ever so lightly to her right heel.

I jumped in with a hasty outer block and sent my right fist to the girl's abdomen. Lynn pulled back just in time, my hand barely grazing the thin cotton of her shirt.

I launched a low, rounded kick, and she parried it with an easy blow of her own. I fell back and instinctively angled my hips so that I was just out of reach, fists raised and ready to counter Lynn's next offense. When it didn't immediately come, I sprung forward, feigning a two-fisted punch while my real attack came in the form of a high kick aimed at her ribs.

My mentor wasn't fooled. She easily countered, stepping into the kick the second she saw my knee rise, and rammed my body with the full force of her weight.

I stumbled.

Lynn rushed forward, kicking and punching in a quick succession of blows. I struggled to block, but I was still off balance from her previous attack. A hard-packed fist collided with my stomach and another with my face.

Lynn sent a quick kick to my shin and gravity shifted from under my feet.

I fell to the side, and my right elbow hit the hard-packed dirt with a *craaaack*. Sand billowed up as something snapped under my skin.

Pain rushed my arm like shards of glass as my control on

my magic splintered and broke.

The pain casting rushed out of me uncalled. It slammed into Lynn and sent her back-first into a nearby palm. Lynn slumped to the ground with a hard thud as my magic dissipated, the casting complete.

"Blast it, Ryiah!" Master Byron swore. His aristocratic face was beet red, a common expression around me. "If you can't control your magic, you're never going to be allowed anywhere near a battlefield!"

I scrambled to my feet, my face aflame. "I'm sorry, sir. I didn't mean—"

"The Black Mage made a mistake." The man puffed his chest. "You shouldn't be here. I don't know what Marius was thinking, granting you an apprenticeship. You may have gotten away with that trickery in your trials, but it will not fly here."

"Yes, sir." My elbow was on fire, and I was too busy looking to Lynn across the way. She had pulled herself up, and her expression was full of pity. She was far too patient— this wasn't the first time my magic had accidentally knocked her into a tree.

It wasn't as if I'd intentionally cast; it just happened. Other apprentices lost control too—but in the two months since my apprenticeship had started, the training master only seemed to criticize me.

"What good is a girl in Combat if she is always embracing her gender's weak-minded ways? Learn to deal with your pain, Ryiah, or go back to a convent."

That's it—

Ella's fingers clamped over my left wrist before I could

retort. I bit down on my cheek until I tasted blood. If I angered the master enough, I'd find myself at the end of more than just his insults, and I had four years left.

A throaty chuckle broke the tension nearby. "If the girls are the only ones who feel pain, then I'm living a lie."

"Your sarcasm, Apprentice Ian, is not appreciated." The master glowered at the tall boy from earlier. "I was simply making a point to Ryiah that she would be better suited elsewhere—"

"For accidentally using her magic?" The boy kept on. "Sir, we've all done that. In my second year alone, I—"

"Perhaps she is not the only one who shouldn't be here!" The master bristled as he turned on me. "Ryiah, see to that arm. You will have to make up the rest of the exercise later."

I couldn't see how with a broken arm, but I didn't bother to reply.

All twenty apprentices stepped to the side to allow me to pass, although none of them met my eyes as I did. Most of them hated Master Byron as much as me; the difference was they had learned to avoid his wrath.

Holding my head high, I began the short trek to the infirmary. At least there would be one bright spot to this day. Alex would be with the rest of the Restoration mages— which meant I would get to see him when I checked into their base.

I'd barely seen my brother since the start of the apprenticeship—our factions kept us busy training in opposite ends of Ishir Outpost. Any excuse to see Alex was welcome at this point.

"Hey, Ryiah, wait up!"

I turned and found Ian jogging to catch up with me. His hair was windblown, and his eyes crinkled as they locked on my own. Even out of breath, the third-year was handsome—not like the prince, but then again, no one ever was.

Ian was just Ian. When the apprentices had arrived at the Academy to pick up their newest recruits, most of the older students had been wary of me. I was the sixteen-year-old girl who destroyed the school's armory during the first-year trials. I was also the sixth apprentice to join our faction's year—a rarity since the Council of Magic only ever selected five students to apprentice per faction.

Ian hadn't cared. The moment the third-year had spotted me, he'd let out a loud whoop and set about to collecting his winnings from the rest of his friends. Apparently there'd been a wager going for which of us first-years would make it; since I'd been considered a long shot during the midwinter duels, Ian had been the only one to bet on me for an apprenticeship.

I was surprised the boy even remembered me from our short time during the solstice ball, but he assured me he'd remembered "everyone that counted."

Since the apprenticeship started, Ian had quickly become one of my closest friends, after Ella. The third-year's sarcasm matched my own, and he knew firsthand how horrible Byron could be. After all, until I arrived, Ian had been the master's least favorite apprentice.

"What are you doing?" I scolded the third-year. "You should be mentoring Darren."

Ian chuckled. "That self-important prodigy? He'll be fine without me..." The boy gave me a disarming smile. "You, warrior girl, are the one who needs help." He hooked my good arm with his own. "That prince has the training master worshipping the very ground he walks on. Darren could be *us* and Byron would still insist he was the next Black Mage."

"Byron's going to stick you with latrine duty." I grinned despite myself.

Ian's green eyes danced wickedly. "He can *try*—but I'll just tell him it interferes with my mentoring, and we know how the master feels about his precious prince."

I laughed loudly. "You are trouble."

"Anything for Byron's least favorite apprentice. It's the least I can do since you took over my torch."

"I wouldn't be so—argh!" I ducked under a low palm's hanging branches and skimmed my bad arm against the side of its trunk.

"You okay?"

"I'm fine." I gritted my teeth. "I just want this pain to end."

"We're almost there." Ian pointed to a set of wooden doors protruding from the base of a large cliff, a quarter of a mile away.

Like most of the city's housing, the infirmary was built into the rocky face of desert crags, a seemingly endless elevation that separated the Red Desert from the northern plains of the capital city, Devon, and the rest of Jerar. I'd always heard tales of a desert city carved into mountains, but I had still been speechless the first day we arrived.

"Thank the gods."

The two of us continued along the dirt path, through the doors, and into the dank, torch-lit passage of the building.

The air was cooler here. There were only two guards posted at the entrance. They recognized us by our apprentice garb and let us in without hesitation. The passage split into three separate channels, and I led Ian down the one to the right.

As soon as we'd taken a couple of steps, I heard the master of Restoration's sharp, clipped voice instructing on the proper *non-magical* treatment for scorpion stings. *Ugh.* Ian and I exchanged looks and entered the Restoration apprentices' classroom.

Normally, one would seek out the city's main healing center to the left of the main corridor, but students were only allowed to be treated there if their injuries were grave enough. If they weren't, we were "lessons" for the Restoration apprentices.

They had to practice on someone.

Master Joan's lecture ceased the moment we entered the classroom. "What are your grievances, apprentices?"

"My right arm." I tried to avoid the curious stares from the rest of Alex's faction. I knew they wanted to be healers, but it still sent an unsettling quiver down my spine. No one should look intrigued—instead of horrified—by our injuries. No one should *ever* be excited to see blood.

"And you, boy." The master fixated her cross expression on my friend. "Why are you here?"

Ian grinned sheepishly. "Too much sun?"

"Out!" The master pointed to the door.

Ian winked at me—fully expecting the master's response—and departed the room with a friendly wave. As soon as he disappeared, several of the female apprentices sighed.

I hid a smile. I wasn't the only one who noticed Ian's good looks.

"Everyone, we will continue the lesson after we have finished Apprentice Ryiah's healing. Ryiah, please list your symptoms so that we can begin to consider a treatment."

I described my injury—pain up and down the arm, swelling, and stiffness in the elbow. I wondered if it was broken.

"Break." Alex was the first to volunteer.

"And how would you confirm the diagnosis?"

"If there are any physical deformities or skin breakage, we wouldn't need to do anything. Those symptoms alone would confirm. If not, we'd project a casting to mirror bone placement." That was Ronan—my brother's friend and sometimes rival, a fellow second-year who'd ranked first in their trial year at the Academy.

Master Joan chose a fifth-year to perform the healing. The girl stood proudly, eyes alight with anticipation as she began her casting. I braced myself—the last time I visited the infirmary for dehydration, a painless casting had resulted in a skin rash and pain for days. *Nothing like trial and error.*

Lucky for me, the girl appeared to know what she was doing. I didn't feel anything above a faint, humming vibration as my arm slowly took on a translucent outline with glowing green lines shining through my skin. My stomach turned a little as I realized those bright orange things were my bones.

There was an unnatural break in the nook of my forearm connecting to the elbow.

"Minor fracture," the girl said proudly. "Nothing we

would need to realign with plating. I would recommend conservative treatment since there is no breakage and her bones do not appear to be displaced."

I swallowed, immediately grateful they would not be inserting metals into my arm.

"How would we treat with magic? And without?"

The same fifth-year replied with the proper response for both. I was thrilled to hear neither detailed anything complex.

"Good. Now splint her arm as you would without magic. Byron will want her to heal naturally since it's not severe."

It was a good thing I was getting used to pain; I'd be keeping this broken arm for weeks.

* * *

When the apprentice finished wrapping my arm and securing it in a sling, I was dismissed.

I started to pass, but Alex called after me.

"How is she?"

There was a twinge in my chest. I'd hoped he wouldn't bring Ella up; it was easy to pretend things were fine when there was a distance between the two of our factions. "She's moved on, Alex."

He swallowed. "Can you tell her—"

Master Joan glowered at the both of us; I couldn't stick around.

My eyes met my brother's. "You need to let her go."

Alex had his chance and lost her. I wasn't sure I would ever forgive myself for encouraging the two of them to try. Heartbreak followed my brother around like the moon.

All it had taken was a couple of weeks.

* * *

By the time I'd returned to the training grounds, everyone had already left for their third session of the day: Strategies in Combat. It was the final class before our afternoon break and my favorite since we'd started our desert training.

I raced across the square to the local regiment's command across the way. There were four long flights of stairs from the fortress's base.

The building contained a large hall for the outpost's commander at its top. Local highborn officials—including Baron Eli—and their regiment of soldiers, knights, and mages gathered and discussed various strategies for dealing with any and all topics of military interest. Though the Crown's Army served the capital and made official decisions in times of war, it was the duty of each city's assigned regiment to enforce Crown law and deal with local issues unless brute force was needed.

I found Ella in the crowd and made my way to the back of the hall. My friend made room on her bench and eyed my bad arm with sympathy. "They only wrapped it?"

"You know the rules. All pain, all the time." Combat apprentices were a glutton for punishment; it was the nature of our faction.

"Still, they—"

"Can you two go whine about your injuries somewhere else?" Priscilla, one row in front of us, shot Ella and me a nasty look. "Some of us are trying to learn."

"She wasn't whining," Ella hissed. "Certainly not like the day you broke *your* shoulder last month!"

"I didn't sound anything like that."

"You made Darren carry you to the infirmary." The words fell from my lips before I could stop them. *Why? Why did I say that?*

Priscilla's eyes narrowed to slits. "Oh, I see."

"You don't see anything, because there's nothing to see."

"You're still pining for him." She rolled her eyes, batting her lashes. "Really, Ryiah, you couldn't be more pathetic if you tried. You're blushing with your little convent girl crush."

My fists clenched. "I'm not—"

"What is this?" Master Bryon came barreling toward the back of the room, sweat beading on his brow. "Have you second-years no respect for your study at all? This is a lecture, not a gossip around court."

Priscilla was quick to throw Ella and me to the wolves. "It was these two, sir. Ryiah kept complaining about her injury and whining that Darren didn't carry her to the infirmary."

My cheeks flamed as the prince, who'd been immersed in a history scroll just moments before, whipped his head around to stare.

"I was doing no such thing!" I avoided Darren's gaze as I turned to face the master of Combat. "I would *never* say that." I hoped the prince would hear my emphasis. "I'm a Combat apprentice, not a damsel in distress."

"She's lying, sir. She's—"

"Enough!" Master Byron cut Priscilla off. "You three are exactly why the apprenticeship should be male."

Our sexist training master was a chauvinistic pig.

The master went on to address Ella and me on our own. "Since the two of you seem to have so much time on your hands, you'll be cleaning the barrack privies with Apprentice Ian during your evening hours for the remainder of this week."

"What about her?" I pointed to Priscilla. "Doesn't she get a punishment too?"

"Are you suggesting I should distrust the Crown's future princess?" The man gave me a look. "Over a lowborn?" The man was a sexist, chauvinistic pig who had grown up in court.

"Ryiah isn't lying, sir." Ella stood and put her hand on my shoulder in a show of support.

"You aren't a source of veritable truth either, Eleanor."

"It's Ella," Ella said through clenched teeth.

"Interrupt me again and you'll get chore duty for a month. Is that what you want?"

Both of us were radiating with rage as the master walked away; I could barely force myself to concentrate on the commander and her regiment leaders at the front of the room.

Ella's fingers tapped against the wooden bench; she was restless like me.

Finally, after what felt like forever but was only the course of ten minutes, I was able to return to the lesson.

Unlike the study we'd had back at the Academy, these courses were formed entirely by first-hand experience.

Today's topic was continuing a three-week lecture on chariot combat. It was what the desert regiments were famous for. That, and the terrain.

Ishir Outpost was located at the northernmost boundary of the Red Desert, which encompassed the entire southern region of Jerar. The city and the rest of the desert's border were made up entirely of tall bluffs and steep crags. There was only one man-made gate that allowed travel between the desert and the rest of the country. The desert's tall, rocky walls overlooked the middle plains and provided perfect vantage points for the Crown's Army in the event of a full-scale invasion on the capital, Devon.

Mostly, the desert's local regiments serviced the bluffs as lookouts in chariots. There hadn't been a war between Jerar and its northern neighbor, Caltoth, in over ninety years.

Supposedly, there were tunnels in those walls to help the central plains evacuate and give the Red Desert's regiment easy passage to the capital.

The chariots were intended to be the first charge with a soldier steering and either a skilled archer-knight or Combat mage leading the attack. The carts allowed mages and knights the ease of a distanced approach that enemies would have a hard time countering with long-range attacks. The Red Desert's regiment was known for their throwing arm, and since Ishir Outpost was the most populace city with the largest regiment, it had become one of the four cities mage apprentices and knights' squires trained in during their four-year apprenticeships.

We switched territories every year. I hadn't known that until the second day of my apprenticeship. Soldiers of the Cavalry were exempt from regional exercises because there was no apprenticeship; they moved onto city placement following their trial year.

Commander Ama continued on to add the finer points of today's strategy, pointing to her comrades as she explained what each leader would do in a chariot attack. The mounted knights would follow up with an armed assault—usually the sickle sword if they were desert natives, or the halberd if they'd transferred from anywhere else. Whatever horses remained were given to the soldiers—with the majority serving on foot with battle axes to break up their opponent's armor and give the knights an easier target. The Restoration and Alchemy mages would remain in the tunnels, equipped for battle, but prepared for healing, and respectively, a last-minute defense.

Ama had left no possibility unplanned. A part of me was awed just listening to her talk. Strategy was no longer something we heard about; the regiment would give us demonstrations later and let us practice alongside them.

Though we went over various techniques for breaking up enemy lines and securing a victory, the one thing the Commander and her leaders never disclosed was the tunnels' location. We knew they were fifty miles apart, but that was it.

Because Jerar's capital had never been under siege, the Red Desert's tunnels had never been used. The laborers who had helped build them had died several centuries ago. The only people who knew their exact coordinates were either dead or currently serving a commanding post in one of the desert cities. The only exception was the royal family.

From everything I'd gathered, the tunnels were Jerar's most safeguarded secret. It hadn't been said directly, but I was almost certain the Crown punished those who disclosed their location with death. There were rumors that those who went looking for them never returned. And then there was the mysterious death of Ishir Outpost's past commander who had been in the prime of his health when a sudden illness had rapidly taken his life after only three years into his reign.

Definitely a secret.

By the time our two hours were over, I had forgotten most of my earlier problems. Priscilla, Master Byron, and my new injury were just small, annoying blips in my otherwise perfect life. Every time I walked away from Strategies in Combat, I felt like I was a part of something great. No one and nothing could take that away from me.

I was an apprentice now for Combat, the most prestigious faction of all. The Academy of Magic had worse odds than any of the other war schools combined, and I'd beat them all.

I wasn't even considered lowborn anymore—as an apprentice mage, I was now afforded the same status as a highborn. Not even squires had that privilege. Magic was rare, important, and so were apprentices.

And in four short years, I would be a mage of Combat.

"You sure look chipper for someone with a broken arm."

Lynn, and Ella's mentor, Loren—a tall, dark-skinned boy with startling blue eyes who my brother loathed—were waiting for us at the stairs.

"Thanks for reminding me." I gave both of our mentors a wry smile as we started the descent to the third floor. The great building hosted four levels: the first was the privies and wash chambers, the second the squire and apprentice mage barracks—depending on whose year it was to field train, we were never in the same city together—the third was the dining commons, and the fourth was for regiment meetings and lessons. It wasn't as grand as the Academy, but it was still impressive.

It was a far cry from my small village of Demsh'aa and the hills I'd left behind.

"Is Ian staying behind to do extra mentoring with Darren today?" Lynn took a seat beside me on the bench. The commons was smaller than the one we'd had at the Academy, and there were only three tables to choose from. Before, there had been over a hundred of us; now there were only sixty, well, sixty-one since I'd arrived: Twenty apprentices from each faction—five for each of the four years.

"I doubt it." The troublemaker was far more likely to be trying to talk his way out of the chore Byron had just assigned. I wished him luck, though I suspected the worst. I said as much aloud.

Ella picked at her plate, avoiding a curry she had deemed too spicy for her liking. "I'm surprised Ian would try when he could have privy duty with us."

"Why would he want to scrub the privies?" I stared at my friend like she had grown an extra head. "He's got the prince as his mentee. He has a card to get out of any chores he wants."

"It's not the chore." Her lip twitched. "It's the people."

What in the gods was she hinting at?

The rest of Combat arrived, so I quickly lost focus on our conversation; the room was distractingly loud. Most of our faction sat at the same table, and everyone's elbows jostled one another as we pressed close.

"Ladies. Loren. I hope you didn't mourn while I was away."

Ian had arrived, looking no worse for wear than usual.

"Did you even talk to Byron?" I asked suspiciously. The third-year seemed too cheery to have just come from a chat with our training master.

Ian took the seat opposite mine as he slid in next to Loren. "Nah. I decided it was a wasted effort."

Ella caught my eye with a pointed stare.

Is she implying Ian chose the privies because of me?

After a moment of awkward silence, I finally cleared my throat. "So is anyone else getting tired of all these mysterious tunnels?" It was a change of subject more than a concern.

My mentor shrugged and then winced as her wrist knocked into Loren's glass. "It doesn't matter much. Jerar isn't going to war anytime soon." She turned to Ian. "What do you think?" she teased. "Are we ready for war?"

The troublemaker grinned. "Why don't we ask our very own royal since it will be his father signing those summons?" He stood up and pretended to scan the row of Combat apprentices for the prince, who was, as usual, missing from the table. "What a shame, my charming mentee is absent. *Again.*"

Darren hadn't taken a lunch with the rest of our faction since we arrived in the desert. Instead, he spent the hour drilling with Master Byron in the training grounds. I wasn't sure whose idea it had initially been—the man hero-worshipped the prince—but I understood Ian's irritation. No one else got exclusive training with the master; Byron was grooming Darren for success and leaving the rest of us—particularly the ones he didn't like—to rot.

I'd confronted Darren about the injustice a couple weeks back, and the prince had just laughed in my face. *"What did you expect, Ryiah? Not everyone is going to treat us like equals. You got lucky with the first-year masters at the Academy, but you are going to have to learn to accept the injustice now. It's always going to be here, especially while I'm around."*

He'd made a good point, even if I hadn't liked what it meant.

Since Ian was Darren's mentor, he took the prince's absence more personally than the rest of us. The third-year didn't trust Darren and the prince's aloof nature unsettled him. Darren's competitive drive only made things worse.

I sympathized. More than anyone else at our table, I understood Ian's plight. I had gone through the same thing the first time I'd met the prince, and it'd taken me ten long months to stop second-guessing his motives.

Normally, the mentor-mentee relationship was a good thing. It gave two apprentices the opportunity to bond over shared trials and common goals in training. Each pairing lasted a year before the partners were switched. We would have two years leading others and two years following them. The varied approach would give us the opportunity to be the best and the worst. The experience was supposed to make us better for it... Ian clearly interpreted Darren's extra training as an affront instead of what it really was: a lifetime of expectation.

I thought there were very few who understood why Darren acted the way he did. I wasn't an expert by any means, but there were things one had to ask. Why was a prince more accustomed to injuries than the rest of us? Darren had never once lost control of his magic in training— and as one of the few apprentices who could pain cast, that was *highly* unusual. It led me to two possible conclusions: Darren was perfect, which he liked us to believe, or he'd trained in far worse conditions than we knew.

"I understand wanting to be best, I do," Ian continued, "but there is nothing wrong with a little bit of amity. Would it kill the prince to take a meal with his factionmates?" He directed the attention to me. "I mean, look at Ryiah. She trains just as hard, but she still manages to have a conversation with the rest of us."

Ella winked at me conspiratorially. "Oh, Darren still has 'conversations' with some people." For a time, my best friend had hated the prince, but that had all been part of a misunderstanding in their past. Now she enjoyed teasing me more than anything else.

I glared at her. She knew very well there was nothing going on between Darren and me. Maybe there had been at one point, but whatever that was—and I wasn't sure it had been anything—it was long gone. Darren's betrothal to Priscilla of Langli, one of the wealthiest young women in the kingdom and my personal nemesis, had made that perfectly evident.

The corner of Ian's eyes crinkled. "That's right. You and Darren are *friends*." He pronounced the last word with mock distaste, grinning. "So how did you do it? What makes the cold-hearted princeling mortal like the rest of us?"

I fidgeted in my seat. The last thing I wanted was for the others to find out about last year's transgression. Especially

Ian. I suspected my feelings for the curly-haired third-year weren't strictly platonic, and I didn't want him to think that I was, as Priscilla put it, "pining" for the prince. *Because I wasn't.*

Ella snorted. "I don't think it's something you would want to attempt, Ian."

The third-year arched a brow and then gave me his most disarming smile. "Ry, just tell me whatever you said to convince him to give up that ridiculous pretense."

"It's not an act." I kept my eyes averted as I muttered, "Darren just has a really hard time opening up to people he thinks are beneath him—"

Ian gave a mock gasp. "*Never.*"

"—But I'm sure after a couple months, he'll realize you *are* trying."

Ian stole a handful of grapes off my plate. "If I didn't know better, I would say you were *defending* him, Ryiah."

"I'm not," I said quickly. Too quickly.

"Did something *happen* between the two of you?" Ian leaned across the table, and I gulped.

"No."

His grin grew wider the longer he stared at my face.

I pushed back from the table, flushed. "Nothing happened!"

"So something *did* happen."

"Maybe it did, but it didn't mean a thing." I snatched my bag from the bench and didn't bother with an excuse. Everyone was watching me, and I couldn't bear their grins.

What had I possibly hoped to gain defending a prince?

TWO

THE SECOND HALF of my day didn't get much better.

I was on my way to the training grounds to begin a lesson on desert castings when I ran into Darren.

"So I heard that you wanted me to carry you to the infirmary."

I gave the prince what I hoped was my most disdainful look. "Your betrothed is a pretty little liar."

A corner of his lips twitched, and I had the distinct impression he was on the brink of laughter. "Don't worry," he said, "I know you'd never accept anyone's help, least of all mine."

We both knew he'd helped last year more times than I wanted to admit. I scowled. "I'm not some inept apprentice in need of rescuing, Darren."

"Even if you *had* asked, I wouldn't have carried you."

This was the person I spent half a year 'pining' over? I must have been mad. "I would *never* ask!"

"I'm not saying it to be mean, Ryiah. You don't need to give me that look."

I continued to glare at him.

"Byron is good for you."

I scoffed. "I don't need another 'adversity builds character' speech. That man is terrible. Where's *your* adversity?"

Darren smirked. "I'm looking at it."

I gave an exasperated huff and went to go find a seat in the back of the stands. I was so distracted, I didn't notice when Ian slid onto the bench next to me.

"Lover's quarrel?"

I glared at the third-year. Ella, Lynn, and Loren were chuckling right behind him. "I hate all of you."

None of my friends paid the insult any heed. Grumbling, I resigned myself to two hours with fools.

* * *

"You heard those Combat mages earlier. Distance is *everything*. Don't get close to the enemy. A mage's life is far too valuable to be wasted in a hand-to-hand fight. If the Crown wants to send in someone expendable, they'll send soldiers, not mages!"

Grimacing, I set to projecting my next attack. Thank the gods the local infantry wasn't nearby today. The master had a particular way of insulting soldiers almost as much as he insulted women and lowborns.

Three hundred yards in front of me was a tall wooden fence plastered with dangling wreaths.

Normally the yard served as a pasture, but today the horses had been stabled—as per the last three weeks of practice. Now, the fence served as an imaginary enemy line and the target. Sloppily woven wreaths represented the weak spots in the opposing forces' defense: the armpit, the eyes, and the plated armor nearest the chest. The goal of the exercise was to hit a wreath with casted arrows—a type of long-range magic similar to the longbow exercises we'd been drilling with every morning for weeks.

If we hit a wreath but the arrow fell or the arrow did not hit our target at all, then our casting was considered a failed attempt.

Most of the second-years, myself included, only had one or two successful castings since we'd begun the afternoon drill. The older apprentices had much better luck.

Chariot attacks with long-range weapons were Ishir's preferred method for attack. As such, Combat mages were the first line of offense. Even though we'd be discharged at the same time as the knights, our castings would give us the ability to reach our targets first. Long bows were usually limited to 120 or so yards, and other ranged weapons even less, but that was *without* magic.

If a mage mastered the technique for long casting, not only would he or she be able to project arrows further than any knight, but eventually heavier artillery as well.

Out of the corner of my eye, I watched Lynn cast out her arrows, one after the other. There was no physical weapon in her hand; her casting was entirely formed by a projection in her mind. Physical shafts manifested in thin air, hovering above her head. The girl strung them back with a flick of her wrist, and then an invisible force launched them across the field.

The arrows soared and embedded themselves deep in a wreath already brimming with arrows directly across from her.

Lynn was one of the better apprentices in long casting; I hoped one day I was half as good as her.

"Apprentice Ryiah, it should not take this long for you to form a casting."

Master Byron's snarl snapped me out of my daze. I hastily cast out three conjured arrows in succession, but my projections were sloppy.

All castings fell short of the target.

As soon as the arrows hit the ground, I let them dissipate, dissolving into empty air. I took a deep breath as I prepared for another casting. This time I wouldn't rush my casting.

"Don't let him get to you, Ry."

I shot Lynn a grateful smile and then returned to the task at hand. I'd let the pain in my arm—and Master Byron—detract me from my focus.

This time I wouldn't be so careless.

I focused on building the length of the arrows and the long elm bowstave in my head. I imagined the horrible, heaving tension from drawing eighty pounds of force against my side.

Then I let the shafts fly, soaring toward the wreath with as much force as I could project.

Halfway into the arrows' flight, I was already building my next projection, concentrating on the mental image with everything I had.

The ground quaked beneath my feet; I dug into it with the heels of my boots, holding my stance and casting steady as I released another set of arrows on my target. Master Byron was testing us, seeing if we could hold focus in a chariot's bumpy floor.

My second and third castings met my target with success, each time at least one of the three arrows hit a wreath.

I kept going. Thirty minutes flew by before I realized it. My luck continued as at least half of my castings met with success, and the others were not far off.

After five more minutes, my stomach turned. Something was churning in my gut as thick perspiration broke out across my skin. I was clammy and nauseous all at once.

My projection flickered in and out in a familiar warning that had nothing to do with the stifling heat.

I called off my magic and dipped my head between my knees as I waited for the dizziness to pass. I'd reached my magic's limits—stamina—for the day.

After a couple minutes, the sensation subsided and I was able to stand.

I straightened, taking in the rest of the class.

With a small flash of pride, I saw that Priscilla, Ella, a third-year named Bryce, and Ray—the lowborn I'd lost to in the previous year's trials—had already quit. Lynn looked like she was about to follow suit, and Darren and Eve were little better. The older apprentices were fading equally fast... though, to be fair, some had been casting with harder artillery than arrows.

During my trial year at the Academy, the Combat master had always urged us to cast until we had nothing left to give. It was the fastest way to build our magic's stamina, but it had always had an unpleasant aftereffect, and more often than not it left us sick, or unconscious.

Now that we were apprentices, our training had changed. After midwinter, we would be actively serving with the local regiment for five months in desert patrols. All of our drills were preparing us for actual combat. Stamina was no longer as important as survival.

No one's power was infinite. The closer we were to our stamina's limits, the slower our magic progressed. Even then, most mages' potential stopped building by the time adolescence was over. A couple might continue on into their early-twenties, but that wasn't the norm. I'd be lucky to reach thirty before my stamina started to decline, even if I kept up a daily routine. It was the main reason our Candidacy took place so often: we needed the strongest Council of Magic possible, even if that meant changing our Colored Robes every twenty years.

"You are preparing yourself for a true-to-life battle," Byron had declared on our first day of the apprenticeship. "If you are approaching your limits, you need to turn back and call off your magic. The only time that I *ever* want to see you fainting is if you are at no risk of danger, or the casting's outcome is worth your life."

In other words, don't do what I did during the first-year trials.

The rest of the class finished minutes later. As soon as they had, Master Byron launched himself into a full-blown speech, praising the prince and insulting the rest of us at the same time. It always ended the same way.

The master occasionally gave Priscilla good remarks, but I was certain they were only for the prince's benefit. Byron didn't even pretend with the rest of us.

"And, Ryiah, stay focused next time. I will not let that arm be an excuse for your casting to suffer."

Today had been my best casting yet. I'd hit the target more times than most of the second-years, and only that one attempt had failed to reach the fence... But, as usual, the master had failed to notice anything other than my faults.

I let the anger slide off me—albeit very slowly—and started my retreat to the dining commons. Our training took place a mile from the main building that housed our barracks and the rest of the amenities. Normally I resented the long walk after a full day of practice, but today I was happy to have some time to clear my head.

My apprenticeship is more important than strangling Master Byron. I repeated the motto over and over again. If I said it enough times, it was supposed to help, but so far there had been no such luck. Each time it was getting harder and harder to ignore his barbs. I'd lost my temper a couple of times during our first month, and now almost three months into our training, the tyrant was still punishing me for it.

"Oops, *so* sorry." There was a horrible jolt as someone barreled into my arm.

One guess as to the offender. *Priscilla.*

"You did that on purpose!" My pain was making me see all sorts of crazy colors, and I no longer cared if the master had rules about casting during hours between lessons. The girl needed to be put in her place. I was done with her antagonistic whims.

It was time to fight back.

"You can't prove it."

I was frothing at the mouth. "Prove it? I don't need to prove it. I'll—"

The prince's hand closed around my good arm before I

could land a punch. His voice was stern. "Stop."

"Stay out of it!" I tried to jerk away, but the prince's grip was iron. I couldn't move. "Darren, let me go."

"Why are you stopping her?" Priscilla's reaction was enough to momentarily detract from my rage, even if the prince was stopping me from giving her the lesson she deserved.

"Do you want a broken arm like hers?"

"She can't beat me," Priscilla scoffed.

Darren chuckled. "Ryiah's not as bad as you think."

I had the pleasure of seeing the raven-haired beauty turn an unattractive shade of red. "What is *wrong* with you? I'm your *betrothed*."

"Priscilla." Darren's patience grew thin. "She's a friend. We've been over this."

The girl let out a frustrated huff and stormed off.

I swallowed, my mouth dry as the crowd parted around us. "Thanks for that."

"It was nothing."

My eyes were still glued to his hand on my wrist. My skin was tingling, and it wasn't because it hurt. It was bringing back memories of a certain night...

Memories I needed to ignore. They meant nothing.

I tugged my wrist, and the prince dropped it like it was on fire.

"How's your arm?" he asked.

"I-it's fine." Why was I stammering? I forced myself to raise my chin and tried a teasing lilt instead. "So, we're *friends*?"

"I told you we were." He was smiling, and for once it met

his eyes.

I sucked in a breath.

The prince was the kind of beautiful that hurt. Dark and tragic, hard lines and crimson eyes, with a crooked curve of his lips that was doing odd things to my insides. Boys shouldn't be able to look like that.

"And here I thought you were the villain to my tale."

"Even villains have a little fun." His eyes hadn't left my face. "But I'm not your villain, love."

Love? My cheeks burned, and I wasn't even sure Darren realized what he'd said. It meant nothing. It was just an expression people said.

"Ry, are you all right?" Ella pushed her way forward with Ian and Loren close behind.

"I'll be fine." I gave a weak laugh and brandished my broken arm. It ached something fierce, but I knew Master Byron would never let a Restoration mage touch it.

"I bet your brother can take a look."

"Really, I don't need—"

"You're so stubborn." Ian wrapped an arm around my shoulders to steer me away, ignoring the prince. "Come on, Ry. Alex doesn't have to fix it, but he can do something for the pain."

Darren's eyes caught on mine as my friends urged me forward. I expected him to make a sarcastic remark about how "pain makes a mage."

"Ask your brother about arnica."

Huh?

The prince disappeared into the crowd, and I was still staring as Ian dragged me away.

Since when does Darren care if I'm hurt?

* * *

Alex was peeling a mango when we found him in the commons. He seemed surprised to see all of us, especially Ella, but he recovered quickly.

"Arnica, huh?"

"Do you know what that is?"

"Of course." His eyes met mine in mild amusement. "I'm just surprised the prince even knew to suggest it. It's not a common ingredient."

Ian turned to my brother. "Well? Can you get it?"

"I can... But I'll need help." Alex's gaze fell straight to Ella standing next to us. She hadn't said one word since we arrived. "The healers keep all their supplies locked away in the main wing. I need a couple of you to distract them while I get the salve. Now would be our best chance, while Master Joan is at dinner."

Ella didn't look at my brother as she said, "Then let's go." She turned to her mentor. "You don't have to come if you don't want to."

Loren smirked. "And miss all the fun?"

A flash of irritation flared in Alex's eyes, but he said nothing.

The five of us began the trek to the infirmary. Ella, Ian, and Loren spent most of the time in animated conversation while my brother and I walked in awkward silence. Alex kept stealing jealous glances at Ella and Loren in the front of our group, and I had to kick him to finally get him to quit.

"Ouch!"

"Stop glaring at Loren!"

"I wasn't."

"You were."

My brother ignored me completely. "Are things serious between those two?"

"They aren't courting, if that's your question." My voice was terse.

"Yet." He kicked at a rock in the sand and groaned. "You have to get me alone with her, Ry. Tell her to go with me when I get the arnica."

"Why?" The last time the two had been in the same room together, Ella had walked in on him kissing a Restoration apprentice. That had been a month ago when they'd still been courting. My friend had told me all about it afterward, sobbing in the barracks and swearing she would never talk to my brother again. She had kept her word, and I never urged her to try.

It wasn't the first time my brother had done this. In Demsh'aa, there was a mile-long list of the hearts he'd left broken in his wake. The difference was that this time my brother seemed to regret it.

He'd never come to me on his knees for one of my friends until her. But it was too late. Ella didn't do second chances, and I wasn't about to lose my best friend to one of my brother's whims.

"Because I made a mistake!"

"You kissed another girl. It's a betrayal."

"I know." His blue eyes bore into mine, and I saw painful regret. His voice was hoarse. "I'll never ask you again. Please, Ry, I know I don't deserve a second chance, but I can't stop thinking about her. I've never... I miss her."

He'd been moping every time we'd crossed paths, blast him.

I growled. "If you make her cry, I will *never* help you again, Alex. Ever."

Alex's face lit up so much that I cringed.

He better not mess this up.

Ten minutes later, we arrived at the infirmary, no worse for wear. Except my arm, the pain had gotten worse.

The five of us entered the building, nodding to the guards as we passed. Three soldiers whistled, and Ian nudged Ella's and my ribs.

"I think you've got admirers, ladies."

I rolled my eyes. "They are probably admiring this bandage."

"Then I admire that bandage a lot."

My eyes shot to Ian's, startled. He was grinning back at me, and I couldn't tell whether he was joking or not.

Alex coughed loudly.

I broke Ian's gaze and pulled Ella to the side. "I think you should go with Alex. We need my injury to distract them."

Ella shifted, uncomfortable. "Does it have to be me? What about Ian? Or Loren?"

"Just talk to him." She trusted me. I hoped I wouldn't regret asking.

"Is this because you want alone time with Ian?"

What? "No!"

Ella fixed me with a skeptical brow. "I'm doing this for *you*, Ryiah."

If I continued to deny it, would she change her mind? I decided to drop the protest. "Thank you."

Loren, Ian, and I crowded the infirmary's desk as soon as we turned the corner. The three of us started arguing loudly with the healer in charge while Alex and Ella snuck past the attendants into the supply room. I kept my eyes open for any passing healers while Ian and Loren continued to point at my arm.

Ten minutes passed, and then Alex and Ella reemerged, proudly concealing a small jar in Alex's fist. My friend looked happier. I wondered if they'd had a good talk.

Ella's eyes caught mine, and she gave a timid smile. I started to return it, and then my face fell as a young woman in a red mage's robes blocked their escape, fixing the two with a steely-eyed frown.

"Apprentice Alex, do you have an authorization for that?" The jar and their guilty expressions hadn't escaped her notice.

The mages behind us were too busy with Ian and Loren to hear.

My brother sauntered over to the healer with an easy stride. "It's just a bit of salve. My sister broke her arm."

Kyra's frown deepened. "You know the rules, Alex."

"It could be our little secret." My brother leaned in close and gave the girl a rakish smile. "Don't you want to keep a secret for *me*, Kyra?"

The mage's cheeks turned pink. "Stop that." But I noticed she said it with a lot less force.

"You know you really shouldn't hide eyes like yours behind those bangs." My brother brushed a strand behind her ear. "People might not see how beautiful they really are."

The girl swatted his hand away with a giggle. "Just this

once, Alex."

"You are a goddess among men." Alex caught her hand and kissed it lightly, winking.

"You should join the healers for a drink one night," she stammered. "We go to the Crow's Nest every Sunday. Will I see you next time?"

Alex grinned. "I wouldn't miss it."

As soon as the girl vanished, Ella snatched the vial from my brother and turned to me, eyes flashing. "Let's get out of here." It didn't take much to ascertain her mood.

"Ella, wait, it wasn't what you—I was helping Ryiah!"

"I don't want to hear it, Alex."

"But I—"

"You just can't help yourself!" Ella cut my brother off with a cold laugh. "It's not your fault—when this girl kisses you or that girl misinterprets your flirting you're blameless. Well, I'm *not* going to wait for it to happen again. *We are done*." She grabbed my good arm and dragged me out of the building, not waiting to see if the rest of our group followed.

I didn't protest. As soon as we were outside the infirmary, I started to apologize. "Ella, I didn't—"

"It's not your fault. You warned me that first day at the Academy. I... I just have this bad habit of falling for the wrong ones."

Thinking about Darren earlier and my reaction to his hand on my wrist, I said sadly, "I think we have that in common."

And like her, I was determined to stay far, far away.

* * *

After a short dinner, we were once again on the practice field for our final lesson of the day. We were separated into two groups: those who could cast using pain, and those that couldn't. Ian, Darren, Eve, Lynn, and I stayed behind with a small collection of older apprentices. Ella, Ray, Priscilla, Loren, and the rest of our faction retired to the far side of the grounds to continue the target casting from earlier.

Now more than ever, I was grateful for the arnica. I was finding it much easier to control my castings when the pain in my arm wasn't fighting my magic.

"No, no, *slowly*, Ian!" Master Byron's command echoed across the chilly grounds. "If you keep that up, you are not going to be able to control the casting."

"*Again*." Darren's voice was thick with sarcasm. The two of them had been trading barbs for the past hour—mostly because Ian kept losing control of his castings. We were supposed to levitate our partners, but Ian hadn't quite mastered the correct pressure to use.

The prince had been tossed into the sand more times than the rest of our group combined.

I wasn't sure whether to laugh or sympathize. Ian was miserable at pain casting.

"Mentees, you are up."

Lynn slowly withdrew the blade from her hand, letting me drift gently to the floor. To my left I heard a loud thump and Darren's subsequent curse.

"Master Bryon, I need to change partners for this exercise. This is ludicrous."

All heads turned to Ian and Darren; the former looked sheepish and the latter, furious.

"Fine. Darren, Ryiah, trade mentors."

I scowled at the prince as we traded spots. "I have a

fracture." His little spat just cost me my arm. *If Ian drops me...*

"Good thing you have the arnica."

Some "friend." I sat down cross-legged in front of Ian, returning to the start position as I reached for a knife. At least it was my turn.

"All right, mentees, this time in your castings I want you to focus on time. Try to hold your partner in the air for as long as you can. Once you feel comfortable, try alternating the pressure and keeping the same two-yards level. Being able to maintain a stable pain casting, no matter the pressure, will help train your magic should you be caught off guard with an unexpected injury." The man paused, his ice blue eyes locking onto me. "Some of you could certainly use the practice."

Maybe you could use the practice bullying someone else. I held my tongue and set to work on my casting. I would gladly practice Byron's drills all night, if only so he could see me try—not that the man would ever acknowledge it.

"If you drop me, I won't hold it against you."

I tried to give Ian a reassuring smile, but that did little to mask the anxiety in my throat. *Concentrate.* I gently dug the blade into the center of my palm, refusing to flinch as the pain roared up along my hand.

The magic was instantaneous, a wavering beast and my mind was the reins. Pain called the unsteady casting, and Ian was instantly hovering in the air.

I inhaled and exhaled, waiting for him to level.

Another minute passed, and I added to the pressure in my palm, alternating between light spurts of pain. Ian remained two yards above.

I took turns nicking my fingers and slicing deeper into my palm, trembling as the pain fought for control. I willed the magic to hold and braced myself as the pain continued to pulse.

My eyes watered and burned. Every little injury opened a floodgate of magic, and if the pain was bad enough, I wasn't always able to hold it back.

I'd broken a barrier—the one that usually kept my pain magic at bay. During the trials, I'd speared myself with a sword and sent an entire building crumbling in its wake. It made sense that so much magic and a near-death experience would leave a large crack in my defense.

Normally people built up to that level of pain casting, slowly, with incremental levels of pain—not the other way around. Master Byron had implied as much when I'd asked. *"They avoid teaching that magic to the first-years for a reason, Apprentice. You lost control of a power you do not— and will not – have control over for many, many years."*

Blinking, I realized that Darren and I were the only ones still casting. The other two mentees—two fourth-years—had already quit.

A couple seconds later, I lowered Ian to the ground, releasing the pressure of the knife. My casting had started to waver and I didn't want to risk my luck.

Ten minutes later, the prince followed suit.

"Well done, Darren." The master directed the mentors to cast.

I braced myself for Ian's inevitable misstep... but nothing happened. The third-year seemed to be concentrating extra hard. I wasn't thrown once.

When Ian's casting started to tremble, he returned me to the ground with the smoothest landing of the night.

If it weren't for my injury, I would've thrown my arms around his neck. "You didn't drop me!"

He winked. "I just need the right motivation."

My heart skipped a beat. *Don't be a fool—he doesn't mean anything by it.*

Darren, still levitating nearby, snorted. "Right."

The third-year shot the prince a sheepish grin. "Sorry, Darren."

The prince arched a brow. "Sorry that I'm not a pretty red-haired apprentice, or sorry that you knocked me into the sand?"

I wanted to knock the prince into the sand with that comment.

"Might be a bit of both, if I'm honest."

My whole face was on fire. I couldn't look either in their eyes for the rest of the lesson.

He thinks I'm pretty?

It was only much later as I was shoveling waste out of the barrack privies that it occurred to me to wonder which one I'd been thinking of.

THREE

"IT'S TIME, APPRENTICES. It's the moment you've all been preparing for."

Yes! I could barely contain my glee; I'd been counting down to the mock battle for weeks. The apprenticeship hosted one in each city at the end of each initial training before we returned to the Academy.

Master Byron marched up and down the row of students, the deep lines of his face set in a glower. "Today Commander Ama and her mages will observe your skills in battle. They'll evaluate your level for field service after solstice."

The other two faction masters, Master Joan from Restoration and Master Perry of Alchemy, took over, detailing their expectations for our simulated encounter. All sixty-one apprentices would be divided into two teams: the second- and fourth-year mentees against the third- and fifth-year mentors. It wasn't intended to be a fair match, but it would give us the opportunity to showcase what we had learned.

"Each of the teams will have a leader from Combat."

Master Byron brandished a black cloth. "Whoever you designate will wear this band around their forearm. If the leader is captured, your team immediately loses, so do yourselves a favor and give the other side a good fight first."

Commander Ama joined the masters and the rest of her infantry under the shadow of a nearby tree. We were three miles outside of the outpost, immersed in a true wasteland without a building in sight. Behind us was an endless expanse of steep cliffs, sand, and desert crags. Strange flowers and crooked cacti dotted the distance.

"This is a true-to-life battle." The commander's shaven head gleamed under the blistering desert sun. "During the exercise, I expect you to treat the opposing team as a true enemy. If we suspect any of you of are failing to do so, you will not like your placement come field training in the spring."

Ella elbowed me with a grin. "You heard her. No special treatment for Ian. He's your *enemy* now."

I shoved her back in good spirits. "Hush."

"Apprentices, report to your teams!" Master Byron's command ripped through the air. "You have two hours and a limited number of supplies to prepare."

Ella and I followed the rest of the second- and fourth-year apprentices to the shade of a large overhanging peak. At its base were fifteen single-horse chariots, a giant crate filled with empty flasks and common desert ingredients used in Alchemy, bandages, and thirty-one sickle swords, the most common melee weapon of the Red Desert regiments.

Third- and fifth-years clustered behind a large mesa a mile away. From the loud clamor carrying through the canyon, I suspected they were already arguing over a leader.

Scratch that, an argument had already broken out for us.

"It should be Darren." Priscilla's drawl rang out above the din. "If *anyone* knows how to lead an army, it's him, not an insignificant lowborn."

"Leaders are fourth-years, not second!" Jayson, a fourth-year and former lowborn, bristled. "It should be Tyra. Last year her advice brought our team victory in Ferren's Keep."

"Darren trained as a knight before the Academy." I had to strain to hear Eve's counter from the edge of the crowd. "He was going to be commander of the Crown's Army like my father."

"Your father is Commander Audric?"

She nodded and my jaw dropped the same time as Jayson's.

No wonder I'd felt so underprepared last year. Eve and the prince had been training for roles in command while I'd still been playing with dolls.

"Let's take a vote!"

"Fine," Priscilla snapped at the crowd, eyes flashing, "you better not be bloody fools."

Jayson looked to the rest of us, hands on hips. "Well? Do you want a fourth-year who knows how to win or Master Bryon's pet, an inexperienced prince who is only in his second year?"

"Darren." Priscilla didn't even hesitate.

"Tyra!" Two Restoration apprentices shouted at the same time.

The rest of the apprentices quickly cast their vote, and it was only after a moment of silence that I realized everyone was staring expectantly at me.

"It's fifteen to fifteen, Ry," Ella whispered.

I swallowed. My sometimes-friend, or the girl Priscilla didn't want to lead? It was tempting to spite my nemesis, but doing so would be a direct slight to the boy who'd helped me more times than I could count.

Darren's lip twitched at the corner of his mouth. It was clear he expected me to vote for Tyra, the same as my brother and friends. And who would blame me? She was older and she *had* led her team to victory...

"Darren." I couldn't let him down, even if I wanted to.

The prince's eyes flared in surprise, and I ducked my head before he could see me blush, but not before I caught Priscilla's scowl.

Apparently she'd wanted me to vote against the prince.

"Only the mentees have chariots." Darren recovered his shock and set to work outlining the strategy for today's battle. "That's an advantage we've got to press. Tyra, how do you feel about offense?"

The fourth-year studied the prince, dark skin glistening under the shade of desert rock. From her expression, it was clear she respected him taking the time to seek her council, even if she wasn't our leader. "We held off a siege last year," she admitted, "but we won concentrating our strike on a small section where the weakest apprentices were located."

Darren gave an approving nod. "I'm sure the mentors will be prepared for an attack like that again. They'll probably alternate fifth- and third-years down the line instead of keeping all of their weakest in one spot, but I wonder..." His voice trailed. "Last year, where did they keep their

Restoration and Alchemy apprentices? Were they helping the defense or hidden away with the leader?"

"Hidden."

"Perfect." The prince straightened and faced the rest of our group. "That's how we'll beat them. *All* of our factions will charge—not just Combat."

A couple of Restoration and Alchemy apprentices stirred, not quite brave enough to voice their protests aloud.

"Restoration, those chariots all hold two riders. Each one of you will be paired with someone from Combat. You have two jobs: steer the cart and see that your partner is safe. The Combat apprentice will be busy leading the assault, so if things go wrong, it will be your job to turn the cart around and heal them when it is safe to do so."

The prince addressed the other faction in turn. "I want Alchemy to start preparing any airborne potions you can think of: liquid fire, gas, sludge, anything that can blind the enemy or help break down their defense. Make as many as you can in the next two hours... Each of you will lead a second chariot strike behind the Restoration-Combat teams. Should things go wrong, you will throw those flasks to startle the enemy, and give the rest of us a chance to escape."

He saved the best for last. "Combat, you already know your role. I want you to cast whatever long-range weapon you are comfortable with. You're going to lead the attack and focus on the left side of the mentor's defense. After we break it, we'll charge the mentor's leader together as a unit, cutting our way through the rest of their defense on foot."

For a moment, there was absolute silence. I was incapable of doing anything but stare. Darren had outlined an entire battle in minutes. Even Jayson and Tyra were speechless.

"We might actually win this," Ella murmured.

I couldn't help but agree.

* * *

Master Byron was counting down from sixty, and we had ten seconds to start.

Alex readjusted the reins of our chariot with a grumble. "Should have known she'd say no."

"You're my partner," I warned. "If you are too busy staring at Ella and steer me into a mentor's javelin, you will be very, *very* sorry."

"*Three.*"

"But Ronan—"

"*Two.*"

"He beat you in the first-year trials," I hissed. "If anyone can protect her, it's—"

"*One.*"

The chariots took off.

Three rows of carts and horses raced across the sandy plain, kicking up dirt and sand as we charged the leftmost enemy lines. Alex and I, along with the rest of the second-year mentees, rode at the center of the formation. Fourth-years maintained our lead, and the Alchemy apprentices covered the rear.

I didn't need to look to know Darren was watching the procession from the top of a southern butte behind us. Our leader needed to observe from a distance. Should something go wrong, he would still be safe from enemy fire, and he could still project commands using magic to amplify his words.

If he needed to, he'd come down to join the fight. A part of me wondered if he wished he were with us, casting attacks instead of directing the force.

As Darren predicted, the mentors had prepared for a strike. Almost immediately I could identify Ian on the far right of their line, stuck between two fifth-years as they held formation. The Alchemy and Restoration mentors hid behind those of Combat. I could see their leader Caine at the very back of the defense, a black armband fluttering in the dry canyon wind.

The mentors weren't taking any chances.

Mentees had an advantage with the chariots, so Caine had known better than to tell his team to try and outrun our attack... But he'd also made a mistake by only utilizing his Combat apprentices to defend. The third- and fifth-years made up only ten against our thirty.

The mentors were in for a surprise.

I launched into my long casting. My pulse jumped as the chariot bumped and groaned. Blast Alex, he wasn't very good at avoiding rocks. I fought to block out everything but the sensation of drawing a bowstring taught against the back of my jaw.

My target was a Combat apprentice second to the left. I prepared the casting until the shaft was strumming with tension and magic, ready to cast.

The chariot drew close, and I recognized my target as Lynn. *Mentor versus mentee*, how ironic. I swallowed and picked the odd dent in her breastplate to visualize.

Then I relaxed my casting's draw, letting the phantom string slide as the arrow zipped across the divide.

Two, three, four… I sent ten castings in the span of a breath. The barrage continued all around me as Combat mentees targeted Lynn and her partner's defense.

At first our castings fell harmlessly, barely grazing the mentors' barrier. But then the wall started to flicker, temporary lapses of a strange purple hue that looked like veins whenever a new casting slammed the defense.

A hundred yards away from the mentors, the Alchemy apprentices joined us, tossing out fire flasks with a practiced finesse. I was grateful all factions, not just Combat, maintained such rigorous conditioning. If they hadn't, Alchemy would never be able to lob such distances now.

The mentors' barrier emitted a loud, ear-piercing shriek. Then the left side crumbled in a cloudy mass of gray and purple haze.

Our missiles began to land hits on the leftmost apprentices. Screams echoed across the canyon walls.

There was a loud, panicked shout from Caine, and then the mentors dropped their remaining defense and what little attacks they'd started to cast.

What are they doing?

"Mentees, fall back!" Darren's panicked voice shook the air.

Alex jerked the reins to the side, and I clutched our cart's railing as it began to swing around wildly.

Before we completed a full circle, the ground beneath us fissured and broke.

Mentees cried out in alarm as their carts tipped over and fell. Horses panicked and took off in every direction. Riders were stranded. Mentee apprentices fought to find balance in the aftermath of the mentors' manmade quake.

"Alex, get up!" I grabbed my brother and attempted to drag him away from our vehicle. When the ground broke, our cart had capsized. I'd managed to roll away unscathed, but Alex hadn't been quite so lucky.

My brother struggled to right himself, using my shoulder to stand while I guarded against potential attacks. In front of us, I could see the rest of our team doing the same: Restoration was retreating to the butte while Combat mentees attempted to hold off the mentors' charge.

We were losing. The mentors had started to push forward with a counter assault. The mentees' first line of defense was dissolving. Fast.

Near the front, Priscilla surrendered; she was surrounded by a pack of fifth-year mentors.

"Don't attempt to take the mentors on! Fall back, fall back, fall back! Alchemy, toss those flasks now!"

"Let's get out of here," Alex wheezed. He didn't have to say it twice. I immediately took off at a sprint—only to realize too late my brother was limping. There was something wrong with his leg. He wouldn't make it out on his own.

I looked across the plain to the mentors just fifty yards behind us. The others were emerging from the fire our Alchemy apprentices had chucked, slightly worse for wear, but still formidable. One of the mentors was casting javelins at a handful of fleeing mentees.

That same mentor spotted Alex...

My brother saw my hesitation and shook his head. "Run, Ry."

I didn't budge.

The fifth-year cast out his spear.

I didn't have time to think. I was already running back with my fist in the air. Seconds later my magic knocked the javelin off course.

I swung Alex's arm over my left shoulder and began to run-walk as fast as I could. The mentor was already preparing his next attack.

Ella appeared, coughing and sputtering through smoke. Without hesitating, she threw Alex's arm around her shoulder and we started to run.

The mentor's next casting missed.

We managed to make it to the butte. I wondered at our luck until the haze cleared and I saw Darren, Eve, and Ray casting defense near the rear. They were keeping the mentors at bay.

As soon as we were close enough to hear without shouting, Darren pointed to a narrow trail behind him. "There's a gulch just past this rock. Keep following the stream until you find the grotto. I surveyed the whole site from the butte. If you can get to the cave, you should be safe for now. I want to make sure we get every Combat mentee out of the canyon before we retreat."

We followed his directions, no questions asked. I could hear the shrieks of pain and explosions of castings gone awry from the other side of the wall.

There wouldn't be many of us fighting for long.

* * *

It was a half-hour later when Darren reached the grotto, half-carrying an injured Jayson as Eve and Ray shielded his approach. Four more mentees had come in after my group, and there'd been eight present when we arrived.

We were down to twenty. We'd lost eleven mentees in that first charge. Only one Combat fourth-year had made it back, and he was gravely injured. We were not in good standing.

The prince quickly set to work outlining our next move. The first thing he did was assess our condition. There were four of us too injured to run—though a couple of Restoration mentees were attempting to fix that. We had nine mentees left from Alchemy, five from Restoration, and only six from Combat. With the exception of Alchemy—who'd had the advantage of a rear escape—most of us were second-years. We'd lost most of the older mentees in the first attack since they'd been leading the first assault.

"From here on out, every casting needs to count. Caine is too smart to fall for our tricks and the mentors already have such an advantage." Darren ran a frustrated hand through his hair. "Eve and I cast a large boulder to block the entrance. That should hold us in this narrow gulch for a while, but there are other ways in, and I'm sure the mentors have already started scouting the rest of the canyon for breaks in the rock."

"Are you sure they won't just try to break your boulder?" Ruth, the second-year Alchemy apprentice Ella, Alex, and I had befriended last year, spoke up. "The mentors have to know your casting won't hold forever, especially against their own magic."

"Caine is not going to sit around and wait." Jayson clutched his bleeding side as two second-year Restoration mentees attempted to treat it. The pained expression he wore made me squirm. "Darren is right—Caine's going to send some of his mentors to scout."

The cave broke into chaos.

"Maybe we should just surrender now?"

"We might've stood a chance in chariots, but there's no way twenty of us can take on so many mentors now."

"They only lost one Combat mage in our attack!"

I waited for the complaints to die out. "We should pick them off one by one."

Everyone's eyes flew to me. It was the first time I'd spoken up.

I forced myself to continue, uncomfortable as I was. "We're outnumbered, but that doesn't mean we can't win. If we limit how many can enter the gulch at one time, we've got a much better chance. It's how the northern regiment won Battle of Daggan's Peak thirty years ago." I'd read all about it in the history scrolls during my first year at the Academy. I'd even cited it during my oral exam in an effort to impress the judges at the end-of-year trials.

"Ryiah is right." Ray gave me an approving nod. "I read the same thing. By barricading the tunnel, the soldiers were able to pick off the enemy one by one since the passage only fit two men at a time."

"The gulch isn't a tunnel." A fourth-year shot us a disapproving look. "It's just a very narrow valley with sandstone walls. It can still fit several mentors at once."

"Yes, but Ryiah's not talking about the entrance. She's talking about the scouts who try to come around the back." Darren shifted from one foot to the next. "The gulch is narrower south of the canyon, and with so many dead ends, it would be hard for the mentors to know which route to take. We can pick them off one by one and reduce the odds before we attempt a full-on assault."

The tight pressure that had been building in my chest was starting to fade. My plan could actually work.

Could it?

"How do you want us to do this, Darren?" Eve was staring at the prince's shoulder. I'd barely noticed it before, but now I could see a huge gash in his vest. There were burn marks, and the skin underneath was a nasty shade of red. One of the mentors must have used fire. I stared at his chest, horrified.

Darren was back to addressing the crowd. "I want Restoration to stay here. All of you do your best to heal the injured members and anyone else we send back. There is no purpose risking your safety now... Alchemy, I want you to guard the front entrance where Eve and I cast the boulder. It will be safer than patrolling, and all of you should have some experience with the sword in case the mentors are able to break the barrier before we return. Jayson will stay with you. He's too injured to help Combat, but at the very least he can keep watch.

"The rest of us will pick off mentor scouts from the southern entrance. It's a long shot, but if we can eliminate at least some of the Combat mentors, we might actually stand a chance."

"But what about you, Darren? Shouldn't you stay behind with the healers for that burn?" a boy protested.

Another: "You're our leader—if you get caught it's over!"

Darren's laugh was cold. "We need every Combat mentee

we have. If I don't fight, it's over either way."

* * *

I descended the butte with careful hands. I was all too conscious of how risky it was to climb loose sandstone... but if Darren had done it, then so could I. Someone had to, and thanks to my reputation for scaling a cliff during Combat's orientation last year, I'd been the first choice now that our leader was injured.

When I reached my last foothold, I jumped, landing lightly in the shallow canyon stream below. The rest of the Combat mentees were waiting for me at the bank. Their expressions ranged from apprehension to fear.

"How many did you see?"

"Four. They were together, but it looked like they were separating at the fork. One of them was Ian. I think another was Bryce. They were headed toward a dead end. The other two were Combat fifth-years, and they were following the stream that leads straight to our camp... I didn't see anyone else following, but it was hard to see past that crag."

Darren took in my report and then issued orders. "Eve, Ray, and Ella, you three will take the two headed toward us; Ryiah and I are going to go after Ian and Bryce."

Our group exchanged nervous glances. This was it.

Ray turned to Darren. "Are you sure you'll be fine— maybe someone should switch?"

"You three have the fifth-years." The prince clamped the boy's shoulder in support. "I'm sure Ryiah and I can take two third-years, injuries and all."

Did that mean he thought I was weak? I wasn't sure.

As soon as we parted ways and started down the trail, I

spoke up. "So what's our strategy?"

Darren's eyes met mine and he smirked. "You really don't know?"

"Know what?" I was suspicious of that mouth; whenever he looked at me like that, well, it wasn't good. Darren didn't always play fair.

"You are so innocent." That maddening grin flashed. "This is going to be fun."

My expression soured. "Because we're going to be beat to a bloody pulp?" Or did he expect me to take on two mentors by myself? Why would *that* be hilarious?

"Think about it, Ryiah." I itched to slap that all-knowing smirk off his face. "Who are the two third-years?"

"Ian and Bryce." I made a face. "What's so special about them?"

"Ian." His eyes were dancing.

"And?"

"And I want you to distract him while I get rid of Bryce."

"You take the weak one and leave me Ian? He's the best in his year!" I glared at the prince. I was good, but even with his shoulder, Darren was still the best in *our* year. That's why Byron had made him the prince's mentor, not mine.

"You're not going to fight him."

"So I'm just what? The sacrificial bait?"

"No."

"Then *what*?"

"I'm going to distract Bryce while you fake an injury. Convince Ian to help you."

"Help *me*? He's a mentor, Darren." Had he gone mad? "Ian's not on our team."

"It doesn't matter." The prince waved my protest away with a flick of his hand. "Ian will help. Just bat your lashes and play the damsel in distress."

"He's not a bloody fool!"

"You'd be surprised." The prince's gaze fell to my mouth. "It wouldn't take much."

Two spots of red appeared on my cheeks. "You're such a jerk!"

"You're only upset because you know I'm right."

"You arrogant, conceited..." *Gah!* Why did he have this effect on me? I held up my hands and glowered. "Fine! *Fine! We'll do it!*"

Darren smirked and pointed to the edge of our trail where the passage became entirely paved in sandstone. A soft light reflected off the walls and into the bright blue sky above. It was just past those rocky structures that our enemy awaited. "You ready?"

Did I have a choice?

* * *

"Ian! *Ian!*" I whisper-shouted as loud as I dared. Bryce was just two hundred yards away, investigating a mysterious noise that had come from whatever Darren had cast. The prince was slowly edging his way out of the shadows as the curious third-year passed him, searching for the source of the sound.

"Ry? Is that you?" Ian twisted his neck and peered into the entrance of the small cave-like formation I was hiding in. "Why are you calling me? I'm not on your t—"

"Ian, I-I'm hurt..." I felt a stab of guilt as I whimpered the lines I'd recited so many times in my head. *You can do this;*

it's for your team. "I got lost—m-my team doesn't know where I am… I n-need to go to the infirmary, and I c-can't walk." Then for good measure: "I-I think I b-broke my leg."

Curse you, Darren, for making me do this!

He couldn't make me do anything I wasn't willing to do.

Blast it, I was just as terrible as him.

"Just stay still! I'm coming in…" The curly-haired third-year was inside the cave in seconds, hazel-green eyes wide with concern.

"Ryiah." He reached out to touch my wrist. "I don't even want to think what would have happened if you'd been trapped here all day."

The words got stuck in my throat. Shame squeezed at my chest. Ian looked so concerned, and I couldn't believe I was doing this.

I wanted the charade to end.

"Ian…" I could see Darren slowly approaching. He was close now.

Ian started to kneel. "Can you stand?"

I swallowed, hating myself. *Ian run. Get out of here before it's too late.* "Ian, I'm sorry."

"Why should you be sorry?" He glanced up so that his eyes were level with mine. His humor was gone, and in its place was an emotion I couldn't identify. The third-year kept his hand on my wrist, swallowing.

"Ryiah…"

There was something about the way he was looking at me, and in that moment, Darren's warning finally made sense.

I was a bloody fool.

"Ryiah," the third-year repeated softly, "there's something

that I've—"

A thunderous wind roared across the cave, and Ian was sent flying face first into the sandstone walls. He crumbled to the floor, unconscious.

"Darren!" I swore at the prince as I raced to check on my friend. "You could have hurt him!"

The prince peeked his head through the cave. "Come on, we need to move."

"I can't just leave Ian here like this. What if the healers can't find him?"

Darren groaned and started inside the cave. "Ryiah, we talked about this. He'll be fine. We have to—"

"Well, well, if it isn't his royal highness and a little minion at his side."

Darren and I almost knocked into each other in our haste to spin around.

Too late. Caine was standing at the entrance of the cave, flanked by two fifth-years and Bryce.

"Caine." Darren's voice was emotionless. "I should have known."

"Really, Darren, you think I'd just send in two defenseless third-years for you to pick off one at a time?"

"You were never known for your brains."

"Well, I know *you*, Darren." The fifth-year smiled coldly. "Always have to be a hero. I knew if I sent in two scouting parties, you'd send your best men after the fifth-years... But you'd be too proud to stay behind yourself."

"Ryiah." Darren's voice was low as he reached for his weapon. "Get behind me."

"Are you joking?" I hissed. "I'm fighting too!"

There was a roar and a flash of blinding light. Flames filled the room in seconds, stopping only inches from our face.

"Aghhhh!"

My magic was the only thing keeping the fire from burning us alive. It wouldn't hold us forever.

"Darren!" His name scraped against my tongue. Sweat beaded along my brow and slipped down the curve of my neck as I attempted to keep the mentors' casting at bay all by myself.

How many days would it take to recover from fire like this? The mentors expected us to surrender before the flames touched our skin, but what if we didn't?

Why wasn't the prince helping me? I couldn't hold their casting forever. This was three against one, and my stamina was depleting faster than normal with the force of their casting. I wasn't meant to take on four mentors by myself.

The prince sliced the curved end of his sword against his wrist and blood dripped down the stone between us.

The fire crackled and spat, retreating one small flame at a time. Darren's casting wasn't just helping my barrier; it was overpowering the fire.

"You can't keep that up forever," Caine shouted.

Seconds later, the fire pushed back and the prince started to shake, his skin ashy and white.

In another minute, Darren's defense would break. The mentors were using the full extent of their power to overtake ours.

Small red splinters were starting to form against the barrier like glass. I could feel the overwhelming heat against my face; the scent of signed hair that was probably my own.

I barely had time to think before I grabbed Darren's hand and thrust my other hand along the barrier's surface.

This time my pain wouldn't win.

"Don't—"

I never heard the rest of Darren's cry as red-hot flames licked across my skin. The pain was relentless and deep; I felt it right down to my bones. The pain chased along my veins like a coursing river, dragging and shoving me down as the magic bubbled and broke.

The pain was a violent storm; it called out and fought for control.

My magic reared like an angry stallion, kicking down walls

Shadows danced across my eyes, a red and orange waterfall of flame. The pain was too much. My legs were quivering. I felt the wave of agony rolling, and the magic threatened to break—

Darren's hand tightened on my own. A sharp swell of coolness flooded my veins, erasing the fire and pain and returning me to myself.

Control.

I was the master of my casting, and he was the master of his.

We pushed back as one. Together, with a shaking step, and then another, Darren and I advanced with the fire billowing back.

We were going to win.

Caine and his friends didn't realize what was happening until it was too late.

The fifth-years and Bryce released their fire, but our force threw them before they could summon a barrier of their own.

The four mentors were sent sprawling to the sand. Two of them were knocked unconscious from a boulder.

Caine and Bryce crawled backward on their arms in an effort to escape.

Darren dropped to his knees with a gasp; he'd breached his limits.

I found myself struggling to stand. When I tried to call on my magic, there was nothing left to cast.

Time for something else.

I drew my blade and staggered cross the sand with the weapon in hand. My legs shook so badly that I stumbled and slipped.

I attempted to push myself back up, but the pain was too much. I couldn't do it.

I was so close…

Caine began to laugh, dirt and blood spilling from his mouth. He wasn't faring any better.

"Surrender, Caine, your time is up."

The fifth-year stopped laughing and blinked. Three dark figures emerged from the sandstone passage behind us. As they drew closer, I recognized Ella, Eve, and Ray—all of them a bit bloodied and bruised, certainly worse than when we parted an hour before. Ray was limping and Ella favored her arm, but they were the best thing I'd ever seen.

They looked even better when they cornered Caine and held three curved blades to his throat.

The fifth-year spat at them and tore off his black armband.

We won. Loud whoops filled the air and I heard rather

than saw Darren collapse.

Ray and Eve ran over to check on their fallen leader. Ella started toward me, but I shook my head and pointed to the cave. I barely had time to murmur "Ian" before my vision, too, faded to black.

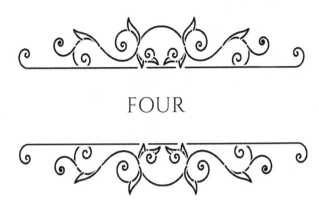

FOUR

"YOU LOOK A lot better today."

I groaned, opening my eyes and wrinkling my nose. I was in the infirmary. The room smelled strongly of herbs and rubbing alcohol, and it was colder than the barracks. My hands and feet were numb.

I sat up with a start. "How long have I been out?"

Ella grimaced. "Almost three full days. That burn on your hand took the longest."

I glanced down at my hand; it was just the barest shade of pink. It didn't even throb.

My friend gave my shoulder a reassuring squeeze. "You and Darren had the worst injuries. Everyone else already returned to the barracks."

"Byron let the mages heal us?" I scanned the room, looking for the prince.

Darren was near the back, one arm hanging off a cot. His black bangs fell to the side, lips slightly parted as his chest rose and fell in deep sleep. *He looks so innocent.* I almost laughed. Darren never looked innocent.

"Well, we *are* departing tomorrow for the Academy." I'd forgotten. "None of the masters want a bunch of cripples holding up our progress. It takes ten days to reach Sjeka, as is."

I couldn't believe we were returning to the Academy so soon. Last year at this time, I'd been drowning just trying to keep up.

Ella grinned at me. "There's a feast tonight for the victors. The masters haven't formally congratulated the mentees yet. Loren said they usually have it the second night, but since you and Darren played such a large role, they decided to wait until you two were out of the infirmary."

Memories of that battle in the sandstone gulley came flooding back. Many things stood out—Ian reaching out, Darren casting our shield, the pain of fire, the sudden strength when I'd been able to take control of my pain casting...

And Ian. Ian flying headfirst into that stone wall.

"So everyone else recovered?" I was suddenly anxious. Where was Ian? How was he feeling?

Does he hate me for tricking him?

Ella nodded and continued on about the feast. I wanted to ask about Ian, but I was afraid of what she might say. Even though Ian had been on the opposing side, I didn't think she'd approve of my tricking him. It was a rotten thing to do to a friend. She probably didn't even know.

If only Ian hadn't been so eager to help me, so innocent.

If only Ian stabbed me in the back before I stabbed him.

* * *

Priscilla found me later that evening, just as I was changing out of my infirmary rags and into a dress. It would be the first one I'd worn since the naming ceremony at the

Academy, and the first one I could call my own. One of the perks of being an apprentice. With my new income, it'd been easy for Ella to talk me into buying it. A nice dress was something special that an apprentice could wear to indicate her new status.

I was a lowborn no longer.

"Caine told me you and the prince spent a lot of time together in that canyon."

I bit back a groan. "What do you want, Priscilla?"

"Whatever idealistic notions you've got running around in that loose head of yours, the prince will never leave me for a lowborn."

Not this again. "Priscilla—"

"My father is the wealthiest baron in the realm. Darren *needs* this marriage."

I needed her to go away, but she didn't seem to be leaving anytime soon.

"Jerar has the greatest army in the world, but if the Crown wants to keep it that way, they need my dowry. No infatuation will change that."

"Just what exactly do you think happened between us?" I pulled the dress over my shoulders, marveling at the way the fabric moved. It was as light as air.

Priscilla just scowled at me. "Just stay away from him."

I rolled my eyes. "I'm not that pitiful little girl you bullied last year. You're never going to send me packing, so you might as well stop trying."

Her expression was murderous. "You think you're special because he wants to be your friend?" She laughed. "A mistress is the best you can aspire to be, Ryiah."

I might never have a prince, but the girl who was once the Academy's pride and joy, save Darren and Eve, was now the worst apprentice here. That counted for something, and I wasn't beyond throwing it back in her face.

"If you'll excuse me, I have somewhere to be." My laugh was cold and unfeeling right back. "There's a feast in your betrothed's and my honor. Some of us didn't surrender during the first ten minutes of battle."

I walked out with the biggest grin on my face... I didn't bother to acknowledge the twinge in my chest.

* * *

"Ry!" Alex caught up to me the second I reached the infirmary's steps. "They told me you were awake!"

"Barely. I just had an unpleasant conversation with my nemesis."

"Priscilla?"

I made a face as the girl flounced past in an armful of skirts.

Alex snorted and held out the nook of his arm. "Well, that takes care of that. Do I have the pleasure of escorting a champion of Combat this evening?"

"Am I your second choice or your first?"

"You're my sister. You're always first."

I grinned. Alex was such a liar, but I wasn't about to call him on it. I already knew Ella was his first choice, and she'd partnered with Loren.

We were in high spirits until I noticed the couple descending the steps below us. Lynn, looking delicate and lovely, was being escorted by a certain curly-haired third-year. I could hear his laugh from yards away. *Ian.*

My pulse caught in my throat. I didn't realize I'd stopped moving until Alex was waving his hand in my face.

"Ry?" My brother tilted his head. "What's wrong?"

My smile was forced. "Nothing."

Alex followed my line of sight with a quizzical brow. "The third-years from your faction. Do you want us to join them? It'd be nice to have some company."

I started to protest, but my brother was already off, dragging me in his wake.

As soon she spotted me, my mentor waved us over. "Ryiah." Lynn's grin was cheery and sweet, everything I was not. "How are you feeling? Ella said you were in the infirmary the entire time."

I couldn't look at Ian. "I'm better now."

"I'm so happy we ran into you." She pressed close. "I wanted to let you know there are no hard feelings for what happened the other day."

She was talking about the mentees' attack at the beginning of our battle. We'd targeted the mages on the left, but it'd been a fair fight... What I'd done to Ian, the reason I couldn't look at him now...

"You've got to do whatever is necessary to win," she finished. "I guess I should be happy it happened to me in the beginning. Ian only just recovered last night. You and Darren gave him a hard time, didn't you?"

I felt like vomiting, and Ian didn't bother to comment.

Lynn looked between us, brow furrowed. "Did something happen?"

"No." Our replies were instantaneous.

The rest of our walk to the ceremony was spent in

awkward silence. Alex kept nudging me with his arm, but my lips were pressed in a hard line. I needed to apologize to Ian, but I couldn't do it in front of the others.

That, and I had the distinct feeling my friend hated me right now. My apology would definitely have to wait.

Our arrival at the hall wasn't any more pleasant. We'd barely made it inside when Ian made an excuse to visit a friend on the other side of the room. Lynn trailed off to find Ella, and I nearly collided with a scowling Priscilla.

Our earlier conversation was instantly remembered: *"A mistress is the best you can aspire to be."*

"Ryiah." The prince stopped me in my tracks. He looked a little worse for wear, perhaps not quite ready to leave the infirmary. His smile was crooked. "Are you ready to be the toast of the Academy?"

He probably thought he was being witty, but when I looked to the prince, all I saw was Ian's face in that cave. I'd betrayed one of my good friends to impress a prince I could never have. Who was the biggest fool now?

I didn't answer and Darren frowned. "Is something wrong?"

I swallowed. "What isn't?"

"What are you—?"

I just shook my head and walked away. I was the queen of mistakes and there was no sign of losing that crown.

* * *

"Tonight we celebrate the incredible prowess of our mentees. This is the first time in a decade that second- and fourth-year apprentices won a mock battle. I take this as a sign of great potential to come, and I hope all of you will keep Ishir Outpost in mind after you've taken up your mage's robes." Commander Ama looked out at the crowd, beaming.

"That said, there are two apprentices who stood out. They demonstrated advanced levels of pain casting with enough control to save their squad. I would like to toast Apprentice Ryiah for her part in this victory, and Prince Darren for his excellent command. May great things come of you both."

I acknowledged the toast with a bitter smile. My victory had come at the cost of a friendship. I wasn't so sure it was deserved.

* * *

Ten days of riding and then they showed us to our chambers.

I couldn't stop staring.

As an apprentice, we were given all the accommodations a lowly first-year lacked: private rooms with the softest sheets, personal fires, a maid, and even an overhanging balcony with a view of the Sjeka coastline, featuring jagged cliffs and the white, foaming waters below. The bedposts were a rich cherry wood, and the cold marble floor was covered in charming rugs.

In each drawer of a well-made cabinet were freshly pressed cloths for drying and additional quilts for cold winter nights. There was already a small shelf with several books for study and a large chaise for lounging.

I wouldn't have to leave my chamber to study. I wasn't sure why the thought made me sad.

I wandered my chambers and found an interconnected alcove with a tub for bathing and a basin for my hands. *My own personal bath.* I practically melted on the spot.

"You ready to see Derrick?" Alex leaned against my doorway with a grin. I forgot all about a nice warm soak. "I paid a servant off to deliver our note."

First-years weren't supposed to associate with apprentices—not that Alex and I were going to follow that rule and wait for the solstice. Our little brother was here.

"Let's go!"

"Keep your voice down," he warned.

We started down the hall and froze. Sir Piers was standing there in the center of the marble, talking to Master Perry and Joan next to the stairs.

The brawny knight looked the two of us over with a nod. He wore the semblance of a smile.

"Welcome back, apprentices."

We acknowledged his greeting with ear-to-ear grins.

"And Ryiah," the knight's voice carried after we had left, "I'm glad you were the sixth."

I was happy to be back.

* * *

"We did not return to the Academy for two months to listen to you romance your factionmates, Apprentice Zyr! If you can't pay attention to your studies, then you clearly have too much time on your hands. I want you mucking the stables until we depart next month." Master Byron's irritated voice cut through the slow murmur of the rest of our class.

I felt a twinge of satisfaction as the fifth-year returned to his table at the corner of the room. For once, the master's wrath wasn't directed at me. It also gave me something to focus on other than my awkward table with Ian and Darren across from Lynn and me.

Why oh why couldn't I have been seated next to Ella and Loren instead?

It was hard to ignore the way Ian refused to acknowledge me. Even though Darren had led the attack in the desert, the mentor-mentee relationship hadn't changed. Probably because the prince's actions were expected and mine were... not.

Each team was supposed to be plotting strategy for desert combat. Byron gave us a topic, and we had a half hour to discuss and present our findings in a circle around the room.

"What do you think about a flash flood casting?"

"Too risky. More complications than it's worth."

"Lightning?"

"Too much stamina."

"Fissure? Fire?" I was growing impatient. Ian had gone from ignoring me to shooting down every idea I had. I wasn't used to this side of him and it hurt. "Direct assault with weapons? Hand-to-hand combat? What?"

Lynn and Darren just sat back to watch.

"Ian," my mentor finally interjected lightly, "why don't you suggest something instead of criticizing all of her ideas?"

"Fine." The third-year met my eyes across the way with a scowl. "How about turning on your comrades? Your friends will never see it coming. Mystery solved."

I winced and hardly noticed as Darren sat up a little straighter in his chair; the prince looked from me to his mentor and back.

"She wasn't out of line."

"Stay out of this, Darren." The third-year shot the prince a look. "We all know Ryiah will do whatever you say."

"That's not true!" My cheeks were pink.

"Really?" He leaned back in his chair. "Was that your idea back there, or was it his?"

My nails dug into my fists, and I refused to look at the prince. "If we'd fought you outright, Ian, we'd never have won."

The third-year laughed loudly enough to disrupt the rest of our class. "You sound just like him."

"Well, maybe I should!" My whole body was flushed. "We won, didn't we?"

"Congratulations." Ian's eyes lacked all of their friendly charm. "You won. And here I thought you were that girl I met at the solstice. Fighting for hardworking lowborns all across the world instead of a backstabbing lackey."

"That's enough." Darren grabbed the third-year by his collar. "I've heard—"

"Apprentice Ian and Your Highness, back to your seats!" Master Byron's gaze landed on me with aggravation. "Apprentice Ryiah, I've no doubt you started this. Go run ten laps around the stadium."

"But—"

"I said out!"

I swallowed. "I'm sorry, Ian." My words were so quiet I wasn't sure he heard them. "I wish I hadn't—"

"Out!"

I was shutting the door and jogging down the hall, but I didn't miss the prince's stormy expression as I passed.

My apology to Ian was a slap to everything Darren

believed. We'd fought hard and we'd done what needed to be done. For me to take it back... I didn't let myself ponder it as I started to run.

There were no winners on that battlefield. Least of all me.

* * *

Darren found me later that evening as I was concluding my evening drills.

"Ryiah." The prince reached down to take my wrist, but I pulled away before he could touch me. My heart began to race, slamming against my chest.

"You can't blame yourself for using every possible advantage to get us that victory," he said quietly.

"Not every advantage is worth it."

"This is about *him*?" Darren's jaw clenched. "You're better than this."

"You're right." My chin rose defiantly. "I'm not you. I shouldn't have traded a friend for victory."

"You're Combat." Frustration rose in his throat. "It's not about friendship. It's about winning."

"So if it'd been me? You would have done the same?"

"I wouldn't hesitate."

His answer hurt, and that was part of the problem. I shouldn't care that it did. And what of Ian and what I'd done to him? That look that passed before I betrayed him in that cave? "Not everyone can be as heartless as you. Power isn't everything."

Hurt flared in his eyes, but a second later it was replaced with arrogance and scorn. "Power is who we are, Ryiah." Darren gave an unfeeling laugh. "If you can't accept that, then you don't belong in this faction, and neither does he."

FIVE

THE NEXT COUPLE of weeks flew by, though they certainly weren't without their grievances. The prince and his mentor continued to silently feud for the rest of the month. There was a budding rivalry, and somehow I'd gotten caught between it. They weren't happy with each other, but that was nothing new.

Now they refused to so much as look at me. Ian was still disappointed and Darren was still... self-righteous and scowling whenever we passed.

Master Byron continued to take out his mounting frustration on me. For once I didn't mind. Drilling until I was ready to collapse was a ritual that brought me peace of mind. Running laps and drilling until my palms were blistered and bruised was a comfort I could grasp. Shouting? Nothing new. All of it was better than dealing with two adolescent boys I didn't understand.

There was also a rumor going around that the master had lost the last Candidacy, coming in third after a former lowborn named Kara.

"I heard he still harasses the Council to exclude women

from mage studies because of it." Ella nudged me over a steaming course of venison and buttered greens. We ate well as apprentices; nothing like the slop the staff served first-years. We even had a separate dining hall. "And then you strolled in like Marius's personal exception."

"No wonder he hates me."

"You *do* seem to have a way of bringing out the worst in people."

I snuck a look around our table before turning to her. "You didn't just say that!"

She grinned. "Poor, sweet Ian? Really, Ry? He won't even talk to us anymore."

"I apologized!"

"He's upset because he cares." Her gaze flit to my brother and back, but I saw it still.

"Like you and Alex?" I countered.

She tilted her head. "Well played. Seems you and your twin have something in common after all."

My victory wasn't as satisfying as I hoped.

Alex had been moping and hiding it for months now. Would that be me someday? I didn't want that mock battle to destroy a friendship I'd just barely begun. Would it have been something else one day with Ian?

I refused to even think about the prince.

Later that night, I found myself lurking outside the stables waiting for Derrick to make an appearance. Apprentices didn't have a curfew or restrictions, but that didn't apply to first-years. Lucky for me, my younger brother was a rule breaker like his sister.

I was blowing into my hands to stifle the winter chill

when he finally arrived.

Derrick shook off the snow from his cloak. "I hate this blasted school!"

"Bad day?" My heart hurt for him; every time Alex or I snuck out to see him, his progress only seemed to get worse. I'd hoped his magic would be as promising as ours, but his stamina had dropped dramatically, and he was still the worst in the class halfway into the year.

Derrick scraped the ice off his boot with the fence post. "I don't think I'm good enough to be a mage, Ry."

"I felt that way many—"

"I want to be a soldier."

I paused. "Not a knight?"

"I don't want to go through a trial like this again. If I'm not named at the end of the year..." Derrick shrugged, but his expression belied his carefree attitude. My brother cared, but he was just too proud to admit it. "At least the Cavalry has better odds."

Gods, he was just like me. I wanted to hug him but I knew he wouldn't appreciate that now. He'd left home for a war school; he wasn't my little brother anymore. Younger, yes, but little, no. In another year, we'd probably be the same height. His voice had even started to change.

"If that's what you want." I swallowed as my mind raced for a happier subject to end with. Tomorrow night was the solstice, and then Alex and I'd be gone. This would be our last visit before his trials at the end of the year.

I wanted to leave him with something to smile about. I knew how hard the Academy could be.

"In Ishir we trained with the local regiment." I rubbed my

gloves together for warmth; it really was cold tonight. "Every morning we spent two hours drilling with the soldiers and knights, not just mages. The things those men and women were able to do, it would make anyone proud to come from the Cavalry... I know it's not what you want to hear, but you don't need to be a mage to be happy, Derrick."

"What about you?" he sighed. "Do you want to give it all up and join me?"

There was a long, drawn-out pause and then a twinkle in Derrick's eye as he finished. "You know, your *favorite* brother?"

I grinned in relief. "Don't tell Alex."

"He already knows." He was starting to smile—that was good! "He's too much of a pansy to fight me for the title."

My stomach rumbled in a long, overdue laugh. Gods, I'd been tense for weeks; it felt good to let it all go.

My brother fidgeted with something in his hand. The odd glint caught my eye and I started.

"Is that...?"

Derrick's cheeks were red. "Yeah."

He removed the ring so I could see it in the moonlight, a simple copper band. It was tarnished with age, with a thick band and an "R" embedded on the surface.

I'd given Derrick that ring years ago. It was actually my ring, and Alex had one just like it. They'd been presents on our seventh birthday.

Four years old at the time, Derrick hadn't understood why he didn't get one too. He'd thought that being twins meant I loved Alex more. It'd upset him enough to throw fits for days... until I'd finally given him the trinket, telling him that the two rings now belonged to "both of my *favorite* brothers."

I hadn't thought much of the ring since, and I wasn't sure Alex still even had his, but after all this time, Derrick had held onto mine.

It warmed my chest.

"Come here." I pulled my brother into an awkward hug, ruffling his hair.

Derrick let me hold him for a second, and then shoved me away with mock disgust. "Don't go all mom on me."

"I'm so proud of you." I really was. "Whatever you choose at the end of the year, Derrick."

He just waved me away with an exaggerated groan.

* * *

"Ryiah, I need help with my coat." Alex's voice carried as he swung open my chamber door without warning.

"Alex!" Ella shrieked his name. "Get *out*!" She grabbed the nearest book off my nightstand and lobbed it at his head.

"Ella?" My brother flushed a very deep shade of red as he realized he had walked in on us getting ready for the solstice ball. We were in underdress, but it was still inappropriate. "I'm—" The book hit his face with a loud slap, and he ducked out of the room.

"He is lucky I didn't cast fire!" she muttered darkly.

"I bet he would have thought it was worth it."

She jabbed me lightly in the arm. "You are not helping at all!"

"He just seems so sad." I sighed. "I'm sorry, I know it doesn't matter much."

She gave me a look. "You are one to talk. Has Ian said a

full sentence to you since the mock battle?"

I cringed. "No. He avoids me at all costs."

"I'll make you a deal." She looked deviously. "I'll talk to your brother if you give Ian a *real* apology instead of moping around like a beaten lamb?"

I bit my cheek. "You've been waiting to say that one, haven't you?"

She grinned. "Perhaps." The girl pointed to the back of my bodice, which was in a shameless state of disarray. "You haven't been practicing like I told you."

I stared ahead at the wall, guilty. Practicing courtly manners and learning how to dress like a highborn had been last on my list of things to do.

I liked the dresses; I just didn't like the work.

"One day I won't be able to help you," she teased. "And then what will you do?"

"Wear my mage's robes?"

"Ha."

* * *

I told myself over and over that I would find Ian at the start of the night, but time trickled by and the room was crowded and loud. I couldn't do it. And then when I was finally ready to approach, I spotted him joking with Lynn and Loren across the way, and I lost my courage.

Coward.

I spent the rest of the night in a packed corner with Derrick and his first-year friends.

Before I knew it, Constable Barrius and his staff were shooing the first-years to bed.

The man scowled as he spotted me amongst the boys.

"You." I was the girl the staff would never forget, and how could they? I destroyed an entire building.

"You want to know who got stuck cleaning up that mess after your trials, girl?"

I ducked and ran.

* * *

I couldn't find Ella anywhere. She wasn't in her chambers and she wasn't in any of the training rooms. The palace bell had just tolled eleven, and after ten minutes, I decided to go find my brother instead. Alex was missing as well.

Well, you did tell her to talk to him.

I considered searching for Lynn and Loren in the ball, but the night was already late, and they were probably still with Ian. I couldn't work up the courage to apologize now.

Fine. I needed a good night's sleep before we set out for the desert anyway.

I shut my door and collapsed on my four-poster bed—dress and all—and then proceeded to stare at the ceiling.

I wanted to sleep, but I was too restless. All I could do was toss and turn. An hour passed and I still couldn't sleep.

With a huff, I searched my nightstand for one of the small vials I kept packed in my bag. A sleeping draught. It wasn't the ideal solution—usually Alchemy's potions left me queasy—but I didn't want to spend the next day falling off my horse on the long trek to Ishir because I hadn't gotten enough rest.

I swallowed the bitter liquid in one long gulp and then lay back down on my bed as I waited for it to take effect.

Everything became quiet, heavy, rhythmic. My eyelids fluttered shut, and I was only vaguely aware that I was still wearing my dress…

The loud clatter of a fallen sconce jerked me awake.

I sat up, suddenly dizzy. Someone in the hallway was cursing. *Inconsiderate fools.* I groaned and shifted on the blankets, but before I could get comfortable, there was a second clatter as the person who dropped the scone tried to replace it, only to drop it again.

That's it.

I staggered out of my room with purpose. The chamber door hit the wall with a thud as I flung it open and tottered into the hallway, blind. I had to squint to see in the darkness, and I couldn't see much.

"Get some decency," I croaked. "Some of us are trying to—" Big yawn. "—sleep in peace."

"Ryiah, is that you?"

I grumbled. "What of it?" The contents of my stomach churned, and it was anything but pleasant.

Oh no. I clutched my ribs. I should have known better than to take a sleeping draught on an empty stomach.

I sunk to the floor with a *thump*. My head spun. Everything spun. I did *not* feel well.

"Are you sick?" The shadow drew closer, and I finally recognized the voice. *Looks like I'll make good on that promise to Ella after all.*

"I should have fought you outright." My words were garbled and weak. He stood just a few yards away. "I'm sorry, Ian, I really am."

The third-year sighed, and the next thing I knew, he was slumped next to me on the cold marble floor. There was a moment of silence—just the quiet intake of breath as we leaned against the wall, shoulder to shoulder in shadows.

His swallow was loud. "You already apologized... I just needed some distance."

"But I—"

"You did what needed to be done. We're Combat. It makes sense."

Is he agreeing with Darren? I twisted my neck. "Then why were you upset?" *Why did you avoid me for weeks?*

"Because I was jealous, Ry." His rasp was so quiet it took me a moment to realize what he'd said.

Then... I was stunned. He'd flirted... I'd hoped... but I hadn't really believed.

"I always knew you liked the prince—"

But I didn't! *"I don't!"*

"—I just assumed one day you'd get tired of waiting for someone you could never have." The boy sighed. "I like you, Ryiah. I always have."

"I like you too!" My face was on fire, and I couldn't believe I'd admitted those words aloud.

"You say that, but I see how you look at him."

"Well then you are a fool for not seeing how I look at *you*!" There the words came tumbling out of my mouth.

Ian was silent. The third-year shifted, and I could sense he was wistful, but not quite convinced.

"Alex. *Alex*, be quiet!" Ella's loud giggling voice carried from the stairwell, and my head jerked in the direction of her voice.

Ian stood.

"Wait, Ian..."

He just shook his head. "Get some sleep, Ryiah." Then the

third-year disappeared into the dark hall, intent on his room.

Alex and Ella stumbled into the light of a nearby sconce, the two of them laughing with their faces flush and red. Neither of them noticed Ian as he passed.

I started to call out, but then my brother grabbed Ella's hand.

My mouth dropped as she turned and whispered his name.

That was all the encouragement he needed. He spun her into his arms and then proceeded to kiss her like he had all the time in the world.

* * *

"What *was* that?"

"A mistake."

My smirk was all-knowing. "That kiss lasted *at least* ten minutes."

Ella blushed. "Ryiah, I really wish we had known you were in that hall."

"So you could kiss him longer?" I yawned loudly. My head throbbed and it hurt to blink; the draught had been a terrible idea. This was not how I wanted to start our trip back to the desert.

And it was *so* cold. Ella fared worse—she hated the snow—but that didn't mean I was any bit happier. The first-years had their nice cozy Academy.

At least in our morning drills we'd been able to stay warm; now there was nothing to keep my blood flowing for a ten-hour ride in the saddle.

Byron wouldn't even let us cast to keep warm. When we were serving in a regiment someday, we'd be asked to conserve our magic for battle. Wasting casting on "mundane comforts" could be the difference between victory and defeat.

"Why were you in that corridor anyway? Seemed like an odd place for a nap."

Ella's question brought me back to focus, but I blanched at responding so close to the others. We were riding out in a two-columned formation, and the icy winds made it easier for people to listen than talk. I didn't want the whole faction hearing about my run-in with Ian, or how he'd insinuated I had feelings for the prince. *That* would be the worst humiliation of all.

Ella gave me look. "I cast a sound barrier. Why else do you think I was willing to discuss Alex?"

I glanced around, but I couldn't see any hint of magic. "Where? How?"

"You can't see it because it's intended to deflect noise, not sight." She grinned. "Watch this." The girl leaned back in her saddle and screamed—outside of the range of our barrier, of course.

Nothing. There wasn't a sound. But there should've been, especially when Priscilla turned around from her saddle and opened her mouth to make a crude remark to Ella for interrupting her quiet, I couldn't hear it, of course.

I made a mental note to ask Ella how to cast that barrier in the future.

When Ella leaned back, I finally told her everything.

She didn't look surprised.

"You can't blame him. He's afraid of getting hurt."

"I would never hurt him!"

Ella shook her head, smiling sadly. "Ryiah, you can lie to

yourself, but not to me. You like the prince."

That was two people—three if I counted Priscilla—now. Did everyone think I was moping after Darren like some lovesick idiot?

You can't lie to yourself.

Was she right? Ella knew me. She was neither a jealous betrothed or a jealous boy.

I swallowed, and a lump stuck to the bottom of my throat. I couldn't like Darren. I hadn't talked to him in weeks.

You left the ball after you saw him dancing with Priscilla.

And there was still that kiss. And that moment in the Academy towers. And that night he took my hand.

Blast it, I didn't even *want* to like him.

"It's Ian that I want."

"Wanting someone isn't enough." Her eyes were somber. "Prove that he comes first."

"What if I can't?" What if the prince was always in my head?

"Then you shouldn't rush a decision."

"What are you going to do with Alex? I thought you didn't want to give him another chance?"

"Your brother." She sighed. "I like him. A lot. More than I should... He can kiss..." Her cheeks were red. "But that was a one-time mistake. For it to be anything else, he's going to have to convince me first."

SIX

"WHEN WE REACH the barracks, I expect each one of you to brush down your steed and put your tacks away before settling into your meal." Master Byron's voice cut the frigid desert air like a knife.

I rubbed my numb hands together, teeth chattering. So much for a warm desert; the plains we passed through had been better than this. Who would expect the hot sands of Ishir to be so cold in January? Our warm breath was the only source of heat for miles.

We'd just passed through the Red Desert Gate. The giant gate was the only manmade barrier separating Red Desert from the rest of Jerar. Sadly, we still had ten miles before we'd reach the city's outpost.

Thundering hooves drew the attention of our group. I peered into the darkness, searching for the source of the commotion, half wondering if we were being attacked, when I recognized the garb of Ishir Regiment riders galloping toward us.

"Master Byron, Master Joan, Master Perry!" the first man practically fell out of his saddle as he pulled to a sudden halt in front of us.

"What is it, soldier?"

"The Red Dune bandits have taken over the Mahj salt mines." The man paused to take in the rest of our party but Master Byron waved an impatient hand for him to continue. "The local infantry couldn't hold them off, sir." His words came out in raspy spurts, "We suspect they're using m-magic."

"Where is Commander Ama?"

"She already left, and s-she requested your party follow them south!"

And there goes any sleep.

* * *

I dug my shovel into the trench, again and again. Sand and rocks scattered around my boots. It was hard, dirty work.

It didn't surprise me that, while everyone else was setting up camp, *I* was the apprentice servicing the tasks no one wanted. Master Byron's dislike had no end to its perks. I longed to be with the other Combat apprentices taking care of the horses, cleaning the regiment's weapons, counting the inventory, prepping the cots... but instead I was stuck here, digging trenches for two regiments.

Alex had been put to work with the rest of Restoration—there were already casualties from the battle of the Mahj salt mines—and he was busy learning and using his magic to make a difference. Alchemy was busy prepping potions to assist with the fight. Both factions were behind the lines, so to speak, so their masters had let them actively participate in the local efforts.

Master Byron, on the other hand, was keeping Combat as far from battle as possible. "They have enough warriors," he'd chastised our group the night we arrived. "What the regiment needs is help around camp."

This was *not* field experience.

Combat apprentices were to see to the upkeep of the fort while the real mages went off to fight. Byron wasn't going to lose apprentices who were "too big for their britches."

The locals couldn't even help because half of them were still barricaded in the mines by the bandits. Some of the soldiers were still trying to get them free. The few farmers who remained at the Mahj oasis were busy preparing meals for the entire camp.

I groaned. Regiment mages were getting *all* of the glory while the Combat apprentices were stuck playing house. This was not the life of a warrior I imagined. I knew it was wrong to be jealous—*especially* when Mahj's local command started to return with injuries—but it was impossible not to sulk after months of preparing for battle.

"You would get a lot further if you stomped your blade along the surface before digging."

And I recognized that voice.

Darren was leaning against a nearby palm, water skin in hand. He'd been one of the lucky ones to patrol the oasis instead of performing menial tasks.

Somehow, I doubted his route included the trenches at the base of camp.

Still…

This was the first time he'd spoken to me in over a month. And he was looking at me right now with a peculiar expression. I wasn't sure what to make of his presence.

The last time we'd exchanged words, I'd told him he was

heartless and he'd told me I wasn't cut out for Combat.

Who would break first? Did it even matter?

I knew he was waiting for me to respond.

I sighed. "Darren—"

"I'm sorry."

What? I blinked twice. I must have heard him wrong.

The prince took a step forward. His hands were shoved in his pockets, his eyes never leaving my face.

"I'm sorry, Ryiah," he repeated. "You were right."

And there it was. A prince of Jerar, the most arrogant boy I knew, had not only apologized, he'd admitted defeat.

The terrible truth? He was wrong.

The one time Darren was wrong, he was wrong about being wrong. The irony wasn't lost on me.

"Combat is Combat." I drew a shallow breath. My apology was long overdue, ever since that night Ian had found me and confessed... Even the third-year had admitted the prince was right. In war, we'd be expected to put the good of the whole over friendship if that friend was a part of the other side. Hadn't I said something similar in my first-year trials?

"You're not heartless," I added. "You were just doing what was best for our team."

"I know." His lip twitched at the side. "I'm not apologizing for that."

Really? I stared at the prince, arms crossed at my chest. *This is his apology?*

"I'm apologizing for hurting you, Ryiah."

I sucked in a sharp intake of breath. *What?*

"I hurt you by hurting him, and for that I'm sorry."

My jaw dropped.

"I'm not like you." He exhaled. "I don't care about keeping relationships or sparing people's feelings. All I've ever cared about is power: how to get it and how to keep it."

"You don't have to explain yourself—"

"But I do." He ran a hand up along his neck. "Eve was my sole exception to that rule, until you."

My throat was as dry as sand.

"I care what you think of me... I wish to gods I didn't, but there it is. Making you miserable and angry makes me miserable and angry." His laugh was bitter. "I've spent the last month hating myself."

I didn't reply. I couldn't if I wanted to. I didn't know what to say.

The prince groaned. "I don't want to be the person to make you mad or cry, Ryiah."

The words repeated, over and over in my head. I was stunned.

"I want to make you laugh," he said. "I want you to make *me* laugh, because gods know you are the only one who can."

My heart was in my throat; the pulse was slamming my veins.

"I don't want to lose you." The words were so quiet I almost missed them. "Our friendship means too much."

I don't want to lose you. Why were those words taking root in my chest? Why were they seeping into my bones, becoming an aching part of me I didn't even understand?

"You can't lose me, Darren." *I don't want to lose you, either.* But I couldn't admit to that second thought aloud. I already cared for him too much as it were.

A lump rose and fell against his throat. "Do you really mean that?"

I nodded and then bent down to adjust a bootstrap, more to busy my hands than anything else. When I finally straightened, Darren watching me, a strange expression on his face.

It made blood pound loudly in my ears. I bit down on my lip, hard. My eyes were glued to his, and I was hit with an overwhelming desire to close the distance between us, to reach out and take his hand in mine...

It's Ian that I want... Was it? Was it really?

"Ryiah." Darren suddenly dropped my gaze, looking anywhere but my face. "If things were... If they were different—"

Screams broke out across the other side of camp. The moment was gone. I dropped the shovel and took off with Darren toward the others.

We caught up to the rest of our faction to find several Mahj soldiers retreating from the northern trail, large burn marks spotting their arms. And blood. Lots of blood. It was pouring down their faces, chests, legs, *everywhere*.

Bile rose to my throat.

"The raiders," one of the men wheezed, "they have magic!"

"O-only ten of them," a female soldier choked. "But t-too much p-power."

"Where's Master Byron?" Caine questioned one of the knights. "We need to alert the regiments."

"With C-Commander Ama's m-men." Ten miles away

helping the regiment recover the southern mines.

But it wasn't the southern mines the raiders were attacking. They needed help now.

The crowd broke out in distress.

"We can't hold them off—"

"We can fight!"

"Wait for reinforcements."

"They are destroying our m-mines. C-can't wait."

"Apprentices, gear up." Darren's voice carried over the chaos. The prince had stepped into command. "We are going to help."

* * *

Ella and I saddled our horses with trembling hands. We were still working up the courage to speak. But what did one say before battle? The masters had never taught us what to say in those final moments of restless silence, the pressure beating on your chest like a drum.

I didn't feel so sure of myself. All this time I'd been so eager to fight, and now I didn't know why. There was nothing exciting about battle.

Any injuries we got would not be so quickly attended to. This wasn't a drill.

I tried to soothe my frantic nerves as I re-checked the reins and tucked my sickle blade into its curved sheath, hiding a dagger in the padding of my left ankle.

We were already dressed for battle in pale linen breeches, a riding shirt, and a vest. I tightened the belt at my waist and futilely wished desert regiments wore armor. I felt exposed with no chainmail and only a thin wooden shield to carry.

"Ella!" My brother crashed into the stables, with

bloodshot eyes and ashen skin. "Tell me it's not true? Tell me you and the rest of your faction aren't going after the raiders on your own?"

"We have to." Ella gave the saddle one final tug of the straps and then swung her leg into the holds. "They could destroy the northern mines, Alex. You know how important those are."

Salt was Jerar's most precious commodity; the mines in Red Desert produced over half the country's coffers. Every single history book mentioned this.

My brother gritted his teeth. "You need to wait for the regiment. Those soldiers can handle it on their own."

"The raiders have mages." I placed a reassuring hand on Alex's wrist. "They need us, Alex."

"But what if they hurt you?" His voice was hoarse. "Or Ella?"

My poor brother. As a healer, all he saw was blood.

"They won't."

"Ella, please…" My brother broke my grip to stand in front of her horse. "Please don't go out there."

"Ryiah's a good mage, Alex. So am I."

"I love you," he rasped. "Don't do this."

The stables were silent. A pin could've dropped and we all would've heard it.

Alex in love? My jaw almost hit the ground. Had the world ended?

"We're not going to die, Alex." Ella's mare shifting restlessly in place but the girl's expression was soft. "You can tell me when we return. If you still mean it then."

He swallowed and stepped back so that we could pass.

Neither one of us were going to die.

I prayed to the gods she was right.

* * *

We'd been riding for almost an hour when we finally located the entrance to the mines.

"There!" Caine pointed to a herd of slaughtered camel. They were heaped in a pile of bloody carcasses next to a pair of toppled caravans, and just further west were two large mile-long pits surrounded by chunks of rock and large slabs of white. *Salt.*

Deep fissures ripped across the salt beds like the claws of a beast. Tremors rattled and groaned, scattering Mahj soldiers and their horses along the ground. The air was lit with battle cries and great flashes of light against the blackening desert night.

I saw blood everywhere. Young men and women were sprawled across ditches and sand, soldiers' garb in tatters and shreds.

There were still twenty or so knights fighting. They fought to press a handful of darkly clad raiders back away from the precious mines and their people.

But it was a losing battle.

The raiders continued to draw closer, bright flares of magic spilling from their hands. They seemed more intent on destroying the mines than on the men fighting them. Already one of the mines had collapsed.

Salt twisted and danced in the wind.

It made no sense. Why were the raiders attacking the mines? How could ten untrained individuals possess so much magic—unless they really were mages as the locals had claimed?

The raiders didn't wear notable robes. They were dressed in loose desert garb, muted browns and blacks with hoods that shielded their eyes. Scarves hid the rest of their faces from view. It must have been how they'd been able to sneak up on the Mahj regiment undetected, blending into the night.

One of the raiders spotted us. *"Leave us."* His command cut across the wind. "I give you the same choice we gave these men here. Return to your camps, and we will let your people live."

"Relinquish our mines, and we will let *you* live," Tyra hollered back.

"This land belongs to the Crown." Darren joined Caine at the head of our party. "We give you one chance to retreat."

The man threw back his head to laugh.

"You filthy bandit!" Caine snarled. "How dare you mock a prince of the realm!"

The man stopped laughing and his eyes snapped to the three apprentices who'd spoken, focusing on the prince.

"Well, well." The gruff raider smiled wide, white teeth flashing. "It's an honor, Your Highness."

Oh no, panic flared in my gut. Stupid Caine—

"Brothers," the bandit roared, "the orders have changed: kill them all. I want that prince's head on a pike!"

"Apprentices, fall back!" Darren roared.

Thunder rolled over us, and then the air lit up with golden light. Bright yellow shards of lightning tore across the sky, and then we were galloping a retreat.

Screams filled the din as Mahj soldiers toppled to the ground; twenty new bodies writhing in the sand.

Men thrashed against the sand as flesh and bone exploded, clouding the air with a thick, crimson mist that spun and twisted in the wind.

"What have we done?" Ella's voice quavered.

We pulled up twenty yards away, out of the direct line of fire.

I didn't know how to answer. Fear had taken complete hold of my body. I clutched the reins, hands trembling and cold as ice. Hysterical screams threatened to break free from my throat; I was mourning the last seconds of my life.

I was a coward. The one time I'd needed to fight, I'd run. Retreating with the rest of our party instead of challenging the others head-on.

Would it have mattered? In those seconds, could we have changed the soldiers' fate?

The raiders had slaughtered twenty men in seconds… And now, now they wanted to kill us.

This wasn't a battle—it was a massacre.

I wasn't the only one who thought it. It was clear that none of us had prepared for this outcome or the realities battle could truly bring.

I tried to speak, but fear lodged itself too deep in my throat. We couldn't run. The raiders had horses, and they knew where we camped. They knew we had a prince.

We had to stay and fight.

"S-shield Darren," Caine finally stammered. "We need to p-protect the Crown!"

"No! We need to—" Darren's protest fell on deaf ears.

We all knew the prince was more important than any of us.

Another deafening boom and the ground below us quaked, just as a bolt of lightning shot out to our right.

It was time to fight.

For once our training worked. The entire faction cast out at once.

Our defense was a large purple globe that crackled and moaned.

The raiders' magic rippled against our barrier before finally fizzling and sliding down to the scorched earth below.

"Pain cast!" Caine gasped. "Now!"

But not everyone could. Ella's eyes found mine. Her lips were white. "Tell Alex—"

"We can't just hold this casting!" Darren's voice cut off the panic filling our dome. "We'll waste all of our magic!"

"We need to target the raiders one by one, like you did to us in the mock battle," Lynn gasped.

"But they are as strong as mages." The quiet voice was Priscilla. Even she was afraid. "We're only apprentices."

"Whoever wants to run, *run*. I'm staying." The prince's reply was defiant.

"No, Darren, they'll kill you!" an apprentice pleaded.

"It's my blasted decision!"

"But—"

Eve cleared her throat. "I'm with the prince."

"Me too," I announced.

In the end, everyone was staying and we were all fighting.

The first thing we did was dismount—there was no advantage on moving ground, and our horses would only hinder us in battle. We quickly laid out a plan of attack, Caine and Darren plotting the course. The rest of us held onto our casting… but the barrier was starting to smell like molten rock. There was a tinkling like glass whenever lightning touched the same spot twice.

It wouldn't hold much longer.

"*Now!*"

On Darren's command, we released the casting and separated into two parties: those who could pain cast, and those who couldn't.

The second group formed a running barrier, launching long casting arrows and javelins with as much force as they could.

The raiders easily deflected their attacks and sent off their own long castings in turn. Lucky for us, weather castings like lightning were too costly for the enemy to maintain.

The rest of us advanced. Using whatever blade we had on hand, we dug deep into our palms, summoning as much warm air and sand as we could. There was loose earth everywhere, providing plenty of debris for our magic. We thrust our castings together, allowing the joint power to fuel the attack.

Our dust vortex began to cut across the fissured plains, fast and deadly in its course. The other apprentices were ready and ducked to the side, allowing the tower of sand to pass. The raiders threw up a barrier and dropped their long castings, unable to see anything beyond the fast whirlwind of sand that blinded their sight.

But then they made a mistake: the raiders cast lightning.

With the heat of the raiders' magic, the vortex's particles fused together and melted. Sand conducted their lightning, and within seconds, the whirlwind transformed into a petrified web of sandglass that retreated to the casters themselves.

The glass shattered their barrier with a *craaaack.*

Molten glass streaked out like a gnarled branch and pierced the raiders closest.

They panicked as they tried to call off their magic—but it was too late for most of them.

Cries and screams ensued as white salt and blood rose, a pillowing cloud, a hazy red clotting the air.

The non-pain casters of my faction charged.

I knelt shakily, retching into the sand. Others around me were doing the same. Ian was on the ground. We'd reached the end of our limits. If we tried to cast again, we would end up unconscious.

I took a rattling breath and then froze.

There was a rustle to my left.

Darren staggered out onto the field, determined to help the rest of our faction. How was he still standing?

The prince always did have more magic than the rest of us.

In the battle ahead, I could make out Ella and Loren with Eve; the three of them were leading an assault on the remaining raiders. Five apprentices, including Darren and Caine, were close behind. Only three of the raiders still stood, but they were burned so badly they were having trouble casting.

I choked back relief. We were winning. Seven dead, three injured...

One of the supposedly dead raiders rose, scorch marks trailing like dark rivulets across his face. The others didn't see him—and Darren, he was too busy casting to notice.

I gave a hoarse cry, but he was too far away.

My boots scraped against sand.

"*Noooo!*" Caine spotted the raider and launched himself forward, shoving the prince to the ground.

The arrow embedded itself in the fifth-year's chest.

Caine didn't scream. Eyes open, mouth shut, he toppled to the ground, soundless, and then he went limp.

Darren struggled to pull himself up and make sense of what happened. Then he spotted Caine and a strangled scream severed the air. Darren charged and his magic roared across the expanse.

The raider who had just feigned death moments before dropped lifeless to the sand.

Then Darren dropped.

I stumbled forward, but then I was on my knees. I couldn't move. Pain was blinding in my head, and I could barely crawl. The pain casting had taken the rest of its toll.

In the distance, I could hear the shouts of the Ishir Regiment. *Thank the gods.* I clutched my ribs and willed myself to breathe. Reinforcements had come.

Master Byron and the regiment mages charged the three remaining raiders, casting heavy metal nets that trapped them in seconds. They sent in groups of men to take care of the bodies, the fallen soldiers and Caine, and then, finally, us.

The last thing I remembered was my twin's face. Bloodshot eyes. Alex. "*Where's Ella?*"

I pointed, and then I shut my eyes.

We were safe.

SEVEN

"HE'S NOT EATING. He hasn't eaten since he woke." The hysteria in Priscilla's voice was rising. "Please, Ronan, do something."

"It's not physical. The only thing that will help is time."

"*That's not good enough*!"

"Apprentice Priscilla, if you cannot keep your voice down, I must ask you to leave." Master Joan's frosty reprimand cut the air like a whip.

The girl let out a shriek and stomped out of the infirmary tent, creating a sharp *snap* as the fabric flapped shut.

I opened my eyes, uncomfortably aware of the pungent scent of blood and sweat all around me. Everywhere I looked, soldiers and apprentices lay in cots. Bandages and vials cluttered makeshift tables and chairs. Healers and Restoration apprentices flit from one patient to the next as they continued to cast and treat naturally depending on each patient's symptoms.

In the cot next to me was Ella. Her black locks were plastered to her neck. She was fast asleep, a bloody bandage on her arm.

A Restoration apprentice noticed I was awake and raced

forward to bring me water. I drank it down greedily; nothing had ever tasted as sweet.

"Alex?"

The apprentice nodded and then turned to the far side of the room. "Alex, your sister is awake."

My brother finished treating his patient and rushed forward, a thick line of sweat staining his forehead as he attempted to wipe it away, only to smear blood and grime in its place. He looked worse than I felt. I wondered how long he'd been here treating the others.

"Ryiah." He sank to the floor with a thud. "Thank the gods you're awake."

"How's she?" I tilted my chin in the direction of Ella.

"Sleeping off a draught." His eyes were bright and watery. "They lost Caine, Ry. The two of you could have died."

I couldn't respond. Caine was a fifth-year; he should've been a mage, not a sacrifice in the desert.

"The masters said they've never lost an apprentice before."

And they wouldn't have, if we hadn't rushed in.

"We saved the last mine." Ella's rasp was weak; she must have just woken up. "If we'd waited... could've cost Jerar."

"You bloody fool." My brother turned to my best friend, his hands balled into fists. "Who cares about Jerar if you're dead!"

"Careful." Her smile was weak. "You might show... all of your cards."

Alex didn't appear to hear. He kept staring at Ella, and there was something about the way he looked at her that made me feel like I was suddenly intruding.

"I... I meant every word in the stables," he rasped.

Definitely shouldn't be here.

"D-don't..."

"Don't what?" He brushed her face, and I immediately averted my gaze. "Ella, that day you walked in... that girl kissed me. I didn't..." His words came out a rush. "You have to know—you're the only one I bloody think about!"

"Alex—"

"Please..." His plea was desperate. "I almost lost you. D-don't make me lose you again."

And it was time for me to leave. I avoided looking at either of them as I stumbled out of the tent, ignoring the protests of healers in my wake. I was well enough to give Ella and Alex some privacy.

As soon as I had left the tent, I found Eve standing outside. She looked upset as she stared out at the rest of the oasis.

"Eve." I walked over to the pale girl. "How is everyone?"

"Caine's dead. Ten knights and one of the Combat mages from Ishir are dead. Half the Mahj soldiers are dead. How are we supposed to be?" Her words were hoarse, and I realized she was close to crying.

I didn't even know the girl *could* cry. She was as infallible as the prince, or so I'd thought.

"Have the bandits talked?" I shifted from one foot to the next, trying to ignore a bout of dizziness. Perhaps I shouldn't have left the infirmary tent so quickly.

"They killed themselves before the regiment could question them. Slit their necks with their own blades as soon as the nets fell."

"Did we find out who they were?"

"They were ours." Her hands trembled. "It's why they kept their faces hidden. I even recognized two of them from the Crown's Army… They weren't bandits or raiders, Ryiah. They were *rebels*. My father's men. Men I knew." Her voice broke. *"Why would they do this?"*

"Rebels?" Our own? "Not Caltothians?" I'd been sure it was our neighbor in the north; Caltoth had been raiding our border for years but refused to admit it. Every citizen in Jerar knew it was a bloody lie. King Horrace wanted our land.

"Commander Ama thinks they wanted to stop our foreign exports. They've already sent word to my father and King Lucius." Her lips were pressed in a thin, hard line. "If some of the mages are leading a revolt, then we can't be sure this won't happen again. Who knows how many others they recruited?"

What if this is only the beginning? Knots twisted in my stomach and I felt sick. No wonder Eve was upset.

There hadn't been a war in close to a century, ever since Jerar signed the Great Compromise. It was the reason we'd held off declaring war on Caltoth for close to two decades of minor border transgressions. To break the treaty was to lose the support of the Borea Isles and Pythus, two neighboring allies.

Not once had I considered a rebellion in our own kingdom. Unlike Caltoth with its extravagant coffers, the Borea Isles with its rising famine, and Pythus with its heavy law, we lived a relatively comfortable existence. The three war schools gave our people—regardless of gender or birth—the chance to rise. Even as merchants, my parents had never once complained about the demands of the Crown.

"Do you think the mages were employed by King Horrace?" Perhaps that was it. Rebel mages paid by a Caltothian king.

"Why else would they turn against the Crown? A mage lives a better life than most highborns."

Why else?

* * *

The following night, on the last evening before we departed Mahj, the locals put together a large funeral pyre for the fallen. Seventy-one bodies were placed on the wooden blocks. When Commander Ama lit the fire, it burned heavily into the night.

Each one of us stood quietly in attendance, solemn in the face of our heavy loss. Many of the regiment leaders from Ishir, and Mahj spoke highly of their men, and even Master Byron gave an earnest speech for Caine. There was something tragic about losing someone so young—and Caine had been so close to his ascension, only five months from earning his black robes of Combat.

Most of the fourth- and fifth-years retired early that evening; they'd taken their comrade's loss the hardest. My heart went out to them. I hadn't known Caine very well, except for that day during our mock battle, but it was clear he'd been a promising student and mentor to those who had known him. His attack in the cave had been part of a show; he'd never been cruel outside of battle.

I glanced around to see how the prince was faring. I'd barely caught a glimpse of him around camp.

Darren looked sickly with lines all too prominent in his

face. Had he eaten at all in the past couple of days? His irises seemed black. No longer garnet, they were two pits of shadow, unfathomable against the red pyre of death.

Eve held his hand, but he showed no knowledge of her presence. The prince watched the dancing orange flames, and I was convinced he saw nothing else.

He looked so broken. So lost. There was an uncomfortable ache in the back of my throat, but what could I do? Priscilla was standing nearby, watching over him like a hawk. And who was I? A friend. He already had Eve holding his hand. *Let him go, Ryiah. He's not yours to save.*

So why were his words playing back in my head? *"I want you to make me laugh, because gods know you are the only one who can."*

After the pyre, the locals prepared a feast. Tradition dictated food and dance to honor the dead. A flask was passed around the circle of us left. A handful of miners returned, playing a set of pipes and drums.

The villagers broke into dance, clapping and laughing as they spun around the sand to a familiar beat. Most of the apprentices watched, but a couple joined in. Alex wasted no time taking Ella's hand.

Loren pulled Lynn to the center of the crowd as well.

For a moment, I stood and it was all I could do to watch. I'd never wanted to dance. I wasn't particularly skilled with a sweeping pattern of my feet, and boys were just as clumsy as me. But just then? I wanted to dance.

I wanted to forget the last couple of days and be swept up into the long desert night. I wanted to send a farewell to the fallen and embrace the living like the others. I wanted to *forget.*

"Ryiah?"

Ian was standing right in front of me, and I hadn't even noticed.

"Would you like to dance?"

He was something real with an ending I could trust. He was the boy with laugh lines and an easy smile.

He was everything I should want.

Don't look back.

"I... I'd like that." My voice cracked as my lips formed a timid smile.

"I'm sorry about the solstice." Ian took my hand in his as he led me toward the floor. "I wasn't ready to give us... a try. But after everything at the mines..." He swallowed. "I'm not going to let fear hold me back... If you'll have me?"

It wasn't just a dance, and as his hand found mine, there was a hot pit in my stomach. If I said yes, I was saying no to something else.

Someone I'd never have.

Do you want to try for a happy ending, or chase after tragedy? The question rang out in the back of my mind.

I refused to look back at the prince as I adjusted the hem of my orange and gold-beaded skirts. This was a beautiful night full of stars that gleamed like glistening pearls.

I deserved to try, didn't I?

The music started up. It was a charming little tune, full of stomping beats and heady drums.

"I'll have you, Ian of Ferren's Keep."

The third-year grinned and tugged me to the edge of the crowd. His hands were hot on my waist, and his eyes were crinkled and soft.

"Dance with me, beautiful girl," he said.

And then he spun me around and around, the speed and the firelight and the heat making us breathless and flushed.

There must have been parts where I stumbled or lost track of the drums, but I hardly noticed. My cheeks burned with the fervent rush of our dance, and I found myself unable to look away, trapped in an endless feeling of right.

Nothing had ever felt as sure as when Ian caught me and slipped, the two of us stumbling to the ground in a laughing haze. We were knee-deep in sand, giggling as we helped the other up.

His hands locked on my arms before I could stand. Flecks of gold danced along his eyes.

"Can I kiss you, Ryiah?"

My eyes locked on his, and then I nodded, cheeks flushed.

We were still in the sand when he took my face in his hands and kissed me.

It was a wondrous kiss, a small thing, full of innocence and courage.

Then Ian pulled back and took me by the hand.

We danced long into the night.

EIGHT

NO SOONER HAD we arrived in Ishir when we were called back to the desert for another patrol. That seemed to be the way of things for the rest of the season and early into spring.

None of our field training mirrored our time in Mahj. If I was honest, we spent most of our time pitching tents and serving as sentries along the soldiers and knights. It was uneventful, but pleasant. We had plenty of time to practice drills, in any case.

As soon as late spring hit, it was time to leave. The final part of each apprenticeship consisted of an ascension ceremony in the capital for the fifth-years, and then a return to the Academy to collect our newest recruits.

For Alex and me and the rest of the lowborns, this was the first time we'd see the capitol and its infamous palace.

"That's the palace?" My jaw dropped.

Ella snickered. "Really, Ry, you act like you've never heard anything about it."

"But it's just so *huge.*"

"I told you that."

"And tall."

"Again, I—"

"And *tall*!"

"Well, now you are just repeating yourself."

Ian sidled next to me. "Wait until you see the inside."

Far past the rolling hills and rocky crags below was a towering palace that seemed to climb straight past the clouds. The King's Road snaked along the clustered hill, a large cobbled trail that snaked between thatched huts, tiny shops, and lumbering temples all the way to the top. Large hanging jacaranda spotted the road, blue and lilac blossoms sprouting along branches as lush grass covered the grounds as far as the eye could see.

At the base of the palace walls was the town square, consisting of more cobble streets and wealthy merchant stalls sporting luxury goods and services.

The palace was enclosed by towering stonewalls. They were at least ten yards high with only one manmade gate at the center of the street. Every so often an even taller pillar protruded from the wall, housing palace sentries with unlit torches and narrow slits lined strategically across.

When the guards let us through, I discovered the palace was made up of the same gray stone and mortar as its fortification. It also housed large, stained glass windows like the Academy and gardens and walkways that went on for days.

The roofs were black along the palace turrets. They cut rounding peaks into the sky. It was so beautiful I forgot to breathe. *This* was where Darren lived? Why had the prince ever bothered to train as a mage? I would've never left home.

To my right lay a long trailing path to the stables, armory, and the massive training grounds for the palace guard, the King's Regiment. The compound was huge. The city regiment had barracks just outside of the walls, and the Crown's Army, I knew, was stationed just outside the city limits. Ten thousand men was much too big a number to fit within the palace walls.

I also knew from our studies that the King's Regiment's housing was in the actual palace itself. As the elite guard to the royal family, the regiment had specific chambers closest to the king and his heirs. There were only fifty knights and mages in its division, but they were usually the most powerful in the land and recruited directly from promotions in the Crown's Army and the Candidacy itself. While the Crown's Army was deployed from time to time to assist with various efforts along the kingdom, the King's Regiment only ever left the palace to accompany the king or one of his sons, like the band I had seen Darren passing with on my way to Sjeka almost two years ago.

To the west lay a continuation of the palace gardens—a place for the courtiers to wander during their residency. I could see highborn ladies-in-waiting strolling the grounds in ornate dress, with coiffed hair and powders perfectly pressed and red, red lips. Young highborn men, off-duty knights, and the sons of high-ranking nobility were seen walking the grounds, placing bets and discussing mundane subjects with a practiced flourish that could only come from a lifetime of court.

"Toss me off one of the balconies if I ever talk like that," I muttered. We had just given our horses over to the hostler and were taking the rest of the path on foot.

Alex, Ella, Ian, and I followed the rest of our factions in through the palace doors.

By this time, I had given up any expectation. The second I entered the enormous castle, I wasn't disappointed. Tile lined the floors in an elegant design, a mixture of red, gold, and amethyst marble. The walls were dark stone, dressed in gold and amethyst tapestries that depicted past battles and monarchy succession. Elaborate gold-plated pillars highlighted the corners of each room, illuminated by the sun through the stained glass above.

Everywhere I looked, corridors branched into twisting passages, stairs, and chambers in a maze. There were so many twists and turns, I didn't know how I would ever find my way out.

"They've got three libraries, two ballrooms, the throne room, a grand dining room for the king's family and special guests, two large halls for the nobility to take their own meals, two kitchens, four servants quarters, a privy at the end of each floor, and at least two hundred chambers besides the ones reserved for royalty and the King's Regiment." Ian couldn't contain the disgust in his tone as he described the palace—down to the exact count of jewels encrusted in its ceilings.

Alex and I made a face; like Ian, we'd been brought up lowborn.

"Surely it's not that terrifying." Ella tried to make light of the situation; she'd spent half of her youth in court. "Jerar *is* the wealthiest nation."

"It's second." All of us jumped as the prince appeared behind us; I hadn't even realized he'd been standing nearby.

"Caltoth is the wealthiest," Darren continued. "We have a bigger army and more land... but they have the ruby and emerald mines in the north. Our coffers don't even come close."

"More wealth than this?" Alex snorted. "Their streets must be paved with gold."

The prince's jaw clenched, but he didn't call Alex on his slight.

The last time the two of them exchanged words, my brother had thrown a fist at his face; I wondered if the prince was practicing restraint out of courtesy for me. "We protect the people with our coin, Alex. King Horrace funds rebels and buys off mages to terrorize our kingdom. You can decide which is worse."

My brother ducked his head as I sucked in a sharp breath. So Darren believed the rebels were bought off by Caltothians like Eve. "Do you—"

"Darren, your father wants to see us." Priscilla's voice rang out like the angry chime of a bell. "You don't want to be late."

The prince's eyes flit to mine for just a moment—the first time in months—but then he continued on down the hall without another word.

A part of me deflated. That was as close to a conversation as we'd come since Mahj. Darren had been closed off from the rest of our faction since the rebels' attack.

Perhaps the change of setting will help. He could finally get over his guilt of Caine's death. Perhaps he'd even talk to his father and convince him to do something about Caltoth once and for all.

What would the king say? Would we go to war? Did they have any idea what Caltoth was up to next? What did this mean for the apprentices?

I was brimming with questions, but it didn't seem like I was going to get answers anytime soon.

Maybe that'll change by the end of the week. I hoped it would.

I'd spent a lifetime thinking war was decades away. Now I wasn't so sure.

* * *

Seven days came and went before I even knew they'd passed. In no time at all, the robe ceremony for the fifth-years ascensions finished and I was in a crowded ballroom filled with hundreds of simpering courtiers and regiment mages who'd come to celebrate the fourteen new apprentices to join their ranks.

"I can't wait until it's us." Ella leaned next to me against the large tapestried wall, gazing out in earnest at the four new Combat mages wearing their black robes proudly. Their faces were flushed with sweet wine, and rumors for where they'd take up station next spread like wildfire. Regiment commanders danced around the room, flitting from one mage to the next to try and recruit the best-ranked mages to their station.

I wondered who would go where. Two girls were ranked last, even though they'd been the first contenders after Caine. That didn't surprise me since the person deciding our rank was Master Byron. The man had led fourteen years straight of female apprentices ranking last.

I tried not to think what that would mean for me—a female and his least favorite apprentice.

But I still had three full years to go.

I took a long swig of something fruity and chilled. "Do you suppose Commander Audric recruits for the Crown's Army?"

Ella pursed her lips. "He hasn't in years. Same with the King's Regiment. You usually transfer in."

We continued our silent survey of the crowd. It didn't pass my notice that Ella had chosen the back of the room since the king and his heir were somewhere conversing with the nobility in the front. She didn't even want to dance with my brother for fear of drawing Blayne's notice.

I told myself it was better this way. I didn't need another night of watching the prince dance with his betrothed. I'd rather support my friend.

Ella started, sloshing her drink. "Is that—"

It was.

The Black Mage was standing in the center of the crowd, wearing his signature robe. Silk black layers cascaded down his broad shoulders, framed by intricate gold designs along the sleeves. There were even small crimson and gold gems spotting the hood. It was a robe every Combat apprentice dreamed of, a robe passed down in nursery rhymes and dreams.

Marius looked uncomfortable in such lavish dress— probably because mages only wore their robes during public ceremonies or court.

Two golden earrings dangled from his left ear, bright

under the flickering castle lights.

I longed to approach him. The man had gone against tradition and vouched for me to become the sixth apprentice of my year. That alone would have been enough to make me worship the man, but he was also the best Combat mage in the realm. The man had won the Candidacy fifteen years ago, and before that, he had served as one of the leading mages in the Crown's Army.

"He won't bite, you know."

Ian's chuckle made me blush. "He's still my idol, Ian. I can't just—"

But apparently I could. Ian was dragging me across the room before I'd even finished my protest.

"Hey, Marius," Ian called, "I think you have an admirer."

I turned the shade of the tapestry behind us as the Black Mage swung around, white teeth flashing. "Is that Master Byron's least favorite apprentice I hear calling my name?" Marius's tone implied a longstanding joke.

"Not anymore." Ian nudged me forward with a grin. "Ryiah has taken over the privilege."

Recognition flashed across the Black Mage's features and his dimples grew. "Ah, Ryiah, well it is only fitting. That cranky old frog *would* hate the first-year I personally nominated." He held out his hand, and I shook it with sweaty palms.

"I'm so g-grateful you vouched for my apprenticeship." My breath was fast and shallow; the words jumbled together like waves. Were my hands shaking too? I felt like a bumbling fool in front of my hero. "I hope I d-don't disappoint you."

The man arched a brow. "The prince was just telling me earlier that you and he led the mentees to victory for the first time in a mock battle in over a decade." *Darren said what?* "Two second-years... why, I might be in the presence of my successor now. What do you think, Ryiah? Are you going to be taking part in the next Candidacy?"

Was I dreaming? This *had* to be a dream. Because in what life would the most powerful mage of the realm be suggesting I was a contender for *the* robe. Not the traditional plain black robe of my faction, but the special robe. *The Colored Robe.* The robe that made a mage the *Black Mage.*

"Well, now you've done it." Ian winked at Marius. "She won't be able to talk all night."

The Black Mage was being called away by a group of boisterous advisors. He sighed wearily. "Politics again... I apologize to you both, but I must return to my Council." His eyes crinkled as they fell on me. "I hope this isn't the last time we talk, Ryiah. I look forward to hearing your accomplishments as the years progress. Perhaps my robe will seem a little less daunting then." Then the man gave a final nod to the both of us and disappeared into the crowd.

"I've never seen you speechless."

I made a face and shoved Ian gently. "You've never put me in front of *him*."

Ian caught my arm and his hand lingered on it just a moment too long. "Another man might be jealous."

"*I'm* jealous." I snorted. "He's a walking prodigy. Who doesn't want to be him?"

"I want to be the man that meets up with you in the palace library." There was a teasing light to his eyes, but for a second, all I could think about was someone else. Why did he have to say library? "What do you say, Ryiah?"

It'd been weeks since we had so much as ten minutes alone together. Code of Conduct forbid the apprentices from *friendly* relations, and we'd barely caught a moment since that crowded dance floor in Mahj when the masters were half-drunk on ale.

"W-what if someone sees us?"

"No one will be in that drafty old place, not with the feast going on all night out here."

"I-I'll f-follow," I stammered. "There's just s-something I have to do first."

"Don't take too long."

The words brought another rush of heat, and I blushed. I'd been thinking about his kiss for months. "I won't."

As soon as Ian disappeared, I inspected the room, searching for the one person I'd yet to locate. I spotted him through the great doors that led through to the grand balcony. While many of the palace chambers hosted small patios of their own, only the main ballroom had views as stunning as the one below. It faced the north, showcasing mountains and hills rolling for miles in lush verdant green.

Beside him was *her*. Wearing a splendid dress of lavender and yellow lace, she looked like she belonged here: the future princess of Jerar. Priscilla's raven curls were done up in the latest fashion, small tendrils escaping an elaborate twist, held high by rose gold clips.

I watched the two of them for a moment—the dark prince and his betrothed. Neither looked happy, and from the way Priscilla's lips and hands kept moving, I suspected they were arguing. The girl thrust her drink onto the rail and stormed off. Darren watched her go with a weary expression.

I hesitated. This probably wasn't the best time to approach him. But after hearing what he'd told the Black Mage, I felt a responsibility to seek him out.

Praying that the prince wasn't in a foul mood, I proceeded with caution. "Darren?"

The young man spun around, shoulders rigid.

"I'm sorry, I didn't mean to startle you..."

Instead of looking to me, the prince searched the crowd behind us. After a moment, the tension left his shoulders and his eyes met mine, seemingly relieved.

"The Black Mage said you gave me half the credit for that mock battle in Ishir." I swallowed. "You didn't have to, it was mostly you."

"I don't give credit unless it's due." Darren's lips held the faintest trace of a smile. "You already know this."

My cheeks burned, and I forced myself to continue. "It means a lot—to have him think so highly of me. He's the best mage there is."

"Ryiah." Darren's eyes seemed to gleam in the setting sun. "You don't need to thank me. You won that acclaim on your own."

"But Master Byron—"

"The master is an idiot. He couldn't see a prodigy if he tried."

My sigh was sad. "He sees you."

"Perhaps not a complete idiot." His lip twitched. "But you can be a great man and still be a fool. Many of our country's leaders could attest to that, were they still living."

"That's your great grandparents you are alluding to." I couldn't keep the grin from my face.

Darren sighed. "People make mistakes all the time—some of us just are in more of a position to leave an impact when we do."

Speaking of power... "What does your father want to do about the rebels in Mahj?" I'd been wondering all week.

The prince gripped the railing tightly, and I could see the white knuckles beneath.

"I'm sorry," I backtracked. "I shouldn't have—"

"They want me to leave the apprenticeship." His words were quiet, angry. "They said it is too much of a risk for me to continue. Because of the rebels."

"You can't leave!"

"I refused." He hesitated and then looked to me, suddenly unsure. "You don't think I'm making a mistake? That maybe I should? Because of Caine?"

"Caine died protecting someone worth saving!" The outburst came unbidden. Was it the wine? "Of course you should stay! People want to see their prince fighting with them!" Definitely the wine. Sweat beaded my brow, and I felt a bit unsteady. I had this strange urge to shake the prince by the shoulders for even thinking of walking away from a destiny any of us would fight to keep. He was the best apprentice of our year, and I didn't want to see him turn this all away.

I didn't want him to leave.

"I put us at risk, Ryiah."

"Those rebels would have fought us whether you were there or not." I swallowed. "You're one of the best apprentices we have. We *need* you to fight with us, not hide out in some palace like a sheltered prince!"

Blast it, what was wrong with my mouth? Why was I insulting the Crown in the middle of a crowded palace?

But Darren didn't look angry. He looked relieved, pleased even, like I had affirmed what he already believed. "Especially if we go to war."

I wasn't sure I had heard him correctly. "Did you just—"

"Nothing is certain." The prince's eyes darted behind my head, and then he lowered his voice. "The Crown is moving in on negotiations with Emperor Liang of the Borea Isles. Once we have his support, we can move forward with Caltoth."

I sucked in a sharp breath. "Are you even supposed to be telling me this?"

"No."

For some reason, I blushed. "Then why are you?"

There was a moment of silence as the prince considered my question, his head tilted to the side. He was studying me, I realized.

All at once, I was back to that day in the desert. His words came flooding back. *If things were different...*

Gods, what had he been about to say? What did he want to say now when he was looking at me like that? When he was telling me Crown secrets in the middle of a ball?

Why wasn't I in the library with Ian?

"What happened to that dress you were wearing that night in Mahj? The one with the beading?"

"T-that?" Blood rushed my face, and I could scarcely breathe. "It's h-hardly appropriate for the palace."

"That's a shame." Darren's garnet eyes refused to leave my face, and I thought I would burst into flame. "I never got to tell you then, but you looked really lovely that night, Ryiah."

Ian. *Ian.* Where was Ian? What was wrong with me?

"I know I shouldn't say this." The prince made a frustrated noise, and he took a step closer. "But I—"

"*Darren!* There you are. Have you any idea how mad Father is? He just spoke to Priscilla—she said that you are staying!"

Darren bristled and took a step back, eyes flashing. "I'm the best mage in the apprenticeship, Blayne. They need me."

"Still trying to be a gods' blasted hero." Ice blue eyes narrowed on me. "You, lowborn, don't you have somewhere else better to be?"

"I was just—"

Darren took a step around me, one arm resting on my arm. "Don't talk to her like that. She's not lowborn, and even if she was—"

"She's special, is she?"

"Ryiah," Darren growled, "leave us."

"No." The crown prince smirked. "Stay."

The two princes were faced off, locked in a silent battle of wits.

I mumbled a hasty excuse and left without a second look back.

I was halfway to the library when I doubled back, realizing I'd taken the wrong passage to meet Ian.

When I turned the corner, I found myself face to face with the heir to the throne. Prince Blayne was dressed stiffly in a blood-red shift and gray trousers. He still wore his dark hair shorter than his brothers, cropped close to his head, with a gold chain bearing the signature black hematite of the Crown gem around his neck. Darren had a similar one, but I hardly saw him wear it.

"Ryiah, is it?" Blayne said my name slowly, distastefully.

Funny, he'd called me *lowborn* before. That had clearly been an act to belittle me in front of his brother.

"Stay away from me." I hadn't forgotten what the crown prince had tried to do to Ella. He might be the heir to the throne, but I carried no respect for someone who tried to assault my friend.

Blayne saw the fear and determination in my eyes, and he laughed. "Oh, so your little friend told you about us, did she? She never did know when to shut her mouth." White teeth flashed like a predator. "Not that I didn't try."

I recoiled, and I was at once grateful Ella was nowhere in sight.

"What do you want?" I was determined to part ways as quickly as possible.

"Ryiah, Ryiah, that is no way to treat a prince."

I said nothing.

"Well, I'll make this short. Stay away from my little brother. He doesn't need power-hungry lowborns making eyes at him in the middle of a ball."

"I wasn't—"

"He won't leave her," he snarled. "Priscilla of Langli is worth a quarter of this country's treasury in gold. You're nothing but a lowborn wench."

"If I'm just a lowborn, then why are you so threatened?" I

knew it was wrong to bait him, but I was growing more enraged by the second.

"My brother has a weakness for strays. I'm here to ensure nothing comes of this twisted little fantasy." He scowled. "He has a duty to the Crown."

"Darren is my friend. Our friendship isn't going to start a war."

"Don't talk back to me, you insipid little girl!"

His hand came down before I'd even realized he'd raised it. There was a loud *claaap,* and then my cheek was on fire, my face jerked rudely to the side as the crown prince withdrew his arm.

Every part of me burned red. "Hit me again," I gasped, "and I'll—"

He slapped me again, only this time I was ready.

My casting hit him full force the second his palm brushed my skin. I sent the crown prince of Jerar colliding against the wall.

"You dare to attack your future king!" Blayne screeched. "Guards, seize her!"

Four of the king's personal regiment rushed the corner and grabbed me, muffling my cries as they held me in place. Two of them were wearing black mages' robes.

"Let's see how brave you are now," Blayne snarled.

I attempted to cast myself free, and one of the mages slammed me against the cold marble floor. I bit the man's hand and screamed as loudly as I could. Blood was dripping down my nose.

There was a shuffle of footsteps from down the hall, and then the mage who I'd bitten went flying.

"Let her go!"

Ian?

"Get the lowborn." Blayne's voice command rang out like a toll.

There was the clamor of boots and a couple heavy gasps as fists connected with flesh, and someone dropped beside me. I twisted in my captors' grip to find Ian. There was a large welt on his forehead. Three additional knights and the mage from before were holding him down.

"I want these two taken to the cellar for—"

"Blayne, I thought you said Father..." Darren's voice trailed off as he entered the hall. There was a moment of silence as the prince took in the scene before him.

Ian and I were held down and restrained by seven of the King's Regiment while his brother stood idly by, brushing blood off his knuckles.

"Ryiah?" Darren faltered. His eyes were livid as he turned on Blayne. "What is the meaning of this? Let them go at once!"

"Stay out of this, brother. That red-headed one tried to attack me, and the boy was no bette—"

"I don't care what she did!" Darren yelled. "Let her go! Let both of them go *now*!"

"This is none of your concern."

"Let them go now or I swear by the gods—"

Blayne made a face, and with the wave of his hand, the guards were called off. "I was doing you a favor, Darren. They are only lowborn trash."

"You think the Council will see it that way if you imprison two of their future mages over a disagreement?

They are *Combat.*"

"The Council does not control me."

The two continued their heated argument as Ian and I attempted to stand. The marble below me was slick with blood—from Ian or me, it was anyone's guess. Probably both.

I started to slide, but Ian caught me before I fell.

"Thanks." I swallowed as his thumb brushed my split lip, and I spotted the bruise that was already forming around his right eye. *I did this.* The guilt was enough to send a wave of nausea to my gut.

What was wrong with me? Why didn't I just agree to Blayne's demand? Why was I so determined to fight for something I didn't even understand?

Ian brushed back a strand of my hair that was stuck to some blood on my face. His green eyes were filled with concern as he gently lifted my chin, checking for injury.

"Did he hurt you?" he whispered.

I shook my head, shamefaced. I didn't want Ian to know the real reason the crown prince had gone after me, what he'd insinuated...

"Well, would you look at that." Blayne's cold laugh cut through the air like a whip. "Looks like I was wrong after all."

"I am done with your mind games, brother."

"Look at them."

Darren's eyes shot to Ian and me. He stilled as he took in Ian's arms around my waist. There was a tightness around his mouth that hadn't been there just seconds before. "We are done, Blayne."

The crown prince just cackled loudly. He wore a smirk as he left the hall.

For a moment, there was only silence.

I needed to say something... but I couldn't even look at him. I still felt his eyes burning the back of my neck.

"I apologize for my brother." Darren's voice was stiff and unnatural. "I'll see two healers are brought to your chambers."

"T-thank you," I stammered, "but we don't—"

"Think nothing of it." He was already walking away.

But Ian wouldn't let the prince go. He stopped his mentee with a meaningful hand on his shoulder. Darren stiffened but didn't order him away. "I know we're not friends," the boy said, "but it means a great deal. What you did. Your brother..."

"I'm sure he was out of line. He usually is."

"Still. *Thank you.*"

The prince appeared uncomfortable.

"I didn't..." Darren hesitated before addressing the third-year. "I didn't know the two of you were courting."

"Since Mahj."

"Congratulations." The prince didn't look at me once as he gave Ian one final nod and retreated down the hall.

There was a snapping inside of my chest. It made no sense.

Why did he sound hurt?

Why did it matter so much if he was?

YEAR TWO

NINE

"DOES ANYONE HAVE a problem with their role?"

I glanced around the field to see if anyone did, but, as I suspected, not one person—even Jayson or Tyra—minded. Darren had proven himself last year in Ishir. There had been no other nominations for a leader in the day's mock battle.

"Good. Now, we have one hour left. That should be enough time for everyone to get to their appropriate station along the bluff. You already have your teams. I expect you to gather as much loose boulder as possible during your off time until one of the others gives the signal fire. When they do, leave your station immediately and come to their aid at once. We will need all the manpower and castings we have to sink the mentee's barge... I don't expect us to lose—we have the advantage. We're mentors this time, but..." The prince's eyes snagged on mine for just a moment before flitting to the rest of our circle. "But I don't want us to be taken for fools either."

Again, a barbed insult meant just for me. It was enough to grit my teeth.

"Is it just me or does the prince seem extra irritable this morning?" My brother followed me off the docks with a shy fifth-year Alchemy apprentice named Barrett trailing silently behind. The three of us were partners for today's mock battle.

"I wouldn't know." Darren and I had barely spoken in months, and every time we had, he'd been unusually curt.

"I thought you two were friends."

"We… I think his brother said something to him."

"Blayne?" My brother's tone was full of unadulterated hatred. Ella had finally disclosed to him why she left court with her parents so many years before. "Why would he involve himself in something that regards you?"

Because he thinks I'm a threat. But I didn't say that aloud. "Because a prince shouldn't associate with lowborns like me."

"Darren is not worth your time if he believes that." My brother didn't bother to hide his bias. "I know you're friends, but perhaps it's time you move on."

I was of the same mind, but it hurt. I still hadn't recovered from the first week we arrived in Port Langli. I'd tried to talk to Darren about that night in the palace and found a cold stranger in his place.

It was like our first year all over again.

"What did Blayne say to you? Why are you acting this way?"

Darren regarded me coolly. "What way?"

"You've barely spoken to me since we arrived. You seem irritated any time I try to approach you. Even now, Darren, you won't look at me!"

"Did it ever occur to you that I am simply tired of you wasting my time?"

I put my hands on my hips. This wasn't the prince. "Why are you lying, Darren?"

"So what if I am?" he snapped. "I don't need to explain myself to a lowborn like you!"

And that had been the end of the conversation. Darren hadn't apologized, and I refused to ignore his callous remark. I knew there was more he wasn't telling me, but until he was ready, I wasn't going to go out of my way to be insulted.

I'd be here waiting for my friend—whenever he decided to return, if ever.

"This is it?" We had reached our assigned lookout, almost two full miles out from the town center.

"It's the last tower west." I pointed to low granite steps that led to a small platform along the port's natural bluff wall. As the most prominent trading post in Jerar, the Crown had made sure Port Langli was well fortified against pirates. That had been a relatively easy feat; the port was a mile-wide cove surrounded by steep bluffs on either side. It hadn't taken much to build a couple of watchtowers along its rim, each armed with a heavy three-man catapult in case it was needed. Any ship approaching would be spotted before it could enter the bay.

Which was exactly what Darren was relying on for today's mock battle. I couldn't believe we were already into our second year of the apprenticeship. Alex and I were third-years now.

"I can barely see the cove!" Barrett paced our lookout with a restless twisting of his hands. The fifth-year was the most anxious apprentice I'd ever met. "Why did the prince post us here? The mentees will never sail this far out. The western bluffs are much too steep to climb, and there's no beach for them to moor!"

"We'll be the last to see action," Alex agreed.

I didn't bother to reply. I had a feeling Darren had stationed us as far away as possible so he wouldn't have to run into *me*. Eve, Jayson, and Tyra were all positioned in the towers along the eastern bluff where there were more approachable shores for a warship to breach our harbor. Priscilla and Ray had posts in the port itself along the front of the beach in case the mentees tried to enter directly. Alex, Barrett, and I were stuck on the western bluff: the side hindered by steep cliff walls and a foreboding surf.

My partners weren't happy—and they weren't even a part of Combat. *Thanks Darren*, I thought sourly. *Your message is loud and clear.*

"Well, we'll make sure to run fast if someone lights their tower's beacon fire," was all I could say. It was cold and windy in our station. The mid-August air was unusually chilly and it had made the bluffs a terrible place to be, especially with the icy chainmail brushing against our skin. No amount of over-layers could shield us from that.

"I'll take the first watch," Barrett offered. He didn't look eager to gather the local rock for our catapult. I couldn't blame him for wanting to avoid the task. I wasn't exactly looking forward to spending the whole day gathering ammunition until the mentees decided to make their move.

If they were smart, they'd just wait for us to freeze to death or wear ourselves out carrying rock under our fearless leader's orders.

"Can't you just cast the rocks here?" Alex grumbled. "You're always casting heavy objects in your drills."

I wish.

"If the mentees take the war barge Darren thinks they are using, we'll need to cast as much magic as possible to sink it." I needed to conserve my magic, not waste it on something I could do by hand.

Alex made a face. "I bet the prince is making his partners do all the work."

I wasn't sure that was true, but I was in no mood to defend Darren. I called out to my brother instead. "Help me with this rock, Alex. I'll be sure to tell Ella if you spend the whole time complaining while I do all the labor."

It was a testament to his affection that he didn't shirk. "She really is wonderful, isn't she?"

I rolled my eyes, but secretly I was pleased. Since Ella had given him a second chance last winter, Alex had kept to his word. He hadn't so much as looked at another apprentice, and he had kept his charm for her and her alone. The two were happy. I could see it in his eyes: he loved her.

It was the way Ian had started to look at me.

It isn't the way I look at him.

* * *

This is useless. I was pouring sweat, and I had to remove my chainmail just to breathe. We'd been at the rocks for hours, and I was ready to lob them at the prince's head. What was Darren thinking? The rocks were only good if the mentees attacked our post. If they attacked someone else's, we were going to have to leave them behind and it would be four hours of wasted effort.

A slow fog had started to roll into the cove. I could barely make out the houses lining its shore, let alone the waters below us.

I called to Barrett, "Can you see anything?" He was currently stationed as guard while Alex and I collected the rock. At first I hadn't thought anything of the damp air, but now I was starting to feel drowsy...

I was beginning to suspect the Combat mentees had cast their first weather assault laced with some sort of sleeping draft that their Alchemy apprentices brewed up.

Barrett yawned. "No, there isn't any... Wait, one of the others just lit their signal!"

I dropped what I was holding and rushed over to the cliff's ledge. Just as Barrett had said, there was a blaze of orange and red in one of the eastern lookouts across the way. It was harder to see in the fog, but it was definitely a fire.

"They must have spotted the mentees' warship!"

The three of us took off for the beacon, sprinting down the winding trail as fast as our legs could carry us. We had almost five miles before we would reach the tower.

What if the others won the battle before we even arrived?

Two miles into our run, I spotted Ella waving frantically for us to stop. She was one station away from the beach and two more from the fire's lookout.

I skidded to a halt.

"We have to keep going," Barrett panted. "Come on!"

"You two go ahead." Alex was right behind me. "I'm going to see what she needs."

"Ryiah!" Ella shouted over the wind. "I need Ryiah!"

"Go!" I shoved my brother toward Barrett and the trail. I

didn't want to think about what Darren would do if he found out I was defying orders, but there was no need for Alex to play a part.

I told myself it would only take a minute to find out what was wrong. Then we could continue on our way.

I caught up to my friend. "Ella, what's wrong? There was a beacon down by the beach."

Her eyes were wide. "I saw it too, but then I saw something else. My partners wouldn't listen, but it doesn't matter. I need someone from Combat…" She grabbed my arm and pulled me to her tower's lookout, pointing to something below in the waters. It was too hard to discern with the fog, just a cluster of shadow.

"I think the mentees are using a longboat," she whispered. "It's fast. It's small. It could easily approach the shore without anyone's notice."

"But the others lit the signal fire." I could see a large barge approaching the eastern bluffs now that I was closer to the lookout. The mentors were firing away. "See, Ella, there's the mentees' warship. We've got to help them."

"It could be a trap."

"Ella, you can't even see anything down there."

"The mentors will be fine without us." She folded her arms. "The fog is only on this side of the coast, Ryiah. Shouldn't we investigate it at least? What if it's the mentees trying to drug us?"

She had a point—and she'd assumed the same as I about the casting. The fog was definitely suspicious.

"Should we warn the others?"

Ella studied the ledge. "We do this on our own, Ryiah. I

don't want the prince blaming us if we are wrong and we confuse the entire faction."

"So how do we get down there?" The fall was steep, and I doubted a climb down the bluffs would go unnoticed if the enemies were truly below.

"Do you remember Priscilla and Merrick bragging about all the secret caverns along the coast?"

"How could I forget?" Priscilla and her vile cousin Merrick, who had just joined the apprentice ranks this summer, had done nothing but talk about the blasted city since we arrived.

Port Langli, or as I liked to call it, Port of the Langli Cousins: each more loathsome than the last.

It didn't help that the younger one was now my mentee.

"I'm almost certain I spotted a cave while I was gathering rock for the catapult," Ella continued. "It doesn't look like a drop you can climb down, but it was an opening and the bottom was filled with water. We could jump in, find the exit, and then surprise the mentees from behind while they are attempting to scale the beach."

If they were there at all.

"But what if there is no exit? What if the tide changes?" I didn't know much about the sea, but one hole in the rock wasn't enough to guarantee another, and if we became trapped...

"We can always cast our way free. You haven't used any of your magic yet, right?"

"Well, no..." I still wasn't sure.

"Then we should be able to cast enough force to break the cave walls. If you and Darren could hold off Caine in that mock battle last year, then you can do this. We probably won't even have to cast."

I made a face. "You are lucky we're friends."

* * *

This is nothing. You've climbed cliffs five times the scale of this drop... I swallowed. That didn't mean I wasn't scared. Climbing I could control; falling was luck.

Ella leaped into the crevice, and then there was a telltale *thunk* as she splashed into the waters below. "Your turn," she sputtered. "Come on, it's fun!"

I struggled to see her, but everything was dark. Fun was the last thing it looked.

Please, don't let this be a mistake. I took the plunge, my tunic flapping along my ribs.

In seconds, I was underwater and writhing in cold. I clawed my way to the surface, spewing icy water and air as fast as my lungs could cough.

"It's s-so c-cold!"

"Let's go." She tugged me along, and I followed, teeth chattering. For someone who didn't like the cold, Ella was finding this entirely too easy.

The walls of the cave were stained blue and green as algae spotted its sloped ceiling. It was beautiful in a lonely, cold sort of way. My entire body quivered by the time we had swam ten minutes, our hands trailing the wall for an entrance.

Finally, after almost ten more minutes of searching in semi-darkness with our arms and legs numb from the cold, we reached the end of the tunnel only to find it covered in the same limestone as the rest of the cavern.

There was no exit.

"It must be underwater." Ella didn't look happy; her enthusiasm must have finally worn off. The current tide meant we were five yards from the bottom of the cave. "I think I can see some light below. That has to be the way the water is getting in. I'm going to dive down and check."

"Be careful," I warned.

My friend smiled, shivering, and then she was gone. I waited nervously for her to return, hoping that our efforts wouldn't leave us trapped in a dark ocean cave.

Ella remerged five minutes later, wheezing water and air. "The entrance is right below us. You'll need to be careful, though. Coral lines the rim, and it's definitely sharp."

"Did you see the mentees on the other side? Did you spot their boat?"

Her face lit up with a grin. "I was right. They're just west of us. I saw Ian and Merrick on the nearby rocks arguing over the best way to scale the bluffs. It's too dangerous to climb and they are stuck."

"Does Merrick know about the cave?"

She shrugged. "There's two second-years keeping guard of their boat right next to the entrance, but they couldn't see me. The cavern is hidden in a high outcropping of rock. They'd have to know exactly where to look to find it. Perhaps Merrick forgot."

"Do you think it will be easy to pick them off?"

She hesitated. "I'm not sure... Do you think Ian—"

I laughed sharply. "He would never fall for that trick twice."

"Well, then we both cast loud distractions in opposite

directions to scatter the group. When a couple of them go to investigate, we take on whoever is left. Hopefully the element of surprise will even the odds. We only need the leader."

"Who's the leader?"

"Merrick." Ugh. A second-year? He wasn't even that good at casting. He must have only gotten the role because he grew up here.

Still, it was as good a plan as any. I dived down after Ella, squinting with salt-burned eyes until I spotted a small shard of light emitting from below. Avoiding the beautiful but deadly reef, I propelled my body through the entrance and into a bright, shallow pool on its other side.

I surfaced. Ella motioned for me to follow, and then we treaded water lightly until we reached the rocks at the base of the cave.

The two of us crouched low and walked on the tips of our toes, climbing along slippery rocks until we could get a good look at the others from our ledge.

The mentees were gathered around a circle, and Merrick was still arguing with Ian in the center of their group.

"I know it's somewhere around here. Priscilla and I used to play in it when we were kids!" So he couldn't remember the cave; that was a relief.

"We've combed this shore for an hour." Ian didn't bother to hide his contempt. He hated Merrick too. "We need to stop wasting time and find a new way up. The mentors are going to realize that barge is empty any minute, and then they will be looking for us. We will lose any advantage we had in surprising them if we continue to look for your precious cave!"

"Fine. Go ahead and be leader—even though *I* am the one who grew up here!" Merrick tore off his black armband and tossed it at Ian.

The fourth-year bent low to pick it up, brushing the sand off his new prize with a self-satisfied smirk.

That's the boy that I'm courting. I started to grin. Ian looked good with the armband, even across enemy lines. He looked forbidden and dangerous, especially after he stood up to Priscilla's bratty cousin.

He's more handsome than an arrogant prince.

Ella elbowed me. "Enough drooling, we need to cause a distraction."

We exchanged grins and sent a rush of power on opposite ends of the shore. There were two loud *booms* and sand went flying to my left as Ella's magic split a boulder in two.

"Show off," I teased.

She shushed me, and we listened as panic broke out around the mentee's camp.

"What was that?"

"They've found us!"

"We've got to get to the boat!"

"No." Ian's voice rang out clearly. "We aren't going back to the boat. Not yet. I want two five-man parties scouting the beach. We don't know that it's them. There is no way the mentors could have already made it back this quickly."

"But—"

"You saw them in the spy glass on the eastern bluffs, did you not? That's three miles from where we are now."

Just as Ella had predicted, Ian split up his team, leaving

only ten behind to guard their boats. Merrick and Ian were the only two Combat apprentices who remained.

"This is too good to be true." Ella's elation mirrored my own. "He's practically unguarded!"

All we needed to do was capture the leader. Even I couldn't believe our luck. "We still have to make it past the others first."

"What if we do another casting close by? He'll be forced to send Merrick and some of the others to investigate."

Ian would never leave himself exposed; he was the best of his year. "He'll wait for one of the other scouting parties to return."

"Fine. Then I'll reveal myself."

"Ella, no, they'll catch you!"

"Yes, but you know Merrick won't be able to restrain himself from going after me. He's just as vain as Priscilla, and he won't be able to resist first capture... And while he's chasing me, it'll leave Ian unguarded. That's the best odds you could have!"

I thought it over. She was right, of course. This was our one chance to capture Ian while the other Combat mentees were away. And if Ian saw that it was me again... well, he might just be too surprised to make the first move. "Okay, let's do it."

Ella darted along the crags until she was two hundred yards away. Then she threw a large casting in the direction of Ian's party and started to run.

Two Restoration apprentices collapsed.

Merrick spotted my friend and took off at a sprint, ignoring his leader's orders as I made my approach.

I leapt out with a casted broadsword in hand, boots crunching against gravel as I lunged.

But something must have warned Ian just in time. The fourth-year spun around with a heavy blade, ready for battle. As soon as he saw me, his green eyes widened, but it didn't cause him to falter.

The two of us immediately engaged—the loud clang of swords colliding as my casting met with his. The rest of the Restoration and Alchemy mentees nearby rushed to help their leader, but Ian waved them off with his free hand. "This is between me and Ryiah," he told them.

"How kind of you." I blocked Ian's swing and cringed under the weight of his blow. There was a reason Darren had struggled so much in non-magic combat against his old mentor. Ian was the son of two blacksmiths. His experience was on full display in our duel.

"Where's your fearless leader?" Ian swung hard to my right.

I fell back just in time, panting. "What?"

"Where's Darren?"

I didn't want to reveal it was just Ella and me. "No one fell for your empty warship," I lied. "They're all waiting inside the cave."

"Interesting." Ian's eyes danced as we continued to trade blows. "Darren was never one to shirk from battle before." There was suspicion in his gaze.

"He thought I'd be the best one to catch you off guard."

"I see." Ian grinned and came at me with a low crescent sweep. I blocked with a wince as part of his blade grazed my thigh. "He's still relying on my weakness for the girl with red hair." He gave me a disarming smile, one that made me falter just the barest second.

It was a second too long. I heard the whistle of metal and then something heavy and sharp crashed into the back of my shoulder—biting deep, *deep* into flesh and bone.

I screamed, the blade vanishing from my hand as my knees skidded against limestone and dirt.

Merrick's head bobbed up above me.

"Byron should have given me a better mentor," the second-year drawled. "That was hardly a challenge."

I cursed as the boy dislodged the throwing axe and held it to my neck.

"You surrender, Ryiah?"

"Yes." I spat at his feet, glaring up at the second-year with his white locks and his cruel violet eyes that were so much like Priscilla's. I could not fight back. In a real battle, I would have already been slain.

I had lost.

I huddled on the ground. My whole back felt like fire—excruciating, searing hot fire. Blood seeped into my tunic and my body alternated between tremors and shakes.

"If Ryiah made it down here, the cave must be somewhere nearby," my mentee continued. He glanced at his leader. "The rules let us torture her for information, Ian. The regiment and our masters can't interfere while we do it."

Ian knelt down to where I was shivering and cursing with pain. "Ryiah," he said quietly, "please don't make me let him. Just tell us where the cave is."

I stayed silent. Giving up the location would cost my team a victory. If the mentees found the caves, they would no longer be trapped at the cliff's base. They'd be able to sneak up on Darren and the rest of the mentors while they were still trying to sink the barge.

"Ryiah, please."

I didn't look at Ian. *Be brave*, I told myself. Whatever Merrick did, the healers would step in as soon as I was unconscious. It was all part of a real mock battle, and a *real* Combat mage would never succumb to torture.

I really thought I would stay strong, but then Merrick swung his axe back into my shoulder—Ian turned his head away—again and again, and I screamed until my voice was hoarse.

The second-year raised his axe a fourth time.

"E-east..." The confession was breaking me, but not as much as that blade.

Merrick pressed down with his axe.

I cried as it carved along bone. "R-right at t-the b-base, in a p-pool." I crumbled into a sob, cradling my side and fighting back tears.

I'd just made our team lose, and all I could think about was pain.

Ian knelt to touch my face, gently, and then called for a healer.

I lost consciousness after that, just seconds too late.

* * *

"Two years. That's two years in a row our mentees have beaten incredible odds." Master Byron's voice was full of unabashed shock as he addressed the crowd of apprentices and Port Langli's regiment. He stood clutching a goblet of wine in his place at the center table of the port's ceremonial hall. "Who would have expected this?"

"A toast to the victorious mentees and their leader Ian. And a special mention to Apprentice Merrick for helping come up with the strategy that contributed to their victory." Commander Chen took over citing the merits of our mock battle to the crowd.

I felt sick to my stomach. Every single one of the mentors was glaring at me, with the exception of Alex. And Ella, because they were mad at her too. I hadn't spoken with anyone since I'd been released from the infirmary an hour before the feast. I knew all of them were waiting to tell me what they thought of my folly.

After the healers had taken me away, Ian and Merrick had led their team to the cavern in the bluffs. From what I'd heard, the mentees cast a climbing rope to reach the top of the cavern's opening and then surprised the rest of my team while the mentors were busy casting at an empty barge.

It hadn't even been a fair fight. Most of the mentors had used up all of their magic by the time the mentees arrived. Darren had been forced to surrender within minutes of their approach.

Mentors *never* lost—with the exception of last year. Now we had an unexpected victory and a humiliating loss.

As soon as the commander's speech ended, I made a beeline for the door. I didn't want to run into anyone on my way to the barracks.

"Oh no you don't!" Priscilla grabbed my bad shoulder, the one that had only just finished healing but was still sensitive to the touch. I cried out as she whirled me around to face the angry mob.

Ella was cornered as well.

I looked to the head table. The regiment was too busy in conversation to notice. Master Byron could see, but it didn't take much to understand he would never intercede on my behalf.

"How could you let that band of weaklings beat us?" Tyra demanded.

Eve looked disappointed. "Merrick told us it was you who told him where that cave was."

"I—"

"Why didn't you try to get help?" someone shouted.

"W-we didn't want to confuse everyone with another fire," I stammered.

"So you decided to play hero." Darren shoved his way to the front of the crowd. "You decided to ignore *everything* I said and go off on your own. At the expense of your team!"

I folded my arms, trying to ignore the pain in my shoulder where Priscilla's hard nails had been. "I made a mistake, but it wasn't *my* strategy that cost the team our victory. You shouldn't have ordered everyone to leave their posts. You left us all open to attack!"

"You were the one who gave up the cave!" Darren's face was flushed and red. "You told them exactly where it was! Without you, the mentees *never* would have made it up those bluffs. Priscilla assured me the west cliffs were impossible to scale and that her fool cousin wouldn't remember the cavern's location!"

"You really expected me to ignore enemy ships?" I yelled right back. "Ella saw their longboat! I wasn't going to run off and ignore it. Maybe you should have told the rest of us what your precious betrothed said!"

His eyes burned black. "What kind of Combat mage are you to give up the rest of your team like that?"

Tears filled my eyes. "I tried, Darren. I—"

"You obviously didn't try hard enough!"

"What kind of friend are you?" Ian had been busy with Commander Chen, but now he'd returned. He pushed past me to glare at the prince.

"This is none of your concern, *Ian*," Darren snarled.

"It is when you are making someone I care about cry." Ian lowered his voice. "I thought I respected you, Darren, for what you did back at the palace... Do you even know what Ryiah went through out there? Did you even stop to ask? Or did you just assume she traded the information for an easy surrender?"

He took another step so that he was in Darren's face, forcing the prince to take an uncomfortable step back. "She was tortured, Darren. I let..." He swallowed. "I let Merrick strike her with an axe four times before she finally gave up the information. The healers spent three days attending to her, or did you fail to notice she was in the infirmary? She's not a coward, and you are certainly not the friend you claim to be if you punish her for what any one of us would have succumbed to." His voice thundered across the hall as he asked his next question. "Or do we need to see how long *you* would last under an axe?"

* * *

I didn't wait to hear what Darren had to say. I didn't wait for Ian to come find me. I left the room, not caring that the others could see me crying. I heard Ella call after me, and

Alex shortly after, but I kept running. Past the barracks, past the village and its busy merchant-laden streets, I kept running until I was sure they had given up following me.

I took the four-mile trek up the winding cliff until I was back at the lookout Alex and I had been stationed at during the mock battle. There were two sentries inside now that the mock battle was done, but I chose to ignore them as I sat down a couple feet away, dangling my feet over the ledge.

Then I cried. I let the angry tears fall until there was nothing left but a crippled set of lungs—too hoarse and too dry to do anything but breathe in and out the night sea air.

Why did I let him get to me? Gods, I wanted to be better than this.

TEN

Dear Ryiah (and Alex—sorry, brother, you always knew I liked her best),

I hope you are both enjoying the second year of your apprenticeship. Does Port Langli have the best mead? If you get time to drink that is. Ha, mages sleep fighting. My trial year in the Cavalry is going well. Sir Piers gave my recommendation to the head soldier who leads it, so I think I am one of the favorites... I like it better than the Academy.

Ry, you were right to encourage me. There is no shame here. The other applicants may not have magic, but they are still honorable and hard working. There's another boy here named Jacob. He comes from Ferren's Keep, where I think you two will train eventually, and he has been a great friend to confide in. He knows all about life as a soldier. His dad is serving in his local regiment, and he says it's always full of action since they are so far north! I know I shouldn't hope for battle, but I think it would be exciting to fight rogue Caltothians one day.

Jacob told me the first station we are placed at after our trial year is a city on the northern border, so I think I might actually get my wish. There's no apprenticeship after we graduate. They just place us and have the local soldiers train us as we serve, which means I might actually be stationed where you will be training in a year or two!

I need to get back to study now, but please write back. I miss you, Ry (and you, too, Alex) so it would be nice to hear from you.

Warmly,

Your favorite brother, Derrick

AT LEAST HE'S happy. I finished my brother's letter with a sigh. A part of me had hoped he'd turn the rest of his trial year around and join the apprenticeship with the rest of us, but it was too much to hope all three siblings shared the same destiny. Besides, he'd been miserable at the Academy. It was better this way.

I put my hands on my head as I faced the mirror. "Why, Ryiah?" I was wearing a dress that cost two month's apprentice wages. It was money I should have sent home.

"So dramatic." Ella grinned at my reflection, adjusting the ribbons at my waist. "You know it was worth it. Wait until Ian sees you in red."

"Ella!"

"All I'm saying is the boys deserve to see us in something besides sweat and grime." She winked as we started out the Academy chamber into the crowded hall where apprentices were making their entrance into the winter solstice ball. "It's not like the Code of Conduct ever gives us any alone time."

That last part was certainly true. Smiles between drills were the most any of us managed. Byron was on us like a hawk. The one time Ian had taken my hand, the two of us had ended up with latrine duty for a week.

Tonight was a reprieve. It helped that the masters would be busy with drinks.

Ella and I descended the ballroom stairs, and I tried not to squirm. Blast that dressmaker in Langli and Ella's compliments; I'd been all too quick to give in. The dress was far too decadent for someone like me.

The material was a striking maroon, with a giant silk skirt and gold tissue-thin gauze beneath it. There were even small gold-embroidered blossoms at the corset that flowered out into a heart-shaped neckline. It was too nice. I felt so out of place in it.

Maybe I should run back upstairs and change?

A sneering voice caught me as I reached the end of the stair. "Are you really wearing the dreadful thing without sleeves?"

I flushed. The dressmaker hadn't had quite enough time to finish the dress in the port, and after seeing the silhouette without I'd decided to leave it unfinished. "I like it this way."

"You shouldn't. Only a whore exposes her arms."

Ella arched a brow at Priscilla. "We expose our arms every day in practice. Why should it matter while she's wearing a dress?"

"We would never allow the dreadful thing in court."

I started forward and Ella's grip turned to steel as she fixated on the prince to Priscilla's left. He had pointedly ignored the both of us since his precious betrothed started talking. "Is Ryiah's dress offending you too?"

His gaze flickered to my face, and I quickly looked away. He didn't say anything, and I only grew more uncomfortable.

To be fair, things hadn't been any different in months. Ever since our fight in Langli, the two of us had avoided one another at all costs. I was still mad, and he was still, well, him.

Ella gave an irritated sigh. "Well, it doesn't matter what either of you think. The court was wearing dead birds in their hair five years ago, so clearly their taste isn't all that bright." She dragged me along, steering me away from the awkward silence.

"You didn't have to do that," I muttered.

"Believe me, I enjoyed it." Ella spotted the two boys waiting for us across the room. "There are our admirers."

Admirers was right. I snorted. Alex was gaping so hard someone needed to put that jaw of his back into place. Lovesick idiot. I was rather fond of my twin now that he was treating Ella like she deserved.

"Ryiah." Ian approached me with a chuckle at the two of our friends. They were already twirling around the room and making up for lost time. "You look beautiful, just like that day I kissed you for luck."

I laughed. "You were such a flirt. I should have slapped you."

"But you didn't." His grin widened. "And now look, you have the most handsome escort of the evening."

My stomach rumbled, and I arched a brow. "Ready to escort me to some food, handsome?"

"Not a dance?"

"Did Ella keep you from eating until you fit in this corset?" I pointed to the tables. "Let's beat the first-years to that, and then we can dance the night away."

"I hope it's not just dancing the night away." His expression was shameless. "Byron's on his third glass of wine."

"Ian!"

"Let's get you some food." He steered me toward the other side of the room. "You'll have plenty of time to say my name like that later."

I choked so hard I almost fainted in my dress.

After swallowing as many tea cakes as the bones in my corset would allow, Ian and I made quick work of the floor, laughing and dancing with my brother and best friend. It was such a change from the year before when none of us were talking. I couldn't help but thank the gods that was over. Tomorrow we'd be heading back out to Langli, and I couldn't wait to see what we'd learn next.

Gods, we were a year and a half into the apprenticeship. It didn't seem real. The first-year had seemed so much longer.

A couple more dances and I could no longer breathe. Blasted corset and all those tea cakes. I made my excuse and then left Ian to dance with Lynn while I retreated to the corner of the room.

First-years and apprentices were everywhere. The whole place was chaos.

I snagged a glass of wine and leaned against a pillar in an alcove away from the rest.

"Have you retired for the evening?"

My hand jerked and part of my wine spilled onto the

floor, narrowly avoiding the hem of my dress.

"Darren." Why was my whole face burning? I'd barely had a sip.

"So you do remember who I am." He leaned against the pillar opposite me with a sigh. "And here I could have sworn you'd forgotten in your efforts to avoid me."

"Why are you talking to me?" I flit my hand around the room. "You've got a whole room of loyal subjects to entertain you in my stead."

"Because I've been a terrible person since we arrived in Langli, and you deserve a better friend."

My eyes snapped to his.

"Yes." His mouth twisted. "Two apologies in the course of a year. What is this world coming to?"

"Why are you apologizing?"

"I'd rather not say." His eyes hadn't left my face, and there was something about the way he was staring that sent a bolt of heat right down to the pit of my stomach. The tea cakes were instantly forgotten.

I gulped, and the wine in my hand was forgotten. I couldn't exchange our usual banter when he had me in knots. I started toward the crowd, but Darren's hand shot out to grab my wrist.

"Dance with me, Ryiah. As friends."

"I..." I froze, looking to Ian across the room. The fourth-year was busy laughing with our friends. He'd just danced with Lynn; surely this wouldn't be any different.

It's just a dance.

I swallowed. I couldn't even lie to myself.

"Please."

I met his gaze. That was a mistake. The second I did, I couldn't look away.

I wanted very much to say no...

But there was another part of me that wanted to say yes. It knew better, of course, but it was screaming too loudly to care. Yes, yes, yes. It was an idiotic, foolish notion, but it wouldn't go away.

You are going to regret this, the sane part of me warned.

Darren led me to the side of the ballroom with my hand in the nook of his arm. People automatically parted in his wake, but I barely noticed. My attention was on him and his hand on my waist as he reached up with the other to put my hand on his shoulder.

"What dance is this?" I mumbled. The music hadn't started, but I knew instinctively that Ella hadn't taught me the steps to the one we were about to begin.

"Don't worry." He smiled. "I won't mind if you step on my feet."

All at once the music began, and I didn't bother to wonder at how the musicians had timed their play to begin exactly when he moved my arm. I didn't stop to think about how everyone else was quiet, how the room seemed to glow in a heady golden light. All I was aware of was the prince's palm on the small of my back and the way my skin burned hot beneath the dress as we moved.

Darren's second hand held mine in the air, and as we traveled across the floor, it seemed so perfect, so easy for him to lead me through the series of fast and slow steps. And it felt right. It felt impossibly, ridiculously right.

I stumbled and tripped, but Darren caught me and turned

it into a low, swooping dip. "I take back what I said to you about that dress in Mahj," he muttered. "This one's better."

My whole face was aflame. "Y-you didn't say t-that when Ella a-asked."

Darren brought me higher and held me upright, his chest rising and falling in time with my own. "That's because I couldn't stop staring, Ryiah."

Like now? My eyes caught on Darren's and neither of us looked away. Gods, this dance was a terrible idea.

"Why?" I couldn't stop myself. The words spilled right out of my mouth. "Why did you go out of your way to push me away? To hurt me after everything you said in the desert? We were friends, Darren." Why this dance? Why now?

It mattered to me so much, and I couldn't take it back. We'd been rivals and friends and everything between, but this last year felt like something else. I was sick of these games. I needed to know what had changed.

His muscles tensed and the dance was finished. "Some things are better left unsaid."

"Wait—"

Darren released me, and I caught the scent wafting from his shirt—a mixture of pine and cloves that smelled so much like my home in Demsh'aa, it brought nostalgia to my chest. But it wasn't just his smell; as soon as he released me, I felt cold and numb and... empty.

"Goodnight, Ryiah."

I watched Darren walk away, cutting through the crowd to Priscilla who stood at its edge, glaring. I continued to stare, oblivious, until Ian found me.

"Are you feeling all right?" the fourth-year asked

anxiously. "You look flushed, Ryiah. Perhaps it's too hot in here..."

But what I was feeling had nothing to do with the room. The temperature could not make me feel like I was suffocating—like something was dying, like something was shattering, breaking into a million tiny pieces as Priscilla took the prince's hand with her own.

Ian pressed his palm to my forehead. "You should lie down. Would you like me to walk you to your chambers?"

"No." Did I really feel this empty all the time? Or was it just that Darren had made me feel whole? What was it that I had felt when he held me? Safe. Whole. Happy. But right now, I couldn't remember any of those things with Ian.

What is wrong with me?

I swallowed as a hard lump lodged in the base of my throat. "You should stay and enjoy the rest of the evening with Alex and Ella."

"Are you sure?" A flash of confusion dashed across Ian's features, but it was gone before I could place it.

"I'm sure."

I walked up the atrium steps in a haze, hardly conscious of Sjeka's beautiful sea as I passed the looming window to the second spiraling stairs of the apprentices' quarters.

As I continued the walk down the long, dark passage, I forced myself to replay the dance in my head. It's an illusion. It's not real. What I feel is not real.

But it had felt real, and I'd felt it before, but never with Ian.

But it wasn't fair. It wasn't right. It wasn't—

"Ryiah!"

I spun around, and my heart leaped out of my chest.

Darren. He was running through the hall, toward me, seemingly uncaring as he knocked over an unlit sconce to the floor. I opened my mouth to tell him to leave or stay or go or any of those things, but before I could get a word out, he grabbed me and shoved me against the wall.

Then he kissed me.

Wildly, possessively, with a hunger that stole the will from my limbs. He kept me up against the wall, kissing me like he couldn't fight any longer, like he was fighting himself and losing to a fervor that would burn him alive.

A loud gasp escaped my lips, and he deepened the assault. His hands slid into my hair, and I felt myself crumble, sparks shooting across my scalp and my skin and my heart until I could hear nothing but the hammering of my pulse.

"I shouldn't have danced with you." His voice was hoarse, ragged. He looked at me and his eyes were two black stars, pulling me in and drowning me. "I knew I shouldn't, and I asked you anyway."

My lips parted before I even realized what was happening. What am I doing?

"No." I shoved the prince away. How could I? What was I thinking? A wave of shame rolled through me. "Darren, this is wrong."

"You can't fight this, Ryiah." He was breathing hard, just like me. "Any more than I can." The third part was so quiet I almost missed it. "And believe me, I tried."

I tried to take a step back and realized he was still pinning me to the wall.

"Let me go."

"Is that what you really want?" His eyes were unreadable.

No. "Yes," was what I heard myself say.

Darren leaned in close, his mouth brushing my ear. "You're a terrible liar, love." Then he kissed me again. Slowly. Once. Twice. Soft moth's wing kisses that made my knees buckle and collapse right out from under me.

And then I was home.

Everything smelled of pine and cloves and him. There was a steady burn rising in me that I couldn't ignore. My whole body was in flames. I was losing myself in what it felt like to be near him. This was what I had wanted. This was what I was missing. This was what I needed.

"Ryiah." My name was barely a whisper from his lips. "Ryiah, I have wanted to do this for so long."

You aren't the only one. Before I could stop myself, I pulled him back to me. My lips hovered above his for just a second before I lost control. And then I kissed him. I kissed him in a way I had never kissed Ian: hungry, hot, angry, desperate, confused, in hate, in madness. I kissed him with everything I had, everything I hadn't wanted to let myself feel.

And then that name came roaring back. Ian.

Oh, gods, Ian.

I threw all my weight into my arms and shoved the prince away.

The moment was shattered in less than a second.

"Ian." I croaked the fourth-year's name and looked up at the prince. "Priscilla." What kind of terrible people were we?

"Ryiah, look at me."

Ian.

Darren touched my face, and I turned away, hating myself.

"Don't do this."

"This was a mistake," I heard myself say. "I'm not—you aren't yourself. We—"

"Ryiah." Darren's eyes burned crimson. "I'm not sorry."

"But what about your betrothal? What about Priscilla?"

Silence.

"Are you going to leave her, Darren? Are you going to throw away an engagement for a lowborn like me?"

His eyes flashed. "It's not that simple. My father—"

"I'm not good enough to marry, but I'm good enough for this?" Sudden fury made it easier to focus. Gods, I'd just destroyed a relationship for another reckless kiss with a cold, unfeeling prince.

Hadn't I learned my lesson once already?

For the first time, he couldn't meet my gaze. "It's not what I want, Ryiah."

And just like that, I understood all the fights, all the reasons he'd kept his distance in the last year. It was the same reason I'd said yes to Ian that night in Mahj.

There was no happy ending for us. We were two rolling clouds set on a storm, and our first casualty was a fourth-year whose only fault was trusting a girl who lied to herself.

"It's not what I wanted either."

"Ryiah, please—"

It hurt to say the words aloud. They cracked and rippled against my tongue. "I'm sorry." And I was. I was so sorry, because he was everything I wanted and everything I could never have.

Gods, he returned my feelings, and I could feel it in that kiss, in this space between us. There was something undeniable between us. It'd been there all along. Like drawn to like, I supposed.

But I would never be a mistress. I would never settle for being the girl he kissed in shadows while he held another girl's hand in front of Jerar. I wasn't a dirty secret, no matter how I wished to be.

I walked away.

And I didn't look back.

There was something breaking in my chest; I prayed it wasn't my heart.

* * *

I found the fourth-year and pulled him to the dark corridor, away from the rest of the crowd. I told him everything, unable to meet his eyes. It didn't take long to accept the truth of my confession—the tussled hair, the smeared rogue, the frayed ends on the back of my dress were all evidence of my betrayal.

The pain in his face was worse than anything he could shout. A part of me wished he would.

"You never loved me, did you? Not even a little?"

Gods, I'd wanted to, but I could only wring my hands. I deserved every hateful thing he thought of me. I already thought them of myself.

"Why him?" The words were angry and bitter. Betrayed. "After a year, he's only hurt you, again and again."

"I wanted it to be you." More than you'll ever know. "For what it's worth, I know you're the better choice."

"You will never be good enough." His voice was

breaking. "Not for Darren. He'll never acknowledge you so long as he's the Crown."

I was never good enough for you.

"I'm not picking anyone, Ian." There was a tightness in my throat. I needed to pick myself. The boy I wanted could never offer me the ending I deserved. The boy who loved me deserved a girl who would put him first, not one lying to keep away thoughts of the first.

"Not the prince?"

"There's no future with him." All that kiss had done was tell me I wasn't ready to fall in love. My life was already chaos, and I didn't need to chase after something I could never keep.

Ian worked his jaw, and his eyes were pained. "For what it's worth, I would have made you happy, Ryiah."

"I know." Gods, if I'd only fallen for the boy in front of me instead. "But I would never make you happy." Not like this. "I'm sorry."

"So am I." His shoulders were rigid. "I... I can't be friends... Not anymore." Even when he was angry, he was still polite.

It only made me feel worse.

His answer was expected. It was deserved. But it still felt like a blade to the ribs.

I missed him already.

ELEVEN

"CONCENTRATE, APPRENTICES. IF I have to say it one more time, I'm going to have all of you take turns serving as your partner's mark for this exercise."

Do not *look at him...*

A surge of heat sprung from my hands, and I sent my casting crashing into the sky. The bolt shimmered in the air, a brilliant flash of gold, and then it was gone. My jaw dropped. *Lightning*. I had just cast lightning.

"Ry," Eve said to my left, impressed. "How did you do that?"

Several others had turned to stare, and I felt myself blushing under their scrutiny. The younger apprentices had been trying for weeks to successfully cast the most infamous of all weather magic... I had been the first one of my year to successfully manage it.

I'd beaten the prince.

"I... I don't know," I stammered. I tried again, holding my breath and summoning the same projection as before. Nothing.

"Weather castings feed off emotions." Master Byron's lecture was dry. "They are a charge to heighten one's magic.

Whatever Ryiah was thinking about before her casting clearly had the intensity she needed. Lightning requires focus, but it channels emotions with it... Apprentice, perhaps you'd like to share what you were thinking of before?" His words had a bitter edge, and I could tell he was disappointed his favorite hadn't been the first third-year to grasp the casting.

"I..." *Darren's lips on mine, a dark hallway with just the two of us.* No, there was no way I was going to tell the class about that. I was trying hard enough to deny it to myself. "I don't remember."

"The charge to produce lightning requires a very intense emotion, one that would not be forgotten so easily." Byron was scowling. "I highly doubt you forgot it."

Why? Why did I always have bad timing? *Why can't I be good at the one thing that demands focus, not fevered daydreams in the middle of a lesson?* Embarrassment crept up the back of my neck, and I willed myself to pretend I was anywhere else, somewhere quiet and alone where the master of Combat couldn't draw attention to my very bright red face.

"Perhaps it's something Ryiah would prefer to keep private." My gaze shot to Darren as he added, "Something she'd rather *not* describe..."

My whole face burned. When I finally looked, I could see Ian scowling at the prince who had turned back to the sky with a not-so-innocent expression.

A second later, there was a bright flash of yellow and a stark white display as lightning crashed in the air above. Only this time it hadn't come from me.

"Well done, Darren!" Master Byron was full of praise for the prince. "What did you use to cast it?"

Darren's eyes found mine. "Something I don't regret."

There was a tightening, something pulling at my lungs. I made myself look away.

"D-don't regret?" Byron was lost, unsure how to respond to Darren's vague answer. The rest of the faction, all of whom had witnessed Darren's and my fights for years, had a pretty good idea. Priscilla was glaring daggers at me. I didn't have the slightest doubt that if she tried to cast lightning from her emotions now, she would be successful. That seemed the last thing on the girl's mind, however, as she stormed out of practice, not caring that we hadn't been formally dismissed.

The master of Combat didn't seem to notice. He was too busy studying the prince and me with a sour expression.

The second Byron released our faction, I took off, not wanting to be there when the man aptly deduced why Darren and I had been the only ones to successfully cast in the day's lesson. I was sure the man would find yet another chore to throw my way if he found out I'd distracted his precious prodigy.

I had just readied myself for the evening meal when I heard a loud crash beyond the barrack walls.

Ella rushed out of the adjoining bathhouse to find me. "What was that?" she gasped. "It sounded like it came from outside."

As the two of us stared at one another, there was a loud curse and a subsequent thud. We raced out the barrack doors to find Ian and Darren grappling on the ground just a couple paces away from the wooden building. The prince had a bloodied nose and Ian didn't look much better, half his tunic was ripped in two and there was a large welt on his shoulder where he had fallen against something hard.

I dove in and grabbed Darren's arm just as Ella went to catch Ian. "Stop it!" I shrieked. The prince stopped struggling, but Ella had to drag Ian back hard in order to get him to cease fighting.

"You just couldn't stop yourself," the fourth-year snarled. "You already have everyone in the kingdom eating out of the palm of your hand. You had to take the one thing that was mine!"

"She was never yours." I could feel Darren loosening deceptively in my grip, readying for another brawl.

"Enough!" I jerked the prince back, throwing his balance off as he fell against the barrack wall. "That's enough!" My whole face flushed. "I didn't choose you, Darren. I chose myself!"

The prince's eyes met mine, and he said the next words slowly. "We should be together, Ryiah. You know this."

"I don't know anything." I turned heel and headed for the commons. The only way I was ever going to hold strong was if I stayed as far away from the prince as possible.

"You can't avoid him forever, Ry." Ella had caught up with me, panting from the run and looking slightly annoyed. "You need to convince him you'll never make that mistake again. He thinks there's still a chance."

"I know." My stomach was tossing and turning, and I felt shame imprinting itself across my face. We'd had the same conversation for days. "I'm just afraid of myself." If I was alone with him and he tried to kiss me again, would I refuse?

I needed to run far, far away.

* * *

It turned out that I would get my wish. Master Byron announced that he had a surprise for us over breakfast. A wonderful, rare, *important* one.

"Port Langli is not like the other cities we train in. Here most of a mage's time is spent on patrols. The threat is not so much war as the prospect of pirates and local thieves. Langli is the wealthiest port in Jerar, our main trading post, our most prosperous harbor. I know you have all grown restless because it's not the fast action you desire. But that's the way of it.

"Lucky for you, Commander Chen has recently received orders from the king. Our local regiment is to deploy five of its own tomorrow on a special assignment that will take them out of the city. The commander has graciously offered up one spot on his ship for a Combat apprentice.

"There is a great probability this will be the only opportunity to serve in a Langli deployment. Missions like this are few and far between. As such, I will be taking a break from your traditional schedule to host a tourney of sorts..."

I drew a sharp intake of breath and heard the excited whispers around the dais. A tourney. A mission. *Deployment.* Everyone was restless, eager to do something besides the nightly rotation as sentries. Our time assisting the local regiment had been too quiet, too peaceful. The opposite of what a Combat apprentice trained for.

"I thought long and hard about what type of competition

we should have. I considered weather casting, which is such a relevant skill to have at sea..." The man paused as his eyes fell on me. "But then I thought better of it."

I scowled. *Of course.* The last thing Byron would want was a tourney centered around a skill I was actually good at. He wouldn't want me to win.

"I asked myself what might be a vital skill to celebrate. What type of casting do I want to reward?" The master was taking his time, basking in our anticipation and focus. "Then it occurred to me. *Non-magic* combat. Time after time, I have had you train without magic, because not only does the experience aid in your casting, it also serves you when your magic runs dry. Because no one's power is infinite, and at some point, you will have to fight without it."

There was a scattered murmur of confusion, dissent, and then curiosity.

Though we spent each morning drilling with weapons and hand-to-hand combat, none of us had bothered to pay our status much heed. I knew my standing in casting: I was better than Priscilla, better than Ray, maybe even better than Ella now. But non-magic fighting? I had never bothered to rank myself.

And I wasn't the only one.

"What type of non-magic combat?"

Byron frowned at the second-year who asked. "You find out when you arrive. You have ten minutes to finish your meal, and then I expect all of you in the training yard. Don't worry about which weapon to bring. I will have the servants bring it for you."

* * *

I was one of the first to arrive. After the master's announcement, I hadn't been able to concentrate on the food in front of me.

So now I leaned against the edge of the rail, wondering what the contest would be. Hand-to-hand combat, sickle sword, long sword, longbow, crossbow, axe, knife, javelin, throwing daggers, staff, or something new? It would have to be something we had already learned, surely. And since the prince was Byron's favorite it would be something Darren was good at.

But he was good at everything.

I hoped it was anything but hand-to-hand combat. No matter how hard I trained, my arms remained stubbornly slim, and there were many boys whose arms bore muscle twice the width of my own. If we were forced into a weighted match, I would lose to the heavier opponent. At least with a weapon, I could keep a distance. I was fast, quick.

Please, I thought, *let it be something I am good at.*

"I hope it's not the crossbow," I heard Ray mutter to my left.

"I hope it *is* the crossbow," a second-year said. "Or the knife."

I wanted the knife too, but I knew better than to hope for it. Byron knew I was good with it. If I knew Byron, he would pick the axe. It was Darren's favorite.

It was also, coincidentally, one of my least.

"Don't look so sure of yourself, Ryiah," Priscilla drawled. "You know it's going to be a fifth-year, not one of us."

She had been on a warpath since the night of the ball. For

once I didn't blame her. If I were in her stead, I'd probably be acting the same. Jealousy was a color none of us wore well.

"It could be a third-year." Darren had arrived. "I happen to be quite good for my age." He looked sideways at me. "Better even."

There was a flutter in the pit of my stomach. *Look away.* Now was not the time to be distracted.

I drew a deep breath, and the corner of Darren's lip twitched in a telltale smirk. He knew *exactly* what he was insinuating.

"Is everyone here?" Commander Chen glanced around and then back to our training master. When Byron nodded, he continued. "Good. Now Byron has been kind enough to let me pick today's weapon of choice."

The breath left my body in a rush. *Yes!*

"Since this city's most common issue is thieves, I thought it best to stick with what my regiment knows best: a street fight with knives."

Thank the gods! I wanted to kiss the bald commander's head. *Thank you for giving me a chance!*

A couple of the heavier apprentices groaned.

"Each one of you will be paired with another student at random. That person may or may not be your year. You will only have one match, and your master and I will judge you according to your performance." He cleared his throat. "After all the matches have concluded, you will be dismissed. Byron and I will take four hours to rank you and post the results at dinner."

What if my opponent is a fifth-year? Suddenly the odds

didn't look so good anymore.

I needn't have worried.

They were worse.

* * *

"Darren and Ryiah."

I stood frozen in place. I couldn't move if I wanted to.

The master frowned and called out again. "Darren and Ryiah, it is your turn for a match."

I'm going to lose. I'd never fought Darren, ever—except in the armory during my first year at the Academy, and that time I had lost. And he hadn't even been trying.

I'm going to lose. I should have hoped for a fifth-year. Then I might have at least had a chance to win.

Swallowing my pride, I followed the prince to a rack of blades beside the commander and Master Byron. I picked up a couple of different knives, weighing them in my hands, testing their grip.

I chose a medium-sized one of quality steel. I wrapped my fingers around the base of the handle so that my thumb overlapped my forefinger. The blade angled up with my wrist, locked and ready to strike. I was ready.

I stood with my feet at shoulder width apart, comfortable and diagonal to my garnet-eyed opponent.

The knowing grin on Darren's face was obnoxiously self-assured. I could hear Priscilla cheering him on loudly to my right. *You should have known Byron would never let you win.*

It was hard to imagine a month ago I'd been kissing the prince, and now I was contemplating the easiest way to strike him down before he struck me.

Let Darren go first, I decided. *Wait for him to make the first move and then disarm him. Don't engage—disarm. Do not take him on without disarming him first!*

"Why so quiet, Ryiah?" Darren interrupted my thoughts as I matched his stride, circling so that we continued to stand across from one another, leaving no side exposed. "I should think you'd be pleased Byron thought us equal opponents." He was smiling and waiting for me to take the bait. He knew just as I did our pairing was not, as the commander had insisted, random.

I stayed silent and continued to study the prince's features, not willing to waste precious energy in banter.

"Gut her like a fish, Your Highness!" Merrick screeched.

I bit down on my lip, hard. It was all I could do not to throw my weapon at my mentee's face.

Darren took the momentary distraction to lunge, striking like a serpent, quick and precise.

I jumped back just in time. I shoved my knife into its sheath and then lunged forward, snatching the prince's right wrist with my right hand. I threw it back behind him while I used my left hand to gouge his eyes.

Darren swore and swung wildly with his left. I quickly pulled his blade arm and myself behind him. At the same time, I grabbed his jaw with my left hand, pulling it left as I attempted to force him to the ground.

Darren wasn't going to lose easily. I could feel it in the way he pushed back. His heels dug into the dirt, legs bracing against my weight. My arm was starting to hurt. The move hadn't worked as easily on him as it did on Merrick during our drills. I kicked off with my weight, letting my feet bear down on his arm as I tried to break the prince's defensive stance.

But I couldn't break it.

All at once, the hand gripping his arm began to shake.

Darren was fighting like mad to break free, and the pressure became too much. I lurched back, barely avoiding the swipe of his knife as I once again drew my own.

"Now it's my turn," Darren told me. His eyes danced as he slashed once left and up and then across to my right in an effort to startle me. I used my blade hand to draw each attack away from my body, but my speed was lessening as he continued to slash in a seemingly random pattern of assault.

I was so focused on blocking that I missed the quick movement when he switched blade hands.

A sharp, biting pain found its way across my stomach. A long line of blood trailed my hips. I tried not to gasp as I fell back, stumbling to avoid his next attack.

Darren pressed forward, continuing his gain.

He used my pain to his advantage and swung down on my blade arm. I cried out, dropping my knife.

The prince brought up his weapon to my throat and held it there.

"Surrender yet, Ryiah?" His hot breath tingled against my ear, and I was unhappy to notice how pleasant it felt in the midst of defeat. His eyes were dancing.

"Yes." I groaned, and Darren spun the knife back in his hand, watching me with humor.

"You put up a better fight than I expected."

But not good enough.

The two of us returned to our seats. Commander Chen

nodded approvingly and then sent me to a regiment healer as the next pairing began.

I glanced at the master. Byron was smirking.

When we were finally dismissed, I was the first to go. I spent the next four hours watching the tide rise and fall from the harbor, studying the way the frothy waves sprayed across the pier.

Ella found me after a while and sat down beside me, leaning her head against my shoulder with a sigh.

She'd lost to a fourth-year.

Hours later, the evening bell tolled and the two of us left the dock. Eager Combat apprentices fought over a list that was pinned to the barracks' door. Even the others from Restoration and Alchemy were present.

Everyone wanted to see who had placed first in today's competition.

"Ry." My brother found me, making his way to the back of the crowd. His eyes were wide.

My stomach fell. Did I place last? Maybe Master Byron would use the contest as another way to humiliate me. Rank me even lower than the second-years. I wouldn't put it past him.

"Well, what did she get? Wait, what did I get?" Ella clutched my brother's shoulders.

"You were tenth, Ella... Ry, you were—"

My brother was interrupted by an angry shriek at the front of the room. "The lowborn placed second? This *has* to be a mistake!"

The "lowborn?" There were only seven of us in Combat, but only one that Priscilla would ever call to her face.

I clutched the pole in support. I hadn't won, but I'd ranked second. Out of the entire faction!

"Congratulations, Ryiah," the prince pushed back to the edge of the crowd. "You must have impressed the commander. You lost to me, of course." He grinned, white teeth flashing. "But there's even better news."

"W-what?" I was still too startled to take in his words.

The prince gave an innocent wave of his hand. "One of the Combat mages dropped out from the mission, so Commander Chen decided to have a second apprentice participate."

Panic seized my lungs. "And who would that be?"

Darren's smile didn't waver.

"You rigged this!" I spat.

Darren raised a brow incredulously. "You wanted to win, and now you're complaining? How was I to know you'd perform so well?"

No one said anything, but I knew what everyone was thinking. They were all just too nice to say it aloud. I hadn't really ranked second. Darren must have told Byron to do it and then talked one of the regiment mages into withdrawing.

The prince stopped smiling with an exasperated sigh. "I didn't do anything, Ryiah."

"But I bet Byron would," I seethed. "I bet he would if you suggested it."

The prince's eyes met mine and there was a challenge. "I suppose you'll never know. And now we are deployed for a month. Alone." There was that look again. That spark in the corner of his eye.

"A month?" Ella gasped as the prince left us in shock.

I wasn't paying any attention. I was watching Ian who had ripped the paper he was clutching into a hundred tiny pieces with his fists balled white around them. His eyes were red, but he said nothing. A moment later, he turned and started toward the sea.

My eyes followed him guiltily until he disappeared from sight.

Priscilla's scowl never left my face.

* * *

"Darren?" I found the prince later that night, drilling in the training yard long after everyone had gone to sleep. Even when we were set to sail first thing in the morning, he was ever dedicated to his stamina.

And this is the reason he'll always be your biggest rival.

The prince's casting ceased as both axes vanished from his fists.

"Yes?" His gaze was hopeful? Calculating? I wasn't sure I could read any of his expressions anymore.

"When we head out tomorrow for our mission... Whatever you think is between us, it's over."

"Ryiah." The prince took a step forward and I took a step back, swallowing. "Ryiah," he repeated. "It isn't a game to me."

"It is when it's all we can ever be."

The prince let out a frustrated noise and the cocky prince from earlier that evening was gone. "Ryiah, you know it's not what I want either—"

"It doesn't matter."

"It does."

Gods, why couldn't he just let me go? Why did he have to

prolong this misery for both of us? There were times I believed he wanted me and times I believed I was nothing more than a plaything, something he could dangle around at the end of a rope.

I couldn't go on this mission and spend a month at sea fighting feelings for someone I could never have. I'd spent the last couple weeks fighting a battle I'd no hope to win.

I was done.

"We're done," I repeated the words firmly aloud. "Do you understand?"

His hands clenched at his sides. "Ryiah, I'm not doing this to hurt you."

"You're hurting me all the—"

"I love you," he interrupted. "Does that mean anything, Ryiah? *Anything at all?* I didn't choose to be a prince! I didn't choose any of this!"

He loves me? No. It didn't matter, nothing he said could change this.

"I d-don't care."

His eyes flashed crimson. "You're lying."

"I'm not." I made myself stand tall with my arms folded. I willed myself for this one moment to not feel anything at all. To appear as heartless and cold as my words.

The prince's expression faltered as a new plea slipped out, desperate. "I can't be friends with you, Ryiah. Not when I—"

"Love me? You're not in *love* with me. It's just an infatuation. It'll pass."

"Is that what I am to you?" His jaw clenched. "An infatuation?"

"Every girl wants a prince. Every prince wants the one girl he can't have. It's hardly a surprise."

Was I made of ice?

"So this is it?" he ground out. "You're not even going to try and fight for us?"

"There's nothing to fight for." The second those words slipped out was the same moment an unforgivable hate crossed his face.

I walked away, but not before he uttered those awful words. *"If there's nothing to fight for, then I suppose we were never friends."*

TWELVE

"ALEX," I CHIDED, "you have to let me finish packing. Byron will have a fit if I am late."

My brother shrugged. "Byron would have a fit either way."

True enough. I groaned and looked to Ella. "How am I going to survive this?"

"You are going to focus on the privilege and ignore the prince at all costs."

"He's a lout, and if he so much as looks at you—" Ella clamped a hand over my brother before he could finish his threat. Alex hadn't taken the solstice or the prince's behavior well.

Then again, who had? My overprotective brother wanted nothing better than to punch the prince in his throat. Ian had attacked him outside the barracks. I couldn't say the thought hadn't crossed my mind—when I wasn't fantasizing other things I refused to admit.

"He won't," I said quickly. My heart stopped, and I prayed that they wouldn't notice the way my hands had suddenly stilled. I hadn't told any of them that I'd pulled the prince aside the night before and finally told him this was done.

I'd hurt Ian and Darren. I'd hurt myself, and gods help me, I'd lost both my friends. My silly sentiments were ruining my apprenticeship. I was going to tear out my heart and feed it to the wolves.

I finished loading the last of my gear into my satchel and hauled the leather straps onto my shoulder.

When I arrived, a little flushed from my run to the docks, I saw that the rest of the ship's crew was already busy at work loading the last of the luggage onto the ship. Darren stood near the back, helping a large man with black braids carry a particularly heavy crate onto the vessel. He looked up when I arrived, but as soon as his eyes met mine, he looked away immediately—but not before I caught a flash of something cold. My heart skipped a beat and my throat became sand, coarse and dry and in desperate need of something I didn't have. *He hates me.*

"Are you the other one?" A loud voice broke my reverie. I turned to see a woman in her early thirties watching me expectantly. Her skin was well weathered and her brown hair fell to her ears, cut in a similar fashion to most men in the regiments. Her eyes were a vivid green, much brighter than Ian's, and she had toned arms I envied—the best yet I had seen on a female mage.

Arms, that no matter how I tried, I would never be able to replicate.

"Y-yes," I stammered. I held out my hand. "I'm Ryiah."

"Well, Ryiah, I'm Andy."

"Andy?" I repeated, unsure if I had heard her correctly.

"My parents had the audacity to name me Cassandra, but you will never, *ever* address me as such unless you want to be made to walk the plank." She grinned in good humor and the laugh lines under her eyes crinkled. "So, Ryiah, you must be feeling pretty special—you and that prince are only third-years and the two of you were the ones to win your master and Chen's competition."

I blush. "Well, I'm not sure if that's an accurate representation—"

She cut me off with a hard slap to the back, one that made me wince and cough at the same time. "Come now, no one with modesty ends up in Combat. Take the praise and embrace it!" She pointed to the bag on my shoulder. "You'd do best to give that to Cethan—he's loading the rest of the supplies with the prince right now. As soon as the two of you are done, come find me and I can introduce the both of you to our leader, Mira."

I squinted at her through the morning sun. "Isn't Commander Chen leading the assignment?"

The tall woman snorted. "Him? No, this trip is for Combat mages only. Well, except for Flint, he is... well, I'm not sure exactly, but I do know he is Caltothian and the king sent him specifically for this mission."

"Andy, stop chatting with the apprentice and get back to work!"

Andy winked at me. "The dragon lady is calling. Best do what she says!" She sauntered off to the front of the ship's hull with a cheerful yet sarcastic response to her leader.

Awkwardly, I set down my pack and went to help Darren and the large man, Cethan, with the rest of the supplies.

"Hello," I greeted the mage. "I'm Ryiah."

The sullen-faced man looked up, irritated, and then gave me a list. "You can start with those crates there. Make sure each has the items I asked for. If we run low on supplies during the trip, we will cut your rations before anyone else, so keep a keen lookout for anything missing."

I set to work counting in silence, trying not to jostle Darren as we took turns pulling the crates open side by side.

It was extremely awkward.

The only time the prince acknowledged my presence was when my elbow accidentally grazed his arm and he snapped, "Watch it!" He said it with so much underlying anger that Cethan shot the prince a wary look.

"S-sorry," I mumbled. *For everything.* He must have heard the strange pitch in my voice because the prince finally looked at me.

"You have nothing to apologize for." His tone said differently. Then, in his most polite, un-Darren-like voice, he added, "Can you pass that crate to your left? I think I miscounted the fish."

* * *

Almost two weeks of cold sweats, nausea, and vomiting. For some, seasickness ends after the first couple of days; for me, it lasted the entire trip.

The lead mage, Mira, noticed right away. One of the first things she told me was that the commander and Byron had made a mistake sending her someone "so useless at sea."

She continued to make similar comments for days.

The night before we reached Dastan Cove, I spent most of the evening clutching the side rails, trying to rid the prickling torment of waves flooding my gut. My skin was pale and clammy. I prayed that the sensation would go away as soon as we took to shore. The night air was cold and biting, and constant blasts sent me quivering from head to toe. I was determined to prove my worth once we hit land.

I was sick of the sea. But most importantly, I was sick of being sick. I hated feeling useless and having the rest of the crew eye me with distaste, like they couldn't believe I was the one who ranked second. They didn't question Darren's presence. *He* had been a great help casting wind to speed our travel. *He* took turns navigating and preparing the meals. *I* spent the entire time clutching the railing.

I couldn't even keep the meals down.

I swallowed hard and cursed myself for never considering seasickness a possibility when I had signed up for a month-long deployment.

"Ryiah, Mira needs you to come back to the meeting."

I glanced up to see Darren watching me with an inscrutable expression.

I sighed and released the rail, trying my hardest to look anywhere but his face. Things had been cold, awkward, and distant between us—almost exactly how they had been when we first arrived in Port Langli eight months back. Of course, now I knew the real reason why.

"I'm coming." At that very moment, I was forced to clutch my stomach and heave into the ocean below.

"She said that you should bring a bucket."

I faltered and my eyes fell to his retreating form in anger and self-pity. He had said it so carelessly, like I was nothing, like I was *no one*. It shouldn't hurt me. Nothing about

Darren should hurt me. I shouldn't allow myself to feel jealous of this wall he had built up between us... but rational thinking had never played its course wisely where the prince was concerned.

I'd lost two friends, and I had no one but myself to blame.

I grabbed a pail and tried to remind myself I had no business wishing Darren would pine for me. I joined the rest of the crew below deck and tried not to let my expression waver as five sets of eyes fell on my haggard face and the bucket in hand.

"So glad you could finally join us, Apprentice." Our leader's voice sounded anything but.

I took a seat silently beside Andy; the mage had the ghost of a smile on her lips.

Everyone else was glaring.

Mira, Andy had told me, was the sister of the Black Mage, Marius. But that was where the connection ended. The brother and sister were as different as night and day. According to Andy, this was because Mira was determined to distance herself from her older sibling as much as possible. She suspected it was because Mira resented his status: *"We Combat mages are a competitive bunch, so it's natural, if we aren't the best, jealousy occurs, especially in families like theirs."*

"As I was just saying, Apprentice, there can be no mistakes in tomorrow's mission. You and the prince will have somewhat a minor role, but it is nonetheless vital that you two stick to your assignment and not allow emotion—or pity—to sway your actions." Our leader was alluding to last night's revelation that our prestigious mission was, in fact, a kidnapping.

For the past week and a half, we'd been memorizing a detailed map of Caltoth's northeastern coast, learning the expected route we would take to arrive in Dastan Cove unnoticed. We had sailed just north of it, approximately a two-day's trek from the seafaring harbor. Flint, our mysterious traveling companion, knew the territory well.

From what I had gathered, he had served as a sentry there before coming to Jerar. He was to be our guide. The three mages would do most of the "blood work" while Darren and I acted as scouts.

At first I'd been uncomfortable. I had prepared for battle, spying on the enemy, stealing an important document or two. Never had I ever contemplated taking a young woman, not much older than me, hostage. She wasn't a mage, not even a fighter, merely the young wife of the baron in charge of the city. Mira and Flint wouldn't even tell us why the woman was important, only that they were under Crown orders to "acquire her."

But then Mira had mentioned the word "rebels," and I'd stopped worrying about the woman's life. That attack in the Red Desert's salt mines would stay with me forever, and I had only to remember the haunted night with the pyres to understand how important our mission really was. Jerar couldn't afford a war. If whatever this girl knew would help save innocent lives, it was well worth it.

* * *

It took me all of the first and second day stumbling across a freezing, pine-infested mountainside to get some semblance of normalcy to my gait. Darren kept shooting me impatient glances. I was slowing our progress down, and we were supposed to be the scouting party.

Eventually, we made it out of the dense forest and up a cold, snowcapped peak that Flint claimed would provide easy vantage for spotting sentries. "They will not have a full guard this far north, but you still need to be vigilant. They might have changed their routine in the year since I left. They think I'm dead, but Caltothians are overly-cautious in everything."

Trying not to wheeze too heavily, I joined Darren along the ledge and did my best to scan the land below, willing the feeling of unsteady ground to pass. Never again would I volunteer to board a ship. All my life I had lived relatively sickness-free. The gods were clearly enjoying a good joke now that I had spent almost two weeks living out the worst humiliation—and symptoms—of my life.

"Take this." Darren held out his water skin, his eyes locked on the city below us.

I took a swig and choked on its contents. I'd been expecting water, not the sweet taste of peppermint.

"It's for the nausea."

I took another swallow, and then another, letting the cold brew settle into my stomach. It brought back memories of my childhood. I was well aware of its benefits, but I was surprised the prince had cared enough to offer it. I'd almost drunk the entire contents before I realized I should've saved some for Darren.

"Thanks." I handed it back to him.

The prince waved the skin away. "That one was for you."

I almost dropped it. "Me?"

"The mint was at the edge of the marsh where we made camp last night. I thought it might help."

I didn't know what to say. After two weeks of silence and short, clipped sentences, this was a miracle.

"Darren—"

"Don't." His words were tired. "You made the right decision, Ryiah. Let's just leave it at that."

But I didn't want to. I bit my tongue and tried to focus on the brightly lit port just past the rocky shores below us. The coastline in Caltoth was a much different kind of port than the one we had left.

The city's harbor was twice the size of Langli. I could immediately understand why Darren called it the wealthiest nation. Most of the buildings in Jerar consisted of timber frames with moderately thatched roofs; below, all I saw was brick: house after house and shop after shop of brick walls and heavy, curtained windows—a luxury that only a king's palace or lord's castle could usually afford. Wide cobblestone paths marked every direction of the streets, and torches were displayed by giant pillars at every corner.

The entire harbor was guarded by as many soldiers as the entire citizenship of Langli.

I drew a sharp intake of breath and Darren noticed. "It's a very important post," he explained. "This is the harbor they ship all of their exports, including the rubies, from. My father said one third of Caltoth's militia guards it—and most of them aren't visible. The ones we see are the ones they want us to see." He paused then asked, "How many?"

"How many what?"

"Sentries." Darren gave me a sideways look. "Mira will

cut our throats if we give her the wrong numbers."

I made a face. "Not yours."

"Well, I still don't want to spend all night freezing while you gawk."

I almost smiled. For a moment, it felt like things were back to the way they used to be between us, before that night at the ball, before the awkwardness at the last ascension. A friendship that was slightly insulting, but with enough undisguised humor to let me know it was at least partially in jest.

After a half hour of counting, and then another hour of matching up Flint's landmarks to their actual positions, the two of us confirmed that the guards' formation hadn't changed. We hurried as quickly and quietly as we could back to camp.

Andy looked happy to see us, but everyone else looked cold and impatient.

"Well?" Mira demanded. The mage's yellow eyes glinted like a cat's in the tiny orange light she was casting. Real fires were out of the question. We couldn't leave any trace of our presence for a patrol to find.

Shadows danced along the strong lines of the prince's face. "Everything is as Flint said."

"Good. Then we set out at first light."

* * *

I straightened the maid's dress and brushed my sweating palms against its clean underskirt, reciting Mira's instructions one final time. Even though I'd just eaten, my stomach was twisting and turning and my hands wouldn't stop shaking. The sun was about to set. It was time to go.

If I failed in any part of my assignment, the mission would fail.

I was sure Mira would've given my task to someone else if she could have, but the task was best given to a woman who could act the part of a lady's maid. Mira was too famous as the sister of Jerar's Black Mage. Andy was far too imposing in size. I was their best bet.

I stepped out into the packed village square and made my way to Baron Cyr's castle. It shone like a gray beacon in mist. There were two guards who watched my progress as I drew close. I handed the one nearest my forged papers and then entered the great doors of the baron's hall with a deep breath and a steady gait.

Trying to appear hurried—as if I'd already been assigned some household chore instead of wandering—I scurried past various servants to the second floor and located Lady Sybil's empty room, just as Flint's instructions directed. I snagged a vase of flowers before knocking once, and then I barreled in and quickly deposited them on the dresser.

Everything was going according to plan.

I scanned the walls for a tapestry. I found it at the corner of the lady's bedpost and then felt underneath for a hidden latch. I twisted and a door swung back, leading into a dark passage that would lead to an unguarded cellar in the back of the castle.

When the door was successfully jammed with a bit of leftover candle wax from the lady's nightstand, I took a moment to admire my work. To the untrained eye, it would be easy to miss the slight line in the otherwise untouched wall and its secret door behind. It was what we were counting on.

I stepped out on the balcony and then pushed my way past two guards, the ladies-in-waiting, and their mistress. The lady was awaiting her husband's return from sea at the balcony, like she did every evening while the baron was away in his travels.

It wasn't dark yet, but I feigned interest in lighting a torch anyway. The other servants would assume I was a bit anxious and overzealous.

Really, I was lighting the signal fire to the others below.

"Miss, miss, what are you doing? The lady does not light that unless her husband is returning!" A lady-in-waiting quickly doused the flame.

Panic reached out and gripped my throat like an invisible hand. The fire had only lasted for a minute. What if the others missed it? Flint had never told us that the torch was ceremonial. Mira was counting on me. They all were.

"Surely the lady does not wish to eat in the dark?" I gave a saccharine smile, trying not to grate my teeth.

The maid gave me an odd look. "She won't—her meal is almost done. She and the little lady Tamora are always done before dark."

"L-lady Tamora?" And then I saw the small child at the lady's right—a headful of black curls like the mother, with wide, innocent blue eyes. She could not be more than five years of age.

My stomach clenched. Lady Sybil had a daughter.

"What did you say your name was?" The maid's stare had changed from annoyance to suspicion.

I swallowed as I realized my mistake. Even a new maid

would know if her lady had children.

A series of shouts and the clamor of a sudden panic below stole the maid's attention away. She and the others rushed to the railing to see what caused the commotion below. I pretended to do the same while silently thanking the gods that Darren had noticed my signal, brief as it was.

Below, on the southern edge of the city's farmland, was a huge, hungry fire eating away at the local crop field and its adjoining pasture, gaining speed. The prince had done well in such a short amount of time.

Men and women were running with buckets of water. Guards were searching the crowds, and there, dressed in a heavy peasant's garb, was the prince. He slunk along the shadows as the city erupted in chaos.

"Your ladyship, you and the child must get back to your rooms immediately!" The maid who'd questioned me was busy dragging the baroness to her feet while the guards secured the railing behind us.

Most of the ladies-in-waiting had already run to their quarters, but two guards stood waiting for the baroness and her child. I would never be able to join them unnoticed, not with the suspicious maid watching my every move.

I needed to do something.

Pretending to busy myself with the lady's belongings, I cast out my magic. At once the maid's mouth and nose were covered in an invisible rag, sealing her airways.

Thirty seconds, that was all I needed.

The maid let out a muffled cry, clawing at the object on her face. The guards and lady started to turn, but I coughed loudly, bringing their attention back to me. The child was too busy clutching her mother's skirts to notice.

Sixteen. Seventeen.

The maid stomped her feet loudly, and I pretended to fall to cover the sound.

Twenty-two. Twenty-three.

"Miss, are you okay?"

I stared up at the guards and shook my head.

One of the guards smiled. "No need to worry, miss. We're very apt at sensing danger."

Are you now? I let the maid's casting disappear and then scrambled to my feet as the maid fell to the floor, unconscious. "Please, sirs," I cried, "the maid has fainted. She needs a healer!"

The two men glanced at one another, and I made myself shrill. "You must take her! I can escort Lady Sybil to her chambers!" The maid was young and pretty. I hoped one of them had a soft spot for the girl, enough to leave their baroness's side.

"It's okay, Red. You can take Mila. Tamora and I will be fine." Lady Sybil's voice was calm and authoritative. I felt a crushing wave of guilt. Her sympathy for her servants would ultimately lead to her demise.

At his lady's command, the guard gathered the unconscious girl in his arms and hurried down the corridor. The other followed Lady Sybil and me down the winding hall to her chambers.

Just as I made a motion to join her inside, the lady turned to me with a stiff shake of her head. "I would like to be alone with my child." Her keen blue eyes watched me, and for a moment I thought I saw a flicker of suspicion. Then she shut the door, leaving me and the other guard outside her chamber.

Well, this wasn't going according to plan.

The big man scowled. "You'd best hide in the servants' quarters, miss." His eyes held the same doubt as his lady and my insides squirmed. "There is nothing more you can do here."

Definitely not a part of the plan.

I hastened a glance to my left and right, a quick study to make sure no one else was watching. The man drew his blade, and I launched my power at him, letting the man hit the wall with a loud thud, and then he crumbled to the floor, unconscious.

I'm sorry. I had no idea if he shared his king's desire for war with Jerar, but he'd been a man trying to do his job before I got in the way.

I knelt and snatched the large ring of keys from the guard's belt. I thrust the key I had seen him use just moments before into the door's lock while clutching the guard's sword in my other hand as I prepared for the lady's defense. There was no way she could have missed the commotion outside.

I needn't have bothered. The others were already there, weapons in hand.

"I'll come with you willingly," the lady begged, "just don't hurt my little girl."

Mira stood in front of the lady while Cethan bound the baroness and Andy held the child by the wrist.

"What do we do with the girl, Mira?" The mage shifted restlessly. "Flint never told us there would be a child."

Mira's cold yellow gaze slit to me. "Give the child to Ryiah. We'll take her with us. Andy, I need you to help me cover the front until we meet Darren and Flint outside."

I hesitated as Andy dragged the child over.

"Are you sure we need to bring the girl?" I swallowed over Tamora's cries. I couldn't imagine hurting such a small, innocent child. "Surely we don't—"

"Are you questioning me, Apprentice?"

I clutched the small girl by her shoulders—they were frail and tiny, like a bird's. Her body trembled violently against my hands. I couldn't bring myself to move.

A sharp, whistling noise—like a whip cracking against air—and the child dropped to the ground. I gasped and looked to our leader in horror. She'd just cast the child unconscious. Tamora now had a small trickle of blood flowing from the left side of her head.

"You didn't need to do that!" I knelt and gathered the girl up in my arms. A kidnapping was one thing, but hurting a defenseless child? Mira was heartless.

"You did well getting us in, Apprentice," she warned, "but if you ever question my orders again, I will *personally* ensure you are thrown out of your apprenticeship for insubordination."

And I thought Byron was as bad as it got.

* * *

Darren and Flint were waiting for us at the end of the tunnel. They were keeping an eye out to make sure our route was safe. The second the prince spotted the limp child I was carrying, his mouth formed a small, hard line. Flint looked surprised but unperturbed.

Mira gave orders for Darren to take over at the front. Cethan and I would stay at the middle of the pack with our hostages. Flint, Mira, and Andy would guard the back.

We took off at a run.

And we ran. Every second, every breath seemed to go on for hours as we made our retreat through an endless sea of green and brown and white. Every once in a while, Flint would shout out a landmark or a direction we missed, but for the most part the only sound was the heavy panting of breath and the crunch of pine needles beneath our boots.

Minutes into our escape, Tamora awoke, but before she could cry, Andy slipped something into my hand. "We were supposed to give it to the mother if she was difficult," she whisper-panted, "but I have a mind she'll play nice so long as you don't let Mira touch that child again."

I shot the mage a small smile and then held the vial to the child's lips. "*Please?*"

Tamora met my eyes, not quite understanding but seeming to trust the pleading tone in my voice. The girl swallowed the potion and was asleep in seconds.

Thank the gods for Alchemy.

Returning focus to the trail in front of me, I hurried to catch up with Cethan. The man was lumbering through the forest like it was nothing, even though the lady he was carrying was easily five times the weight of her child.

"You can't be mortal," I wheezed.

The corner of the mage's lip twitched, but that was it. Cethan was too in control of his emotions to chuckle or laugh. I took it in stride anyway. He didn't smile for anything.

After three hours of running, climbing, and small bursts of hiding, we reached the camp we'd left behind the night before. All of our stuff was still hidden deep under brush, and the others quickly set to work locating our sleeping rolls and the rest of the supplies, including a much more comfortable change of clothes—it hadn't been easy running in a full skirt, but thankfully I'd had on my most comfortable boots beneath.

Cethan and Andy took charge of our hostages. Lady Sybil refused to speak, except to ask for her daughter. Her eyes were red, undoubtedly from crying, and she had dark welts across her cheeks from where the gag had cut too tight. Her wrists had been rubbed raw from constant jostling during the escape, and yet despite everything, she still remained strong. Her keen blue eyes were unfazed.

Flint set out our supper: cold jerky and two fresh loaves he'd managed to steal during the hour he'd been patrolling the castle's exit. Everyone exhaled loudly at the scent of fresh bread. At sea we'd survived on almost nothing but overly salted meats, barely preserved vegetables, and *very* stale baker's rolls that Andy had lovingly renamed "rocks."

I watched Lady Sybil cradle her sleeping child and swallowed hard. The lady refused to eat. It was hard to imagine a woman like that—one that was brushing the strands of hair out of her daughter's eyes and adjusting the pale silk ribbon on the waist of her dress—was responsible for the rebel attacks in the desert. What was so important about this woman? She was only a baroness with no relation to the monarchy in Caltoth. She wasn't even a mage.

Darren took a seat between Andy and I on the log. In his

hands, he was rotating a bit of his bread over and over again, watching Lady Sybil with an unreadable expression. I didn't say anything, but I knew instinctively he was wondering the same thing I was. I knew he carried the weight of Caine's death on his shoulders, and I could see him trying to figure out the baroness's role in all of this. We weren't allowed to question the prisoner. Mira had made *that* very clear on our first day out at sea, but it didn't stop us from wondering.

Somehow, my hand found a way to his. Darren looked up, startled, and I gave it a small squeeze. We'd accomplished an important task for our country... even if we didn't know what is was yet.

The prince cracked the barest of a smile, and then his eyes fell to our interlocked fingers. My heartbeat stilled. I knew I had overstepped my bounds, that I should let go before it became more than a friendly reassurance, but then I saw his expression: not anger, not longing—grief, the same look he'd worn during the funeral pyres in the desert.

Darren wasn't thinking about me. He was thinking about all the lives we had lost in the rebel attacks.

"It wasn't your fault," I whispered.

The prince didn't say anything. The only indication he had heard me was the tightening of his hand.

Just tonight, I decided, I would let it remain.

* * *

We had been traveling all day with relatively no rest. Our pace was slower than the day before, but not by much. Mira was convinced the Caltothians would be flooding the forest at any moment.

We had just settled into to a quick break to finish off the

remains of our water when the low crunch of leaves alerted our leader of approaching enemies.

"Cast now!"

Mira's warning came just in time. The rest of the group threw out a barrier. Arrows began to rain down from above, hitting the magicked wall and then sliding harmlessly to its side.

Someone groaned to my right, and I saw Andy had not been so lucky. One of the enemy's missiles had gotten to her before the defense.

I started forward to help, but Cethan grabbed my arm and pointed to Tamora, grunting. Our first responsibility was to the mission, not a comrade. Still, I hesitated a moment longer until I saw Darren approach Andy.

Mira shouted for us to run—that she, Darren, and Andy would hold the Caltothians off as long as they could. When it was safe, they would follow, *if* they could.

The fate of Jerar relied on this mission. Comrades came second.

So I ran.

The sun was already setting. Bright shards of light shot through the trees and blinded me as I followed Cethan and Flint along the trail. I could hear the shouts, the pounding of footsteps, the whistle of things cutting through air, but I ignored it all and focused only on the girl in my arms and Flint's breathless direction.

We must have run for an hour before the clamor of fighting finally died away. It made me anxious, scared for the others. How was Andy faring with her injured arm? Where was Darren? What would happen if our leader, Mira, were dead?

Cethan, Flint, and I slowed down our progress to double check the landmarks nearby.

There was a snap in the brush behind us, and I swung around ready to cast—

It was only a deer.

Cethan grabbed my arm and we continued our trek, more careful not to leave a trace now that we were close to the ship. Flint followed behind, scattering needles and dirt over our path so that it wouldn't be quite so obvious which direction we'd taken.

Finally, after an hour of cautious hiking, we located our ship. I handed Tamora over to Flint, and he and Cethan loaded the small paddleboat with the two hostages and our supplies and then paddled out to our ship anchored deep in the waters a quarter mile beyond the shore. I stood guard at the beach, scanning the tree line beyond it for any sign of an enemy—or the others—approaching.

After the first half hour of waiting, Cethan returned. Flint had chosen to remain on the ship with our prisoners. I knew the big man and Andy were close.

"You can search the woods, if you like," the man told me quietly after the first hour had passed. It was too dark to see anything past the rocky beach now. Both of us were growing anxious as the minutes wore on. Mira would have wanted us both to guard the ship, but it was evident the man's thoughts mirrored my own.

"I—wait, Cethan, look!"

A small glow of dim orange light cut a swatch along the tree line ahead.

"Is it them?"

We watched warily as the shadows drew closer, ready to cast at a moment's notice. The thunder of blood was so heavy and frequent, I couldn't hear anything over the hammering of my pulse. *Please*, I begged, *please be the others*.

As the figures drew closer, Andy and Mira's faces materialized in the darkness.

Cethan let out a long, ragged breath. He ran forward to help Andy, while I half carried our leader to the paddleboat next to shore. Both of their knees seemed to give out the moment we set them down. Their faces and arms were streaked with sweat and dried blood.

"Did the prince make it back before us?" Mira croaked.

My lungs stopped and my hands dropped the oars I'd been about to hand to Cethan.

Andy swore as she realized my reaction.

"I'm going to find him." The words were out of my mouth in an instant.

Mira's stern gaze met my own defiant one. "We will wait for him, Apprentice. You must remain on the beach. The prince knows where to find us, and I need you here to serve as a lookout, not a hero."

"What if Darren's lost?" I challenged. "What if he's hurt and can't make it back on his own?"

The woman glowered. "Believe me when I say it would be a tragedy I'd take to heart. But it is unwise to—"

"He's a *prince*. I thought you served the Crown!"

"He's not the heir," Mira cut me off shortly. "Therefore, Darren is expendable in certain situations. The mission we serve right now is one of those."

"But—" *What kind of mission is more important than a prince's life?*

"I am done arguing. We will wait for him here, for as long as we can." Mira had already turned her back, ordering Cethan to take them to the ship.

"I'll stand watch with Ryiah." Andy stepped off the boat, groaning.

Mira glared at the woman. "You had better not try anything."

Andy put a firm hand on my shoulder and tried not to wince. "I'll make sure Ryiah remains here. I know my duty."

The leader kept her eyes on the two of us for a moment longer and then indicated for Cethan to continue paddling.

As soon as they were out of hearing, the mage spun me to face her. "Lightning," she said, "if you see it, whatever you are doing, get back to the beach. I will try to hold off the enemy as long as I can—but if it gets too much, Mira will make us leave without you."

"What are you—"

"Go, Ryiah. Go find Darren."

* * *

I tore across the dark forest. Long, black branches reached out like fingers to scrape across my skin. I cast out small balls of light, launching them in every which direction, trying to find any sign of the prince or where he'd gone. The cold air whipped across my lungs like a knife. My frantic breathing was coming out in quick, sharp gasps.

Darren could be anywhere. The others had said they'd been forced to separate two hours ago. Andy wasn't sure if he had gone deeper into the woods, or east toward the beach. One thing was certain: he wouldn't have gone south unless he'd been captured.

I retraced my trail, following familiar landmarks and calling out as loudly as I dared.

As the minutes ticked by and there was still no sign of Darren, my searching became frantic. My quiet shouts gave way to desperate shrieks. I no longer cared if the enemy soldiers spotted me.

I knew Mira would be furious if she found out I was casting giant beacons of light and screaming at the top of my lungs, but I was too far from the shore for my leader to stop me.

Rational thinking had given way to panic, and there was nothing holding me back.

"Darren!" I screamed. *"Darren!"*

It had been an hour and a half since I started. My castings had begun to falter, and while I knew it was reckless to use up all of my magic, I couldn't bring myself to stop.

I made it back to where the soldiers had first spotted us. A handful of bloodied bodies littered the clearing in front of me. This was where Mira, Andy, and Darren had first held off the enemy...

All of the bodies bore Caltothian insignia. I exhaled slowly. The prince was safe, for now.

He must have taken a different path. Or maybe he was lost. Or perhaps he had already made it back to the beach and was wondering where I was. I hadn't seen any signs of lightning yet. Andy was still waiting for me.

I had run the whole trail back, thinking I would find

Darren somewhere waiting—possibly too injured to continue
the way to the ship without my assistance. Now, I took my
time, carefully examining each and every bit of ground in
hopes of a trampled branch, bent grass, a footprint in the
leftover winter frost, anything that would point to Darren or
where he had gone.

At one point, I thought I saw something—a bit of dried
blood smeared against a rock, as if Darren had been using it
to prop himself up—but no matter where I turned, the
clearing was empty.

He's probably already on the ship, I told myself quickly.
You must have missed him on your way in. I continued to
prowl the forest back, shouting and casting in every which
direction.

It started to rain.

After a couple minutes, my clothes were soaked through.

"D-ar-ren," I tried again. My teeth were chattering and it
was hard to speak. I tried to swipe at the raindrops that were
blurring my vision, but they were falling in sheets. I could
barely see two feet in front of me. "Darr—"

I broke off, crying out as a searing pain tore in and out of
my left side. I barely had a second to register the pooling
blood above my hips before a loud, swooshing noise came at
my face and I was sent staggering to my knees.

With all the magic I could muster, I cast out from all
sides, hoping to hit my attacker before he landed another hit.
I didn't have any time to prepare. I threw forward the first
projection I could think of: fire.

But it was a mistake. The flames were quickly doused by
rain. I cursed myself for wasting so much magic on the

wrong casting. I hadn't been thinking. A Caltothian soldier behind me kicked my back, and I fell flat into the mud, barely rolling out of the way in time to avoid a heavy boot from crushing my neck.

"I found one!" the enemy shouted.

I heard two sets of loud boots slapping against the wet ground. I tried casting again, but my magic was gone. I'd spent four hours expending my force in my desperation to locate the prince. The fire had cost me my last bit of magic. I was weaponless except for a small blade tucked into my boot, but I couldn't reach it from my current position.

The footsteps were right beside me, and I shoved my hands deep, deep into my open wound, screaming. I forced the pain to bend to my will, calling out the branch of magic that belonged to me and me alone.

And then I pain cast everything I had.

* * *

I woke up to a sea of silver falling from the sky. It was beautiful. One of the stars brushed my face, and then another, and I was surprised to feel a calm, cooling sensation as they caressed my skin, dancing across my brow, my nose, and finally the curve of my jaw.

Finally. *Peace.*

I blinked and realized with a start that the silvery stars were actually glittering flakes of snow, and that I was definitely not enjoying a peaceful death. Every inch of me throbbed like it had been slammed against a wall, repeatedly. My head spun and every time I tried to move, my vision seemed to fade away, leaving me with a black haze and small clusters of shadow I could only assume were some of the forest pines a little further away.

My stomach felt like it was on fire, especially just above my waist where one of the soldiers had managed to stab me with his knife. *Of course*, I acknowledged, *I made it much worse with my pain casting.*

The casting. The Caltothians. Had the soldiers presumed me dead? Had my magic worked? If it hadn't, where were they now? How much time had passed? Biting back a cry of pain in case any were still nearby, I forced myself to sit up and see through the dizzying fog to my surroundings.

Two men and one woman in Caltothian armor were splayed out below a large boulder to my right. I immediately felt sick. The granite behind them was stained red and their bodies were crumbled at odd angles. There was no movement in their chests, the breath stolen from their lungs. Blood covered the grass beneath them.

Three. I had just made my first, second, and third kill— before I had even obtained my mage's robes. I bent over and vomited into the grass. There was no pride, no justice, just the appalling sense that I had lost my innocence. That I was a monster.

It didn't matter that they would have killed me first. Seeing the three lifeless soldiers—still so young and strong and now stained forever against a rock, never to take another breath—left me with a nausea so fierce I could barely breathe without cowering against the ground in a pale, clammy sweat. I had known I would kill in Combat, but I had always pictured the glory. Now my opponents were here, and they were real, and all I saw was blood.

And then I saw Darren. A strangled cry escaped my lips,

and I dove forward to the fourth person I had missed at the edge of the rock's base, hidden by one of the men whose armor had initially blocked my view.

I knelt beside the prince, listening desperately for a heartbeat, but I could hear nothing over the hysterical screaming in my head.

You killed him! You killed him, you killed him, you killed him!

I felt frantically for a pulse, but it was the same. My hands were quivering too badly to tell. I saw the blood pooling underneath his hair, but I refused to acknowledge it.

He'll wake up, you'll see. He's only unconscious! I tried shaking his arms. I tried yelling. I tried pleading with the gods.

But nothing happened.

Slowly, tremors took control of my limbs and I began to tremble uncontrollably. *He's dead.* I was crying and screaming. My sobs were so loud they drowned out the beating in my heart.

Darren is dead. My ribs were cracking apart, crumbling into jagged shards. White ice plunged into my chest as invisible hands choked my lungs until I could no longer breathe.

"You made the right decision, Ryiah. Let's just leave it at that." His words brought a flood of memories, and my tears turned into a flood. An avalanche of emotion and self-hatred came rushing out and reminded me that the fallen prince was more than a friend, more than the wrong decision I had pretended he was.

The first time I saw Darren, in the mountain overpass, his

cold garnet eyes met mine in haughty condescension. If someone had told me back then that he would be the one to break my heart, I would have laughed in their face. But now my heart was breaking, shattering, crumbling into pieces that would never heal.

In the midst of my tears, I saw a stark flash of lightning high above the trees. Andy's warning. They hadn't left, but they would be leaving soon. Could I make it in time? Now, if I ran, would I make it?

But it doesn't matter. It doesn't matter one bit because I am not going anywhere. I could never go back to Andy, my faction, my family and friends knowing I was responsible for killing *him.*

I was dirty, tainted, a lowborn of no significance. The prince deserved better than a sobbing murderer at his feet. I forced myself to wipe away the tears, not caring that I had just smeared blood and dirt across my face in the process. I stood with my back to the prince and scanned the clearing for any sort of flower that I might be able to set beside him: I couldn't recreate a funeral pyre, but I could give his body one last thing of beauty before the Shadow God came for his soul.

But then I remembered we were too far north, still in the months of winter. I couldn't even give Darren something beautiful, something to take with him now that he was gone.

My tears became hysterical and my legs gave out. I kneeled in the mud, sobbing. *What have I done?*

Something brushed my shoulder, but I barely felt it; the rain was drowning out everything as I fell away...

Ryiah.

The rain had his voice. It hurt how real it sounded, catching the slight lilt to his tone—a hint of music edged in humor and bitterness, a mixture of darkness and light.

I told myself I didn't deserve to hear it.

Ryiah.

This time it was louder, and for a moment, for a moment I believed.

"Ryiah." A rough hand gripped my shoulder and jerked me around. And then, suddenly, I was face to face with Darren.

The prince was sitting across from me, cradling the back of his head, the strangest expression on his face.

"I... I thought you were..."

Darren winced, keeping a hand on my shoulder as he studied my face. "You don't give me much credit," he said hoarsely, "if you thought one of your castings would kill me." He meant it as a joke, a play on the vanity he always wore around the rest of our faction, but it only made me cry harder.

"How...?" I couldn't finish.

"I was on my way back when I heard you calling, but by the time I got there, the Caltothians had found you... I was about to jump in when you pain cast... If I hadn't cast my shield—well, let's just say your pain casting has gotten a bit stronger since the first-year trials."

I couldn't look at him. I was too afraid if I did I would see I was alone, that this scene was all just a figment of my imagination, a way of coping with my loss. What he said made sense, but it was just too simple, too easy.

"Ryiah, look at me."

I kept my eyes fixed to the hem of his sleeve, but then Darren lifted my chin so that I was forced to meet his eyes. Silent tears slipped down my face.

My breath hitched.

He's here. He's alive.

It should have made the tears stop, but they only seemed to come down harder.

"Why are you still crying, Ryiah?" His words were almost a whisper. "Why were you away from the boat?"

I just shook my head, not trusting myself to speak.

"You came back for me." He was on his knees as he inched closer. My chin was in the palm of his hands. "Why?"

"B-because..." *It's my duty. You're the prince. No matter what, we are friends.*

I didn't say any of that.

"Be-because I'm in l-love w-with you."

His chest stilled and I heard myself add softly. "But I don't want to be."

Darren sucked in a sharp breath. "I thought you told me..." That this was an infatuation? That it would pass?

"I didn't. I mean, I—"

"Be with me." His voice was hoarse. "I'll call off the engagement as soon as we get to the palace."

There was a moment of elation but it broke just as fast. "You can't—"

"Gods blast it, I don't care!" His eyes beseeched me to listen, to believe. "Ryiah, I love you." There was anger and desperation burning in twin garnet stars. "I'm tired of following their rules. I deserve one good thing. One good

thing for always doing what they want, being who they want me to be. I..." Darren's grip on my hand tightened. "I want *you*, Ryiah. Just say the words, and I'll do it. I'll find a way to convince my father."

I could barely breathe. Every inch of me was singing and crying out. The words were fighting to rise and I was hard-pressed to stop them. I *didn't* want to stop them.

He doesn't know what he is saying. Both of you are drunk on emotion. He isn't being rational; you aren't thinking clearly. Who's to say the king will even let him call off the engagement? And most importantly: *Could it be this easy?*

I realized I didn't care.

I'd chosen him all along. I was tired of fighting feelings for the one person I could never have. Maybe I could have him; we would make this work.

"Darren—"

The sky lit up, and I froze.

Lightning. The ship!

That was the second time in... ten minutes? How much longer would they be able to send out that warning before they left.

"Get up!" I pulled Darren off the ground, and my whole body was shaking. I'd pushed myself to my limits, but I couldn't rest now.

"Ryiah, what are you—"

"Andy cast lightning!" It was the signal our whole crew agreed upon during our plans.

Darren didn't need any more explanation. He broke into a run with my hand in his. I stumbled along, as best as I could.

The wound in my stomach, the dizziness, none of the

aches from earlier had subsided, but somehow the warmth of Darren's fingers in mine gave me strength to continue. I couldn't remember how close we were to shore. I didn't let myself think about what would happen if the others were gone. I just kept running, running knowing that even if they were, I'd won.

Darren was alive.

If the gods had chosen to grant one wish, I was happy it was mine.

THIRTEEN

"THE THREE OF you almost destroyed an entire mission with your reckless conduct. Never have I been so disappointed by the amount of insubordination in all my years of service. Andy and Cethan, I have no choice but to recommend you for disrobement. Ryiah, you don't even have your robes, but make no mistake, I will be suggesting the end of your apprenticeship as well."

Darren cleared his throat as Flint applied a new bandage to the wound on the back of his scalp. His hard lines were every inch the affronted prince. I recognized that look from our first-year at the Academy. "You would rather I die, Mira?"

The leader scowled. "We are all very pleased to have recovered you, Your Highness. It was not my intention to leave you behind, but you were well aware of our orders."

"There were orders to recover our hostage by all means. As those two demonstrated, my sacrifice wasn't necessary to those means."

"It could have been—"

"Will my father see it that way? I'm here alive and we have what we came for."

"Your Highness, you can't possibly—"

"But I will. If you punish those three for seeing to my rescue, I will make sure *you* are disrobed and thrown in the Gilys prison for treason."

She exhaled with a gasp. "My loyalty is to the Crown!"

"And it will stay that way, so long as you follow my orders." His command was like ice.

The leader spent one moment studying his face, weighing the words of his threat, and then stormed off to check our course, lest she counter a prince.

Darren turned to us and his gaze softened. Andy and Cethan had done the impossible. Without them we'd never have made it out of Caltoth. When the first soldier had appeared and Andy shot out her lightning, instead of retreat, she'd fought while Cethan refused to cast the wind for the ship. With only non-magical Flint and two hostages, Mira had been forced to wait offshore.

Our leader had been furious.

There'd only been a handful of men, and by the time Darren and I had burst through the clearing, they'd just finished combat with the final one. According to Mira, they should have retreated to the ship the moment they caught sight of the enemy.

"She won't try that threat again."

"Thanks for that." Andy gripped the prince's forearm with a hobble. Her grin was bright against her sun-darkened skin as she left.

Cethan just grunted in the prince's direction and trailed after his friend to the front of the deck.

Then it was just the two of us. We were alone for the first

time since we'd boarded the ship the night before. Andy and Cethan had taken turns at our recovery when they weren't seeing to Andy's own extensive list.

Darren stepped out to lean against the deck's railing. I followed him. A moment of awkward silence followed as we both stared out at the ocean.

Here was my chance to take back the words I'd never gotten to say in the forest. *I want to fight for us.* I could walk away and save my heart for the turmoil that came next.

My feet wouldn't move.

"What we talked about in the forest—" Gods, how I wanted to tell him I couldn't, but every part of me was screaming, fighting for a chance. We deserved this. We'd spent too many years fighting feelings that left us half mad and delirious. "I want to be with you, too."

There was a sudden intake of breath as his pupils widened and his hand gripped the rail. I could see the fast rise and fall of his chest. Darren hadn't been expecting me to say yes. "It's not going to be easy, Ryiah." His voice was hoarse.

"I know."

"We have to keep us a secret until I have his approval. I… I don't want to, but…" But it was obvious. If Priscilla caught wind of our decision, her father would reach out to the king. He had too much control with her dowry. "I need to address my father in person, a letter won't be sufficient, not if we want this to work."

I'd fought my feelings this long, what were a couple more months? *You can't court a prince; they'll never accept it.* I shoved the despair to a deep cavity in my chest.

After yesterday, we deserved to fight for *us.*

"I... I want this to work." Gods, I'd dreamed of something like this for years.

Darren brushed a strand of hair from my eyes and sighed. "I just wish there was an easier way for both of us."

Hadn't we been wishing that for years?

He took my hands and gently tugged me to his side of the rail. Then his arms locked around my waist, pulling me to his front. "No matter what happens, Ryiah, I'm not going to give you up."

I nodded and he pressed his lips to my forehead.

No matter how hard it gets.

I wasn't sure whether that last part was his promise or mine.

* * *

"Langli may be a beautiful city"—Ella's horse dipped its head, attempting to steal a cluster of tall, high grass—"but I'm happy we are moving on."

I'd returned to Langli near two months back, and now we were back on the road for the capital. Another fifth-year ascension, only this time there was more riding on the line than a ceremony.

I gnawed on my lip as my eyes slid over to Darren, riding a couple spots in front of the faction. He was in the middle of a debate with Eve and Ray and a couple of the fifth-years they were friends with. After a couple seconds, he looked back, sensing my stare, but he didn't look away.

My pulse stopped. I wanted to cross the distance between us and grasp anything besides empty air. We'd shared a couple of desperate, hungry kisses on that ship before we'd reached the shore. Now we were back to playing as if things hadn't changed.

It was like there was some invisible cord holding us in place, trapping us in a daze we couldn't break... until Eve tapped the prince's shoulder and Darren turned back to his dialogue with the others.

His back was to me.

I continued watching him, memorizing the confident way he spoke and the way he drummed the saddle with his long, lean fingers until Ella reached over to wave a hand in front of my face.

"Hey," she chided, "enough of that!" Leaning in, she added, "We've still got a week to go before we reach Devon."

I'd told her everything weeks ago.

"Those long, anguished looks are worse than your brother and me," she added.

For that, I managed a smile. "I know your aim hasn't gotten any better since the two of you started those late-night practice sessions. What were they for again?"

"Ssssh!" She clapped a hand over my mouth—well, she tried to. Her swat missed, and she almost swung out of the saddle, laughing. "If Master Joan or Byron catch one whiff of that, they'll send us to latrine duty for a month!"

They already had. Twice.

At least the faction knew they were a couple. I had to suffer through Priscilla and the prince.

The last two months, I'd been easily distracted and it'd shown in my performance. Too much of my time was spent watching that girl and wishing I were in her stead. The rest of that time was daydreaming about when I would take her place.

My potential was at a standstill, and I had only myself to blame.

Glancing back up front, I saw Priscilla had joined Darren's party. My stomach twisted just looking at her run her fingers up his arm like he was hers.

I hadn't been able to do so much as hold his hand.

My whole face was on fire, but I managed a deep breath. Ella was right. One more week, and then we could finally be together.

"You know Alex is worried." Ella interrupted my thoughts. "He says you shouldn't get your hopes too high."

I frowned. "I know exactly what I'm setting my hopes for."

"He's just trying to protect you. We both are."

"Well, tell Alex, if he really cares, he will keep his opinions to himself." I regretted telling him the truth. He'd never liked the prince and now... "This isn't a mistake. I don't tell my brother how to go about his relationships— gods only know he's made more mistakes than me." I immediately regretted the choice of words when I saw the flush on Ella's face.

My friend pulled away, putting more space between our mares. "If anything, Alex's mistakes should tell you he has a point. He knows how a man thinks. He knows how they act. He—"

"Alex isn't Darren," I interrupted. "He doesn't have any idea what it is like to be a prince."

Ella gave me a meaningful look. "Do you?"

"More than him!"

Ella sighed. "I wish you would hear him out, Ry." A part of me wondered if she shared his opinion. Ella had a complicated past with Darren too.

"He needs to apologize first."

"Alex just wants the best for you, even if he is making a mistake in the way that he goes about it. He remembers what I told him about Blayne, and then that time when Darren hazed you during your first year... It's hard for him to forget that. He's your brother, and I know more than anything he just wants to protect you."

I glanced to the right of our procession where the Restoration apprentices rode. My brother stared right back. I straightened in my saddle and glared straight ahead. I was the Combat mage. I could protect myself.

* * *

I'd just handed off my reins to the palace hostler when something smooth and squared was pressed into the palm of my hand. A note? I glanced back, but the shaggy-haired stableman was already hurrying away.

Curious to see what the paper said, I hurried to my assigned chambers in the palace without a second look back. Then I locked my door and read the scrap of crumbled parchment:

R,

Meet me at the palace gardens in one hour. Wait near the statue of Morteus. Look for an old hag with a long, gray braid.

-D

What? I hadn't expected to see the prince until he talked to his father later that night... We couldn't be seen together, so what was this?

I made a quick attempt to wash from the morning travel and then fumbled around my bags for the right thing to wear. I held out the dress I'd worn to the solstice ball, but it was far too nice, and I had no idea what Darren had planned. Would I even see him at all? He wanted me to find an old woman, so there was no point in dressing up for him.

Ultimately, I decided on a simple blue cotton dress that wouldn't draw attention. I pinned my hair back in a makeshift twist and then left to find the gardens.

When I reached the statue, there was a hunched figure in a red cape with a long, gray braid sticking out the side of her hood. I approached her nervously. "Ma'am?"

The figure spun around, and I gasped when *she* withdrew *his* hood, chuckling. It was the prince wearing a wig, pressing one finger to his lips as he beckoned me forward.

"Darren!"

"Gran." He pulled the hood back low over his face and grinned. "Are you ready for a real tour of the palace?"

I scanned the gardens, suddenly anxious. "What if someone recognizes you?"

"The only servants who know this disguise are loyal. The rest?" He smirked. "They are too blind to see who is right there in front of them."

"What about your father? Don't you need to talk to him?"

"The king can wait." His face contorted. "The moment I tell him my intentions, I will be yelled at from dawn until dusk." Darren took a step closer and took my hand in his. It felt *so good* after weeks of watching him do it with someone else. "Before I subject myself to that, I'd like to spend time with the girl who convinced me she was worth it in the first place."

My whole face burned. I still wasn't used to Darren talking to me like... like I was special to him—like we were a boy and a girl together, instead of two forces colliding in a storm.

"There's that blush I was hoping for." His eyes warmed. "I was beginning to think you didn't care."

"Priscilla paraded you around in front of me for months." My other hand was on my hip. "What did you expect me to do?"

He grinned. "So you *were* jealous."

"Of course I was. You didn't have to watch me and Ian—"

Darren ducked under a nearby willow and dragged me behind him.

"Darren, what are you doing?"

The prince put a finger to my lips, eyes dancing wickedly. "Would I kiss Priscilla like this?" He didn't give me a chance to reply, his hot mouth was on mine in an instant and I forgot my own name.

Gods. My hands twisted around his neck as his lips parted mine.

When he finished, I was weak-kneed and lightheaded, floating on clouds.

Darren released me with a groan. "I forgot what that was like."

So had I. I'd remember it, but the memory was a candle to the flame of the moment. I swore I caught fire every time.

"I should take you on this tour before someone spots us."

Darren's eyes fell back to my mouth, and he didn't seem interested in leaving. "If we stay here any longer, I won't make a very convincing grandmother."

I didn't want to do anything but grab Darren and let him make good on that threat.

Focus, Ryiah.

I swallowed quickly. "Right, let's take that tour shall we... Gran?"

Darren grinned and held up his hands, taking a step back. "All right. Let's start with the kennels. There's someone I want you to meet."

* * *

"So you are the one who's put the prince out of sorts." A large man with a gruff voice and three missing front teeth beamed down at me. He'd introduced himself as Heath. "'Course I shuda known that it could never be that other one. His highness has never once taken *her* to meet Wolf."

"So who is Wolf?" I glanced between the two. I hardly knew anything about Darren's life in the palace. To say he was a mystery was an understatement. I didn't even know Heath's role.

The man chortled. "Not who. What." He motioned for me to follow through a large building that served as the kennels. Inside was a large enclosure where twenty hounds relaxed on comfortable oak panels. A second set of steps led up to another platform where even more of them slept. Against the wall were large bins for food and water, and a large door led to a grassy pasture where the dogs could roam during certain hours while the servants supervised. The falconry was just a bit beyond, and I could hear the angry bird cries across the room.

"Is Wolf a hound?" There was a pit in my stomach, but I forced myself to ignore it.

At the mention of his name, a thin, shaggy mutt lifted its head from the middle of the pack. Unlike the sleek, muscled palace hounds, this animal was frail. Clearly not used for the hunt. It was scrawny with gray matted fur and timid brown eyes peeking out of the long gray hairs that practically covered its face. It didn't look dangerous, but then old man Crawley's dog hadn't either.

"Come here, boy."

I turned quickly to look at Darren. The tone he'd used to call Wolf forward was so different from what he usually used that I almost couldn't believe it had come from him.

Darren didn't notice; he had already jumped the fence.

Wolf sprung to life and launched himself into his master's arms. The dog yipped and thumped its tail so loudly I was afraid someone might think there was an attack.

Foreboding filled my chest. I knew what was coming next.

Darren glanced back at me. "Are you coming, Ryiah?"

I hesitated for a moment. Maybe. Maybe I could do this. I took a step forward and gripped the gate's handle, my knuckles white with trepidation. One of the hounds trotted forward to sniff at my fingers, and I leaped back, retreating to where Heath stood a couple feet away from the gates. My hands were slick with sweat, and I wiped them nervously against the skirt of my dress.

"I... I can't." My throat was dry and the words came out scratchy and odd—like I was choking on sand.

Darren frowned. "What do you mean you can't?"

"I mean…" I clenched and unclenched my fists anxiously. "I just can't, Darren."

"Ryiah." Something about the prince's voice made me look up. "Are you afraid of dogs?"

I forced myself to hold his gaze. "When Derrick was five, one of them attacked him. I was only eight. We'd both grown up playing with our neighbor's dog, Bo, and then one day it just turned." My breath hitched, and I made myself exhale. "It was terrible. Crawley had to—he couldn't call Bo off—he had to…" I couldn't say it. The blood and those glassy eyes afterward…. "And then Derrick had to spend two weeks being treated—we, um, we couldn't afford a healer, so it was up to my parents to tend to his leg… It's fine, now, but I—ever since that I just…"

Darren hadn't once taken his eyes off me the whole time I was talking. Now he straightened and approached the gate's fence with Wolf trailing behind. When he reached the edge of the enclosure, he rested his arm on the top of the barrier's railing. "Ryiah, I want you to come here."

I stared at him, wide-eyed. "You are mad if you think that I'm going inside."

"Ryiah," he said patiently. "You want to be a war mage. Facing your fears is part of that."

I thought my fears would involve other things.

Darren read the protest in my eyes.

"You can." His eyes held pity. "Ryiah, Bo was sick. It happens with the hounds when they are bitten by an infected animal, or even one of the strays. There's no known cure when it happens. There was nothing you could have done differently." He patted Wolf's head and the dog yipped affectionately. "Heath and the rest of the kennel's staff know the signs. You are safe. Now come meet Wolf." There was a smile as he looked down at the shaggy-haired mutt; the kind I so rarely saw on the prince. "He's the only family member I can promise will give you a warm reception."

I forced myself to take a step forward, and then another, until I was in front of the gate. Darren nodded encouragingly as I unbolted the latch and timidly stepped through its entry, every hair on end.

Darren held out his hand, and I took it, hoping he wouldn't notice how clammy my fingers had become. I let him gently tug me closer to Wolf and then held myself rigid as the mutt eagerly sniffed at my boots. The other hounds remained at a distance, seeming aware of my obvious discomfort, or perhaps a testament to their training and obedience.

Wolf yelped, and I dropped Darren's hand, heart slamming into my ribs. For a second, all I could see was the cold, hard axe and Bo whimpering in a pool of his own blood.

"It's okay, Ryiah." Darren's voice broke through the haze as his hand found mine again. "Wolf just wants you to pet him."

The hammering in my ears lessened, and I forced myself to look away from the prince and down to the panting gray dog at my feet. The dog looked up at me and thumped its tail, then whined again.

"He's a bit needy. I'm afraid I've spoiled him."

I took a deep breath and reached out to touch him. Wolf

yipped and jumped up to meet my hand. I stumbled, unable to stop myself from pulling back in fear, and landed on the ground with Wolf bounding right on top of me. Wolf lodged his head at my throat, and I shrieked, arms held up against my face only to feel his warm, wet tongue against my skin. I lowered my arms, embarrassed, and the dog darted in to lick my face.

Meanwhile, standing above me was Darren, shaking with laughter.

I timidly began to pet the dog, still keeping one eye on his teeth while I shot Darren a half-hearted glare. "I could have been mauled!"

"How? Being licked to death?" Darren crouched down with a grin to rub Wolf's neck. "This one is a coward. The palace cats tease him about it all the time. The hounds chase them and then they take their frustration out on Wolf because he's not fast like the rest of them. He's only a stray."

I couldn't help smiling a little as I shifted to a crouch, still petting the dog. *This isn't so bad. Bo was like this too, before it happened.* "A stray?"

Darren nuzzled his dog's neck, seemingly unconcerned that he was getting white and gray fur all over his dress. The perfect, immaculate prince had a weakness after all. "When Wolf was just a pup, I found him wandering the palace grounds... I'm not sure exactly how he got through the gates, but it was raining and he was nothing more than a pile of bones, so I took him to Heath. I was only ten..." He suddenly stopped, and when I glanced at his face, it was pained. *What happened?* "I brought him to my first hunt."

"Is that how he got his name?"

Darren's hand faltered on Wolf's neck. "It was." There was another long pause. "During the hunt, one of the men broke his legs falling down a ravine and his horse didn't survive the drop. A pack of wolves attacked. The soldier and I managed to kill three, but Wolf managed two. He couldn't have been more than six months at that time."

It sounded like an ordinary childhood tale, but there was something dark he wasn't telling me. I could see the memory as a garnet storm in his eyes. Whatever that day had been, there was more to the tale than he was telling me.

Still, I knew better than to push. It'd taken this long for the prince to open up about his past at all.

I rubbed Wolf's belly, pleased to note the anxiety I'd been feeling had all but disappeared. Wolf was making excited yips and rubbing his back against the ground so that Darren and I had no choice but to continue patting his stomach. "He's not so bad," I admitted.

The storm was gone as the prince rubbed a hand along his neck and smiled. "Wolf has had me wrapped around his finger since the day we met. There hasn't been a day gone by that I've been in the palace and not visited this kennel."

"He better not be with that filthy animal of his!"

Darren and I glanced at each other: both of us recognized the voice. Prince Blayne couldn't be more than two minutes away from the kennels.

"Why he thinks it's appropriate to come here before seeing to his family is—"

"This way." Darren led me to the back of the enclosure. He gave a nod to Heath and the man strode off in the direction of his brother with a smirk. A moment later, he and

Blayne exchanged words—Blayne demanding to see his brother while the kennel master insisted he hadn't seen Darren all day.

"Let's go."

I turned sharply. There was a tunnel I had never seen before—it had come from one of the panels in the wall. "Where did that—"

Darren yanked me through the door and slammed it shut just as Blayne's voice reached the hounds' enclosure.

"You see, Your Highness? Your brother isn't here." I didn't get to hear the rest of their conversation; Darren and I were already running through the tunnel as fast as we could in the dark. I was mostly blind. Darren dragged me through the musty passage with a small casting of light—he seemed to have the turns memorized. There was no way I wouldn't have fallen on my own.

I crinkled my nose as we reached the end and Darren halted behind something solid. The entire place smelled like mold and cold, dank earth. "Where *are* we?"

"The servants use this tunnel to feed the animals. It's the shortest route directly through the kitchens. Cook gives them the leftover scraps. It helps the hounds keep up their stamina."

Darren did something to the wall and a door swung open to a very hot room teeming with steam and the tempting aroma of fresh roast and stewed vegetables.

"What's this—why is a beggar woman in my kitchens?" A hefty man in cook's robes flushed, cheeks red as cherries as the prince dropped his hood. "Your Highness!"

The prince gave the man a reassuring pat on the shoulder.

"It's fine. Has Blayne already been down here?"

"Your insufferable brother has already been down here twice." The cook made a face. Apparently he and Darren had some kind of rapport. "I told him you were probably with that mutt."

Darren grinned.

"He's set to check the training grounds after the kennels, so you've bought yourself a half hour before he returns."

"Thanks, Benny."

The cook nodded and Darren led me through the back of the servants' hall to the fourth floor of the palace.

"Did you want to see the Council of Magic's chamber?"

"Of course I do!" I couldn't contain my squeal. The room was off limits to everyone but the Crown and the Colored Robes.

Darren tugged me along to a narrow corridor at the right, and then up another flight of stairs past stained glass windows and powerful tapestries of previous kings. We must have walked another ten minutes before we finally reached an elaborate set of doors, stained black with metal engravings that stated, "Council of Magic: Official Chambers" and then in smaller writing, "Do not interrupt. Meetings are by appointment only. Please see Artemis to schedule."

"Who's Artemis?"

"One of the palace scribes. She's not a particularly cheerful woman. I wouldn't recommend sitting next to her at any of the dinners if you can help it." He swung the door and then froze.

I collided with his back just as someone screeched.

"You have no right to enter this chamber! What are your names? Explain yourself at once!"

Darren's face lost all of its color, and I peeked over his shoulder. Three Colored Robes and King Lucius, along with a group of what look liked the king's advisors stood around a map of Jerar and its surrounding territories. Two guards strode forward and Darren swore under his breath. "Run."

The two of us took off, racing down the hall, ducking into random passages as Darren led us on in a mad dash to avoid the two guards chasing us. Darren kept changing stairwells and halls so quickly I lost track of where we were.

"Almost—just a little bit further!" Darren turned down a wider hall than the rest. Gold, real gold sconces lit the passage and there was a lush rug padding our steps. I followed, clutching my ribs—I had forgotten how much faster Darren could run; my heart felt like it was about to explode from my racing pulse.

"In here!" The prince turned a key and then yanked me into the room behind him. He threw off his cloak and the wig and tossed them into a trunk at the foot of the bed. At that same moment, there was a loud knock on the door. The guards had arrived.

I ducked behind the doorframe and Darren swung open the handle with a bored expression.

"Your Highness."

"What is it?"

"I'm so sorry to disturb you, Your Highness, but we think an elderly lady and a young woman might have passed by here. We just want to make sure that you didn't see them."

"An old woman and her granddaughter?" Darren spoke a

little too loudly. "You must have been nipping at Cook's wine, Torrance. No one has been anywhere near this hall but me."

"My apologies, Your Highness, we were on orders to check all the rooms."

"The only one with a key to this chamber is myself—and, of course, Father."

One of the guards muttered something unintelligible and then cleared his throat. "Of course, Your Highness, please excuse me for the error. You said you never saw them?"

"I didn't. But if I do, I will be sure to send word."

"Yes, if you do, please let us know."

Darren leaned against the doorway and folded his arms. "Tell me, Torrance, what did you think?"

"The old woman? It's hard to say who she was."

"Didn't you say there were two of them? What was the younger one like?" I couldn't see Darren's expression, but I could tell from his tone that he was grinning. If I'd been standing closer, I would have kicked him. *What is he thinking?*

"I'm sorry, Your Highness, I—"

"I'll bet she was pretty." I could practically hear his laughter. "Did you think she was pretty, Torrance?"

"I'm not sure. I barely caught a glimpse, Your Highness."

Darren sighed. "That is all, you may go. And you too, Cyrus."

As soon as Darren had shut the door, I glared at him, arms crossed. "Are you mad?"

His eyes danced. "I'm allowed to have a little fun at your expense, Ryiah."

"If they find out it was me——"

"They won't." The prince took a step forward, still smiling.

"But…" I never got to finish my thought. Darren's mouth was on mine, and all protests were lost in the blink of an eye.

And then we were on fire.

I broke for air, gasping. My heart was racing, my legs were shaking, my head was spinning, and I couldn't think. I couldn't—

Darren's hand grazed my waist as he pulled me back to him. "Ryiah," he said.

The two of us stumbled across his chambers. Behind me I heard the thud of something loud. Books falling to the floor?

Darren pressed me against his bedside table and kissed me again, slowly, one hand cradling the back of my neck. Unable to stop, I slid my hand under his shirt and felt him swallow. His chest was hard with smooth ridges and curves against the lean muscle. I trembled. I wanted to run my fingers along every inch of him, and it scared me how badly I wanted to do it *now*.

Darren's hand ran down my ribs, my waist, my thigh, and then hooked up under my knee. I had to bite my lip as he pulled me even closer, not caring that the hem of my dress was riding dangerously high. Every part of me was burning hotter and hotter, and I knew we should stop, but I couldn't bring myself to move even if I wanted to because, gods, Darren's hands were on my skin and in my hair and my entire body was aflame.

His breathing wasn't so steady either. His mouth fell to my shoulder and a whimper escaped my lips. *Was that really me?* I started to pull away, embarrassed, but Darren took my chin and kissed me hard, biting the bottom of my lip until I gasped.

My nails dug into his shoulders, and I kissed him back, melting and burning and unable to keep my hands to myself. Gods, I was losing myself in what it felt like to be near him. Darren was dangerous, driving me to forget everything and everyone but this moment, and I didn't ever want it to end.

Any semblance of control was broken. The prince choked my name, picking me up and throwing me onto his bed. Soft pillows feathered my fall. Darren's face was flushed and his eyes were wild as he pushed my wrists up against the frame.

I held my breath, my eyes locked on the two dark smoldering stars bearing down on me.

"You have no idea what it is I want to do to you," he whispered.

The only sound in the entire room was the frantic beating of my heart slamming against my chest until I was sure it would break.

And then there was a loud knock on the door.

"Open up, brother, I know you are in there. The guards saw you."

The two of us jumped. Darren practically fell from his bed as I darted to a corner of the room, the two of us in a mad panic.

Darren motioned for me to hide behind one of the heavy brocade curtains hanging at the opposite end of the room. Then he cleared his throat loudly and made his way to the door, cracking it open only a smidge to glare at his brother on the other side.

"What do you want, Blayne?"

"I have been looking all over for you. Father expected you to report to him as soon as you arrived."

"I was busy."

"Busy?" Blayne's tone was instantly suspicious. "Doing what? Avoiding your duties to the Crown? Priscilla said she hasn't seen you all day. This better not be about that lowborn, brother. I have no more patience for whatever silly infatuation you've got parading around in that thick skull of yours."

The prince stiffened. "Ryiah is not lowborn anymore, and even if she were—"

Blayne ignored him and rattled on. "What you need is a good lay, Darren. I've seen how that redhead looks at you. Tell her whatever she needs to hear, and the rest will take care of itself. Then you can get back to what's important, like your role in this kingdom—or have you been training so long as a mage that you forgot you were also a prince?"

Darren's knuckles on the door's handle whitened. "I know my role," he said shortly, "and where my duties lie. I will report to Father within the hour."

"Well, see to it that you do," Blayne snapped. "I can't be the only one who takes my role seriously. What Father sees in you, I will never know."

Darren slammed the door shut and then waited until his brother was out of hearing distance before he turned to me. "I'm sorry you had to hear that."

I stepped out of the curtain, sick to my stomach. Even without the knowledge I'd been present, Blayne had still managed to make me feel worthless. *"Tell her whatever she needs to hear, and the rest will take care of itself."* His words made me realize how close Darren and I had come to fulfilling his twisted prophecy.

This time when the prince took a step toward me, I flinched. Darren's shrewd gaze missed nothing.

"You are upset."

"I-I'm not upset," I stammered. "I j-just didn't think things would h-happen s-so fast."

Fury darkened the prince's face. "I would never ask you to do anything you didn't want to, Ryiah. I'm not my brother. I would never try what he and Ella—"

"I-it's not that." I was stuttering, and I knew my cheeks were now as red as my scarlet-red locks. "But..."

"But you can't stop thinking about what my brother said."

I couldn't look at him.

A hand entered my vision and tipped my face. Darren's eyes met mine, and there was a grim smile on his face. "Blayne's wrong," he promised quietly. "I love you, Ryiah. Nothing is going to change that."

FOURTEEN

With my best impression of nonchalance, I exited the castle's formal ascension chambers and followed the remaining throng of apprentices into the grand ballroom. Everyone was chattering on in excited voices. Even the ornate torches seemed to reflect the evening's enthusiasm, flickering wildly along the hall and dancing off the many-colored windowpanes surrounding it. The orchestra was already playing an upbeat march and the heralds were having particular fun announcing the newly graduated mages to the awaiting crowd of nobility.

I scanned the mass for the one apprentice who had been noticeably absent throughout the entire ceremony. For the past week, I'd barely slept, tossing and turning, dreaming of that moment Darren finally appeared and put all my fears to rest. Five days had never passed as slowly as they had the past week.

"Ryiah, would you like to grab something to drink?"

I started, drawn out of my thoughts by my best friend's question. She and Alex had appeared at my side while I'd been too busy searching the crowd.

"Ella," my brother's response was filled with irony, "can't

you see? She's waiting for *him*."

I glared at Alex. "You don't need to be so cruel."

My brother made a frustrated noise. "You don't need to be so naïve."

"Like all those girls you courted before Ella?" I stood my ground. I would *not* let his doubt get to me. Not tonight. "Darren's not a hopeless flirt like you!"

"Ry, Alex, stop it!" Ella shoved herself between us and then scolded my brother. "Alex, your sister is old enough to make decisions for herself. The least you can do is support her."

My brother stared at her incredulously. "Don't pretend to agree with her, El. You told me last night—"

"It doesn't matter what *we* think." She glowered. "We are here for her, and we'll support her because that's what—"

I never got to catch the rest of her reply. The royal herald had just announced the arrival of the Crown.

"King Lucius and his royal highness, Prince Blayne."

The king and his eldest son entered, their icy blue eyes spawning a sudden chill as they made their way to the front of the room. They bore matching blood-red cloaks and tight-fitted brocade that highlighted their health as well as the golden thread and gems that lined their heavy, chained fastenings. The room went silent in their approach—although it hardly seemed possible from the heavy pounding in my ears.

I watched as they settled into their chairs, waiting.

There was an odd moment where everything was still, and then the herald continued.

"Prince Darren, second-in-line to the throne."

I started toward the front, eager to catch a better glimpse.

"And his betrothed, Lady Priscilla of Langli."

The loud clang of metal brought the eyes of everyone—including *him*—to me. I stood frozen in place, pale and unmoving as ice, while a red-faced servant bent to pick up his serving platter from the hard marble floor. It had been unceremoniously knocked from his arms just moments before.

I didn't hear the loud gasps coming from the crowd around me. I barely noticed the red stains that now covered the hem of my blossoming skirts. My eyes were glued to the indifferent prince staring back at me.

He was still betrothed?

What about us?

Why was he looking at me like that?

Like I was nothing. No one.

Like that moment in the Caltothian forest had never happened. Like this was all a mistake.

Two pairs of hands took hold of my arms and gently led me to the back of the room, out of the attention of others, while I watched the dark-haired stranger and his lady resume their procession.

"Ryiah?"

I watched as the young man took his seat beside the king and his heir, with Priscilla close by. Not once did the stranger's gaze stray from her face, nor did he hesitate to kiss her hand and laugh easily at something a nearby courtier said in response to the lady's question.

"Ry, if you want to retire early, I'd be happy to join you." Ella's voice was strangely muted, like she was speaking through glass. Her voice was distorted and muffled, more like one long humming stance than a question.

What is happening? Why was he smiling at *her* like that? I kept staring, waiting for a break in the façade. Just the barest hint that he wasn't enjoying himself, that he felt something—anything—other than the nonchalance that was plastered all over his face.

"You should just take her now." My brother's hushed whisper seemed even further away. "Before she does something rash."

His father forced him into this. My breathing became calm, steady. That was it, of course. Darren needed more time to talk the king around. It wasn't something either of us had prepared for, but we would find a way.

Warmth returned to my limbs, and I found that the numbness in my legs and arms had receded. I hugged my arms to my chest. He loved me. So I would wait. I had already waited three years, what would a little more time be?

"Please excuse me." My voice caught. I didn't bother to look to my brother or friend as I pushed my way through to the hall. Faces passed by in a blur, though it was only as I entered my chambers that I realized why.

Tears.

I might be willing to wait, but I could not very well stand by while Priscilla paraded the boy I loved in front of me.

I could not pretend.

* * *

I waited, counting out the opening and shutting of chamber doors until I was certain the last apprentice had returned from the palace's late night ball. I waited for an additional toll from the great bell tower and then stealthily exited my chambers, careful not to slam the door and draw the attention of any loitering servants or guards posted nearby. Most were too busy cleaning up after the feast to notice, but one could never be too careful.

I drew my cloak close and passed the women's hall, continuing on past the men's and then finally up the many flights of stairs and twisting corridors—retracing my steps once or twice—in an effort to locate Darren's chambers.

"Excuse me, miss, no one can pass this point without an official summons." Just as I reached the final hall, I found two guards blocking its entrance. The one who had spoken was eyeing me with a skeptical expression and the other was tapping his scabbard. Tick. Tick. Tick. Neither looked particularly willing to let me pass.

I'd been expecting as much. I let the hood fall from my face so that they would recognize me as one of the apprentices. "Please, if you could tell Prince Darren it's Apprentice Ryiah. I am sure he will make an exception."

The first guard yawned loudly. "Lady Ryiah, if we interrupted the Crown for every person seeking audience, we would be out of a job."

"Yes, but I'm not—"

"Let her in, Sirus. I can vouch for this one *personally*."

Every hair on my neck stood on end. I knew that slick voice like the back of my hand. Blayne. Bells of alarm rang out loudly in my ears, but I tried not to let the panic show in my face. Why was *he* coming to my aid? He hated me.

Something was wrong.

The guards lowered their weapons and stepped to the side

as the heir to Jerar escorted me forward. I tried not to flinch as he tugged me along, a deep sense of foreboding consumed me as we reached Darren's chamber. The last time the two of us had crossed paths, Blayne had made it perfectly clear what he thought of the lowborn girl who shared a friendship with his brother. And then I'd attacked him. Even if Darren had informed his brother of his intentions, I highly doubted Blayne had forgiven me for *that*.

I hesitated at the door, wondering if Blayne planned to witness my confrontation with his brother.

"Go on. Knock." The words came out silky and dangerous, with a hint of disgust that was fully evident now that we were past the guards' hearing. I chanced a glance at Blayne's face and saw the malignant curve of his lips.

Rapping twice against the dark wood, I waited, my stomach in knots. I heard the soft pad of boots against carpet, and then the door swung open to reveal Darren, half dressed in dark breeches and a loose cotton shirt. Dark bangs fell to the side of his face—but it wasn't enough to shield the guilt that flared in his eyes for just a moment before quickly melding into cool indifference.

Darren's mouth hardened into a small, thin line. "What are you doing here, Ryiah?"

My whole body went cold, and for a moment I couldn't believe it was Darren standing in front of me. There hadn't been a single hint of emotion in his address.

"I need to talk to you." I was trying my best to sound calm. "Alone."

The prince's gaze slid to his older brother, and then back to me. His expression didn't waver. "There is nothing to discuss."

"Darren." My voice cracked. *"Please."*

Blayne, who up until now had been a smug spectator leaning against the frame of Darren's door lazily, snorted rudely. "My dear," he drawled, "my brother has given you his answer. Pick up your lowborn pride and leave before this gets worse. I only brought you here so you wouldn't assault those poor guards trying to get over here in the first place. I am well aware of your *temper*." He pronounced the last word distinctly.

I ignored Blayne and kept my eyes locked on the one person who mattered. "What did they say to you, Darren?" My pulse raced. I could feel my heartbeat in my throat. I swallowed and forced myself to continue. "I'll wait... If you tell me you need more time to talk your father around—"

Blayne let out a high-pitched laugh.

"Ryiah." Garnet flames stopped me midspeech. "I don't want you to wait."

It was as if someone had just plunged me into a bath of ice. "What do you mean?"

Darren was silent.

I felt hysteria rising. "Darren." I took a step forward, ignoring his brother's sharp intake of breath, and took the prince's hand. "Don't do this. I..." My voice caught. *"I love you."*

The prince frowned and looked pointedly to his brother. "Might we have a moment alone?"

Blayne's blue eyes narrowed in suspicion, but he stepped back with a curt glance at me. "Remember," he snarled, "if you try anything, I will have the guards over here at a moment's notice."

I glared back at him. "I believe your brother asked for some privacy."

Anger webbed across the heir's features, but before he could retort, Darren jerked me into his chamber and shut the door.

Then it was just the two of us facing one another, no noise except for the quiet beating of my chest and Blayne's pacing outside the room.

"Why won't you talk to me?" I sounded pleading, even to my own ears. I hated it, but I had no control over my emotions, and he was breaking every part of me in his silence.

"I am making the best of a bad situation. It will be best if you don't make a scene."

"A scene?" My voice was shrill. "Darren, you told me you were leaving her! Why are you still betrothed to Priscilla?"

"You know why."

"I thought you were tired of following rules!" I shouted, furious. "You told me—you *promised* that day on the ship— even if things became hard you wouldn't give up on us!"

The prince didn't respond. I closed the distance between us and grabbed both of his shoulders, shaking him. "Darren, look at me!"

He shoved me away angrily. "What do you want me to say, Ryiah? I made a mistake."

For a moment, there was only silence.

Tears burned my eyes. "We aren't a mistake."

"You had to know we never would've been able to marry." His eyes were fathomless. "Even if I had somehow convinced Father to break off my engagement to Priscilla and court you, it never would have lasted long."

I couldn't breathe. All I could hear was the angry pulsing of blood.

"You coward!" I picked up the nearest object I could find—a large glass globe—and lobbed it at his head. *"You aren't even trying to fight for us!"*

Darren dodged the globe easily, and there was a loud shattering as millions of tiny shards misted the air between us.

"You shouldn't have done that, Ryiah," he said.

The chamber door swung open as Blayne and the two guards from earlier strode in, weapons raised.

I dropped my hands and let the two men bind my wrists, two sets of rough hands dragging me away from the prince. "All this time, I respected you for trying to prove you were more than a prince, more than some privileged highborn!" I spat at him. "It's a shame to find out you are no more than your father's whipping boy!"

Darren stopped looking indifferent. Now the expression he wore was livid. "You want to know the truth?" He shouldered his way past the guards so that he was inches from my face. Blayne watched the both of us with keen interest. "I never loved you."

"Liar!" I wrestled with my restraints, but the guards were too strong.

"I never loved you." Darren's laugh was cold and unfeeling. "Did I want you? Of course, I would've been a fool not to... But love? Well, that's just something one claims to win certain privileges."

"You are lying!" I couldn't believe him. I wouldn't. He was only trying to hurt me to make this easier. It was like our first year at the Academy: he was protecting me, I knew it. *He had to—*

"Ryiah, Ryiah." Blayne's tone was scornful. "Surely you know better than that. Think about it. When has a prince of Jerar ever married a commoner? Darren didn't want to court you. He wanted to bed you." He sneered. "Why do you think he was so quick to end things after you turned him away?"

"No." My whole body was shaking. *"No!"*

"I'm sorry it had to come to this."

I couldn't speak—not without bursting into angry sobs, and I would *not* let him see me cry.

"You should leave now, Ryiah." Darren's voice was void of emotion.

My hands trembled violently, and I couldn't stop gasping for air. *What was wrong with me?* I felt like my chest was being ripped apart at its seams.

"Guards, take her away." Blayne had stopped looking entertained. "This has gone on long enough."

You do not control me. Before the guards could drag me away, I slammed a heel into each of their boots and then bit down on my tongue until it bled, letting the momentary pain send enough magic for my bonds to break.

Then, before the men could stop me, I gathered my skirts and ran.

I could hear Blayne's shouting and Darren's mumbled response. I kept waiting for the pounding of angry boots behind me, but it never came. Darren must have convinced the guards to let me go.

"I never loved you." I threw open the door to my chambers and slammed it shut behind me. *"Love?"* I threw myself onto the bed. *"That's just something one claims to win certain privileges."*

Darren was the world's greatest liar, or I was the worst kind of fool.

Either way, there was no victory to be held. Everything had played out exactly the way Alex had warned me it would. I had chosen to fly—was it really any wonder the fall would be so steep? My breathing hitched and an unbidden sob tore its way across my chest.

Then the tears came...

I wasn't sure they'd ever stop.

They did, eventually.

But that only made it worse. I was still crying, screaming, dying inside.

I didn't remember falling asleep.

YEAR THREE

FIFTEEN

"LISTEN UP, APPRENTICES. I don't want you parading around like a bunch of girls at a convent because you have an audience during today's drills. This morning's exercise was downright shameful."

"Is the entire court going to be watching all year?" The words burst from my mouth before I could stop them. I couldn't help it. The first half of our day, the palace nobles had been everywhere. Watching the morning run and warm-ups around the practice yard, commenting during the non-magicked weapons drills, placing bets on our prowess and rooting for favorites. It was like our first-year trials all over again.

The highborns had returned to the palace grounds for lunch, but there was always the threat they could return.

Master Byron scowled as the rest of the class turned to watch his reply. "Yes. This is one of the court's favorite activities when the apprenticing mages and squires are stationed in Devon. The king *encourages* it. Do you have a problem with spectators, Apprentice?"

I bit my lip. There was no point arguing with our training master, hadn't I learned that by now? "No."

Byron's stern gaze slide to the rest of his audience. "Anyone else?"

Silence.

"Good. Now that Apprentice Ryiah has withdrawn her complaint, let's resume what matters, shall we?" The man paced the field. "This year's castings will be particularly poignant. Mentors, you will be casting on command. Mentees, I leave it up to you to form the appropriate deflection."

"How do we know which casting to defend ourselves with?"

I cringed as I watched the master of Combat turn on the second-year who'd spoken, an anxious-looking girl named Tully. His face was a mottled shade of red.

"Common sense. And practice. Lots of it. Do not interrupt me again, Apprentice." The training master cleared his throat with a retching cough. "*As I keep attempting to say*, these drills will build up your reserve to a multitude of attacks... I am sure most of the fourth- and fifth-years will be ready to advance to free exchanges, but the first month I would like the entire faction to train together. Now, everyone take your positions."

The class quickly dispersed, and I found myself trailing after Ella and her new mentor Bryce to the end of two parallel lines. Both apprentices avoided looking directly at one another as they waited for the drills to begin. I cringed inwardly. Ella's pairing was almost as painful as mine. Bryce was one of Priscilla's friends and shared many of her condescending views. This morning he'd made the mistake of telling his mentee she was a fool for consorting with lowborns. Before my brother and I had even risen, Ella had already thrown the entire contents of her porridge into the highborn's face.

Now she had latrine duty for a week.

Needless to say, the two were at an uncomfortable impasse.

Still, I had to think animosity was better than guilt. Ella could at least channel her frustration into her castings. With my fifth-year mentor, I had already made a fool of myself holding back in a misguided attempt to spare him. Two times during the morning's non-magic sparring I had received a stiff reprimand from Byron and an unpleasant bruise where my new partner's blows landed.

I vowed not to let pity affect my actions for the rest of the afternoon. The last thing I needed was for the master of Combat to assume I'd gone soft.

Taking a deep breath, I took my place beside Ella, shifting my feet into a comfortable stance as I faced off against the curly-haired fifth-year five yards across from me.

Ian met my eyes without expression. He hadn't said a word to me since our unfortunate pairing, not that I could blame him. He'd heard the rumors about the last ascension, that I hadn't really chosen myself.

It was a second betrayal he didn't deserve. And this time he was angry. He'd had enough time to mourn in Langli. Now he was angry.

Not unlike what I felt for another.

I shoved the thought away as soon as it came. I wouldn't, *couldn't* think about the prince now—not unless I wanted to spend the rest of the day fighting back tears. And I was done crying. I'd had three weeks of that during our trek from the palace to the Academy and then back again. If anything, that experience taught me exactly how heartless I'd been to Ian.

I deserved the fifth-year's silence.

But it made things extremely awkward. Mentors and mentees were supposed to trade advice and feedback. Suggestions. It wasn't exactly possible if you weren't speaking to one another.

"And begin. Mentors, *ice!*"

I barely had time to throw up my defense as Ian cast out an onslaught of icicles. Sharp, spinning torrents of water tore into the metal shield I'd cast as defense. An unfortunate choice. Within seconds, his ice had frozen my metal and sent a sharp burn down the wrist bracing my casting.

Ian released his casting just as I dropped the shield to the floor. My whole arm stung as our castings dissipated into thin air. Stupid, stupid, *stupid*. I knew better than to cast iron against ice. My guilt was going to ruin my training if I kept forgetting to *think*. Ian could handle himself—any feelings of ill will were buried behind a stone wall of silence.

I was the one who needed to focus.

Massaging my arm, I forced myself to straighten back up and take in the rest of the class around me. I was relieved to see I wasn't the only one who had cast metal... but then it came to my attention that the only mentees foolish enough were second-years. The rest of the fourth-years had used fire.

I nodded to Ian for him to start again and then cast out a barrier of flames. At that exact moment, Byron called out, "Wind!"

I barely had time to fall back before a huge gust of fire

came sweeping toward me. Ian ceased his attack immediately, but it was too late for my pride. I could hear Priscilla's tittering laughter a couple spots down.

I turned my head to glare at the girl and immediately regretted it when I noticed the prince watching me.

My pulse stopped.

I couldn't breathe.

I couldn't think.

I couldn't *move*.

"Keep drilling, apprentices. I didn't tell you to gawk!"

What was wrong with me? I swallowed the bitter taste in my mouth and made myself block out everything but the green-eyed fifth-year directly across from me. My mentor's blank expression gave no hint to his feelings. If he was secretly pleased I was making a fool of myself in today's lessons, he gave no sign of it.

"Fire!"

At least this time I was ready. Before the flames had even traveled half the distance between us, I had a spiraling tunnel of sand chasing across the field to squelch them. There was the sizzling hiss as sand collided with fire and then a loud clap as the flames died.

The remains of sand sprayed across Ian and the mentors closest.

Several of them—including Bryce—shouted insults. They stopped their own castings to brush sand off their clothes and skin, glowering. Master Byron issued the command to stop and then came barreling down the field to stand directly in front of me.

"*Have you lost all common sense, Apprentice?* I told you

to defend yourself, not show off in front of the entire faction! You are supposed to conserve your castings! *Conserve!"* He took a deep, exaggerated huff. "Your little display just cost you an unnecessary amount of magic. Flashy casting doesn't win a war. The mages fool enough to use it will be long dead while the rest of the enemy mages are left standing."

Why me? If I'd been anyone else, Byron would have seen fit to offer a short rebuke and move on. But never with me.

"Yes, sir."

"If you can't control your castings, then you don't belong in Combat."

I stayed silent.

With a satisfied grunt, the master retired to his post near the second-years and called out his next command. Byron remained there for the rest of the exercise. Not once did his hawk eyes leave my face.

* * *

By the time our drills had ended, I was ready to collapse. As soon as we were dismissed, Ian brushed past me in a hurry to spend as little time together as possible. Ella joined in my slow march to the commons. My friend knew better than to say anything. Instead, she linked elbows and sighed loudly.

Students hurried past us, eager to beat the others to the evening meal. Ella and I took our time. This year was different, and neither of us had been prepared for how much.

When Byron had first announced our new city was Devon, I'd thought it was a joke. A very cruel, very sadistic joke.

And then, after we returned from picking up the second-years, I'd found out he was serious.

We really *were* stuck in Devon.

The capital was different. Ishir Outpost and Port Langli were important, but neither of them could compare to a regiment ten times their size. The Crown's Army trained, if it was at all possible, harder than anyone else.

The army was so large the capital had built four training arenas—a small one inside the palace walls for the King's Regiment, and three much bigger grounds outside the city where the army's soldiers, knights, and mages spent their days endlessly drilling until they were called upon for service. It was ten-miles east of the palace. The site housed an enormous armory, never-ending stables, two bathhouses, two outhouses, three cook's camps, and an impressive expanse of tented housing just south of its arenas.

It was the city regiment we had the highest chance of being placed in after our ascension. That was the first thing Byron had told us when we arrived the night before. It was for that reason alone I had dried my eyes, taken a deep breath, and told myself to forget the past three weeks.

I needed to toughen up quick, or risk becoming the laughingstock of not just my faction but the Crown's Army.

That, and I was done with my body's traitorous reaction any time the prince looked at me. I couldn't survive two more years of this apprenticeship if I let myself feel. I was done with misery. I would *not* let my learning be squandered by a broken heart.

"Ry! Ella! What took you two so long?"

I made a face at my twin. "It's been a long day." Alex was already seated on one of the outdoor tables with a mountain of noodles piled high on his plate. Beside him sat a couple of his factionmates and Lynn and Ray—none of which bore half the servings my brother did.

Ella's mouth hung open in shock. "You know the cook has to feed the whole camp, right?"

Alex grinned. "Only the ones that arrive on time. After that? It's fair game."

I snatched a roll off his plate before he could stop me. "After that, we'll just take from you."

The one good thing to come of the ascension's disaster was that my brother and I were back to old terms. He'd forgiven me for being pigheaded, and I'd forgiven him for disapproving of a relationship that was clearly never meant to be.

Alex rolled his eyes and then changed the subject. "How was casting? Lynn was just telling me Byron yelled at you in front of the entire faction."

"How is that different from any other day?"

Alex didn't let it go. "What did you do?" He lowered his voice. "Please tell me you finally gave the prince the thrashing he deserves—" My brother didn't get to finish. Ella had elbowed him, hard, in the chest.

I stared at the sky in frustration. I wanted to move on. I did. But no matter how hard I tried, there was always something or someone there to remind me. Alex knew this, of course. Since the ascension ceremony, he had tried to keep his outrage to a minimum, but it still slipped out whenever he wasn't careful.

Alex swallowed guiltily. "Sorry, Ry."

I stood up, ready to fill up a plate of my own and leave the uncomfortable exchange behind. "Don't be. If I couldn't be imprisoned for attacking a king's son, I probably would have done just that." I left the table without waiting for a response.

* * *

A flurry of days, and then weeks, swept by before I even had a chance to catch my breath. I quickly got used to the stifling conditions of Devon's giant training camp and the constant presence of the king's court in our early morning practices. I even got used to interpreting the stony silence of my mentor.

I avoided the prince at all costs.

Before noon every day, Byron had us wielding axes. The sword was the weapon of choice for the Crown's Army, but far be it from our master to pick anything but the prince's favorite blade instead.

Out of all the battleaxes, we drilled with the poleaxe and halberd most. The training master was quick to point out how easily they could break enemy lines. We spent most of our days nursing wounds from slashed mail or dented armor.

When we weren't drilling on the ground, we fought as cavalry, against one partner or a cluster of teams. The axes made a formidable opponent against crowds. Their haft was ideal for mass attacks on horseback.

We learned when it was better to bludgeon and slash, when to thrust with the spike's head, and how to disarm an enemy in a slight of hand.

It was an endless cycle of drilling, but by the end of the second week, I had no reservations going up against Ian. He was a formidable opponent; being the son of a blacksmith brought many advantages. Any time I held back, I got a painful reminder why that was a mistake.

Ian still wasn't talking to me, but he treated me like an equal. If he'd really wanted to hurt me, he could have held back in his attacks. There was nothing worse for a warrior's training than an easy teacher, and for that I was grateful.

Our midday lessons were spent in one of the camp's largest tents. Crown's Army meetings were held inside the palace walls, but for our training purposes the tents would do. Local command, including Eve's father, Commander Audric, and even the Colored Robes made an appearance from time to time to assist with lecture. Most of the military's special strategies were released on a need-to-know basis—especially given past rebel activity—but the officials did give us plenty of other things to consider.

The majority of the time, men and women of the Crown's Army stayed on base training, enforcing Crown Law, and assisting Devon's local farmers. Only a small grouping regularly patrolled the countryside. The army was too expensive to house in the capital, so the camp was at the city's outskirts.

The soldiers who resided in camp took care of its upkeep and any services that needed rendering. Units took turns cooking, cleaning, hunting, and building to keep the costs to a minimum. Still, the commander made it clear the army's salaries alone ate away at the Crown's coffers. Housing a large army was an incredibly expensive feat.

While we didn't get to learn as many specifics as I'd hoped, the leaders did spend a great deal of time addressing each mage's role in the event of a siege. Devon was the most important city of Jerar, and as such there were certain tasks that needed to be seen to first.

I was so distracted with all of our learning that I'd almost forgotten the mock battle was the following day.

To calm my frazzled nerves, Ella suggested we spend an evening outside of the barracks... Which was exactly how Ella, Alex, and I found ourselves in one of Devon's local taverns the night before the big fight.

Interestingly enough, we weren't alone. Half the factions' apprentices and some of the Crown's Army were already crowding the tables by the time we arrived. The Lusty Wench was, apparently, a local favorite.

Waiting for the others to get back with the drinks, I pulled out Derrick's most recent letter and read:

Dearest sister (and Alex who never writes back—for shame!),

I'm a soldier! I know, I know, you never had any doubt, but it is still such a relief to be out of Demsh'aa for good. I love our parents dearly, but I believe the three of us have all seen enough herbs to last a lifetime, eh?

They already have us stationed along the northern border... I've only been here two months, but the Cavalry instructors weren't exaggerating. There's already been two raids since we arrived. Both times I was asleep, and by the time my section of the barracks was awoken, the enemy was gone.

I know it's not good thinking, but I really hope I get to serve during the next one. Some of the others are already bragging that they made their first kill. I don't want to kill anyone—I know I will have to; it's only a matter of time— but I would like to serve Jerar and keep those Caltothians out.

How is the apprenticeship? The two of you are still surviving, I'm sure. Gods, I don't envy that. It's so nice to be serving instead of drills and lessons.

Write back and say hello to your pretty friend Ella. Tell her if Alex messes this one up, I'd be happy to prove not all men in our family are halfwits. Ha.

—Derrick

I set my brother's letter down with a chuckle. It might be my most challenging year yet, but at least Derrick was having a good time. Someone should be.

Alex snorted loudly, having finished the letter over my shoulder just moments after. "That little pest is full of himself now that he's made himself a man."

Ella grinned. "I don't know, Alex, Derrick *is* a handsome boy."

Alex choked. "He's three years younger!"

I let them continue their banter. I couldn't wait to be stationed up north with Derrick next summer. Everyone knew Ferren's Keep was one of the four cities the apprentices trained in, and it was only a half a day's ride to the border from there. I had missed many things since Alex and I had first set out for the Academy three years ago, and my family—especially Derrick—I missed the most. Already my younger brother had matured from a feisty twelve-year-old into a young man. The Cavalry didn't have a four-year apprenticeship period like the other war schools, but I still couldn't believe Derrick was a soldier.

Next year couldn't come soon enough.

"Do you think we will lose? We're mentees this time."

I glanced up over my plate of roasted boar to frown at Ella. She was talking about the mock battle. "You think we will?"

"We are mentees. The odds aren't exactly in our favor."

Alex put his arm around the girl's waist. "We won our first year, and we were the underdogs then."

"Yes, but we won because Ry was able to bat her eyelashes at Ian instead of fighting him. Somehow I don't think that tactic would work quite as well this year."

"Hey!" I huffed indignantly. "I can fight him."

"Sorry, hun, but he *is* your mentor. I've seen the two of you in practice." My friend looked sympathetic.

I cringed. She was right, of course. Ian *did* beat me most of the time. The last two months Byron had let the fourth- and fifth-years cast on their own. Without the master's split-second commands, I'd struggled to keep up with the random assault of attacks. Still, I liked to think I had done better than most of the other fourth-years, and Ian was the best *fifth-year*, not fourth.

That, and I was still better than Ian at pain casting. Darren and I were better than *all* of the fifth-years who could pain cast... but that didn't really matter when the third-years were still much better than our second-year mentee teammates.

Overall, the mentors still outperformed us in casting *and* physical prowess.

"If you think about it, since we started the apprenticeship, the mentees have won every year." Ray joined us at our table, drinks in hand.

"That's true." Ella stirred a cider with her finger. "And that's uncommon enough as it is. Perhaps the streak will continue."

The tavern was noisy, but not so much so that I couldn't hear the door swing open for its newest customers, especially when the whole room went suddenly silent.

I swung around in my seat just in time to see Priscilla, Darren, and Blayne appear in the entry, all conversing with an unknown companion at their right.

My blood turned to ice. I was all too conscious of *his* presence. I fought myself to keep from staring.

I shouldn't have gone out tonight.

To redirect my thoughts, I studied the stranger instead.

The girl was of islander descent like Lynn, with the same straight black hair and almond eyes. The material that made up the stranger's gown and cloak was something I had only seen once before, in one of the merchant stalls in Langli. A special Borean silk.

What really caught my interest was how the girl held herself. When she spoke to the crown prince and his brother, there was no hint of awe, no fear, none of the usual signs of someone addressing their better. Either the stranger knew Blayne and Darren very well, or she was royalty.

"Is that...?"

"*Princess Shinako!*" I watched as Lynn ran up to greet the girl in the fine dress.

The princess instantly broke off her conversation to embrace her old friend. The two started to exchange excited chatter, but Blayne interrupted with a curt, "Shina!" The princess rolled her eyes, and then Blayne grabbed her arm, whispering something that made her scowl.

The princess murmured an apology to her friend and then shoved her way past Blayne to strike up a conversation with his brother instead.

"What do you think he said to her?" Ray wondered.

"It's Blayne." Ella's gaze followed the princess, sympathetically. "So probably something horrible."

Alex darkened. "If I ever catch him *or* his brother in an alley alone..."

"You won't do anything." Ella gave my brother a sharp look, but her voice softened as she added, "Because if you do, you'll be thrown in prison, and what life would that leave *us*?"

Alex gripped my friend's fingers tightly.

Neither of them said anything more. They didn't need to.

I turned to Ray, feeling uncomfortable with the exchange. I was happy for Alex and Ella, I was, but every time I saw how easy it was for them, a dark, gnawing jealousy began to eat away at my chest.

Ray gave me a nudge. "Romance only slows you down."

I tried a smile and found it came a bit easier than it would've three months back. "Thanks."

"What are you thinking for tomorrow's strategy?"

The tavern door swung open again, and I found my eyes unwillingly tearing toward it. A second later, I regretted the action when I realized who it was.

It took Ian even less time to spot me. The moment he did, irritation crossed his features.

The fifth-year turned heel and strode back through the

exit.

Ian would not be partaking in the festivities tonight, not as long as I was part of them. The door slammed shut and I heard Ray's low whistle.

"Guess it slows others down too."

SIXTEEN

"WHY SHOULD *HE* lead?"

The entire grouping of second- and fourth-year mentees swerved their heads to look at me. Even Ella and Alex looked surprised.

I held my ground and repeated myself. "We didn't even vote. Darren shouldn't get the role of command just because he's a prince. There are other fourth-years who would like the opportunity to try."

"Like you?"

I swallowed as Darren's gaze fell to me. For a moment, he almost looked hurt, but any residual surprise quickly morphed into indignation.

"I led us for two years."

"And only once to victory, which you wouldn't have been able to do without me." It felt good, I realized, to speak out.

"Last year we failed because of your and Ella's flagrant disregard for orders."

"Your orders were wrong."

"I was the leader. Even if my orders were wrong, you should have listened to me!"

"So I should just blindly follow an idiot?"

"*Enough*!"

Both us stopped arguing as Eve stepped in between us. The girl, usually soft spoken, was unusually loud.

"I don't want to hear about any more of our past battles. We won one. We lost one. For everyone's sake, I am going to offer myself as commander. I don't agree with Ryiah's assertion that Darren was chosen for his bloodline. I happen to think he is very good at leading, but I do think it would be a nice change to let someone else take the reins for a day. And, no, Ryiah, I don't think it should be you. You and Darren are too much alike. Both of you are risk-takers. It's time we had someone who approached things more cautiously."

I bristled at that last insinuation. The idea that Darren and I were the same in anything irked me to no avail. I was *not* reckless. Darren didn't look too happy either.

"I second Eve." Ray stepped forward, shooting me an apologetic smile. I remembered our first-year trials and the stunt I had pulled during our duel. *Maybe I was a little reckless.* I couldn't fault him for his vote.

"I as well."

"Me too."

Within seconds, the mentees had all agreed to a change of leadership. Even Ella and Alex. The only person who did not was Priscilla, but she was outvoted.

"Sorry, Ry," Ella murmured as Eve launched into strategy talk. "I'm sure you would have done well, but I think everyone knows Darren would not be very cooperative if it was you, and we need all of us working together to win this."

I sighed. Once again the prince had found a way to make

my life difficult. No one wanted me as a leader if it meant our most powerful fourth-year was against it.

How could I have ever fallen for someone like him?

We spent the next hour following Eve's directives. I had to admit she knew what she was doing. Having a father in charge of the Crown's Army had made her the ideal commander for a mock battle in Devon. She had the Alchemy apprentices busy mixing magicked oils to strengthen the weak armor our team was supplied. Restoration was already scouting the southern district, looking for possible safe houses to mark with our agreed upon sign.

Combat, of course, was busy planning the attack. Eve led the discussion, citing the best and worst locations for an ambush.

The entire city had been evacuated for our mock battle. All around the edges of its agreed upon border were families of merchants, farmers, nobility, and any of the King's Regiment and Crown's Army who had received the day off. They were all watching alongside our factions' masters and Commander Audric.

It was intimidating.

For the day's event, each team had been allotted five horses, six breast plates, five chain mail shirts, a handful of wooden shields, six poleaxes, five halberds, a rucksack of woolen bandages and salve, and a small barrel filled with the ingredients Alchemy needed to cast their potions.

We quickly divvied up the components and gave the second-year mentees the magically-fortified plate armor, halberds, and horses. They would need the most advantage and plate armor was too heavy for quick movement on foot.

Eventually, it was time to begin.

* * *

I fell hard, my palms slapping the ground and the rustle of small metal ringlets ringing in my ears. Moments later, a spiraling torrent of ice slammed into the wall behind me, just inches from where my head had been. I barely had time to choke out a small gasp of relief, and then I was on my feet, sprinting as fast as my legs could carry me.

I threw up a barrier behind me and prayed it would hold. It was a costly casting—something I usually didn't like to invoke since the sphere tended to drain my magic's stamina much faster than a shield. It was a combination of phantom currents: steel, wind, and crackling power all thrust into a giant purple globe. But I didn't have time to predict my pursuers' next casting, not while I was out in the open.

My feet pounded along cobblestones as I searched for a safe house, wishing desperately I had remembered Eve's instruction from earlier that morning. The mock battle had been going on for three hours, and I already seemed to have forgotten most of our strategy.

"You can't run forever, Ryiah!" Laughter echoed down the street.

I kept running.

Alex and the rest of his Restoration mates had spent twenty minutes going over the safe houses. Our signal was supposed to be a small splatter of mud at the bottom right corner of a doorway, inconspicuous to all except one who knew exactly what to look for... but try as I might, I could not spot any in the buildings I passed.

I must've heard wrong.

I knew a safe house had to be somewhere close—just two shops further and I would be crossing into the northern half of the city where the mentors patrolled. At the start of our pre-battle planning, the masters had assigned us the southern section. Which meant, if I didn't pass a safe house soon, I would be forced to turn back and face my two attackers alone. It was reckless to go into mentor territory, and there would be no help there.

If I found a safe house nearby, I could get another Combat apprentice to help me take on my two followers. The houses here weren't just a haven for Restoration and mentees in need of healing, they were also where Alchemy and Combat mages could confer until they were ready to come back out of hiding. If I fought the mentors pursuing me now, I would win—but it would cost almost all of my magic to do so. And who knew how much attention the attack would draw. If more mentors spotted me, I'd be forced to surrender in a second.

I needed help.

This was exactly what Eve had warned against. It was the reason she had asked us to patrol and scout in pairs. Our team was counting on the fourth-year mentees to secure victory—all but one of our Combat second-years had already surrendered during the first two hours of battle. More than ever we needed my magic.

The original plan had been for the Combat mentees to travel in packs of two: one fourth-year and one second-year each, with Eve, Darren, and their second-year mentee as our sole grouping of three. We'd been instructed to carefully scout the city limits and take out any solo Combat mentors who might be foolish enough to enter the southern territory alone.

Unfortunately for us, the mentors had also traveled in packs. Which was how, when we did cross paths, Priscilla, Ella, Ray, and I lost our mentee partners as well as their horses in a lightning-quick skirmish.

Now we were all separated, scattered across the city, seeking the others we had lost track of before. I thought I'd seen Ella take off east—the direction I'd been heading in— but everything had happened so fast, and I wasn't sure of anything anymore. I'd been cut off from the others when the third-years had caught up to me twenty minutes back. Theo and Merrick had refused to give up chase, and I'd spent most of my energy ducking and dodging since.

There. I sprinted toward the doorway with the telltale sign. The casting I'd been holding onto was starting to give me a headache; I needed to end it now before I wasted any more of my magic. I dropped my casting just as I tore open the door to find Priscilla, two of Alex's Restoration mates, and Ruth staring wide-eyed at the street behind me.

"You idiot!" Priscilla screeched. "You led them right to us!" But before I could argue, she had shoved her way past me and cast out a large assault of flying daggers. One of the mentor's own blades caught her shoulder and the highborn swore loudly.

I stumbled back after her, panting heavily, and helped Priscilla's casting. One of the blades hit Theo's horse and it reared, throwing off its rider.

Merrick tried to take on his cousin directly, but a large

torrent of power knocked him off his feet before he had the chance. Priscilla and I raced forward with our halberds and got the two mentors to surrender before they could cast out anything else.

As soon as the mentors said the words, Priscilla and I went back into the safe house while a healer on the sidelines came to escort the two out of the city. The woman bore a red silk robe that proved she wasn't a part of battle in case any of the others came across her while she escorted the surrendered apprentices to the palace infirmary.

"Erik, do you have any more of that healing balm? It looks like Ry needs some for her leg, and I need you to see to my shoulder."

My head swiveled to Priscilla. I couldn't keep the surprise from showing on my face. Now that we were out of danger, she was still helping me.

"Don't look so surprised, lowborn. I'm not about to let my disgust for you as a person keep me from trying to secure a victory." Priscilla's tone was anything but kind.

Well, *that* at least made sense. She wanted to win, even if it meant playing nice. Temporarily.

I took a steadying breath as the Restoration apprentice treated the deep gash on my leg. It'd happened when I'd tried to save Phillipe, my second-year partner. *Much good it did me.* "How long have you been hiding out here? Have you seen any of the others?"

Priscilla sniffed. "I got here a half hour before you did. And no, I haven't been reckless enough to risk my neck without backup. I have no idea where the others are."

"I think we should find them." I helped the apprentice

finish wrapping my leg.

"Are you mad? You only just got here!"

"But what about Ray and Ella? What if they didn't find each other like we did? We can't let the mentors pick us off one by one! Like Eve said, we only have strength in numbers when we are going up against the mentors."

"We should wait for them to find us. How do you know they aren't already together? Maybe they are with Darren and Eve."

"Priscilla, don't be a coward."

"I helped you, didn't I?"

"Well, help me again. Help the mentees win."

"I am helping. I'm helping the mentees in here right now."

Ruth interrupted Priscilla. "You know Ry is right. You two have to find the others. Eve's plan stated you were only to use the safe houses if you were injured or alone. Once you have help, you need to go back out there and fight."

* * *

Priscilla kicked a pebble across the street, sulking, as she studied the houses behind us. We were back-to-back scouting as we made our way through the southern streets of Devon. Both of us were looking for any of our teammates, another safe house, or potential enemy mentors.

"I hope you know what you're doing."

I didn't respond. All of my concentration was directed on the path in front of me. If we came across a pack of mentors, we needed to spot them before they saw us. We could not afford to get caught off guard. Again.

"Don't think that I didn't know you were trying to steal

Darren away from me in Port Langli."

That caught my attention. It took all my effort not to divert focus as I snapped, "Priscilla, now is not the time."

"But it's the only time I don't have to worry about running into you with your pack of friends. So, yes, now *is* the time whether you like it or not."

My blood was racing, and I knew it had nothing to do with the stagnant landscape in front of me. I forced myself to swallow. "It was a mistake. I thought he loved me." It hurt to say the words aloud, especially because if I said much more, I knew the pain would come flooding back, and I'd be powerless to stop it. No matter what I said or how I acted, I still loved him. It was a disease I was fighting to cure.

"Let me let you in on a little secret, lowborn: he doesn't love me either."

I stumbled and barely had time to catch myself.

"He never has. Probably never will. But that's the way of the Crown, and you of all people should know better than to try and change it. If you want proof, just look to Shina—excuse me, *Princess Shinako*—the next time the two of them are together." Priscilla sounded bitter.

"What are you talking about?"

"People like Darren place power above everything. If Blayne hadn't secured that princess, Darren would have done so himself. It doesn't take a fool to see what *he*'s after."

"You don't love him?" I still couldn't get over her admission.

Priscilla laughed. "Love Darren? Of course not. Love is for fools not smart enough to see the path in front of them. That's the difference between you and me, Ryiah. I see the truth and accept Darren for what he is. You just see what you want to see. It's why I will wear the crown and bear his children while you are left wondering why you were never good enough."

I wanted to turn around and tackle her to the ground. She was deliberately using this mock battle to bait me. The highborn knew I wouldn't dare attack her while we were being observed by an audience. "You wouldn't be jealous of Shina and me, if you weren't afraid of losing him."

Priscilla laughed scornfully. "Losing him isn't the same as loving someone. I want power, same as anyone else. I shouldn't have to worry much longer, though, since his father moved up our wedding."

I felt as if the ground had slipped right out from under me. "W-what?"

"That's right. The night of the ascension ceremony, right after you made that whole scene with the platter, the king announced the new date. You'd already left the ballroom by then, of course, but then again it is your nature to rise to dramatics anytime something is not going your way. Like the pig's blood. Really, Ryiah, it was a harmless hazing."

"*Stop!*"

"What are you—"

I turned around and slammed my palm over Priscilla's mouth and dragged her to the side of the closest building to our left. Not one moment later, a cluster of mentors appeared, one of them wearing a black armband. It was Ian.

Priscilla stopped trying to claw my hand and let out a low gasp, pointing at my mentor. I nodded. Now we knew who was commanding their team. Again.

We stayed in hiding until the patrol had passed, and then we looked to one another.

"We should follow them," I said before she could speak. "We should try to pick them off one at a time."

"We can't be heroes, Ryiah. We need to find the others first."

The two of us stared at each other stubbornly.

"Fine." I was done arguing, and it was time for a compromise. "Let's follow them and look for the others at the same time. It's possible they know where the rest of our team is and are heading in that direction anyway."

She sighed. "Fine. But don't do anything daft, Ryiah. We both know you have a reputation for doing reckless things."

I glared at her. "If you waste any more time insulting me, we'll lose sight of them."

The two of us took off in the same direction as Ian and his two accomplices. We trailed stealthily behind, using the tracking skills the Ishir regiment had taught us during our desert stay.

We had gone on for about twenty minutes when we caught sight of another safe house.

Priscilla raced ahead to see who was inside while I kept a lookout nearby, hidden behind some brush. A minute later, Priscilla emerged with Ella. I breathed a sigh of relief. My friend was still okay, and I could see Alex and another Alchemy mentee inside.

Ella followed Priscilla to my hiding spot. She wore a funny expression. Probably at the idea of Priscilla and me as partners.

The three of us continued tracking the mentors to an

armory on the northern side of the city. We'd just set up watch a quarter of a mile away when a loud crash sounded behind us.

Before I even had the chance to cast up any sort of defense, Ella and Priscilla were sent sprawling into the wall behind me. I whirled around to find Bryce and Loren smiling.

"Surrender?"

Ella and Priscilla attempted to stand. Bryce cast out two swords at their throat and Loren pressed his poleaxe against mine. "Don't try anything," Loren warned. "I don't want to hurt you if I don't have to."

"Bryce," Priscilla's voice was sickly sweet. Ella made a gagging sound, but our teammate continued. "Please, let us go, or at least me. You can trust me. You *know* me."

The mentor laughed shortly, not swayed by his friend. "You're such a liar, Priscilla. The second I let you go, you'll free these two lowborns to impress your betrothed." He cleared his throat. "Surrender now. Say the words, or this will get a lot worse."

Ella's eyes shot to me, and I swallowed. I could see her question: *would I pain cast to try and set us free?* Loren's blade was close. If I could press into it...

"Don't even think about it, Ryiah. We've been following you three since that safe house you pulled Ella out of," Loren said quickly. "If you do, our first order of business after we take out the three of you will be to get your brother and his friends. We won't give them an option. We'll just let them burn. Wonder how long it'll take the Restoration mages to treat Alex in the infirmary afterward?"

My stomach clenched, and I could hear Ella struggling. I knew Loren was a friend, but in that moment, I hated him for playing my twin against me. I opened my lips to speak.

With a huge flare of light and a loud boom, the ground shook.

A rush of thick gas flooded the air around us.

I couldn't see anything as I choked back my breath. I could hear crying and someone shouting, but everything was hazy. A second later, I lost control of my balance.

As I fell, I wondered absentmindedly which Combat apprentice—mentee or mentor—had cast enough magic to make the rest of us weak enough to lose track of our limbs.

Two sets of arms gripped mine and pulled me up, running and dragging me out of the fog. I followed as best I could, but I wasn't much help. At some point I must have lost track of consciousness, because the next thing I knew, cold water was being splashed into my face.

I spit out a mouthful of water, sputtering.

My vision cleared and I discovered Darren and Ray clutching a bucket with Eve leaning against a bedframe behind them. We were in another safe house, only this one didn't have a Restoration or Alchemy apprentice in sight. Ray saw the question in my eyes and said, "They were caught," by way of explanation.

"Where are we?"

"Just south of Ian's hideout."

"Why did you only rescue me?" Because that's what this was, I realized, a rescue.

"Because you are the most powerful fourth-year, and we only had time to save one of you." Darren didn't look at me as he said it.

Eve cleared her throat. "The mentors have been systematically combing the south. We've had to change hideouts three times, and there are always more nearby."

I was lying awkwardly on a bed. I forced myself to try and sit up. It was surprisingly easy.

Eve noticed my shock.

"We gave you one of the Alchemy mentees' special drafts." She pointed to the empty vial beside me. "I had the girl make two in case we needed to get away in a hurry by using that gas. Hopefully we don't have to use the other."

"What's our plan?"

"You are going to distract Ian's guards while the rest of us ambush his hideout." She said the words matter-of-factly, like it wasn't a big deal that our entire plan hinged on my performance.

I stared at her. "But the guards are Lynn and Morgan! They are both fifth-years, Eve. If they only see me, they are going to suspect a trap. They'll know I'd never be foolish enough to attack them alone."

"If you tell them you are pain casting they'll be wary. You and Darren are the most powerful in the faction. The mentors will be too busy watching you to notice when Darren, Ray, and I come out from behind."

"You think so?"

"It's our best chance."

* * *

While the others waited in the shadows of a building to my right, I made my approach, coughing loudly in case my footsteps weren't enough to draw the notice of the two mentors guarding the armory Ian was in.

Lynn's face fell, and Morgan didn't look too happy either. "Great," the girl muttered, "I thought she had already surrendered."

"Are you really this foolish, Ryiah?" Morgan wanted to know.

I shrugged. "I can pain cast, or did you forget that? I can have the two of you gone like that." I snapped my finger and then tossed my chainmail to the ground so they could see my bare arm.

In my other hand, I produced my weapon.

The door to the armory swung open to reveal Ian, who'd heard the commotion outside. He frowned when he saw me standing there alone. "It's not just you, is it?"

"Ian, run!" Lynn screeched. "Morgan and I can hold her off—*go*!"

I slammed the halberd's axe end into my left wrist, biting back a scream as I sent an eruption of power into the air around me. I was hardly conscious of the pain. Raw magic had taken over my thoughts.

I called upon every last ounce of magic I had and launched it at the three mentors as hard as I could. I heard their scattered cries, a thud of metal and explosion, and then, somewhere, Ian's shout of surrender.

I started to release my magic and the ground gave way beneath me.

Instantaneous darkness. *Victory.*

SEVENTEEN

IAN'S AND MY mentorship only became more strained
after the mock battle. The worst part of my day was during
Byron's lessons in the apprentice study upstairs. Going over
potential battle strategy with someone who barely talked to
you was tedious. It was like prying teeth from a rabid
animal: you were always afraid of the bite. I could tell Ian
was still trying very hard to be polite—painfully so—but
every once in a while his efforts would break and there'd be
a flash of anger in his eyes or a snappy retort that reminded
me just what he really thought of me.

It had only been made worse by Byron's evaluations. The
master delighted in tearing apart every solution Ian and I
came up with. No matter what strategy we suggested, it was
never, *ever* good enough. We were the two troublemakers
the master despised, and so his lessons were just one more
way to repay our years of insolence.

Which was what led me to the Academy's snowy practice
yard this evening, in an effort to clear the frustration that had
been building since the day we arrived two months back.

I'd barely started my drills when I caught sight of Darren
exiting the Academy with a training sword in hand. As soon

as he saw me, his expression darkened. "Coming or going?"

His words were so distant, it was like we were strangers. And it hurt.

Was this the first time we'd spoken since the ascension, excluding that day of the mock battle? I suspected it was, though I'd worked hard to block out as many memories of the prince as possible.

"Why?" My voice was hard and cold. I was proud it didn't waver. "So you can make sure you're not stuck in the same place as me for more than a second?"

"I'm trying to keep things civil between us. You've never been known for your easy temper."

"My temper goes hand in hand with your benevolence."

Darren's hand on his blade tightened. "You don't know anything about me, Ryiah."

"I know *exactly* who you are." I took a step forward, and another, until I was standing right in front of him. Then my words turned to ice like the ground beneath my boots. "You are the selfish, spineless son of a king who is too afraid to be his own man. You would rather hide behind your status than fight for something that could actually mean something." There, that felt *good*. It was one of a thousand lines I'd recited in my head. "And it's a shame, really it is, because, according to you, I was the one true friend you had besides Eve."

Something flared in the prince's eyes, but it was quickly replaced by a malicious smile. "That's where you are wrong. We were never friends, Ryiah. I was only telling you what I thought you needed to hear."

I shoved at Darren, but he was ready and caught me by the

wrists, holding them high above my head. He leaned in so that I was forced to stumble back.

"Do you remember our first year at the Academy? I said something to you once, in the library." His breath was hot on my face and my cheeks flushed—from anger or something I was unwilling to admit, I wasn't sure.

"I remember you saying a lot of mean things," I spat.

"I told you not to trust a wolf." His words dripped like honeyed venom. "Because it would only ever want to break you." Darren let out a small, harsh laugh. "Haven't you figured it out yet? I'm the wolf, Ryiah. I guess what I really should have told you was to never trust a prince, but that's not quite as memorable."

I broke free of his grip with an angry jerk of my wrists. Then, before he realized what I was planning, I slapped the prince across his face. Hard.

He said nothing, which only infuriated me more. *Say something, you coward!*

Tears spilled down my face. "I hate you," I whispered.

Darren nodded once, and then turned and walked away. Leaving me there. Alone.

Again.

I hate you.

* * *

By the time we returned to Devon after the winter's solstice, I was more than ready to face a cold season at camp. The frost in the Crown's Army training grounds was a welcome distraction. With the bitter cold, I was able to forget my unpleasant mentorship and the breaking I felt around Darren. In a way, the frozen earth was exactly what I needed.

It froze my heart.

Almost as soon as we arrived, we were deployed to assist the Crown's Army with King's Road patrols up and down the central plains of Jerar. In truth, we were probably only stationed in the capital two or three weeks at most; the rest of our time was spent in active duty. Since they were regular patrols, we didn't see much battle. The days were spent hunting down bandits or helping out local regiments with their training.

I didn't get to see Derrick. We only traveled as far north as the base of the Iron Mountains and as far south as the Red Desert Gate.

Every morning we drilled and trained alongside the Crown's Army mages, and it was during that time we really got to learn what service would be like in Jerar's largest regiment. None of the men or women were quite as fun as Andy from Port Langli, but they were still a good source of entertainment. They gave opinions freely, the most valuable were which territories to serve and what commanders to stay away from.

"If you want action, it's best to take a position north," Hannah stated. She was one of the few female Combat mages traveling in the same unit as me. "It's messy, what with all the rebel activity and border disagreements, but it's the best place to be if you really want to make something of yourself. Most of the mages who enter the Candidacy have served in Ferren's Keep or one of the border towns at one point or another. And if you have any mind to become a candidate, I suggest you do the same."

"It's also the territory with the highest death count," Brennan, another Combat mage, supplied. "So keep that in mind. You might be brave and you might be strong, but it means nothing when you come across a lot of Caltothian mages and you are without backup. My best mate died in his second year of service because he thought he could take on five of them on his own during a routine raid. We lose a surprising number of Combat mages up north because of our faction's heroic tendencies... It's not to say you won't find glory—they memorialize every one of our deaths and the Crown supports the deceased's family heavily—but every bit of fame has its price."

Ella stared at the man curiously. "So you're not one for fame?"

Brennan snorted. "Of course I am. I spent my first ten years in Ferren's Keep building up a fancy reputation."

"Why did you leave then?"

"The north is no place to start a family. If you have half a mind to fall in love, don't do it there."

* * *

In no time at all, we had finished our final patrol and it was time to return to the palace for the fifth-year's ascension ceremony.

I swallowed as I unpacked my belongings. In one year's time, it would be *my* turn.

Assuming I don't ruin my chances by stabbing a prince or two.

I had only seen Darren and his brother once since we arrived. I preferred to keep it that way. The little time I had spent in their company already had been far from pleasant.

Blayne had gone out of his way to insult me, and all the while Darren had looked at me like I was a cockroach in need of smashing.

Yes, I was going to stay far, far away from the prince and his entourage, as much as humanly possible.

Well, that's what I told myself, in any case. And I really was doing well—until I ran into Priscilla on the third night. The girl made a face as soon as she spotted me.

"Why aren't you at that musty old tavern with the rest of your lowborn friends?"

I stared at her. Even for her that was unusually curt. "I don't need to explain my actions to you." To be honest, I was pretty sure Alex and Ella had wanted some time alone without me tagging along, but I wasn't about to tell her that.

"You stayed behind looking for *him*, didn't you?" Priscilla laughed brazenly, and it was then that I realized the wine goblet in her hand.

"Are you drunk?"

"No." She hiccupped. "Because if I were, I'd be sure to throw this in that harlot's face."

Not me? I wasn't the *harlot* she hated?

I prodded, curious. I had nothing better to do, in any case. "Who is bothering the great Priscilla of Langli?"

"Don't mock me, lowborn. It makes you look graceless." She covered her mouth and belched. "Like *her*. Why don't you take a nice long stroll to the library and see exactly why you should never chase after your precious prince."

My pleasure instantly dissipated. There was only one reason Priscilla would send me to see him, and that meant it would hurt me. *She* was upset and drinking wine at the prospect of lost status. *I* would be broken.

I shook my head. "I have no care to see Darren's newest conquest."

"Well, Blayne will when I tell him how much time Darren has spent romancing that future wife of his. The two of them have been inseparable since we got back." She sneered, "It's like when we were kids, only now they spend late nights in his chambers... and no, I am not lying, Ryiah. His servants confirmed that to me just last evening." She dropped the goblet and let it clatter to the ground.

The girl grabbed me by the shoulders and swayed. "They were talking about marriage. I heard them." Her laugh was haughty and mad. "Though why a princess would choose a non-heir over a crown prince is beyond me."

"I'm sure you heard wrong." The words were thick on my tongue.

Priscilla pursed her lips and released me with a stagger. "I won't lose my chance at the throne to you *or* a Borea Isle princess. The Crown needs my dowry *and* Shina's. Blayne will put a stop to this. I know he doesn't want to waste another year trying to secure another engagement. Blayne *has* to marry above his brother. The only two higher than Shina are the princesses in Caltoth and Pythus, and believe me when I say neither of those countries—or their ambassadors—like Jerar enough to support a marriage. I know what Darren is trying to do, and it won't work. The king will never make him his heir."

Is that what this is about? Is Darren trying to convince his father to make him crown prince? Suddenly it all made sense. It explained why he was pursuing Princess Shinako.

He was trying to steal Blayne's betrothed right out from under him. The prince was more ruthless than I'd ever given him credit for.

I'd heard of families feuding in the old scrolls, but there hadn't been a fight over the throne in ages. Strife between the royal family was bad for politics, and it was even more foolhardy while Darren was pursing magehood and there were rebels and possibly a Caltothian war.

Would the Council of Magic force him to give up his robe? Council Law stated an heir could not become mage. But maybe they would change that. They'd already bent the rules to let a member of the royal family participate.

Was everything Darren ever did a play for power?

My head was spinning from the possibility, and Priscilla's words were ringing in my ears. Maybe I really didn't know him. *Love must really be blind.* Four years of knowing Darren and it had taken me until now to see him for who he really was. A wolf, a power-hungry, ruthless wolf who had tricked everyone, including his own flesh and blood. And I'd had to hear it from the girl I spent four years believing to be my enemy.

The irony was that my real enemy had been there all along right in front of me. Smiling crookedly and convincing me we were friends. Trying to seduce me for the thrill of the chase. Chastising me for not trusting him that first year in the tower stairs at the Academy… Telling me he loved me in our apprenticeship.

And then tossing me aside the second I jeopardized his dreams. I wasn't what he'd wanted all these years. I'd merely been a diversion in his pursuit of the crown.

I never should have trusted a prince.

* * *

During the night of the ascension ceremony, a huge fight erupted in the great hall. I wasn't there to see, but I heard about it when Loren and Ray joined us in the tavern for a nice dinner to celebrate our new status as fifth-years.

"You should have seen it!" Loren laughed. "Blayne may be fit, but he doesn't have a chance when his brother uses his magic."

"Yes, but Blayne gave Darren a good shiner at the beginning."

"And then Blayne was out cold. The king couldn't stop laughing! You would think he'd be angry, but he actually enjoyed his sons' brawl..."

I concentrated on my stew and tried not to listen closely as Alex and Ella quizzed Loren and Ray on the action. I didn't want to know. It just made Priscilla's words that much more true.

I'd just braved another large sip of the steaming hot liquid when Ian swung open the tavern door. He looked handsome in his black mage's robe—such a change from the training breeches and linen shirts apprentices wore. He pushed back some unruly curls and then spotted me at one of the far tables directly across from him.

I'd been so busy the past couple of months, training and not letting myself think about anything except the apprenticeship, so it was a sudden jolt to the lungs when he nodded in my direction and pointed to a small table in the corner.

Ella and the rest of my friends were too absorbed in

conversation to notice. I didn't bother to excuse myself before making my way over to the newly ascended mage.

I didn't know what Ian wanted, but I thought it was safe to congratulate him on his new status.

"Thanks." Ian scratched at his arm and seemed to have a hard time meeting my eyes. "Care to join me, Ryiah?"

I sat. And then waited, drumming my fingers against the table's rough wood, waiting for him to say whatever it was he'd planned. I owed him that much.

Maybe he will finally tell me what he really thinks of me.

Ian drew a long breath. "I'm sorry I was so cold… I wish I could have said it sooner, but I needed time."

"I'm sorry I hurt you." I forced myself to speak. "You deserved much better than me, in any case."

He swallowed and looked away. "For what it's worth, I really thought the prince cared… I know what I said, but at the time, I was just trying to hurt you."

"Well, it looks like we were both wrong." *I wonder,* I thought, *what it means that I chose someone as cold as Darren over someone as kind as you?*

The Combat mage held up his ale. "A toast to better love in our futures."

I joined him. "May the ones we love, love us much better."

Silence.

Then: "Have you received any offers?"

He nodded. "A personal request from Commander Chen in Langli. Apparently my performance in the port's mock battle impressed him."

"Are you going to take the position?"

"I already have. He was at the feast earlier when I accepted."

"You'll have good company." I smiled. "There's a mage who goes by Andy in their regiment. She's got the same humor and reckless disregard for authority you and I share. And you'll like Cethan, too. I served with him during that mission. He's a quiet brute, but he's steady."

Ian took another sip of his drink thoughtfully. "Where do you think you'll end up?"

"Wherever they'll have me."

He gave me a strange look. "Ryiah, you and Darren are the top of your year. You'll have commanders lining up to beg you. Don't forget it was *your* pain casting that won two mock battles, and you've still got a year to add another victory to your belt."

"I won't get any good offers when Byron gives me my ranking. Even if I'm second only to Darren—which I'm not sure that I am—it doesn't mean much if I am at the bottom of our rank during the ceremony. Byron despises you, but he still gave Lynn the worst rank because she's a girl. Everyone knows the two of you should have placed first and second. Me? I'm a girl *and* Byron hates me—I'll be dead last in a procession of six."

Ian shrugged. "It won't matter. It didn't for me. Chen didn't choose me because I placed fourth. He chose from what he saw when I trained in Langli."

I sighed. "Well then, I definitely won't be stationed near you. We lost the mock battle that year, and Ella and I were the ones to cause it."

He gave me a crooked smile. "I guess not. But I'm certain

tonight won't be the last time we cross paths. The Candidacy is only two years away. Maybe we'll finally get to have our duel? I know you've been dying to test your prowess in an arena. We are each one of the best in our years. Who knows which one of us would win?"

I lifted my mug. "To our future match."

Ian winked. "To my beating you."

YEAR FOUR

EIGHTEEN

IN THE FOUR years since I had walked through the Academy's doors, I'd come a long way from the girl who had struggled to cast a tree limb on fire. Unfortunately, my first day in Ferren's Keep didn't attest to that... I was too busy counting down the hours until I could see my younger brother.

"Apprentice Ryiah, if you fancy my lessons pleasant enough to daydream in, then clearly I've been too soft on you. This is the third time today your head has been in the clouds. One week polishing the regiment's armory starting tomorrow, and if I catch you at it again, I will not hesitate to triple your time!"

Of course he wouldn't, the old crow.

Ella elbowed me lightly in the stomach, and I gave her a helpless shrug as soon as Master Byron's back was turned.

"Pay attention!" she hissed. "You really don't want to spend the next year scrubbing mail, do you?"

Another voice chimed in. "Yes, and *I* will never forgive you for jeopardizing my training, Ryiah!"

I glared at the sour-faced boy in front of me, another of Merrick's bratty fourth-year friends. Not once had I been bestowed with a sweet-faced mentee to train.

Byron had undoubtedly chosen this one on purpose.

I made a face. "Your training was already jeopardized long before you met me, Radley."

The rest of the day's lessons finished with much difficulty on my end. My overconfident mentee had a flagrant disregard for all of Byron's cautionary measures, and I spent a good amount of time nursing injuries when he went too far in his castings. Especially during the final drill.

Radley still seemed to think the only thing that mattered in pain casting was power, which meant he didn't bother to practice any semblance of control.

I had to remind myself that revenge was less important than performance. I needed to spend my final year carefully crafting my own pain castings. I'd improved greatly over the last four, but so had Darren and Eve, and I so desperately wanted to excel in something.

I was tired of being third in everything, and I would've been lying if I didn't admit it would be nice to watch the look on the prince's face when he lost. Someone needed to knock Darren off that pedestal—he'd been enjoying its light for far too long. It was time for someone else to shine, and I wanted it to be me.

I could have sent my ungrateful mentee flying into the tall pines behind us, but I chose to focus my energies on a carefully exerted force. Stop and start, change direction, send my crackling lightning flying to the side only just in time— all from a small blade's pressure on my forearm.

I glanced to watch Darren with Merrick. He and Ray were sharing the same mentee this year. Another stark clash of light flashed and the familiar smell of burning wood wafted from where his bolt landed just inches from mine. *Was that deliberate?* I stared at the prince and saw a small upturn at the corner of his mouth. He was trying hard not to smirk, but I knew, I just *knew*, that he had done that last casting on purpose.

I straightened and prepared for a cut that would show that smug prince exactly who he was going up against… and then stopped myself. *What am I doing?* I didn't let Radley's castings get to me, so I certainly wasn't going to let Darren's.

Me. This year is about me. I took a deep breath and focused on imitating my last casting, flexing my magic as I pulled back a second sooner. Perfect. Now just ten more minutes and we'd be dismissed.

And then I could finally seek out the one person I'd been looking forward to.

* * *

"Is this what my no-good brother has become? A soldier who falls asleep at pubs?"

Derrick's head shot up with a start, and I laughed as the drink he'd been resting beside spilled all over his table. "Ry!" He was out of his stool in a second.

Laughing, I embraced my younger brother, who had grown even taller in my absence. And bigger. He now carried twice as much muscle, and my head only went up to his chin. When he released me, I could barely contain my gaping jaw.

"You're huge!"

One of the soldiers who'd been sitting next to Derrick

choked on his roast. "They feed us well, and this one has an appetite. He won a contest against everyone else in our station."

Just like Alex, I thought wryly. *Some things never change.*

"Did you just arrive today?" Derrick dragged me over to an empty chair.

"We did." I grinned. "I rode all night to get here."

"By the gods, Ry, Ferren's Keep is a good three hours from Tijan! You are mad! Weren't you riding two straight weeks before this?"

I gave a weak wave of the hand. "It was worth it to see my favorite brother."

Derrick grinned, dimples forming at the corner of his cheeks. "You're such a bad liar, Ry. You only say that now because Alex is nowhere in sight... Where is that lug anyway? Why isn't he here visiting me with you?"

"He's coming tomorrow. He told me to tell you there was no way he was going to spend another night in the saddle." I snorted. "He had really bad sores from this last ride in the mountains, and unlike us, he's not exactly warrior bred."

Derrick snickered. "Trust Alex to become a healer. That's about as dandy as it gets."

I yawned. "We shouldn't mock our poor brother just because he likes to be comfortable. I don't know about you, but there are certainly days I dream of leaving Combat behind and taking up something easier instead."

"But you never would."

"No. But it's a nice fantasy, especially when Byron spends all his time ripping me apart."

"Is he worse than Sir Piers?"

"You have no idea." I took a bite of my brother's dinner, or what was left of it. "Besides, Piers always believed in me. Byron is just looking for ways to make me quit."

"Our commander out here is like that. But I think it's because he cares and doesn't want to see us unprepared."

"Byron doesn't care if I'm prepared or not. He just wants me gone."

"Surely he's like that with everyone?" That question came from one of Derrick's female comrades.

I smiled weakly. "Only the women—and one of my friends when he was with us. But, no, it's mostly me. The master *loathes* me."

Derrick looked amused. "Because you're stubborn."

I sighed. "Because I'm everything he hates. But enough about my miserable existence. Let's hear what life is like for a soldier in Tijan. How has the action been up north?"

I must have asked the right question, because the next thing I knew, every single soldier in the place was bellowing over the other to tell me their wildest stories since coming into service. My brother and his cohorts had had quite the adventure in the year since they started, and some of the older men had tales as far back as two decades.

I spent the rest of the evening listening to tales about border raids and the pranks the soldiers liked to play against one another in their downtime. It was nice to see how happy Derrick was with his new friends.

Much glory was given to mages, but it was the soldiers who were always the first line of defense. It was a fact I'd tried not to ponder too heavily when I thought about Derrick, especially when I remembered that he was stationed along the border where most of the fighting took place. Neither he nor his comrades seemed too concerned, or if they were afraid, they hid it well. But I worried. Because that was the only thing a sister could do.

Still, it was meant to be an evening of festivity, not solace. My brother was one of the best in his year, and he was not a fool. He would be smart about any action he took, and I knew he trusted me to do the same. I forced myself to smile and enjoy the rest of the night.

By the time I finally said my good-byes and saddled my horse, it was two hours past midnight. I was fighting sleep and not looking forward to the three-hour trek back to Ferren's Keep. But if I missed the morning warm-ups with the regiment, Byron would notice, and then I would be stuck cleaning the armory for the rest of my apprenticeship. So it was one night without sleep, or ten months of polishing armor. I chose the former.

I just hoped the next day would carry on much faster than the first.

* * *

"You feeling all right, Ryiah?"

I just shook my head and laid it back on the table while the others continued their morning meal.

Ella patted my back sympathetically. "She didn't get any sleep."

"Derrick and his friends kept you up that late?" Alex guffawed. "That oaf should have sent you on your way after an hour."

"I wanted to see him," I mumbled without raising my head. If I did, the room would start to spin, and then I'd be right back where I started.

"A lot of good that did you."

"I only have to get through the rest of practice, and then I'll get to sleep."

"You forgot the armory," Ella reminded me.

I groaned. *Why does Byron have to hate me so much?*

After the second bell, I followed Ella out of the dining commons to Combat's training grounds. Ferren's Keep, like the other three cities we had trained in, was as different as could be. Which meant, of course, that our training was different as well—though just *how* different, I hadn't expected.

First things first, the keep was actually *inside* a giant fortress built into one of the Iron Mountains. Like Ishir Outpost, the rock city provided a safe refuge for its inhabitants, but it had the added bonus of a dense forest and raging river just south of it.

The fortress was as large as the king's palace in Devon with a similar wall guarding its face. The fortress hosted row after row of sentry posts and a high tower to its north. Add to that an endless supply of lookouts and a guard at every possible entrance to monitor the people's coming and goings, and it was easy to see why our training focused on defense instead of what we were used to, offense.

"The balance of power favors the defender." That was the first thing Commander Nyx said when we arrived. "This keep is impenetrable so long as our regiment continues to make it so."

During our non-magic drills, we spent a good deal of time running back and forth along the narrow sentry wall, taking turns with our partner as one attempted to scale it while the other employed various techniques to hold them off.

Those "techniques" had included longbows and crossbows—the two favorite weapons of the keep's regiment, whose main role was servicing the wall as a sentry.

We also trained with knives since they were easy to carry during a climb.

Then we practiced loading and unloading the heavy catapults, after taking turns aiming heavy piles of rock at landmarks below.

The last exercise was the worst. I was already so tired from a lack of sleep and the morning warm-up. By the time we'd started the catapults, my arms shook so badly that I dropped two large stones I carried. The third time, one landed on my right foot. I spent the rest of practice limping through my drills.

Byron, of course, deemed my injury "not serious enough" to warrant a trip to the infirmary. I hated the man almost as much as the prince.

At the end of practice, I chanced a peek under my boot to see how "serious" my foot really was and shuddered at the spotted purple and red bruise in its place.

"Where did you get that little nasty from?"

I turned my head and realized a woman with short-cropped blonde hair was examining the foot cradled in my hands. I immediately dropped it. She had steel gray eyes and a permanent frown, which meant she could be only one person: Commander Nyx.

I cringed. The last thing I wanted was the leader of Ferren's Keep's regiment to consider me soft.

Especially if I wanted a chance of being offered a post next year.

The commander stepped forward, still squinting at me. "It was the catapults, wasn't it?"

I nodded mutely.

"If you have time to swing by my chambers during lunch, I've got some bruise balm for it. I tend to keep some on hand whenever the squires or apprentice mages are stationed here. Someone always manages to drop those rocks at least once a day for the first week or two."

Is she really this nice, or is it a test to see if I'm weak-willed enough to accept her help? I'd heard rumors about how Nyx got her post... You had to be a very tough sort of woman to beat out hundreds of other knights for Jerar's highest command up north.

I decided I didn't want her aid either way. Alex had helped me that second year back in Ishir, but that had been for a broken arm, not a bruise. What was Byron always saying? *"Pain is how we build strength."* Well, I could certainly use some after today.

"I'll be just fine, but thank you for the kind offer."

The woman cracked a toothy smile. "Wise choice. I've offered it to two others so far and you are the first to turn me down. I can't respect anyone who coddles themselves."

A wave of relief washed over me. I would not be one of those apprentices she marked off her list for potential service, at least not yet. "Who were the other two?"

She chuckled. "Check the dining commons. Byron and I have a little game we play every time he brings his apprentices to my keep. I give him the name of any apprentices foolish enough to accept the help I offer, and then he orders them a week without rations to help them build their resistance to pain. It saves my cook's stores as well, so we both win."

I was doubly glad I had refused her offer. One night without sleep and a throbbing foot was bad enough; I did not need to withstand a week of starvation as well.

"Be sure to tell Byron I refused your offer. He doesn't like me much." It was reckless, but I felt a lit bit braver now that I hadn't fallen for her hoax.

Commander Nyx's eyes crinkled. "He doesn't like me much either, but his methods work. Have no fear, Apprentice, I'll make sure to put in a good word... What is your name?"

"Ryiah."

"Well, Ryiah, welcome to Ferren's Keep."

* * *

In the next couple of days, three more Combat apprentices went a week without rations as our training got more intense and they caved to Nyx and Byron's scheme. I'd been delighted, at first, to find out Radley was one of them.

But then my mentee became more nasty than usual, and it was even harder to resist casting him into the steep forest drop beyond us.

I was so consumed with fighting off my growing dislike of my mentee that I almost forgot about the prince.

Until the afternoon I ran into him and Priscilla arguing quietly outside the men's barracks. The girl was clutching a letter in one hand and brandishing her fist with the other. I heard her shout "Shina" before I turned heel and left. I didn't want to hear anything else. I didn't need to.

When I ran into Darren later that day, I avoided his gaze. I was sad and upset, and I wasn't sure which one was worse. Depressed that I still wasn't over him? Or angry that I hadn't known him at all?

For a while last year, I'd entertained the notion that maybe the prince did care. I'd told myself his father forbade him. Threatened his life even. Poor Darren, he'd had no choice in the matter. He loved me, but he'd been powerless to stop his family.

But that dream had not reconciled with his words at the Academy and the fight on the night of Ian's ascension ceremony. Darren hadn't been afraid to disobey the king then. No, he had openly fought for the princess he wanted and tried to make himself his father's heir. That Darren was fearless, and not the least influenced by what his vile family said.

Seeing Darren's letter from Princess Shinako only made the truth that much worse.

Between drills, weekly visits to see Derrick, the occasional armory chore, and all the extra lessons with Ella I could manage, I quickly lost all track of time. I didn't really lose track of Darren, but then again that had never been an option.

As much as I might wish it were.

NINETEEN

"I SECOND EVE."

"Darren."

"I also vote for Eve. She did a great job in Devon."

"Eve for me."

"I nominate Ryiah."

At that I gave Ella a grateful smile. I knew our fifth year was critical and what it would say if we lost, but I really, *really* wanted a chance to try. And this was my last year to do it.

"I second Ryiah." Ray gave me a rueful smile, perhaps to make up for voting for Eve the year before.

"Well, I vote for Darren," Priscilla said shrilly. "I will not follow a lowborn."

"We vote with Priscilla. We want the prince." Merrick and Radley made no attempt to sound impartial.

"Ryiah," Alex and all four of his comrades spoke at once. I grinned. Restoration's pride wasn't at stake the way it was for Combat, so the fifth-years in his faction were more open to change.

"Ryiah. Give the poor girl a chance. If she wants to risk commanding this year, it will be her fate on the line if we lose. All of us know Byron will blame her anyway." Ruth winked at me from her circle of Alchemy mentors.

The rest of the class spoke out. Eve made a bold move and took herself out, voting for me in a pleasant twist of fate. Darren and I were tied... it came down to a third-year boy in Alchemy.

I stood tall. "You should vote for me because everyone deserves a chance. That's how we all became apprentices, isn't it? We were allowed to try... So you should let me try." I smiled sweetly, and the boy blushed. *Beat that, Darren!*

Darren stepped forward and said loudly, "You shouldn't pick Ryiah because she's lowborn and reckless—"

I made a choking sound.

"—And did you hear why the Academy's armory had to be rebuilt the year before you started? That was because *Ryiah* made a rash decision that brought the whole thing down and almost killed herself *and* Ray here. The only reason she didn't die was because *he* was able to save them. If she does that this time, who knows what will happen?"

I broke free of Ella's hold. I didn't even care that all of the mentors' eyes were upon me. I was done trying to ignore the prince.

I would not let Darren sabotage another part of my life.

"You and me," I growled, "duel. Pain casting. Now. Let's see which one of us has more control *then*."

"You know I would win," Darren shot back, "and at least *I* didn't resort to petty flirtation to sway someone's vote!"

"Flirtation is hardly the same as insult!"

"It's not an insult if it's true."

"You called me lowborn and reckless!"

Darren arched a brow, and I longed to swipe the smirk off his face. "Well, you *were* born in Demsh'aa and that decision *was* reckless. I was only stating fact."

"You know exactly what you were implying, Darren. Don't you dare try to—"

"I want Eve."

Both of us turned our heads to face the boy we'd been fighting over. We had forgotten all about him.

"I want Eve too," another girl from Alchemy spoke up. "I want to change my vote."

"Both of you are wasting our time. I vote for Eve as well."

Before my eyes, I watched as the rest of the mentors turned against Darren and me with the exception of Priscilla, Ella, Ray, and Alex, who loyally kept their votes. When it was all said and done, Eve beat out Darren and me for the second year in a row.

Eve walked over to the both of us. "I don't want the two of you distracting everyone else from what needs to be done. Both of you can scout the grounds below the wall. When you're done, report to me and we will station two of our third-years as sentries in whatever location you deem best. This way we'll be warned before the mentees arrive and I won't have the two of you hindering the rest of our planning."

My face fell. "How will we know what to do during the battle if we spend the whole time before it scouting?"

"Yes, Eve, how will I know my role if I'm out counting trees?" Darren's tone was incredulous. "I'm one of the most valuable apprentices you have."

"You should've thought about that before you decided to

stage a fight during the middle of our vote." Eve gave her friend a discerning look. "You two will be stationed next to me during the actual battle. But until then, you scout. Understand?"

* * *

"Have you heard anything yet?"

I glared at Darren. "I thought you were keeping track of the bell tower."

"I *was*," he snapped, "but you kept bringing us further into the forest, and I can't see it anymore... I was hoping we'd be able to hear it, but—"

I threw down the charcoal I had been using to map our location. "But what?"

"I think we are too far out."

"You couldn't have mentioned this sooner? How many tolls do we have left?"

"Just the ten minute warning bell before it begins."

I stood up with a start. "Darren, we are *twenty* minutes away from the wall!"

"That was when we didn't know where we were going." Darren's tone was anything but helpful. "Now we do. If we run we should be fine."

A bloodcurdling scream ripped across the clearing.

I whirled around to stare into the woods behind us. "What was that?" Did the battle already start? *Leave it to Darren to lose track of our time.*

"I'm not sure." The prince was staring in the same direction as me. He seemed puzzled. "All of the other mentors are at the keep, so why would a mentee attack one of their own?"

"Maybe they know we are out here? It could be a trick."

Darren scoffed. "But why would they think we'd help?"

There was a loud boom and the ground beneath us shook violently. That same second, a chorus of men's shouting started just north of us.

"I don't think it's the mentees trying to trick us." I reached for my scabbard at the same time that Darren cast out three bolts of lightning into the sky, one by one. They flashed directly above us.

My lips parted in surprise. "What was *that* for?"

Darren grabbed my arm and started to run, dragging me behind him. "A distress call."

I stumbled along, trying to keep up. "Caltothians?"

Darren released me and pointed to the same path we had taken from the keep. It was at least fifteen minutes from the fortress.

I started to walk toward it and then froze. Darren wasn't following. "Darren," I whispered loudly, "what are you doing?"

"I'm going to find out what's happening."

I stared at him. "Are you mad? What am I saying, of course you are! Darren, you can't. Who knows how many of them there are?"

"Ryiah, this is not a request. I am *ordering* you back to the keep. Warn the others." His garnet eyes flashed. "I'm a prince and you're my subject. Now is *not* the time to question me."

I ignored him. "Darren, you can't do this on your own. You need me."

"I need you to do what I..." He gave up when he caught

my expression. "Fine," the boy snapped, "but, Ryiah, no heroics. I will *not* have your blood on my hands."

"So kind of you to care." I couldn't keep the sarcasm from my reply.

"I mean it, Ryiah."

"Are we going or not?"

* * *

I followed Darren, darting from one tree trunk to the next and peering out into the shrubbery ahead. It was hard to see. The sun was almost completely blocked by the towering pines crowding the sky... but what I did see through narrow shafts of light was alarming.

Five knights, four men and one woman, were tied and bound in a circle on the ground. Scattered nearby were three bodies with blood pooled around their necks. Their heads were severed, with just a small patch of skin connecting the neck to the body. I recognized one of them as a soldier from the keep's regular patrol. The young man had occasionally escorted me on my weekly visits with Derrick.

My chest tightened. *Kai.* He was my age. He'd once told me he missed his old comrades in Tijan... Now he would never see them again.

The sun's next ray revealed a large gathering of men and women in dress I did not recognize. Caltothians. Their clothing blended in with the surroundings—dark brown breeches and long green tunics, covered in thick brown cloaks that hooded their faces.

One of the first things I noticed was that there was no chainmail or plate armor anywhere on them. *That must have helped them catch the keep's regiment by surprise.* Without the rustle of metal rings, the enemy had managed to blend right in with the rest of the forest... until a passing patrol had come across their place of hiding.

Who knew how many more would've been captured had it not been the day of our mock battle? Most of the keep's regiment had been dismissed to view the affair from the keep's towers; only a few had been assigned to patrols.

"I count fifteen, but there might be more out back." Darren's voice was barely a whisper.

The Caltothians seemed to be arguing over what to do with the remaining hostages, although it was hard to know for sure as they were all speaking at once. Only short fragments of speech carried over to where Darren and I hid, crouching.

At one point, one of the Caltothians strode forward and grabbed a prisoner by the back of his braid. She brandished a knife against the base of his throat and shouted something to the others. Another Caltothian rushed forward to pull her back, but it was too late. The woman dropped her grip and a thick spray of blood spewed from the man's neck.

One of the hostages let out a muffled cry.

My fingernails dug into Darren's arm so deep he bled. I dropped it immediately. Three soldiers—and now one knight—were dead. I glanced at the prince and saw fury. He shook violently and his fists were white and hard.

"We've got to do something," he growled. "I can't just watch them slaughter my people."

My throat burned, and I forced myself to whisper. "I can light a fire." I could see it now. "I could cast one large enough to get the Caltothian to investigate... I know they probably won't send all of their men, but they might be confident enough to leave only two or three guarding the prisoners since they're already bound."

Darren's jaw clenched, and for a moment he looked like he was fighting himself. Finally he said, "You need to go far enough that it takes them a while to return. I can handle the ones who stay behind, but I need to know you'll hide as soon as you've got their attention." He ran his fingers through his hair. "I'll help the hostages back to the keep, but you need to promise me you'll stay safe until I can send help."

I squinted into the trees. The woman was already pointing to another one of our knights. I needed to go. *Now*. Before the others found the same fate as the man with the braid. I stood and Darren grabbed my arm.

"Don't you dare get caught." His voice was oddly strained.

"Why?" The words fell from my lips before I could stop them. "Why would you care?"

Darren looked away from me. "Just don't."

* * *

I sprinted through the trees, leaping over jagged granite and forcing my way through thick brush as I raced across the dense forest. I needed to get as far away from the Caltothians—and the Keep—as possible. It was hard to keep track of time as I ran. I needed to put at least ten minutes between us. I wanted to do more, but I was afraid if I spent any more time running, another knight would die.

I came to a stop in front of a towering pine. Just behind it was a thundering white stream. The river would keep the fire from spreading west, which was where I would seek shelter.

The pine's thick smoke would draw the Caltothians out, and there was no chance the Ferren's Keep regiment would miss it.

I placed my palms on the trunk of the tree and set to work projecting my casting. The pine was close to a hundred yards—at least twenty yards taller than the rest of its surroundings. It would take much more power than normal to exert a casting of this range, but I hadn't used my magic once that morning. I had a full reserve to draw from. And pine burned fast.

In five minutes, I had the highest branches roaring in red. A thick gray cloud straddled the sky. The top quarter of the pine was engulfed in flames.

I released my casting and stumbled back, slightly dizzy. The distance had been a greater effort than I expected. Still, the fire was burning high and there was no missing its smoke. Darren would see it any second.

I raced over to the stream and then, standing in the shallow shore, cast a cursory brush of wind to displace any dirt I had marked with my steps. The rest of the river was too powerful and too fast to swim. I could feel its undercurrent dragging at my feet.

Summoning a controlled current of wind, I transported myself to the other side. It took a great effort to carry my weight across. Self-levitation was always costly, but I didn't trust myself to balance on a log. The river was too dangerous.

When I reached the other side, I immediately dropped my magic and sprinted into the thick forest beyond. My heart was racing and every breath sounded louder than before. I clawed at blackberry brambles and forced myself to keep on running anywhere with brush so that it would be much harder to track the path I'd taken.

* * *

I wasn't sure how much time had passed. I was crouched behind a tree, watching, waiting. I had heard shouts for a while now, but none of them had come close to where I knelt hidden. I couldn't see anything except for a few yards in front of me, but I was confident I wouldn't be caught off guard. After finding my spot, the first thing I'd done was cast a thick mess of dead leaves in a large radius surrounding me.

I would hear my attackers before they found me.

When the shouting got closer, I was able to count eight or nine voices. Relief flooded my chest. I'd been afraid most of the Caltothians would stay behind. My plan had worked.

Darren is freeing the hostages right now.

I took a deep breath, and then choked as I breathed in a new scent. Either the Caltothians had Alchemy potions on hand, or they had a Combat mage in their midst. I recognized that foul stench from the mock battle in Devon—it had come with the mentors' fog. It was the same poisonous vapor that had made me lose control of my body.

I had to move. The thick silver fog was spreading fast; any moment it would reach my tree line…

I made a split second decision to rip off my tunic and wrap it around my face so that my ears and mouth were covered. Then I ran, ringlets of chainmail clanking against my skin now that the tunic was not there to muffle their hiss.

"There! You see her?"

Orders called out behind me, but I didn't dare look. I cast out a giant sphere at my back and sprinted deeper into the forest.

To my right a tree exploded in flames.

I ducked right and started to dive and twist among the trees and rock, hoping to lose the party tracking me. But I had no such luck. The shouting drew closer.

And the castings were multiplying.

They most definitely had a mage. And from the number of castings so far, they had at least three, if not more. A well-trained war mage couldn't cast as many attacks as the ones I was avoiding now. Not at once.

At some point, I came across the same river from earlier. The burning tree was just beyond it, now a towering, spiral of flame.

My stomach fell. I had to cross. Every other direction, I was surrounded. My pulse raced and I could barely breathe. My vision swam in front of my eyes. I could not maintain the defensive sphere and levitate at the same time.

My magic was depleting fast.

I sent a swift plea to the gods and dropped my defense, casting myself into the air. It would only take me twenty seconds to cross.

But a biting pain tore into my thigh before I had even completed ten. The sudden shock shattered my concentration and my casting fell away.

And then I fell into the raging stream below as I lost control of my magic. It was too late to attempt another casting—it was impossible to focus. White water swarmed me, and I was thrust under its surface. I spewed liquid as I fought for air, only to be tossed again in the stream's plunging rapids.

The river was ice cold, and the sharp pain in my thigh became more intense. Red blood and white waters threw me against the current, beating my body with every river rock along the way. I fought to the surface each time, only to get sucked under and then out. My fingers were rubbed raw from scraping against rocks.

I couldn't cast, not with the collision of pain and water choking my lungs. My legs were numb, and it was becoming harder and harder to swim. I couldn't see anymore. Darkness was grabbing me, pulling me under.

My arms held on the longest, but eventually those two slowly slipped away...

All at once, I was conscious of gold. Sunlight streamed down from above, blinding me. I was at the surface. I could breathe.

There was shouting in the distance. My ears were pounding too heavily to recognize it.

My entire body ached, and my skin felt like ice.

I opened my eyes and saw that the raging river had fettered out into a shallow stream down the river's bank. I had washed ashore. There was a deep gash in my left leg. An arrow had struck it and part of the shaft was still in it.

But I was still alive.

"We found the mage girl!"

"Get her bound and gagged. She might be able to pain cast!"

I tried to move, stand, anything, but my limbs were still catching up from the cold.

I tried to cast, but my vision just spun and spun and a sharp pain probed at my head until I was forced to vomit the contents of my breakfast onto the sand beside me.

I couldn't escape. I needed to do exactly what the Caltothians feared. I needed to create more pain. I blinked at the shaft in my leg. *If I could just roll myself onto my side.*

I shifted just slightly and pain tore into my thigh. I screamed. Magic came rushing out, and I thrust as much of it as I could muster into the band of enemies racing toward me.

But I missed. My lightning missed its mark.

And now I didn't even have pain magic. Not unless I wanted to lose consciousness summoning more.

Two pairs of hands pinned my arms and legs to the ground. My hands and feet were bound in a matter of seconds, and then an oily cloth was shoved into my mouth as another wrapped it in place.

A face entered my vision, and I saw the same woman who had killed the knight squinting down at me. Her lip was curled in disgust.

"Who else is with you?" she demanded. A large wad of saliva landed on the side of my cheek. "Hold up your fingers for the count of your men."

I trembled. I would not tell her anything. From Derrick's past accounts, I knew I was going to die no matter what. Caltothians never kept prisoners. But at least I would not die a traitor.

The woman slapped me hard across the face. My lip split open from the impact.

"Tell me and I will let you live."

Never. I shook my head and tried to ignore its unwelcome

spin.

"Kinsey, shouldn't we keep this one?" one of the men probed. "She put up a good fight. If we break her, I bet it would be worth our time. We could use another mage—"

"You know the orders as well as I do, Wade. No survivors."

"Not if we don't tell them."

"Do you really want to take that chance?" Kinsey drawled. "Two times a traitor would only bring a slow and painful death."

The woman pulled out a curved dagger. It was the same blade she had used to slit the knight's throat. She cradled it against the side of my face. "One more chance before I gut you like a fish," she crooned. Her blade carved a shallow cut across my neck.

Be brave, Ryiah. I shut my eyes. I would spend my last moments of life envisioning something more pleasant than the ugly face of my enemy.

What would I see in my last breath, I wondered. Derrick's laughing face, Alex's crooked grin, or my parents' kind smiles?

Kinsey cackled. "Enjoy the Realm of the Dead."

Darren.

In my last moments, I saw *Darren.*

A sharp sting was followed by the withdrawal of pain and the shrill cry of a woman's scream. I opened my eyes and realized that I was not, in fact, dead. I touched my throat. The blade had only nicked it.

I was very much alive. Still injured and without most of my magic, but I was alive.

The woman who'd brandished the knife was not so fortunate. Kinsey lay face down in the sand next to me, dead. A javelin was in her back.

All around me were panicked screams.

Sensation returned to my limbs. I propped myself up with my elbows so that I could take in the scene around me. Was it too much to hope? Had someone seen my casting in the keep?

All around me were great flashes of light and smoke. The heat from the forest fire was growing: the air was sweltering. Any residual cold from my icy bath had faded quickly in its presence.

The Caltothians guarding me were busy, engaged in a battle of sorts with two others in the clearing ahead. It was hard to make out my rescuers' faces, but I could tell from the way they fought that they were winning.

Only three of the Caltothians were mages, and one of them—the woman who had threatened me—was already dead. The enemy soldiers were hiding behind their mages. Only one of them was an archer; the rest carried swords.

There was another great blast of magic and a storm of knives rained down from the sky. The enemy shrieked and scattered.

The only two still standing were the Caltothian mages.

After another great blast of magic, the mages were forced to flee, leaving me behind as they regrouped to the other end of the clearing. As they traded sides, my rescuers drew forward, one leading the way while the other guarded his back.

I choked back a cry of relief. It was Darren and Eve.

He'd come back for me.

The prince set to work on my bonds. "Just couldn't stay out of trouble, could you, Ryiah?"

"Mmmph." The gag was still in my mouth. When it finally came free, I turned to Eve. "How did you find me?"

"I went looking for the two of you when I saw the lightning. Then I saw the smoke and found him." Eve shot out another barrage of weaponry at the enemy mages and checked Darren's progress. "How are those ropes coming?"

"Not fast enough," he said through gritted teeth. "Whoever bound them wanted to make sure she stayed that way."

"Well, make it faster." Eve's skin—already so pale—was even more so. There were beads of sweat trailing down from her brow to her chin. Her violet eyes were bloodshot, and I could tell from her stance it was costing her a great deal to continue to hold the two mages off with her casting.

"Got it." Darren hacked off the last bit of leather rope and then stilled as his gaze caught on something in the trees ahead.

He cursed and Eve sucked in a sharp breath as she and I looked. "There's more."

"It's the ones from before." Darren's voice had lost its edge. "They must have spotted the smoke."

My stomach fell. *More* Caltothian mages. The barrier Darren and Eve had cast was already faltering. The two mages Eve was holding off were growing confident. A couple more castings would shatter it.

"I can't pain cast." My panic returned in light of our newest discovery. "I've already reached my limit." Not unless I wanted to kill the others and myself in the process.

"There are three of them." Eve's voice was labored from her continuous casting. "Plus the two we've already been fighting. We might have been able to take on two, but—"

"But we don't have enough magic left to take on all five." Darren's statement was void of emotion. "The new three haven't even touched their magic. They'll have full reserves."

My voice quavered. "Then we don't fight."

"Yes." A lump rose and fell in the prince's throat. "Ryiah is right. We need to run."

"On my count," Eve said, "we drop our casting and flee east."

I glanced to Darren and saw him pocket the blade Kinsey had dropped.

"One."

What is he doing?

"Two."

He was facing the wrong direction.

"Three."

There was a loud whoosh as the prince and Eve released their magic. I hardly noticed it—I was too busy tackling Darren to the ground. A heavy mist of sand rose up around us as I wrestled the knife out of the prince's grasp.

"Ryiah!" Darren spat through a mouthful of dirt. "Let me go!"

"You are not going to be a hero today, Darren!"

"That is not your decision to make!" He struggled to break free of my hold. When he found the effort harder than he expected, he glared at me. "Let me go or I'll cast you off."

"You can try, but I'll still—"

At once, an ear-splitting screech rang out across the forest floor and I went flying back into the shallow stream behind us. A second later, Darren landed to my right. There was a loud slap as his body hit the water. We barely had time to catch our breath before the trees began to tremble and groan.

The two of us scrambled to stand just as the first pine fell. One by one they all broke free of their giant roots. Great towers of flame were crashing down all around us.

"What's happening?" I squinted, trying to see through the thick cloud of smoke. I could hear screaming. "Is it the regiment?" *Had help arrived?*

"I don't—I can't see any..." Darren started to sway. I was close enough to steady him just before his knees buckled and collapsed.

"Darren?"

"Eve." His entire body was a series of tremors. "She..." He pointed and his chest heaved up and down, too fast to count. "She had the same idea as..." He couldn't finish, choking on his words.

My heart stopped. I'd been so focused on stopping Darren that I hadn't bothered to consider what Eve might do.

Somewhere in the burning forest to our right was a pale girl with ash blonde hair and violet eyes that had just closed for the last time.

Darren was having trouble breathing. I could feel his ragged breaths, in and out, his shoulders shaking. I hated him, or I wanted to, but my grip still tightened on his arm.

Eve had never intended to run. Neither had the prince. *I*

had been the only one foolish enough to think we would—
Darren and Eve had been too busy plotting how to let me and
the other one survive. Because there was only one way any
of us could evoke enough magic to take on five mages in our
weakened state.

Pain casting. By death.

Eve had given her life to save us.

And that's when I saw it—a dark silhouette making its
way along the flickering river of flame. I strained to see
through the smoke. Was it Eve? Had Darren been wrong,
was she alive?

The limping figure was much too tall.

"Darren." I shook the prince's shoulders and said in a loud
whisper, "Darren!"

He didn't hear me.

"Darren, we've got to get out of here!"

I could see more clearly now. It was a man, one of the
mages from before. He was making his way among the trees,
one palm in front of his face as he parted the flames in his
path.

I drew a sharp intake of breath. The mage still had magic.

Angry eyes met mine as he spotted me from across the
clearing.

I was done waiting. I shoved Darren back behind me and
pulled out the blade I had stolen earlier. I wasn't going to let
Eve's sacrifice be in vain. I lifted it to my wrist.

Darren's hand clamped down on my fist while the other
sent my knife skittering into the stream behind us. He'd
recovered fast. "Don't you even think of it!" he snarled.

"Darren, you're a prince of Jerar!" The man was almost

out of the fire. "I can't let Eve's death be for nothing."

His eyes were hard. "I couldn't stop Caine or Eve, but by the gods, if I must die, I want to die knowing it is not because everyone is proffering themselves up as sacrificial lambs every time I'm in danger!" He released my wrist and handed me my cut bonds from earlier. "You are not going to die today, Ryiah. Now take these."

He took a shuddering breath as he forced himself back into command and away from the grief somewhere buried in his eyes. "That mage must have used up quite a bit of magic to hold off Eve's casting. I still have some of mine, and you have this rope... If you want to fight, then fight, but don't you dare sacrifice yourself for someone like me."

My lips parted in surprise. *Don't you dare sacrifice yourself for someone like me?* That didn't sound like Darren the Wolf at all. It sounded like the boy I'd fallen in love with.

Now is not the time to question things. I studied the landscape, knotting and unknotting the leather cord in my hands. The mage had finished crossing the flames and was now running toward us. He still had quite a distance to come, but he would reach us soon enough. *A mage employs every resource he has. We don't spend years training in both types of combat just so you can shirk your duties the second you've used up your magic.* I bit my lip. *You're still a warrior, Ryiah, so think like one.*

I pointed to a thicket a quarter mile away half covered in ash. "There's a steep ravine just east of that brush. When I was looking for a place to start the fire, I almost missed it."

Darren drew a sharp intake of breath. "So the mage

wouldn't be able to flee east. We could cut him off if we can lead him to it."

The two of us both took off at a sprint. It only took me a second to realize my mistake. There was no way I could breach the distance in time. The searing pain in my thigh was a quick reminder why. I hobbled after Darren, my pace no faster than a brisk walk. I was skipping, half dragging my leg behind me as the mage drew closer. The man still hadn't cast—it was a good sign that he was conserving his magic—but he would be upon me in less than a minute.

Darren looked back to see where I was and stopped running.

The prince raced toward me just as the mage raised his hands.

I ducked and a series of sparks shot out across the distance between us. The mage's magic collided against a barrier not two feet in front of me. There was a loud crack and then Darren's casting shattered, shards of glass splintering the air around me before subsequently vanishing with Darren's magic.

"Get behind me," the prince gasped. The mage was already calling upon his next casting.

I shook my head and took a stand stubbornly beside him.

There was less than five yards spanning the distance between us and the Caltothian. We could not outrun him if we tried. And judging from Darren's last casting, we wouldn't be able to out-magic him either.

"If we are going to die today," I told Darren, "let's make it the best fight of our lives."

Before he could stop me, I threw myself forward with the

leather strap high above my head. I paid no attention to the agony in my leg. I cut the distance in half, springing into the air with the balls of my feet. The thick rope shot straight up and then I let my elbow bend and snap.

There was the satisfying crack as the leather met the mage's shoulder, and then I fell to the ground, doubled over in a pain so terrible I couldn't think. I heard Darren roar and shut my eyes against a huge flare of light. Two men's screams were followed by a loud thud.

I opened my eyes. My surroundings flickered and spun, over and over. My stomach ate at me from the inside. Something was piercing my abdomen. Black and red swarmed my vision, and I could barely make out the dark heap in the grass next to me.

Then I heard the short, sputtering coughs as the person struggled to breath. There was a hoarse gasp and then a terrible moan.

Darren.

I reached across the distance and tried to find the prince's hand. My fingers caught his, and I held on tight. I knew it was wrong, but I didn't care. I couldn't speak. My pain was building and building, and all I could do was shut my eyes and pray to the Shadow God that death came swiftly for us both.

"Ryiah," Darren gasped, "I'm sorry I made a mess of everything." He tried to laugh and then choked, sputtering for air.

Something broke in me.

Pain was deafening my senses, but an unrequited anger rose when I heard Darren utter what he thought would be his last words. An apology. For everything. In his dying breath, the prince wanted to tell me he was sorry.

And that's when I realized Priscilla was wrong. I was wrong.

Whatever he'd put me through, Darren was good.

The prince could have waited for the keep's regiment, but as soon as he'd freed the others, he had come back for me.

Like Eve, he'd never had an intention of fleeing when he told me to run.

Those were two times Darren had chosen to save me instead of himself.

A prince of Jerar had decided a lowborn's life was more important than his own.

I heard the crunching of pine needles and the mage's labored breathing as he drew close.

I let my hand fall limply to the side.

"Ryiah?" Darren's voice rose.

I didn't respond. I let my eyelids flutter shut.

"Ryiah!"

I held my breath.

"She's a pretty thing," the Caltothian declared. "I can see why you wanted to keep her alive."

"Don't you look at her!"

"You can't stop me, boy. You are dying yourself." The mage laughed raucously.

There was a sudden clatter, and then Darren gave an ear-shattering scream. It took everything in me not to move.

"You shouldn't have tried to pain cast," the man addressed the prince, "not against me."

I exhaled and began to inch my hand slowly, closer and

closer to my abdomen. As soon as my fingers closed around the dagger embedded in my stomach, I took a deep breath and waited. One. *Two*.

The soft crunch of grass alerted me just as the man stepped on the ground near me. I kept my hand frozen in place. There was the rustle of movement, and then I cracked open one lid, just in time to catch sight of the man hovering over the prince.

The mage held out his hand and a shimmering orb of fire appeared in his palm. "I would have made your death quick, like the girl's," he told him, "but since you tried to trick me, I'm going to let you burn. *Slowly*. I want you to feel every second of it."

I didn't waste another moment. I wrenched the blade free and lunged, slashing at the back of the mage's leg with all the strength I had. I caught the steel along the curve of his thigh and dragged down, deep, *deep* into his calf and fell back with a cry.

Then the pain took over.

My whole world reared up around me as blackness took hold of my sight.

I lost consciousness to the man's screams.

TWENTY

I COULDN'T SEE. Couldn't breathe. Couldn't feel.

All I could do was listen.

The pounding of my heart, and the murmur of something faint. His voice.

One whispered word. Over and over.

Ryiah.

TWENTY-ONE

"I'M ALIVE?" THOUGH I'd spoken the words aloud, they still seemed at odds with my memory. *Wasn't I supposed to be dead?* Dead with Darren and Eve in the northern forest of Jerar? Surrounded by burning pines as I bled to death from a fatal wound to my stomach?

Which brought me to my next question. *"How?"*

Derrick snorted. "That would be the first thing you ask us, wouldn't it?"

Alex, meanwhile, was glowering down at me with Ella clutching his arm. "You must have a death wish," he bellowed. "This is the fifth—no, the *sixth*—time I've had to visit my sister in an infirmary because she thinks she can take on the world by herself!"

"Alex, that's not fair," Ella interrupted. "Most of those were because of mock battles. You can't blame your sister for—"

"I don't care what they were for!"

"Alex!" Derrick looked annoyed. "Don't yell! The healers!"

"I will yell if I want to. I'm going to be a healer too!" my twin shouted. *"The lot of you are fools for choosing Combat.*

Fools! And you, Derrick, choosing to be a soldier—did you not hear that four of your own were murdered? Slaughtered like pigs for a butcher! What kind of idiot signs up for—"

"All right, Alex, that's quite enough." Ella tugged on my brother's arm with an apologetic look to me. "Later," she mouthed as she escorted him firmly out of the room.

"So," I said weakly to my last remaining visitor, "he's mad at me again."

Derrick guffawed. "Alex is always mad. Just because the rest of us live exciting lives is no reason for that grouch to bring you down." He paused. "Besides you and Prince Darren—"

Darren! I'd forgotten all about him! "Is he—"

"Of course he is." Derrick grinned. "You two are the talk of the keep right now. All the squads heard about how the two of you risked your lives to save the regiment! I wouldn't be surprised if they made a song about it the next time they find themselves at a tavern!"

I cringed. The last thing I wanted was to hear my "deeds" memorialized in drunken song, especially when the only thing I had done was almost die... "Eve," I asked suddenly, "did she—"

"She's dead, Ryiah." Derrick's voice lost its humor. "It was quick, if that helps. Stabbed herself in the chest. I overheard Master Byron telling someone it was a 'mage's last stand,' whatever that means."

I swallowed. When someone willingly brought on his own death to exert an extreme pain casting, it was known as the mage's last stand, but I'd only read about it in scrolls. "Eve was a hero," I said softly. "Without her magic, Darren and I would've died."

"Probably why the prince is in Devon."

"Darren left the apprenticeship?" I sat up with a start and then regretted it immediately. My whole body roared in protest. "Why would he...?" Why wouldn't he after what happened?

"He didn't leave it."

"But you said—"

"He's visiting that girl's father. Eve. He said it was something that couldn't be put in a letter." Derrick looked sideways at me. "The prince is nice, actually. I don't understand why Alex hates him so much."

"He was here?"

"He was here for the first four days. Granted, two of them he was recovering in the cot next to yours, but he came back even after that. And that girl you hate? Priscilla. She caused a huge scene when she saw him in here."

"How...?" I cleared my throat and tried again. "How am I...?"

"Alive?" Derrick was amused. "Ryiah, you were never dead. No matter what our charming brother might claim, Restoration is not that good. The prince gave a full account to Commander Nyx. The two of you were fighting that last Caltothian when you pulled that dagger out of your stomach—madness, really—and caught the man off guard by slashing at his leg." He frowned. "You lost consciousness right after, but the prince was able to finish the job. He wasn't faring much better, but he still managed to carry you a couple miles before the regiment arrived. They brought you two to the keep while the rest of the mages put out that fire you started. In case you are wondering, Ry, a quarter of the northern forest is now gone. It's going to take years to grow back."

The whole time my brother was talking, I couldn't help but remember the one thing that'd been bothering me since I awoke: the dreams I'd had. The ones where I kept hearing Darren's voice. He'd been saying my name. Over and over. Had that been real?

What does it matter? Nothing has changed.

"Ryiah? Are you still listening?" Derrick looked concerned. "You probably need rest," he surmised. "I should leave... All of the apprentices were delayed by the fire, but now that you are better, I expect the masters will want to set out tomorrow for the Academy."

* * *

"Apprentice Ryiah?"

My eyes flew open, and I found the commander of Ferren's Keep standing over me, her steel gray irises studying my face. My pulse jumped and I sat up with a start. This time with much less pain than before. "C-Commander Nyx?"

"I am sorry to wake you, Apprentice, but I have a matter that cannot wait."

I waited for her to continue.

The woman pulled a chair to the side of my cot and leaned forward. "I have already spoken with the prince, but I need to know if you saw anything strange—anything at all that might merit questions—the day of the mock battle?"

The confusion must have shown on my face because she tried again.

"Anything odd, Ryiah. Anything that struck you as contrary with the Caltothians?"

I shook my head. "I'm not sure I understand what you're asking."

The woman sighed and stood up, pressing the chair legs back with a loud squeak. "If you think of anything, no matter how silly or minute the detail might seem, please send for me."

I nodded and promised to do just that. The woman left the room with a wish for my speedy recovery, and then I was left once again with an overwhelming fatigue. I drifted off quite quickly, but as I did, one question pressed at my thoughts: what was that about?

* * *

The second week after we'd arrived at the Academy, Darren finally returned from his visit to Devon. I was at odds with his presence. I couldn't hate him like before, not after what had happened. I didn't know what to think.

I spent the next couple of days lost in my own dance of drills and meals with my friends. At one point, I turned around to ask Eve her opinion, and then caught myself. I had a sickening moment where that day in the forest came rushing back, and I decided to retire early that night.

It was as I was turning the corridor to my room on the Academy's second floor that I finally came across the prince. He was not alone.

"Now is not the time to discuss our wedding!" I entered the hall just in time to see Darren slam a chamber door in Priscilla's face.

The girl let out a loud shriek and picked up a nearby vase

and threw it against the wall. It shattered into a mass of tiny shards, wilted flowers, and water flooding the floor. Then she turned around and caught me staring.

"He wasn't just visiting her father," she sniffed. "He was with *her*. My friends in the palace tell me everything."

I didn't know what to say. Once again my chest was being ripped at the seams. I felt torn between three states: pity for myself who loved such a capricious person, pity for Priscilla who spent her whole life fighting girls like Shinako and me to keep the prince and her position in court, and then frustration at Darren for saving my life and being so heartless and power-hungry in the same breath. Why couldn't a person just be good or evil? Why couldn't Darren pick a side? I was tired of trying to guess which one he was on, and it was beyond aggravating when my heart was involved.

"The day I am crowned princess will be the best day of my life," Priscilla continued. "Believe me when I say you are lucky to be lowborn, Ryiah. A highborn's struggles are more tiresome than you could ever know."

There. That was the reason I didn't pity her. Not truly. "One, my status as apprentice means I am no longer 'lowborn,'" I snapped. "And two, my struggles are just as relevant as yours."

The girl rolled her eyes.

"I find great pleasure in knowing that it is one of your own who is stealing him away," I told her flatly.

"And here I was trying to be polite!"

"You are wasting your breath. Any pity I feel vanishes every time you open your mouth."

The girl stopped smirking. "You have grown vain in light of your magic, Ryiah. Were we friends, I might use my influence to have Byron give you a higher rank at our ascension. A shame, you could be the best apprentice of our year, but you'll still be ranked last."

"I'd rather be last than align myself with you."

The girl glared at me. "You are making a mistake."

"Her only mistake is talking to you. Why don't you find some other hallway to haunt with your presence?"

I grinned as Ella sidled next to me on the stairs. Priscilla stomped off to find better company, and I turned to Ella. "Thanks."

"She's afraid of you. Priscilla knows you have power and it scares her. Last thing she wants to do is make enemies with the future Black Mage."

I snorted. "I find that highly unlikely."

Ella looked thoughtful. "Maybe. And maybe not."

* * *

The Academy turned to a winter wonderland with the first-years' lights decorating the castle just in time for solstice.

I enjoyed a good feast and then left my brother to dance with my friend.

It was strange to be surrounded by so many eager-faced first-years and know that I'd been one of them, enthusiastically sharing in drinks and laughs, just four years before. I still had five more months at Ferren's Keep, but the ascension took place in Devon, not Sjeka. Tonight would be my final night within the Academy walls.

"Feeling nostalgic?" Darren appeared beside me in the

snow. I started. I hadn't even noticed him exit the doors.

The two of us were standing under a pillar of icicles and trees glowing violet under the first-years' lights.

"I spent so much time dreaming about becoming a mage." My words were barely a whisper. "I don't think I'll know what to do with myself when it becomes real."

"I doubt that." The prince's expression was wry. "I think the second you are ranked, the commanders will vie to give you a spot in their regiment."

That was the second time someone had told me that. I still didn't believe it. "I hardly think that will be the case."

"I do."

An awkward silence followed, and then Darren cleared his throat. "I never got a chance to ask," he said quietly, "how you were faring. After the battle."

"Are you asking me now?"

"I am."

"I'm fine." I couldn't think of what else to say. Anything else felt like a betrayal to myself.

"I'm glad."

I made the mistake of meeting his eyes and saw... I'm not sure what I saw. My emotions were running so wild I couldn't trust myself. Every inch of me was screaming at his proximity and my skin was fighting to make contact.

He'd only been nice for a moment. That was all it took to bring back that rush I needed to forget.

"Thank you..." I swallowed. "For coming back for me that day. I'm sorry about Eve... I know she meant a lot to you."

"She..." I could hear the break in his voice as he said it.

"She didn't deserve to die. Not for me."

"I'm sorry."

"So am I." Now he sounded angry and his eyes flared crimson. "Her death will not go unpunished."

"What are you going to do?"

"When I returned to Devon, I met with my father. The Council and his advisors have been averse to take action, but this time it's different. The Caltothians have grown bold— sending that many men to attack our northern post. Our men and women depend on that forest for lumber, and now a quarter of it is burned to the ground. The daughter of the Crown's Army commander is dead. Several of the regiment? Dead. You and I were almost killed." He clenched his fist. "I admit the nobles could look the other way while half of Jerar is destroyed—they are that opposed to war—but they can do little to ignore Father after he found out his own son was almost murdered."

I bit my lip. "So we are going to war?" The Great Compromise had been in place for almost a century. It seemed impossible.

Darren looked away. "As soon as my brother and I secure our marriage dowries to finance his army."

Oh. How could I have forgotten? It must have been because he was standing so close to me, eyes burning like fire, robbing me of the last year and a half. Darren was still Darren. Just because he was kind did not mean he loved me, or that he wasn't a prince. It didn't matter how he looked at me. Nothing had changed.

* * *

That same night, I arrived at my chambers and shut the

door softly behind me. It was only after I heard the lock click into place that I let myself breathe. I felt myself slip to the floor, fingers tracing the wooden panels above as my heart pounded traitorously hard in my chest.

Why do I do this to myself? Why does he have to be kind? Why can't he be cruel? It wasn't fair. Darren had broken my heart. And he continued to shatter it every time he looked at me.

We couldn't be friends. We couldn't be enemies.

So what were we?

* * *

It was the worst winter I could remember. We could see every breath we took. Ella and I were beyond miserable.

Then we were deployed in one of the keep's regular patrols.

"What do you mean, we have to camp in the snow?" my friend whispered, outraged. She was smart enough not to complain in Master Byron's presence, of course.

"For this next week, I want you to go completely without using your magic," the training master had said. *"Absolutely no casting. Unless we come across a raid, I want you to learn how to survive a harsh winter climate without using your powers. The soldiers and knights do it all of the time. This will help prepare you for a position in the northern regiment. Your magic will be needed for battle, not comfort, and as such, I expect the next week to reflect this. Afterward, we will resume our regular lessons. "*

"Madness," I told her, grinning, "absolute madness."

She elbowed me. "Don't mock me, Ry. By the second night you, too, will be wishing for summer."

"Not as much as my dear brother, I expect."

Ella blushed. "Yes," she admitted ruefully, "I suppose I'm not the only one."

"He wants to marry you, you know."

"I know." Her face was in flames. "I'd be a fool to say anything but yes. I love the both of you more than what is healthy, I'm sure."

At least someone would get a happy ending.

* * *

"Commander Nyx!"

The woman paused. "Yes, Apprentice?"

"You asked me to find you if I remembered anything strange?"

The commander's haggard gaze transformed to one of keen interest. "Yes, Ryiah, I am so sorry. Please forgive me, my mind was elsewhere."

I shifted from one foot to the next. "I'm sure it is nothing of importance," I stammered, "but I remembered something..." I was sure I looked foolish. I felt like a fool, that was for certain. I'd been plagued with nightmares of that battle for months.

And then I'd remembered.

"One of the mages called herself a traitor. A man was arguing with his leader whether or not to take me as a hostage, and she asked him if he really wanted to defy their orders. She said 'two times a traitor would only bring a slow and painful death.' I didn't think it then, but now it struck me as an odd thing to say... What did she mean? Why would a Caltothian be 'two times a traitor'?"

The commander smiled. She never smiled. It made every

inch of my skin crawl. "Have you ever considered a position up north?" the woman wanted to know. "Ferren's Keep, perhaps?"

My ill ease was immediately forgotten. *Is she offering me a position before my ascension ceremony?* "I've thought about it."

"Well, if you decide that answer is yes, you would be guaranteed a place in my regiment."

I couldn't breathe. "Really? But you don't even know my rank yet, and Byron…"

"I judge a person by their merits, not hearsay," the woman interrupted. "And you, my dear, have impressed me far more than any of your factionmates. You passed an initial test half your year failed, and then you saved my regiment. If I were to go by hearsay, then I must tell you the northerners are singing you nothing but praise. Either way, you will always have a place in my keep." She reached out to grasp my arm firmly. "We need more fighters like you, Ryiah."

"And Darren," I said weakly. "He helped save your regiment too."

The commander's gaze seemed far away. "Yes," she said, "I suppose he did." Then her focus cleared. "Nonetheless, I am sure he will be stationed close to the palace. He might be a mage, but he's still a prince. I believe the king has been generous in allowing him to spend so much time abroad."

I nodded, feeling silly I'd forgotten. Of course he wouldn't accept. The prince would serve a much higher rank close to home in the Crown's Army.

I didn't understand why I had felt it necessary to remind her of his prowess. The whole country knew. Was I so desperate to spend the rest of my life fighting alongside the prince? I should've been happy to finally free myself after spending so much time together. *Why in the name of the gods was I trying to keep him here?*

* * *

"If I wanted to be saddle sore," Alex griped, "I would've joined Combat, not Restoration."

"Calm down, big brother," Derrick teased. "You'll have plenty of time to grow fat and old after your ascension."

I snickered as Alex glowered at Derrick over his meal. "You might think yourself wise because you've enjoyed two winters in this gods' forsaken place," he said brusquely, "but there is nothing wrong with choosing a comfortable life."

"A shame you fell in love with a Combat mage."

"A shame indeed." Alex looked wistful.

"You know Ella wants to be stationed up here, right? She hates the cold, but she still wants the glory." Nothing was more fun than teasing my twin, especially in the recent months. It was obvious to everyone except him how deep he'd fallen. The poor sap didn't stand a chance.

Alex made a face. "I will make it my mission to talk her around."

"You only have a couple more weeks," I replied snidely, "and then we'll be in the capital."

"You grow more insolent every day." Alex threw a piece of his toast in my direction. I dodged it easily. "Must be your inflated sense of pride. You and Derrick are one in the same, nothing but a bunch of overfed peacocks."

"That we are." Derrick snickered as he turned to Alex with a sly grin on his face. "Well, if your ladylove declines to join you south, I would be happy to have her stay up north with Ryiah and me. Ella grows lovelier every time I set eyes on her." Derrick ducked just in time to avoid Alex's fist.

The innkeeper barked at Alex to stop riling his customers.

I shot my embarrassed brother a grin. "You know Derrick only teases you because you are so easy to rattle."

"Yes," Derrick added, "that and I'm afraid I've grown restless. Eight months is far too long to go without fighting any Caltothians." He shrugged. "Those drills my commander puts us through are no use. I'm not accustomed to peace."

"It's not peace," I reminded him tersely. "It's the quiet before the storm." I glanced at Alex. "And you, even if you two aren't stationed together, she'll wait for you. All you have to do is ask. I, for one, would love to have another girl in this family."

Alex turned a deep shade of red and busied himself with his stew.

Derrick picked up the conversation, steering me toward a much-needed debate on the merits of a two-handed axe. I became so engrossed in conversation I almost missed the tolling of the midnight hour. Alex and I groaned our apologies to Derrick and then retired to the stables for our final night's ride to the keep's barracks.

In a couple short hours, we would be back on King's Road, headed for the palace... Only this time we would leave it as mages.

TWENTY-TWO

"I HAVE NEVER been more terrified in my life." Alex was writhing in his best clothes—a silk-lined tunic and fresh-pressed breeches. Ella reached out to straighten his hem and then pushed back his bangs, laughing.

"Master Joan is much less intimidating than Byron," she teased. "It'll be over before you know it. And just think, when it is, you'll emerge looking handsomer than before in a red Restoration robe."

I smirked. "And if not, at least your face will match the rest of you."

Alex paled and Ella gave him a quick kiss in the cheek, wagging her finger at me as she did. "Leave your poor brother alone," she chided. "If he gets any more nervous, he'll sweat through his shirt. I hardly think we can find another in time for the ceremony."

I fingered my own garb. I felt exposed in the dress I was wearing—a soft lilac thing with a bodice that felt much too tight. It didn't seem right to wear something so feminine going into an ascension for Combat, but Ella had assured me that was exactly why I should. *"You're a woman,"* she'd insisted. *"We're already a minority in all of the war schools—not just our own faction as mages. It would do good to remind the audience that we can be both."*

And so now here I was, unable to breathe—which I must admit was becoming a common occurrence around Ella during important occasions in general—and dreading the rest of the evening. Master Byron's attitude toward me hadn't grown any better in the last couple of months, and I'd no doubt what my standing would be at the end of the ceremony. Even though I had Commander Nyx's offer to hold onto, it did little to sway the deep sense of foreboding that was growing more prevalent by the second. In less than an hour, I would have to face the world as a fifth-rank mage.

By the time Ella had finished adjusting Alex's new tunic, it was time to go. I gathered the hem of my dress and followed my brother and friend into the palace's throne room. There was a red- and gold-lined rug that trailed down the center of the great hall, folding several times on tall steps before finally resting under a large gold-adorned throne marked with plush red cushions and thick golden arms. The king studied the apprentices as we entered.

One by one, each of us kneeled before him and then separated into three distinct rows: Restoration closest to the front and Combat at the rear.

Prince Blayne sat in a less ornate chair than his father, but he still looked regal and cold in a matching hematite and steel crown. He had an air of extreme boredom as each apprentice entered, with only the slightest note of interest when his brother appeared.

Behind the throne, three massive stained glass windows cast rays of light across the hall and onto the side risers at either end where the nobility and our younger factionmates sat watching. Several members of the King's Regiment stood guard at the front and back of the room while the Council of Magic and Crown Advisors sat in a small stand to the left of the king to watch the proceedings from their own special box.

The three faction masters strode forward to begin our rite. Ella giggled into her hand and pointed. Master Byron looked beyond miserable standing between Master Joan and Master Perry. From his strained tone, it was obvious he would rather be anywhere else than close quarters with the two female mages.

"...To defend all those in need of rescuing."

We all answered in unison. "I solemnly pledge."

"To speak the truth to all questions asked. No matter the consequence."

"I solemnly pledge."

"To be loyal to your commander in trying times. To exercise caution before magic."

"I solemnly pledge."

"To be brave in times of danger. To obey Crown and Council Law in all matters of service."

"I solemnly pledge."

"To be kind in times of need. To only fight when it is necessary. "

"I solemnly pledge."

"To be a mage of honor and valiance. To always put the Crown before yourself."

"As a mage to the Crown and Jerar, I solemnly pledge."

Commander Joan took a step forward to call on her

Restoration mages, one by one. When she called Alex, he was given the third rank. Though we were supposed to remain silent during the entire ceremony, it did not stop me from letting out a small shriek and Ella from clapping almost hysterically loud.

Master Perry went next with her Alchemy mages. Ruth was given first-rank. I should have known. She always was the best of her faction. I watched her, envious, as she returned back to her seat.

Then it was time for Combat.

Master Byron stood proudly as he called, "In the matter of first-rank ascension, I would like to call forward our very own Prince Darren, second-in-line to the throne and now first-rank mage of Combat."

I watched as the prince left his position in line to kneel before his father, his brother, and then, finally, Master Byron. When he arose, a servant handed him a silken black robe. Darren's face was expressionless as he slid the smooth mage's robe over his regular clothes, letting the hood rest on his head for just a moment before it slid back onto his shoulders.

There was a hushed silence as Darren turned back to face the crowd. I lost my breath. Blayne might wear the heir's crown, but Darren was the one with power. Whatever I might think of him, the prince had earned that robe.

Darren returned to his seat beside Priscilla. I waited with bated breath. Who would Byron name next? The only other male in our faction or the future princess of Jerar? I was sure he wanted to name Ray, but the master would not be so quick as to snub a girl of great influence.

Ella nudged me with her arm. "Ryiah."

"Shhh." I nudged her back. "I'm trying to hear who he picks."

"Byron just called your name!"

"You're joking."

"No. I'm not." She jerked her chin to point in the direction of the throne.

All the blood rushed from my face as I realized she was telling the truth. The training master was glowering at me from his position beside the king. I hastily pulled myself off the cold marble floor and raced over to stand before the throne. I kneeled before King Lucius, Prince Blayne, and Master Byron.

"Ryiah of Demsh'aa, I award you second rank for your—" The man paused uncomfortably. "—your outstanding apprenticeship. I'd be a fool to ignore power when I see it, even if you are a—" He coughed. "—a woman. Please stand and accept your new status as a second-rank mage of Combat."

I stood, hardly conscious that I was sobbing. I only realized it when the servant handing me my robe touched the side of my face and showed me my tears. "Not many mages cry," she told me kindly, "but I like to think it's the best of them that do." I nodded, wetness staining my cheeks, and then let her help me with my robe.

Then I turned back to face my audience. I could hardly see straight, tears were blocking most of my vision, and by the time I reached my seat, my sight had cleared just enough for me to find my place beside Ella.

"You blubbering mess," she teased, "you are making a

fool of yourself."

"I d-don't care." And it was true. I was smiling so hard my face hurt.

Master Byron called Ella next—much to our mutual shock. The girl almost screamed when he said it. And then it was time for Ray.

Priscilla was last. When the dark-haired beauty left the podium, she was seething, anger piercing the gaze of any person foolish enough to meet her eyes.

I, for one, had trouble containing my glee.

The herald called for the newly ascended mages to take the ceremonial banquet in the king's dining hall. Having never before partaken in the meal—apprentices were always directed to the ballroom with the rest of the visiting mages and court—I was eager to see how it transpired. Only the Council of Magic and the king's family were allowed to dine with us.

I took my seat between Ella and Alex. Within seconds the room had filled with the rest of our year, chattering on in quiet but excited voices as they found their place along the table. At the very front sat the three Colored Robes, King Lucius, and Prince Blayne.

I did a double take when I realized who was still missing.

Two seats down from me, I heard Priscilla complaining to one of Ruth's factionmates. "I told him not to go anywhere, but did he listen to me? Of course not. Well, when Blayne finds out he is off with that trollop again—"

The chamber door swung open to reveal the non-heir and Princess Shinako clinging steadfastly to his arm. My pulse stopped. *Dear gods, no.* I was so close to being free of him.

Couldn't he just wait until tomorrow to proclaim his love for her? Even on my happiest day, he'd found a way to ruin it.

King Lucius looked up at his son and the crown princess of the Borea Isles, startled. Blayne clutched his wine goblet, his face tight with rage.

Darren cleared his throat loudly. "Everyone, please stay where you are." The whole room fell silent. "Princess Shinako and I have an announcement to make, and I want all of you to bear witness."

No. No. No. Why is he doing this now? My eyes sought Darren's, but his attention was focused on the king.

"Father." The prince took a deep breath. "You promised if I secured a dowry equal to Priscilla of Langli, I would be free to break off my current engagement in favor of that opportunity. You have said that Jerar is our utmost concern, and its strength triumphs all."

Priscilla's face went white as a sheet.

Prince Blayne pushed back his chair, spitting wine as he cried, "He did not give you permission to steal *my* future wife, you ungrateful, power-mad—"

Darren held up his hand. "I am not stealing her, *brother*."

Blayne sat down with a suspicious glare. "Then what is the meaning of this ridiculous speech?"

"Princess Shinako and her father have been kind enough to guarantee us the sum of her dowry and a pledge of support—equal to what the two of you would receive once wed—in exchange for the same pledge from us and a dissolution of your intended marriage. We received a signed letter from Emperor Liang just this morning."

"Father, this is madness!" Blayne turned to the king in

horror. "Tell him to put an end to this!"

The king scowled at his oldest. "Let him speak, Blayne. I must admit even I am intrigued."

"Not only have I secured Jerar more wealth than any daughter of Langli, I have also given my dearest brother the opportunity to marry a princess from Pythus and amass an even greater dowry and support for this great country."

"The king of Pythus would never marry one of his daughters to me!" Blayne's face was as red as his venison.

"Perhaps you haven't tried hard enough to please him." Darren didn't look perturbed.

"Father!"

"Silence, Blayne!" the king snapped. "Your brother has done a great thing for us. Foolish, but great. I will not be so blind as to deny it would benefit us greatly, and you most of all." The man turned to Darren. "Very well, your previous engagement has been ceded in favor of this new proposal. Pending the signed pledge, of course."

The door slammed shut. Priscilla of Langli had just left the room.

The king chuckled and indicated for Darren and Shinako to take a seat.

"That is not all, Father."

The king stopped laughing to stare at his son, his eyes narrowing. "Isn't it?" His tone held a warning.

"No. It's not."

My heart began to slam against my chest so loud and so fast I was sure the whole room could hear it.

Darren's eyes found mine.

My fork clattered to the floor.

"I wish to secure a new engagement with the dowry Princess Shinako has so generously bestowed."

"I gave you what you wanted." The king's eyes were furious. "You are free of that Langli girl. Anything more and you have overstepped your—"

"I wish to marry Mage Ryiah of Demsh'aa."

Several people exclaimed at once. My brother choked on his water. Ella grabbed my arm. The king clutched his knife so tightly his knuckles were white.

"Absolutely not!"

I just sat there, motionless. *This isn't real. It* can't *be real. It's a dream.* I watched Darren, standing there in front of his father with his back erect.

"I believe Master Byron just deemed Ryiah one of the most powerful mages in this room," Darren said slowly, "and if we all know Byron, he is nothing if not stingy in his praise where women are concerned."

The training master's face went up in flames. Somehow I knew his praise was anything but voluntary.

"In fact, it was Shina, excuse me, Princess Shinako's only stipulation that the dowry she so generously bestows go to Mage Ryiah specifically, was it not?"

The princess nodded demurely, smiling. "Yes, it is the least I can do. Darren and I are good friends. Nothing would please me more than his happiness."

"So you see, Father, there is absolutely no one who would benefit me—or Jerar—more than Ryiah of Demsh'aa. You said strength triumphs all, and Ryiah's dowry and status would certainly bring the Crown strength." Darren pulled out a scroll tucked into the sleeve of his robe. "Your advisors have already given this union their full blessing. Here is a letter stating their support…"

"*This is ridiculous!*" Blayne shrieked. "*Father, do not let him marry that lowborn!*"

"Your Majesty." Marius stood with the two Colored Robes at his side. "The Council of Magic would be in full support of this union. We think it a very wise proposal."

The king stood, fists clenched. When he finally spoke, it was strained and full of unspoken rage. "Then it appears this girl is indeed Jerar's best interest." The man turned to his youngest. "Congratulations, my son, on your new betrothed."

King Lucius strode out of the room without another word.

* * *

The moment the king and his heir departed, the room became chaos. I flew out of my chair, slamming the door behind me as I tore into the hallway beyond. My heart was beating so fast I was afraid my ribs would explode. I could barely breathe; air was coming out of my lungs in quick, choking gasps.

I hunched over, leaning against the side of the wall while the room rose and fell all around me in a frenzied whirl. I stayed there for a couple of minutes, breathing in and out, in and out, until the room began to seem a bit more static.

The door opened and closed behind me.

I turned and saw Darren standing there. "I was looking for you."

When I didn't reply, he made himself speak.

"I know you are mad at me." The prince took a step forward and then stopped himself. His eyes found mine, and he took a deep breath. "If you'll let me explain—"

"You lied to me."

"I did." His gaze didn't waver. "I lied, and I lied, and I lied to you. Over and over. I know what I did. I know what I said. I wanted to make you hate me."

"But why?"

"Why, Ryiah?" Darren made a frustrated sound. "Because what kind of prince would I be if I let my love for a lowborn blind me from the fate of my country?"

A lowborn? Tears stung my eyes and I turned away, biting back a sob.

Darren's hand clamped down on my arm, and he spun me around, eyes blazing. "I needed to do the right thing." His face was flushed. "Don't you see, Ryiah? I would have been exactly what you accused me of—a coward—if I'd let my love for you blind me from what has been happening all around us! I know you despise me for what I did, but when I went to my father that day, he told me that we were going to war with Caltoth. That hundreds of our men were going to die, and if I chose to marry for love over wealth, I'd be ensuring millions more." He cursed. "He was right. I couldn't marry you without a dowry, not unless I wanted people like Caine and Eve to die every day, all so I can have a bit of selfishness."

I shoved him away. "But you never told me, Darren! You made me *hate* you!"

Darren caught my hand in his, and I trembled. "I had to." His voice was hoarse.

"Ryiah, I was willing to jeopardize the fate of this country just for a chance to be near you. I needed you to hate me, because it was the only way *I* could do the right thing."

"I thought you were in love with Princess Shinako. Or that you were trying to impress your father so he'd make you his heir." I could barely get the words out.

"So did my brother. So did everyone." Darren's laugh was bitter.

My hand fell away and I took a step back, shaking. I had cried myself to sleep for the good part of two years. My heart had shattered every time he looked at her.

Darren said the next words so quietly I almost missed them. "I kept telling myself it was better than them assuming the alternative."

"What was the alternative?"

"That I had never gotten over you." Darren slammed his fist against the wall. "That I was still madly in love with a girl who hated me by sight. That Shina loathed my brother and cared for a young man in her home country. That we were both trapped in arranged marriages, wanting nothing more than to find a way out. That every time I fought with you, I was really fighting myself, wanting nothing more than to grab you and kiss you and tell you that it was all a mistake. That I missed my best friend and the taste of your lips, and every night that I dreamed, it was only ever of your face."

My heart slammed across my ribs, and I couldn't seem to breathe.

His eyes found mine. "Ryiah…"

I forced myself to speak. "You and Shina planned this?"

"We grew up together. I knew she hated my brother. She always has. When she arrived for her engagement and told me she couldn't stand the thought of marrying Blayne, I told her about you. The two of us were miserable. At first we just shared in our misery that we had to marry for duty, but then it occurred to me that maybe the gods had intervened on our behalf. The emperor wanted a new treaty with Jerar—he knows war is coming, but who was to say the treaty had to be from an arranged marriage? All my father ever cared about was a dowry. It took us a while to convince the princess's father. We had to be careful in our correspondence, but when I finally returned home after the battle in Ferren's Keep, Shina pulled me aside to tell me he'd finally agreed. We still had to get my father's advisors to agree to his letter, but it wasn't that hard when any fool could see it would only bring Jerar more wealth than before."

Darren paused. "I knew we would have to wait for the ascension. We needed to have the Council present, and until a few days ago, they'd been busy along the northern border, meeting with local commanders and their regiment to make sure our defenses were sound after the incident at Ferren's Keep."

"After you started talking to Shina," I said quietly, "why didn't you say anything to me?"

Darren looked away. "I wanted to tell you, Ryiah, but after everything I'd put you through, I couldn't bring myself to say it.... *Because what if it didn't work?*" He swallowed. "And then that day at the Academy, you told me you hated me. You wouldn't even *look* at me."

"I couldn't." The words were barely a whisper.

"I believed you." Darren's voice cracked. "I started to

think you were better off if I left you alone. But then that day at Ferren's Keep, you saw what I was trying to do and you stopped me. You hated me, you had no reason to let me live, and you still wouldn't let me die—*even if it would save you.* I kept thinking about that when I left for Devon. I thought maybe I'd been wrong. That you didn't hate me."

I held my breath as Darren stepped right in front of me. "That maybe you still might love me." His hand found mine. It was shaking. We both were.

"Because I still love you," he whispered desperately.

"I..." I swallowed. "I never stopped. I wanted to." I was rambling now. "I hated myself that I couldn't... That I wasn't strong enough, that I—"

Darren pulled me to him, and the rest of my words fell to the floor.

He kissed me.

And as he did, I smelled pine and cloves.

I tasted cinnamon.

There was only one word to describe it. One word that came rushing back after all of this time.

Home.

How could I have forgotten?

Darren was *home.*

* * *

When we finally broke for air, the prince was grinning.

"Who would have thought," he teased, "that the girl who tried to get me kicked out of the Academy—"

"That was Ella!" I shoved Darren, and he caught my hands in his.

"It was both of you." His smile was wicked. "As I was

saying, this girl who tried to get me kicked out of the Academy, this girl who tried to light me on fire, this lowborn girl I absolutely couldn't stand—"

I scoffed. "Please! You insulted me, mocked me, tricked me, lied to me—"

Darren's hand lightly clamped over my mouth so that the rest of my speech was muffled.

His eyes found mine. "Let me finish, love."

My heart skipped a beat.

"That somehow, this insufferable girl would become the one person I am forever, hopelessly, *madly* drawn to against my will and possibly even my better judgment."

I smiled faintly. "I don't think either of us had a choice in the matter."

"The higher powers are probably having a good laugh at our expense." Darren touched the side of my face, eyes gleaming. "Though perhaps they are right about this one."

I started to lean forward and paused. "Wait. Does this mean you were behind my ranking tonight?" My heart stopped. It was him. Of course it was Darren. *I should've known Byron would never give me second rank willingly.*

Darren's expression was amused. "I can assure you I had nothing to do with it. I was as surprised as you were—not that you didn't deserve it, of course, but that Byron could move past his... er, difficulties where you are concerned." He paused, and then a devious smile spread across his face as he caught sight of someone behind me. "But I bet I know who did."

"Who?" The only person I could think of was Commander Nyx, and she was still north at the keep. There was also considerable doubt that a woman would ever be able to influence a man whose reputation was built on a hatred of their gender.

"Why don't you see for yourself?"

I spun around and found myself face to face with none other than the Black Mage himself, Marius.

"Hello, Mage Ryiah," the man said smoothly. "Did I not tell you we would talk again? Congratulations on your engagement, if I might add."

"It was you," I stammered. "You convinced Byron to rank me second?"

"I merely reminded your headstrong master what a fool he would look should a woman win the next Candidacy... I must say I'm sorry I hadn't corrected his egregious bias sooner, but as it is with most politics, I am slow to catch on." The gold hoop hanging from his ear glimmered, dancing off the windowpanes behind us. "As to second rank, well, my dear, he did that all on his own. I suspect the Ferren's Keep commander would've made his life difficult if he had shunned a northern hero."

I blushed. "I'm not a hero."

"My dear, each one of us is a hero. The irony, of course, is that most will never receive the title. Bask in the recognition, for I suspect it shall not last as long as one might hope, especially with the rumors of Caltoth..." He cleared his throat. "But enough of that. Drink. Dance. Be merry. You are a mage of Combat and betrothed to a prince of the realm. What more could you desire?"

Nothing.

But then a thought occurred. "A black robe would be

nice."

Darren gave me a sideways glance. "What are you talking about? You are already wearing one."

My eyes were dancing. "Maybe like the one Marius is wearing."

"With the gold lining? Ryiah, only the Black Mage..." Darren stopped talking as he realized what I was implying.

Marius smiled. "Yes," he surmised, "I believe I was right to bet on you that day at the Academy. Your future, dear Ryiah, has just begun."

And now an excerpt from

CANDIDATE

THE BLACK MAGE BOOK 3

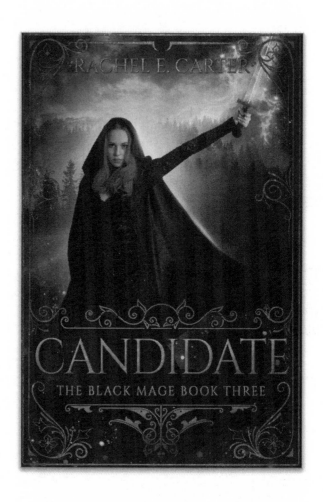

ONE

DARREN LAUGHED SOFTLY. It was like water—the sound of a stream cascading down rock, low and unhurried. Silky. Confident. "You don't really think you can beat me, Ryiah."

I put my hands on my hips. "How would you know? We've never dueled before."

"I beat you in that contest when we were apprentices in Port Langli."

"Yes, but we didn't fight with *magic*." I shifted from one foot to the next as the prince arched a brow and gave me a knowing look. He tapped his fingers against his wrist, and I could tell he was torn between dismissing my challenge and outright intrigue. Prince Darren of Jerar, second-in-line to the throne, was nothing if not proud.

But he was also stubborn. Like me. And I knew he wasn't thrilled by the prospect of dueling his future wife.

I bit my lip, considering how to convince him otherwise. I watched as Darren's eyes fell to my mouth. Suddenly, I was quite sure I knew the answer. Senseless attraction had made the past five years a misery for the both of us, but now it was going to help.

"How about a wager?"

"A wager?" Darren's tone was instantly suspicious. "What kind of wager?"

I took a step forward and lightly laid my palm against his form-fitting tunic. I had to swallow as I felt the flat layer of hard muscle beneath. *Control yourself, Ryiah.* Now was not the time to be noticing things like that. *I* was the one who was supposed to be seducing him.

"Careful, Ryiah." The prince smiled.

"I win and you join me in Ferren's Keep." Ha. We'd spent the past week arguing over where the two of us were going to be stationed.

"You know I need to remain at the palace."

"Then win and you won't have to leave."

"What's my counter?"

I spoke without thinking. "Anything you want."

"*Anything?*" Darren's eyes met mine, and my stomach dropped. A flush crept up the side of my neck and stained my whole face crimson.

"I... I didn't mean t-that," I stuttered.

"Then don't lose." His eyes danced. "Isn't that what you just told me?"

I folded my arms and stared him down stubbornly. "Fine," I said, "but if you get 'anything,' then I get to add another condition. If I win, you have to make peace with Alex the next time the two of you cross paths."

The prince cringed. He and my twin had a strained relationship at best, and even after the night of the ascension, Alex was still wary of the prince. He'd told me the morning after, four days back.

Which was ironic because Darren's brother, the crown prince of Jerar, *hated* me. Although to be fair, I shared the sentiment. There was no one I despised more than Prince Blayne.

"Well, it's a good thing I plan on winning." I looked up and found Darren smirking. Gods, even when he was arrogant, he was attractive. Or maybe it was because of his smug self-assurance. It made me want to slap that silly smile off his face, and then grab him by the collar and kiss him breathless. Not necessarily in that order.

I concentrated on tugging my hair back into a knot—anything to appear unaffected. "Vanity doesn't suit you."

The prince just gave me a knowing smile and pulled himself off the wall, lazily walking to the center of the training court. I followed him until the two of us were standing three yards apart in the center of a large stone dais. The palace's practice court was much smaller than the outdoor ones we'd trained in during our apprenticeship, and it was also twice as elaborate. I suspected it was because we were in the nation's capital, where more coin was devoted to pleasure than practicality.

Normal arenas were in the dirt, outside under a radiating sun with a bare picket fence to serve as the perimeter. Here, inside the palace of Devon, we stood on a raised stone platform surrounded by large, white pillars and a curved base of cushioned benches. On the same side as the empty seats was a thick glass wall, reinforced by a regular supply of the Alchemy mages' resistance potions.

This way the king's court could relax in leisure without the threat of a knight or mage's attack gone awry.

On the opposite side, where we'd just come from, was a small alcove featuring a display of training weapons and spare armor. Darren didn't bother to take any—he already had the most powerful weapon at hand. His *magic*. As Combat mages, we were able to cast any weapon we needed, and while we'd outfit ourselves in real battle, this was only a duel and we'd both agreed the outcome would be decided by sheer prowess alone.

"Are you ready, Ryiah?" Darren grinned.

I studied his stance, hoping for a small hint as to what his first attack might be. I'd spent five years studying his form in casting, and while the prince was good, no one was perfect. He still had tells just like the rest of us. They might not be as obvious, but they were there. If Darren were to cast a weapon to hold he'd likely adjust his right hand—just the slightest widening of his fist to grip a handle. Likewise, he'd be more likely to dig in with his right heel were he to prepare for a substantial casting from his center of gravity, something akin to a heavy torrent of wind power or flame.

Right now, on the day I needed to read him the most, the prince was a blank slate. I scowled. "I'm ready."

"On the count of three." Darren's eyes met mine. "One ... Two ... *Three.*"

The two of us threw out our castings at once, our magic rising up and exploding in a collision of brute power and force.

And then we were flying back.

Each of us slammed against a pillar on opposite ends of the arena. I barely had time to cushion my fall with a casting of air before I was staggering forward, running back toward

Darren with a hand raised and magic flowing from my palm.

But he was even faster.

I narrowly ducked as a series of whistling daggers soared past my ear. Swiping a loose strand of hair that'd fallen from it's knot, I met the prince's gaze.

"Having fun, love?" The words were full of unspoken laughter.

"Aren't you?" A blade appeared in one hand as my other sent off a blinding flash of light. The air lit up, and for a moment, there was only gold as I barreled forward, bringing my sword up and then down in a vertical slash. I threw all my weight into the heat of the attack.

But Darren was waiting. The sound of two metals colliding sent out a noisy ring across the dais.

I withdrew and threw up a pine shield just in time to counter his cut.

"Nice touch."

"I learned from the best." I paused. "Well, *second* best."

He snorted.

We continued to trade blows for parries, but within minutes, Darren was walking me backward across the dais with a maddening smirk. His weighted blows were stronger than mine, and my arm started to strain against the heavy hits I was blocking, but only occasionally issuing.

I made a split-second decision to lunge forward with my shield. Darren blocked the move easily, but that was my intention. While he was distracted with the blow, I changed my sword to a knife.

He registered my decision a second too late as I threw a crescent cut low and out. I caught the side of his leg just before he fell back, and I was rewarded with a loud rip of cloth and the trickle of red.

I jumped out of the way of the prince's counter.

"Should have known you'd choose the knife."

"It always was my favorite."

We regarded one another for a moment in silence, our chests rising and falling after the first ten minutes of battle. I'd drawn first blood, so I won by standard duel etiquette. But we were playing for more. We trained for Combat, and Combat trained to win. We were war mages. Our definition of winning was surrender—or death.

I adjusted my grip. *One victory down, and one more to go.* I lifted my hand at the same time Darren lowered his. Our eyes met and power burst from our fingertips. The dais rumbled and groaned, and I leaped to avoid a large fissure as Darren cast out a magicked globe, shielding himself from the storm of arrows I'd sent flooding down from the ceiling.

This time there was no rest.

Fire tore a line across the fissure, sprouting even more flames as it chased me to the edge. I spun and doused it with a flurry of ice, listening to the snap, crackle, and hiss as the flames met with cold.

For a second, heavy steam fogged up the arena. I shut my eyes and called up a memory for the next casting.

Darren and me. The night he told me he didn't love me. Blayne laughing in my face while the fathomless prince watched, unfeeling, as my heart crumbled to a million pieces.

My fingers tingled, and I felt the warm static building in my arm. These were the memories I needed. Weather magic wasn't like a normal casting—it was fueled by emotion. Extremities were best. And my years with Darren had certainly given me a large assortment to choose from.

"I told you not to trust a wolf, because it would only ever want to break you... Haven't you figured it out yet? I'm the wolf, Ryiah."

A hot surge of anger leaped out of my core. I mentally harnessed the emotion and channeled its magic, letting the searing heat surge along my veins. Then, I released my casting.

A jolt of lightning struck Darren's barrier and shattered it. There was a shrill, earsplitting noise as his casting splintered like glass.

Darren released his magic and sprinted across the platform, a magicked sword in each hand.

I sent out a large funnel of fire, but the prince crossed his arms midstride and the flames came barreling back. I had just enough time to duck to my left, and then a terrible smell met my nose.

I lifted a hand to my head. The fire had singed off part of my hair, just above my right ear.

When Darren came again, I was ready. Ice shot out across the short distance between us and met with the prince's swords. His metal froze over, webs of glistening frost spreading from the tip to the handle with a shrill crack.

He dropped his castings with a growl—nothing like the biting sting of frozen metal—and looked to his palms. They were now reddish-black.

I was torn between guilt and glee. I knew how that felt. I'd had that same casting done to me when I was an apprentice.

But I was here to win.

I barreled forward and prepared to end our duel with a knife to his neck. Or that was what I'd planned. But, like usual, Darren was one step ahead of me.

The second the steel started to materialize in my hand, Darren tackled me midstride.

Before I could get a good focus, my casting disappeared—concentration broken by his attack—and we both hit the hard stone floor with a loud *thud*.

I felt the jarring impact in my side rather than the full at my back. I had somehow grappled my way so that Darren wasn't quite pinning me flat—one leg in and one out.

He was trying to wrestle me to the floor, but I knew the second he had my shoulders, the match was as good as over. I would never be able to break the full weight of his hold if I couldn't push forward. I simply didn't have the mass to win a contest with my arms, but that didn't mean I couldn't fool Darren into thinking I'd try. He and I had never fought in hand-to-hand combat, so I could only hope that meant he hadn't been paying attention during my training in the apprenticeship.

Pretending to gasp, I made a huge deal out of struggling back and forth to break free. Darren took the bait. He leaned forward to pin me back and my second leg snaked free. It took me all of two seconds to dig my first heel into his hip and pivot to the side.

It was enough to give me some leverage against his weight.

I threw myself forward using my second leg to kick up

and off the ground, rolling the prince underneath me. I was up.

But I was sitting too far back. Darren's reflexes were too fast. Or maybe he'd expected the move. His hips threw me, and I toppled forward, palms slapping the ground while he used the strength in his torso to flip-roll me. Hard.

I landed on my back with a curse. My lungs were on fire, and I wasn't sure I hadn't broken something in that twist. White-hot pain ate away at my ribs, and Darren had my arms pinned to the stone ground.

"Time to surrender, love. Don't fault yourself. It's not every day someone goes up against a first-rank mage."

I grumbled an unladylike word, and Darren laughed, his whole body shaking.

"You're insufferable."

Darren stopped and his eyes met mine. The look he gave me was enough to forget the terrible pain in my chest and bring on a whole different kind of heat. "Well, I don't believe that for a second."

Blood rushed my face as the prince leaned in.

"Admit it." Darren's mouth was close to my ear. "You aren't suffering in the least..." His hand traced circles along the inside of my wrist. A trail of shivers followed wherever his fingers went. "*Are you*, Ryiah?"

I swallowed. For the first time, I was conscious of the fact we were the only two in the room. And we were on the floor, which suddenly didn't feel quite so uncomfortable and cold.

Not when he was looking at me like that. Like...

I had a sudden flashback to that day in his chambers two years before—to what had almost transpired the last time we'd been truly alone.

Gods, I hadn't been able to keep my hands to myself. And neither had he.

The memory made me blush even now.

Darren noticed and his lips curved in a half smile, his eyes hooded. "That's what I thought." With those words, he closed the distance between us. I detected the faint spiciness of his breath, like cinnamon and heat and *ice*. Something that was dangerous and dark and, to be honest, exactly what I wanted.

I knew we needed to treat our injuries, especially mine, but...

"If you are going to kiss me," I said brazenly, "you should do it now."

The corner of his lips turned up. "Oh, I intend to."

Author's Note

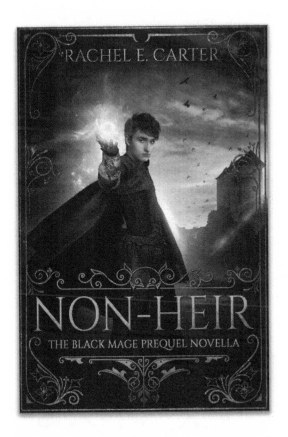

Want to read Prince Darren's backstory before he met Ryiah at the Academy of Magic?

Sign up for Rachel's newsletter on her website so you can receive the exclusive e-novella and be notified of new releases, special updates, freebies, & giveaways!

ACKNOWLEDGEMENTS

I'll say it and say it again, I would be nothing without my READERS. This new edition is here due to some lovely readers and reviewers who gave the best feedback on the whole Ian-Ryiah-Darren fiasco in the original edition. This book is also a gift to every Darren fangirl, because let's face it, he's my favorite too.

As always, FAMILY and FRIENDS and the AUTHOR COMMUNITY played a part, as well as my amazeballs EDITORS (Hot Tree Editing) and COVER ARTIST (Milo).

Lastly, *huge* thank you to my PROOFERS of this new edition for taking time out of their busy lives to spot all the typos and whatnot I missed: TIFFANY KIMBRELL, NIKKI ALLEGRETTI, COURTNEY HOOVER, SHAWN HOWZE, and RYAN TEMPLE. Again, you guys went out of your way to selflessly help me with this book and I can't thank you enough!!!

ABOUT THE AUTHOR

RACHEL E. CARTER is a young adult and new adult author who hoards coffee and books. She has a weakness for villains and Mr. Darcy love interests. Her first series is the bestselling YA fantasy, *The Black Mage*, and she has plenty more books to come.

Official Site:

www.RachelECarter.com

Facebook Fan Group:

facebook.com/groups/RachelsYAReaders

Twitter: @RECarterAuthor

Email:

RachelCarterAuthor@gmail.com

ALSO BY RACHEL E. CARTER

<u>The Black Mage Series</u>

Non-Heir (e-novella only)

First Year

Apprentice

Candidate

Last Stand

61507375R00234

Made in the USA
Lexington, KY
12 March 2017